Praise for

AMIN MAALOUF

Winner of the 1993 Prix Goncourt
and

Samarkand

Winner of the Prix des Maisons de la Presse

"A rich historical romance... that exudes a distinct *Arabian Nights* flavor... Mysteries and their solutions are deployed with masterly authority in this accomplished novel by one of the best European voices to have emerged in the last decade."
—*Kirkus Reviews*

"Remarkable... Maalouf has written an extraordinary book."
—*The Independent (London)*

"Maalouf is a strong storyteller... Throughout the novel, the reader is treated to lovely set pieces that evoke medieval and early modern Central Asia."
—*New York Times Book Review*

"Prop up an extra pillow against your head. Pop open a drink. You are in for a sumptuous read... Amin Maalouf is an artful writer who can bring the story into your bedroom like IMAX with Surround Sound, but who never allows the momentum to bog down the details. You'll find yourself wide open to the poetry and history along with the white-knuckle adventure."
—*Small Press Magazine*

"This is a splendid novel... structured as a thriller... and brings together love, intrigue, tyranny, creativity, and the timeless power of the word..."
—*Choice*

Samarkand

AMIN MAALOUF

A NOVEL
translated by Russell Harris

Just
demanding
:)
Aug 26th 2020

INTERLINK BOOKS

An imprint of Interlink Publishing Group, Inc.
NEW YORK

To my Father

This edition first published in 2004 by

INTERLINK BOOKS
An imprint of Interlink Publishing Group, Inc.
46 Crosby Street, Northampton, Massachusetts 01060

ISBN 978-1-56656-293-5

Printed and bound in the United States of America

To order or request our complete catalog,
please call us at **1-800-238-LINK** or write to
Interlink Publishing
46 Crosby Street, Northampton, MA 01060
e-mail: info@interlinkbooks.com • website: www.interlinkbooks.com

Contents

Look 'round thee now on Samarcand,
Is she not queen of earth? her pride
Above all cities? in her hand
Their destinies?

Edgar Allan Poe (1809–49)

At the bottom of the Atlantic there is a book. I am going to tell you its history.

Perhaps you know how the story ends. The newspapers of the day wrote about it, as did others later on. When the *Titanic* went down on the night of April 14, 1912 in the sea off the New World, its most eminent victim was a book, the only copy of the *Rubaiyaat* of Omar Khayyam, the Persian sage, poet, and astronomer.

I shall not dwell upon the shipwreck. Others have already weighed its cost in dollars, listed the bodies, and reported people's last words. Six years after the event I am still obsessed by this object of flesh and ink whose unworthy guardian I was. Was I, Benjamin O. Lesage, not the one who snatched it from its Asian birthplace? Was it not among my luggage that it set sail on the *Titanic*? And was its age-old journey not interrupted by my century's arrogance?

Since then, the world has become daily more covered in blood and gloom, and life has ceased to smile on me. I have had to distance myself from people in order to hear the voice of my memory, to nurture a naïve hope and insistent vision that tomorrow the manuscript will be found. Protected by its golden casket, it will emerge from the murky depths of the sea intact, its destiny enriched by a new odyssey. People will be able to finger it, open it, and lose themselves in it. Captive eyes will follow the chronicle of its adventure from margin to margin, they will discover the poet, his first verses, his first bouts of drunkenness, and his first fears; and the sect of the Assassins. Then they will stop, incredulous, at a painting the color of sand and emerald.

It bears neither date nor signature, nothing apart from these words which can be read as either impassioned or disenchanted: *Samarkand, the most beautiful face the Earth has ever turned towards the sun.*

BOOK ONE

Poets and Lovers

Pray tell, who has not transgressed Your Law?
Pray tell the purpose of a sinless life
If with evil You punish the evil I have done.
Pray tell, what is the difference between You and me?

OMAR KHAYYAM

1

Sometimes in Samarkand, in the evening of a slow and dreary
day, city dwellers would come to while the time away at the dead-
end Street of Two Taverns, near the pepper market. They came not
to taste the musky wine of Soghdia but to watch the comings and
goings or to waylay a carouser who would then be forced down into
the dust, showered with insults, and cursed into a hell whose fire,
until the end of all time, would recall the ruddiness of the wine's
enticements.

Out of such an incident the manuscript of the *Rubaiyaat* was to be
born in the summer of 1072. Omar Khayyam was twenty-four and
had recently arrived in Samarkand. Should he go to the tavern that
evening, or stroll around at leisure? He chose the sweet pleasure of
surveying an unknown town accompanied by the thousand sights of
the waning day. In the Street of the Rhubarb Fields, a small boy
bolted past, his bare feet padding over the wide cobblestones as he
clutched to his neck an apple he had stolen from a stall. In the Bazaar

of the Haberdashers, inside a raised stall, a group of backgammon players continued their dispute by the light of an oil lamp. Two dice went flying, followed by a curse and then a stifled laugh. In the Arcade of the Rope-Makers, a muleteer stopped near a fountain, let the cool water run in the hollow formed by his two palms, then bent over, his lips pouting as if to kiss a sleeping child's forehead. His thirst slaked, he ran his wet palms over his face and mumbled thanks to God. Then he fetched a hollowed-out watermelon, filled it with water, and carried it to his beast so that it too might have its turn to drink.

In the square of the market for cooked foods, Khayyam was accosted by a pregnant girl of about fifteen, whose veil was pushed back. Without a word or a smile on her artless lips, she slipped from his hands a few of the toasted almonds that he had just bought, but the stroller was not surprised. There is an ancient belief in Samarkand: when a mother-to-be comes across a pleasing stranger in the street, she must venture to partake of his food so that the child will be just as handsome, and have the same slender profile, the same noble and smooth features.

Omar was lingering, proudly munching the remaining almonds as he watched the unknown woman move off, when a noise prompted him to hurry on. Soon he was in the midst of an unruly crowd. An old man with long bony limbs was already on the ground. He was bare-headed with a few white hairs scattered about his tanned skull. His shouts of rage and fright were no more than a prolonged sob and his eyes implored the newcomer.

Around the unfortunate man there was a score of men sporting beards and brandishing vengeful clubs, and some distance away another group thrilled to the spectacle. One of them, noticing Khayyam's horrified expression, called out reassuringly, "Don't worry. It's only Jaber the Lanky!" Omar flinched and a shudder of shame passed through him. "Jaber, the companion of Abu Ali!" he muttered.

Abu Ali was one of the commonest names of all, but when a well-read man in Bukhara, Cordova, Balkh, or Baghdad pronounced it with such a tone of familiar deference, there could be no confusion over whom they meant. It was Abu Ali Ibn Sina, renowned in the Occident under the name of Avicenna. Omar had not met him, having been born eleven years after his death, but he revered him as the undisputed master of the generation, the possessor of science, the Apostle of Reason.

Khayyam muttered anew, "Jaber, the favorite disciple of Abu Ali!", for, even though he was seeing him for the first time, he knew all about the pathetic and exemplary punishment that had been meted out to him. Avicenna had soon considered him as his successor in the fields of medicine and metaphysics; he had admired the power of his argument and only rebuked him for expounding his ideas in a manner that was slightly too haughty and blunt. This won Jaber several terms in prison and three public beatings, the last having taken place in the Great Square of Samarkand when he was given one hundred and fifty lashes in front of all his family. He never recovered from that humiliation. At what moment had he teetered over the edge into madness? Doubtless upon the death of his wife. He could be seen staggering about in rags and tatters, yelling out and ranting irreverently. Hot on his trail would follow packs of kids, clapping their hands and throwing sharp stones at him until he ended up in tears.

As he watched this scene, Omar could not help thinking, "If I am not careful, I could well end up a wretch like that." It was not so much that he feared drunkenness, for he and wine had learnt to respect each other, and the one would never lay the other low. What he feared was the idea that the mob could break down his wall of respectability. He felt overly menaced by the spectacle of this fallen man and wanted to distance himself from it. He knew, however, that he could not just abandon a companion of Avicenna to the crowd. He took three solemn steps, and struck a detached pose as he spoke firmly and with regal gesture.

"Leave the poor man alone."

The gang leader who had been bent over Jaber came and planted himself upright in front of the intruder. A deep scar ran across his beard, from his right ear to the tip of his chin, and it was this puckered profile that he thrust towards Omar, as he uttered in judgment, "This man is a drunkard, an infidel." Then he hissed out the last word like a curse, "a *failasuf!*"

"We want no *failasuf* in Samarkand!"

A murmur of approval arose from the crowd. For these people, the term "philosopher" denoted anything too closely associated with the profane Greek sciences, and more generally anything that was neither religion nor literature. In spite of his tender age, Omar Khayyam was already an eminent *failasuf* and as such a greater catch than poor Jaber.

The man with the scar had certainly not recognized him, since he turned back to Jaber, who was still speechless. He grabbed him by the hair, shook his head three or four times and made as if to smash it against the nearest wall, but then suddenly released him. Although brutal, it was a gesture of restraint, as if the man while showing his determination hesitated to commit a murder. Khayyam chose this moment to intervene again.

"Leave the old man alone. He is a widower. He is sick — a lunatic. Can't you see, he can hardly move his lips."

The gang leader jumped up and came towards Khayyam, poking Khayyam's beard.

"You seem to know him quite well! Just who are you? You aren't from Samarkand! No one has ever seen you in this city!"

Omar brushed aside the man's hand haughtily but not abruptly enough to give him the excuse for a fight. The man took a step back, but persisted, "What is your name, stranger?"

Khayyam hesitated to deliver himself into their hands. He tried to think of some ploy. He raised his eyes to the sky where a light cloud had just obscured the crescent moon. He remained silent and then uttered a sigh. He longed to immerse himself in contemplation, to enumerate the stars, to be far off, safe from crowds!

The gang had surrounded him and some hands were brushing against him. He came back to himself.

"I am Omar, son of Ibrahim of Nishapur. And who are you?"

The question was for the sake of form only. The man had no intention of introducing himself. He was in his home town and he was asking the questions. Later on Omar would learn his name. He was a student called Scar-Face. With a club in his hand and a quotation on his lips, he was soon to make all Samarkand tremble, but for the moment his influence only extended to the circle of youths around him, who hung on his every word and gesture.

Suddenly his eyes lit up. He went back towards his disciples, and then turned towards the crowd triumphantly and shouted, "By God, how did I not recognize Omar, son of Ibrahim Khayyam of Nishapur?

Omar, the star of Khorassan, the genius of Persia and Mesopotamia, the prince of philosophers!"

As he mimed a deep bow, he fluttered his fingers on both sides of his turban and succeeded in drawing out the guffaws of the onlookers. "How did I not recognize the man who composed such a pious and devotional *rubai:*

> *You have broken my jug of wine, Lord.*
> *You have barred me from the path of pleasure, Lord.*
> *You have spilt my ruby wine on the ground.*
> *God forgive me, but perchance You are drunk, Lord."*

Omar listened indignantly, but worried. This provocation could provide an excuse for murder on the spot. Without wasting a second, he shot back his response in a loud, clear voice lest anyone in the crowd be fooled. "I do not recognize this quatrain. Indeed this is the first time I have ever heard it. But here is a *rubai* that I myself have composed:

> *They know nothing, neither do they desire to know.*
> *Men with no knowledge who rule the world!*
> *If you are not of them, they call you infidel.*
> *Ignore them, Khayyam, go your own way."*

Omar really should not have accompanied the words "men with no knowledge" with a scornful gesture towards his opponents. Hands came at him, grabbing his robe, which started to rip. He tottered, his back struck someone's knee and then landed on a cobblestone. Crushed under the pack, he did not deign to fight his way out but was resigned to having his clothing ripped from him, being torn limb from limb, and he had already abandoned himself to the numbness of a sacrificial victim. He could feel nothing, hear nothing. He was closed in on himself and laid bare.

So much so, that he viewed as intruders the ten armed men who came to break up this sacrifice. On their felt hats they wore the pale green insignia of the *ahdath*, the town militia of Samarkand. The moment they saw them, his assailants drew back from Khayyam, but to justify their conduct they started to shout, "Alchemist! Alchemist!", calling upon the crowd as their witness.

In the eyes of the authorities being a philosopher was not a crime, but practicing alchemy could mean death.

However, the chief of the patrol did not intend to enter into an argument. "If this man is in fact an alchemist," he pronounced, "then he must be taken before the chief *qadi*, Abu Taher."

As Jaber the Lanky, forgotten by all, crawled towards the nearest tavern, and inched his way inside resolving never to step foot outdoors again, Omar managed to raise himself up without anyone's help. He walked straight ahead, in silence. His disdainful mien covered his tattered clothing and bloodied face like a veil of modesty. In front of him, the militiamen bearing torches forged ahead. To the rear followed his attackers, and behind them the group of gawkers.

Omar did not see or hear them. To him the streets were deserted, the country was silent, the sky was cloudless, and Samarkand was still the place of dreams that he had discovered a few years earlier.

He had arrived there after a journey of three weeks and, without taking the least rest, had decided to follow closely the advice of voyagers of times long past. Go up, they had suggested, onto the terrace of Kuhandiz. Take a good look around and you will see only water and greenery, beds in flower, cyprus trees pruned by the cleverest gardeners to look like bulls, elephants, sturdy camels, or fighting panthers ready to leap. Indeed, even inside the wall, from the gate of the Monastery, to the West and up to the China Gate, Omar had never seen such dense orchards and sparkling brooks. Then, here and there, a brick minaret shot up with a dome chiseled by shadow, the whiteness of a belvedere wall, and, at the edge of a lake that brooded beneath its weeping willows, a naked swimmer spreading out her hair to the burning wind.

Is it not this vision of paradise that the anonymous painter wanted to evoke, when, much later, he attempted to illustrate the manuscript of the *Rubaiyaat?* Is it not this that Omar had in mind as he was being led away towards the quarter of Asfizar where Abu Taher, chief *qadi* of Samarkand, lived? He was repeating to himself, over and over, "I will not hate this city. Even if my swimming girl is just a mirage. Even if the reality should be cold and ugly. Even if this cool night should be my last."

2

In the *qadi's* huge *diwan* the distant chandeliers gave Khayyam an ivory hue. As he entered two middle-aged guards pinned him by the shoulders as if he was a violent madman — and in this posture he waited by the door.

Seated at the other end of the room, the *qadi* had not noticed him as he gave out a ruling on some affair and carried on a discussion with the plaintiffs, reasoning with the one and reprimanding the other. It seemed to be an old quarrel amongst neighbors, consisting of tired old gripes and pettifoggery. Abu Taher ended by loudly showing his weariness, ordering the two heads of family to embrace, there and then in front of him, as if they had never quarreled. One of the two took a step forward but the other, a giant with a narrow forehead, objected. The *qadi* gave him a mighty slap on the face at which the onlookers trembled. The giant cast a quick look at this chubby, angry, and frisky man who had had to hoist himself up to reach him, then he lowered his head, wiped his cheek and complied.

Having dismissed this group, Abu Taher signaled to his militiamen to approach. They reeled off their report and replied to questions, having to explain how they had allowed such a crowd to gather in the streets. Then it was the turn of Scar-Face to give his explanation. He leant towards the *qadi*, who seemed to have known him a long time, and started off on an animated monologue. Abu Taher listened closely without revealing his own feelings. Then, having taken a few moments to think it over, he gave an order, "Tell the crowd to disperse. Let every man go home by the shortest route and," addressing the attackers, "you all go home too. Nothing will be decided before tomorrow. The defendant will stay here overnight and he will be guarded by my men, and none other."

Surprised by being asked so speedily to disappear, Scar-Face made a feeble protest but then thought the better of it. He wisely picked up the tail of his robe and retreated with a bow.

When he was alone with Omar, the only witnesses being his own confidants, Abu Taher pronounced a mysterious phrase of welcome: "It is an honor to receive the famous Omar Khayyam of Nishapur."

He revealed not the slightest hint of emotion. He was neither sarcastic nor warm. His tone was neutral, his voice flat. He was wearing a tulip-shaped turban, had bushy eyebrows and a gray beard without mustache, and was giving Khayyam a long piercing gaze.

The welcome was the more puzzling since for an hour Omar had been standing there in tatters, for all to see and laugh at.

After several skilfully calculated moments of silence, Abu Taher added, "Omar, you are not unknown in Samarkand. In spite of your tender years, your knowledge has already become legendary, and your talents are talked about in the schools. Is it not true that in Isfahan you read seven times a weighty work by Ibn Sina, and that upon your return to Nishapur you reproduced it verbatim from memory?"

Khayyam was flattered that this authentic exploit was known in Transoxania, but his worries had not yet been quelled. The reference to Avicenna from the mouth of a *qadi* of the Shafi rite was not reassuring, and besides, he had not yet been invited to sit down. Abu Taher continued, "It is not just your exploits that are passed from mouth to mouth, but some very curious quatrains have been attributed to you."

The sentence was dispassionate. He was not accusing but he was hardly acquitting him — rather he was only questioning him indirectly. Omar ventured to break the silence. "The *rubai* Scar-Face quoted was not one of mine."

The *qadi* dismissed the protest with a gesture of impatience, and for the first time his voice took on a severe tone. "It matters little whether you have written this or that verse. I have had reports of verses of such profanity that I would feel as guilty quoting them as the man who spread them about. I am not trying to inflict any punishment upon you. These accusations of alchemy cannot just go in one ear and out of the other. We are alone. We are two men of erudition and I simply wish to know the truth."

Omar was not at all reassured. He sensed a trap and hesitated to reply. He could see himself being handed over to the executioner for maiming, emasculation, or crucifixion. Abu Taher raised his voice and almost shouted, "Omar, son of Ibrahim, tent-maker from Nishapur, can you not recognize a friend?"

The tone of sincerity in this phrase stunned Khayyam. "Recognize a friend?" He gave serious thought to the subject, contemplated the *qadi*'s face, noted the way he was grinning and how his beard quivered. Slowly he let himself be won over. His features loosened and relaxed. He disengaged himself from his guards who, upon a sign from the *qadi*, stopped restraining him. Then he sat down without having been invited. The *qadi* smiled in a friendly manner but took up his questioning without respite. "Are you the infidel some people claim you to be?"

It was more than a question. It was a cry of distress that Omar did not overlook. "I despise the zeal of the devout, but I have never said that the One was two."

"Have you ever thought so?"

"Never, as God is my witness."

"As far as I am concerned that suffices, and I believe it will for the Creator also. But not for the masses. They watch your words, your smallest gestures — mine too, as well as those of princes. You have been heard to say, 'I sometimes go to mosques where the shade is good for a snooze.'"

"Only a man at peace with his Creator could find sleep in a place of worship."

In spite of the *qadi*'s doubting scowl, Omar became impassioned and continued, "I am not one of those for whom faith is simply fear of judgment. How do I pray? I study a rose, I count the stars, I marvel at the beauty of creation and how perfectly ordered it is, at man, the most beautiful work of the Creator, his brain thirsting for knowledge, his heart for love, and his senses, all his senses alert or gratified."

The *qadi* stood up with a thoughtful look in his eyes and went over to sit next to Khayyam, placing a paternal hand on his shoulder. The guards exchanged dumbfounded glances.

"Listen, my young friend. The Almighty has granted you the most valuable things that a son of Adam can have — intelligence, eloquence, health, beauty, the desire for knowledge and a lust for life, the admiration of men and, I suspect, the sighs of women. I hope that He has not deprived you of the wisdom of silence, without which all of the foregoing can neither be appreciated nor preserved."

"Do I have to wait until I am an old man in order to express what I think?"

"Before you can express everything you think, your children's grandchildren will be old. We live in the age of the secret and of fear. You must have two faces. Show one to the crowd, and keep the other for yourself and your Creator. If you want to keep your eyes, your ears, and your tongue, forget that you have them."

The *qadi* suddenly fell silent, but not to let Omar speak, rather to give greater effect to his admonition. Omar kept his gaze down and waited for the *qadi* to pluck more thoughts from his head.

Abu Taher, however, took a deep breath and gave a crisp order to his men to leave. As soon as they had shut the door behind them, he made his way towards a corner of the *diwan*, lifted up a piece of tapestry, and opened a damask box. He took out a book, which he offered to Omar with a formality softened by a paternal smile.

Now that book was the very one that I, Benjamin O. Lesage, would one day hold in my own hands. I suppose it felt just the same, with its rough, thick leather with markings that looked like a peacock-tail and the edges of its pages irregular and frayed. When Khayyam opened it on that unforgettable summer night, he could see only two hundred and fifty-six blank pages that were not yet covered with poems, pictures, margin commentaries, or illuminations.

To disguise his emotions, Abu Taher spoke with the tones of a salesman.

"It's made of Chinese *kaghez,* the best paper ever produced by the workshops of Samarkand. A Jew from the Maturid district made it to order according to an ancient recipe. It is made entirely from mulberry. Feel it. It has the same qualities as silk."

He cleared his throat before going on.

"I had a brother, ten years older than I. He died when he was as old as you. He had been banished to Balkh for having written a poem which displeased the ruler of the time. He was accused of fomenting heresy. I don't know if that was true, but I resent my brother for having wasted his life on a poem, a miserable poem hardly longer than a *rubai.*"

His voice shook, and he went on breathlessly.

"Keep this book. Whenever a verse takes shape in your mind, or is on the tip of your tongue, just hold it back. Write it down on these sheets, which will stay hidden, and as you write, think of Abu Taher."

Did the *qadi* know that with that gesture and those words he was giving birth to one of the best-kept secrets in the history of literature, and that the world would have to wait eight centuries to discover the sublime poetry of Omar Khayyam, for the *Rubaiyaat* to be revered as one of the most original works of all time even before the strange fate of the Samarkand manuscript was known?

3

That night, Omar tried in vain to catch some sleep in a belvedere, a wooden pavilion on a bare hillock in the middle of Abu
Taher's huge garden. Near him on a low table lay a quill and ink-pot,
an unlit lamp and his book — open at the first page, which was still
blank.

At first light there was an apparition. A beautiful slave-girl brought
him a plate of sliced melon, a new outfit, and a winding-scarf of
Zandan silk for his turban. She whispered a message to him:

"The master will await you after the morning prayer."

The room was already packed with plaintiffs, beggars, courtiers, friends,
and visitors of all sorts, and amongst them was Scar-Face, who had
doubtless come for news. As soon as Omar stepped through the door
the *qadi*'s voice steered everyone's gaze and comment to him.

"Welcome to Imam Omar Khayyam, the man without equal in
knowledge of the traditions of the Prophet, a reference that none can
contest, a voice that none can contradict."

One after another, the visitors arose, bowed, and muttered a phrase before sitting down again. Out of the corner of his eye, Omar watched Scar-Face, who seemed very subdued in his corner, but still had a timid smirk on his face.

In the most formal manner, Abu Taher bid Omar take his place at his right, making a great show of dismissing those near him. He then continued, "Our eminent visitor had a mishap yesterday evening. This man who is honored in Khorassan, Fars, and Mazandaran, this man whom every city wishes to receive within its walls and whom every prince hopes to attract to his court, this man was molested yesterday in the streets of Samarkand."

Expressions of shock could be heard, followed by a commotion which the *qadi* allowed to grow a little before signaling for quiet and continuing.

"Worse still, there was almost a riot in the bazaar. A riot on the eve of the visit of our revered sovereign, Nasr Khan, the Sun of Royalty, who is to arrive this very morning from Bukhara, God willing! I dare not imagine what distress we would be in today if the crowd had not been contained and dispersed. I tell you that heads would not be resting easy on shoulders!"

He stopped to get his breath, to drive his point home and let fear work its way into the audience's hearts.

"Happily one of my old students, who is with us here, recognized our eminent visitor and came to warn me."

He pointed a finger towards Scar-Face and invited him to rise.

"How did you recognize Imam Omar?"

He muttered a few syllables in answer.

"Louder! Our old uncle here cannot hear you!" shouted the *qadi*, indicating an ancient man with a white beard to his left.

"I recognized the eminent visitor by his eloquence," Scar-Face could hardly get the words out, "and I asked him who he was before bringing him to our *qadi*."

"You did well. Had the riot continued, there might have been bloodshed. You deserve to come and sit next to our guest."

As Scar-Face was approaching with an air of false submission, Abu Taher whispered in Omar's ear, "He may not be your friend, but he will not dare to lay into you in public."

He continued in a loud voice, "Can I hope that in spite of everything that he has been through, *Khawaja* Omar will not have too bad a memory of Samarkand?"

"I have already forgotten whatever happened yesterday evening," replied Khayyam. "In the future, when I think of this city, a completely different image will spring to mind, the image of a wonderful man. I am not speaking of Abu Taher. The highest praise one can give to a *qadi* is not to extol his qualities but the honesty of those for whom he has responsibility. As it happens, on the day I arrived my mule had struggled up the last slope leading to the Kish Gate, and I myself had hardly put my feet on the ground when a man accosted me.

"'Welcome to this town,' he said. 'Do you have family, or friends here?'

"I replied that I did not, without stopping, fearing that he might be some sort of crook, or at the very least a beggar or irksome. But the man went on:

"'Do not be mistrustful of my insistence, noble visitor. It is my master who has ordered me to wait here and offer his hospitality to all travelers who turn up.'

"The man seemed to be of a modest background, but he was dressed in clean clothes and not unaware of the manners of respectable people. I followed him. A few steps on, he had me enter a heavy door and I crossed a vaulted corridor to find myself in the courtyard of a caravansary with a well in the center and men and animals bustling all about. Around the edges, on two floors, there were rooms for travelers. The man said, 'You can stay here as long as you wish, be it one night or the whole season. You will find a bed and food and fodder for your mule.'

"When I asked him how much I had to pay, he was offended.

"'You are my master's guest.'

"'Tell me where my generous host is, so that I can address my thanks to him.'

"'My master died seven years ago, leaving me a sum of money which I must spend to honor visitors to Samarkand.'

"'What was your master's name, so that I can tell of his acts of kindness?'

"'You should give thanks to the Almighty alone. He knows whose acts of kindness are being carried out in His name.'

"That is how it came about that I stayed with this man for several days. I went out and about, and whenever I came back I found plates piled high with delicious dishes and my horse was better cared for than if I myself had been looking after him."

Omar glanced at this audience, looking for some reaction, but his story had not caused any looks of surprise or mystery. The *qadi*, guessing Omar's confusion, explained.

"Many cities like to think that they are the most hospitable in all the lands of Islam, but only the inhabitants of Samarkand deserve the credit. As far as I know, no traveler has ever had to pay for his lodgings or food. I know whole families who have been ruined honoring visitors or the needy, but you will never hear them boast of it. The fountains you have seen on every street corner, filled with sweet water to slake the thirst of passers-by, of which there are more than two thousand in this city made of tile, copper, or porcelain, have all been provided by the people of Samarkand. But do you think that a single man has had his name inscribed on one to garner gratitude?"

"I must confess that I have nowhere met such generosity. Would you allow me to pose a question which has been bothering me?"

The *qadi* took the words out of his mouth: "I know what you are going to ask: how can people who so esteem the virtues of hospitality be capable of violence against a visitor such as yourself?"

"Or against a poor old man like Jaber the Lanky?"

"The answer I am going to give you is summed up in one word — fear. All violence here is born of fear. Our faith is being attacked from all sides by the Qarmatians in Bahrain, the Imamis of Qom, the seventy-two sects, the Rum in Constantinople, infidels of all denominations, and above all the Ismailis in Egypt who have a massive following right in the heart of Baghdad and even here in Samarkand. Never forget that our cities of Islam—Mecca, Medina, Isfahan, Baghdad, Damascus, Bukhara, Merv, Cairo, Samarkand—are no more than oases that will revert to being desert if neglected for a moment. They are constantly at the mercy of a sandstorm!"

Through a window to his left the *qadi* expertly calculated the sun's passage. He stood up.

"It is time to go and meet our sovereign," he said.

He clapped his hands.

"Bring us some fortification for the journey."

It was his practice to supply himself with raisins to munch on his way, a practice much imitated by those around him and those who came to visit him. Hence the immense copper platter that was brought in to him piled high with a mound of these pale treats for everyone to stuff their pockets.

When it was Scar-Face's turn, he grabbed a small handful, which he held out to Khayyam with the words, "I suppose that you would prefer me to offer these to you as wine."

He did not speak in a very loud voice, but as if by magic everyone present fell silent. They stood with bated breath, watching Omar's lips. He spoke.

"When one wishes to drink wine, one chooses carefully one's cupbearer and drinking companion."

Scar-Face's voice rose a little.

"For my part, I would not touch a drop. I am hoping for a place in paradise. You do not seem anxious to join me there."

"The whole of eternity in the company of sententious *ulema?* No, thank you. God promised us something else."

The exchange stopped there. Omar hurried to join the *qadi*, who was calling him.

"The townspeople must see you ride next to me. That will dispel their impressions of yesterday evening."

In the crowd gathered around the residence, Omar thought he could make out the almond-seller concealed in the shadow of a peartree. He slowed down and looked around for her, but Abu Taher badgered him.

"Faster. Woe betide you should the Khan arrive before us."

4

"Since the dawn of time astrologers have proclaimed that four cities were born under the sign of revolt, Samarkand, Mecca, Damascus, and Palermo, and their words are truth! These cities have only ever submitted to government through force. They follow the straight path only when it is traced by the sword. The Prophet reduced the arrogance of the Meccans by the sword and it is by the sword that I will reduce the arrogance of the people of Samarkand!"

Nasr Khan, the master of Transoxania, a bronzed giant in flowing embroidered robes, gesticulated standing in front of his throne. His voice caused trembling amongst his household and visitors. His eyes sought out amongst those present a victim, a lip that might dare to tremble, an insufficiently contrite look, the memory of some treachery. By instinct everyone slipped behind his neighbor, letting his back, neck, and shoulders slump, and waited for the storm to pass.

Having found no prey for his claws, Nasr Khan grabbed armfuls of his ceremonial robes and in a fury flung them one after another into a pile at his feet, yelling insult after insult in the sonorous Turco-

Mongol dialect of Kashgar. According to custom, sovereigns would wear three, four, or sometimes seven layers of embroidered robes, which they peeled off during the day, solemnly placing them on the backs of those whom they wished to honor. Behaving in such a manner, Nasr Khan showed that day that he had no intention of gratifying any of his numerous visitors.

As with every sovereign's visit to Samarkand, this was to have been a day of festivities, but any trace of joy was extinguished in the first minutes. Having climbed the paved road leading up from the Siab River, the Khan effected his solemn entry by the Bukhara Gate at the north of the city. He smiled with his whole face, making his small eyes seem more deeply set, more slanting than ever, and making his cheekbones glow in the amber reflection of the sun. Then suddenly he lost his good humor. He approached a group of some two hundred notables who were gathered around the *qadi* Abu Taher, focusing a worried and almost suspicious gaze upon the group in whose midst was Omar Khayyam. Apparently not having seen those he sought, he abruptly made his horse rear up, jerked hard on the reins and moved off, grumbling inaudibly. Rigid on his black mare, he no longer smiled, nor did he respond with the slightest gesture to the repeated cheers of the thousands of citizens who had been gathering there since dawn to greet him. Some of them held up petitions, composed by some public scribe. In vain, for no one dared to present his petition to the sovereign, but rather applied to the chamberlain who leaned over again and again to accept the sheets, mouthing a vague promise to take action.

Preceded by four horsemen, holding aloft the brown standards of the dynasty, followed on foot by a slave naked to the waist and bearing a huge parasol, the Khan crossed the great thoroughfares lined with twisting mulberry trees without stopping. He avoided the bazaars and went along the main irrigation canals, called *ariks*, until he came to the district of Asfizar. There he had had set up a temporary palace, directly adjoining Abu Taher's residence. In the past, sovereigns would lodge inside the citadel, but since recent battles had left it in a state of extreme dilapidation, it had had to be abandoned. Now, only the Turkish garrison would periodically erect its yurts there.

Having observed the sovereign's bad humor, Omar hesitated to go to the palace to give his respects, but the *qadi* urged him, no doubt in the hope that the presence of his eminent friend would provide a favorable distraction. On the way, Abu Taher took it upon himself to brief Khayyam on what had just transpired. The religious dignitaries of the city had decided to boycott the reception, accusing the Khan of having burnt down the Grand Mosque of Bukhara where armed opponents had entrenched themselves. "Between the sovereign and the religious establishment," explained the *qadi*, "the war rages on as ever. Sometimes it is overt and bloody, but most often clandestine and insidious."

It was even rumored that the *ulema* had made contact with a number of officers who were exasperated by the behavior of the prince. His forbears used to eat with the troops, they said, omitting no occasion to state that their power derived from the bravery of their people's warriors. But from one generation to the next, the Turkish khans had acquired the regrettable habits of the Persian monarchs. They thought of themselves as demi-gods, surrounding themselves with an increasingly complex ceremonial that was incomprehensible and humiliating for their officers. A number of the latter had thus consulted the religious chiefs. They took pleasure in hearing the officers vilify Nasr and accuse him of having cast aside the ways of Islam. To intimidate the military, the sovereign reacted harshly against the *ulema*. Had not his father, a pious man moreover, inaugurated his reign by cutting off an abundantly turbaned head?

In this year of 1072, Abu Taher was one of the few religious dignitaries who managed to maintain close ties with the prince, visiting him often in the citadel of Bukhara, his main residence, and receiving him with solemnity each time he stopped at Samarkand. Certain of the *ulema* eyed warily Abu Taher's conciliatory attitude, but most of them welcomed the presence of this intermediary.

Yet again the *qadi* easily fell into the role of conciliator. He avoided contradicting Nasr, profiting of the slightest glimmer of an improvement of his humor to buoy up his spirits. He waited until the difficult moments were over, and when the sovereign returned to his throne and Abu Taher had seen him finally settle himself firmly against a soft cushion, he undertook a subtle and imperceptible resumption of control which Omar watched with relief. Upon a sign from the *qadi* the chamberlain summoned a young slave-girl to pick up the robes, which were abandoned on the ground like corpses after a battle. Instantly, the atmosphere became less stifling, people discreetly stretched their limbs and some chanced to whisper a few words into the nearest ear.

Then, striding towards the space in the center of the room, the *qadi* positioned himself in front of the monarch, lowered his head and said nothing. The maneuver was so well-executed that after a long silence, when Nasr finally declared, with a strength tinged with fatigue, "Go and tell all the *ulema* of this city to come at dawn to prostrate themselves at my feet. The head which is not bowed will be cut off. Let no one attempt to flee, for no land can give shelter from my anger," everyone understood that the storm had passed and that a resolution was in sight. The clerics had only to make amends and the monarch would forego taking harsh measures.

The next day, when Omar again accompanied the *qadi* to the court, the atmosphere was hardly recognizable. Nasr was on his throne, a type of raised platform covered with a dark carpet, next to which a slave was holding up a plate of crystallized rose petals. The sovereign would choose one, place it on his tongue, let it melt against his palate, before nonchalantly holding his hand out to another slave who sprinkled perfumed water on his fingers and wiped them attentively. The ritual was repeated twenty or thirty times, while the delegations filed past. They represented the districts of the city, notably Asfizar, Panjkhin, Zagrimach, Maturid, the bazaar corporations, the trade guilds of coppersmiths, paper makers, silkworm breeders, and water-carriers, as well as the protected communities: Jews, Parsees, and Nestorian Christians.

They all began by kissing the ground. They then raised themselves up, and made another bow, which they held until the monarch signaled them to rise. Their spokesman uttered a few phrases and they went out backwards, it actually being forbidden to turn one's back to the sovereign before leaving the room. A curious practice. Was it introduced by a monarch over-keen on respect, or by a particularly distrustful visitor?

Then the religious dignitaries came, awaited with curiosity but also with apprehension. There were more than a score of them. Abu Taher had had no difficulty convincing them to come. Since they had shown their feelings to ample extent, to persevere in that path would be to ask for martyrdom, which none of them desired.

Now they too presented themselves in front of the throne, each bending as low as his age and joints would allow him, awaiting the sign from the prince to rise. But the sign did not come. Ten minutes went by and even the youngest of them could not remain in such an uncomfortable pose indefinitely. What could they do? To rise without having been authorized would be to expose themselves to condemnation by the monarch. One after another they fell on their knees, a pose that was just as respectful but less exhausting. Only when the last kneecap had touched the ground did the sovereign make the sign that they might get up and leave with no further ado. No one was surprised by the turn of events. That was the price to pay. Such is the order of affairs of the kingdom.

Turkish officers and groups of notables then approached, as well as some *dihkans*, headmen from neighboring villages. According to his rank, each kissed the foot or shoulder of the sovereign. Then a poet came forward to recite a pompous eulogy to the glory of the monarch, who very quickly looked ostensibly bored. With a gesture he interrupted the poet, made a sign to the chamberlain to lean over and gave the order that he was to transmit. "Our master wishes the poets assembled here to know that he is tired of hearing the same themes repeated, he wishes to be compared neither to a lion nor an eagle, and even less to the sun. Let those who have nothing else to say depart."

5

The chamberlain's words were followed by murmurs, clucking, and a general din from the twenty-odd poets who had been awaiting their turn. Some of them even took two steps backward before quietly slipping away. Only a woman stepped out of the ranks and approached with a steady tread. Quizzed by Omar's glance, the *qadi* whispered, "A poetess from Bukhara. She has herself called Jahan, meaning the vast world. She is a fickle young widow."

His tone was that of rebuke, but Omar's interest was only heightened and he could not turn his gaze away. Jahan had already raised the bottom of her veil, revealing lips without make-up. She recited a pleasantly worked poem in which, strangely, the Khan's name was not mentioned one single time. Praise was given to the Soghd River which dispenses its bounty to Samarkand and then to Bukhara before losing itself in the desert since there is no sea worthy of receiving its waters.

"You have spoken well. Let your mouth be filled with gold," said Nasr, pronouncing his usual phrase.

The poetess lent over a huge platter of golden dinars and started putting the coins into her mouth one by one as the audience counted them aloud. When Jahan hiccupped and almost choked, the whole court, with the monarch at the fore, let out a laugh. The chamberlain signaled to the poetess to return to her place. They had counted forty-six dinars.

Khayyam alone did not laugh. With his eyes fixed on Jahan, he tried to work out what emotion he felt towards her. Her poetry was so pure, her eloquence so dignified, her gait so courageous, but here she was stuffing her mouth with yellow metal and being subjected to this humiliating reward. Before pulling her veil back down, she lifted it a little more and cast a glance that Omar noticed, inhaled, and tried to hold on to. It was a moment too fleeting to be detected by the crowd but an eternity for the lover. Time has two faces, Khayyam said to himself. It has two dimensions, its length is measured by the rhythm of the sun but its depth by the rhythm of passion.

This sublime moment between them was interrupted by the *qadi* tapping Khayyam's arm and bringing him back to himself. Too late, the woman had gone. There were only veils left.

Abu Taher wanted to present his friend to the Khan. He uttered the formula, "Your august roof today shelters the greatest intellect of Khorassan, Omar Khayyam, for whom the plants hold no secrets and the stars no mystery."

It was not serendipity that made the *qadi* note medicine and astrology out of all the disciplines in which Omar excelled, as they were always in favor with princes; the former to try and preserve their health and life, and the latter to preserve their fortune.

The prince's expression cheered up and he said that he was honored. However, not being in a mood to engage in intellectual conversation and apparently mistaking the visitor's intentions, he chose to reiterate his favorite formula, "Let his mouth be filled with gold!"

Omar was taken aback and suppressed a retch. Abu Taher noticed this and was worried.

Fearing lest a refusal offend the sovereign, he gave his friend an insistent and serious look and pushed him forward by the shoulder but to no avail. Khayyam had already made his decision.

"Would my Lord be so kind as to excuse me. I am in a period of fasting and can put nothing in my mouth."

"But the month of fasting finished three weeks ago, if I am not mistaken!"

"During Ramadan I was traveling from Nishapur to Samarkand. I had to break my fast with the vow that I would complete it later."

The *qadi* took fright and all those assembled fidgeted, but the sovereign's face was blank. He chose to question Abu Taher.

"Can you tell me, you who have knowledge of all the minutiae of the faith, can you tell me if putting gold coins in his mouth and taking them out quickly thereafter constitutes breaking the fast for *Khawaja* Omar?"

The *qadi* adopted his most neutral tone:

"Strictly speaking, anything that goes into the mouth can constitute breaking the fast. It has happened that a coin was swallowed by accident."

Nasr accepted the argument, but he was not satisfied. He questioned Omar:

"Have you told me the real reason for your refusal?"

Khayyam hesitated for a moment and then said:

"That is not the only reason."

"Speak," said the Khan. "You have nothing to fear from me."

Then Omar pronounced these verses:

> *It was not poverty that drove me to you*
> *I am not poor, for my desires are simple.*
> *The only thing I seek from you is honor*
> *The honor of a free and steadfast man.*

"May God darken your days, Khayyam!" murmured Abu Taher, as if to himself.

He did not know what to think, but his fear was tangible. There still rang in his ears the echo of an all too recent anger and he was not sure if he would again be able to tame the beast. The Khan remained silent and still, as if frozen in unfathomable deliberation. Those close to the Khan were awaiting his first word as if it were a verdict and some courtiers chose to leave before the storm.

Omar profited from the general disarray to seek out Jahan's eyes. She was leaning with her back against a pillar with her face buried in her hands. Could it be for him that she was trembling?

26

Finally the Khan arose. He marched resolutely towards Omar, gave him a vigorous hug, took him by the hand, and led him off.

"The master of Transoxania," the chroniclers report, "developed such an esteem for Omar Khayyam that he invited him to sit next to him on the throne."

"So now you are the Khan's friend," Abu Taher called out to Khayyam when they had left the palace.

His joviality was as great as the anguish that had gripped his throat, but Khayyam replied coolly:

"Could you have forgotten the proverb that says, 'The sea knows no neighbors, the prince knows no friends'?"

"Do not scorn the open door. It seems to me that your career is marked out at court!"

"Court life is not for me; my only ambition is that one day I will have an observatory with a rose garden and that I will be able to throw myself into contemplating the sky, a goblet in my hand and a beautiful woman at my side."

"As beautiful as that poetess?" chuckled Abu Taher.

Omar could think of nothing but her, but he did not reply. He was afraid that the smallest word uttered carelessly might betray him. Feeling a little light-hearted, the *qadi* changed both his tone and the subject:

"I have a favor to ask of you!"

"It is you who has showered me with your favors."

Abu Taher quickly conceded that point. "Let us say that I would like something in exchange."

They had arrived at the gateway of his residence. He invited Khayyam to continue their conversation around a table laden with food.

"I have thought up a project for you, a book project. Let us forget your *Rubaiyaat* for a moment. As far as I am concerned they are just the inevitable whims of genius. The real domains in which you excel are medicine, astrology, mathematics, physics, and metaphysics. Am I mistaken when I say that since Ibn Sina's death there is none who knows them better than you?"

Khayyam said nothing. Abu Taher continued:

"It is in those areas of knowledge that I expect you to write the definitive book, and I want you to dedicate that book to me."

"I don't think that there can be a definitive book in those disciplines, and that is exactly why I have been content to read and to learn without writing anything myself."

"Explain yourself!"

"Let us consider the Ancients — the Greeks, the Indians, and the Muslims who have come before me. They wrote abundantly in all those disciplines. If I repeat what they have said, then my work is redundant; if I contradict them, as I am constantly tempted, others will come after me to contradict me. What will there remain tomorrow of the writings of the intellectuals? Only the bad that they have said about those who came before them. People will remember what they have destroyed of others' theories, but the theories they construct themselves will inevitably be destroyed and even ridiculed by those who come after. That is the law of science. Poetry does not have a similar law. It never negates what has come before it and is never negated by what follows. Poetry lives in complete calm through the centuries. That is why I wrote my *Rubaiyaat*. Do you know what fascinates me about science? It is that I have found the supreme poetry: the intoxicating giddiness of numbers in mathematics and the mysterious murmur of the universe in astronomy. But, by your leave, please do not speak to me of Truth."

He was silent for a moment and then continued:

"It happened that I was taking a walk round about Samarkand and I saw ruins with inscriptions that people could no longer decipher, and I wondered, 'What is left of the city which used to exist here?' Let us not speak about people, for they are the most ephemeral of creatures, but what is left of their civilization? What kingdom, science, law, and truth existed here? Nothing, I searched around those ruins in vain and all I found was a face engraved on a potsherd and a fragment of a frieze. That is what my poems will be in a thousand years — shards, fragments, the detritus of a world buried for all eternity. What remains of a city is the detached gaze with which a half-drunk poet looked at it."

"I understand your words," stuttered Abu Taher, rather at sea. "However, you would not dedicate to a *qadi* of the Shafi ritual poems which smack of wine!"

In fact, Omar would be able to appear conciliatory and grateful. He would water down his wine, so to speak. During the following months, he undertook to compile a very serious work on cubic equations. To represent the unknown in this treatise on algebra, Khayyam used the Arabic term *shay*, which means "thing." This word, spelled *xay* in Spanish scientific works, was gradually replaced by its first letter, *x*, which became the universal symbol for the unknown.

This work of Khayyam's was completed at Samarkand and dedicated to his protector: "We are the victims of an age in which men of science are discredited and very few of them have the possibility of committing themselves to real research. The little knowledge that today's intellectuals have is devoted to the pursuit of material aims. I had thus despaired of finding in this world a man as interested in the scientific as the mundane, a man preoccupied by the fate of mankind, until God accorded me the favor of meeting the great *qadi*, the Imam Abu Taher. His favors permitted me to devote myself to these works."

That night, when he went back towards the belvedere that was serving him as a house, Khayyam did not take a lamp with him, telling himself that it was too late to read or write. However, his path was only faintly illuminated by the moon, a frail crescent at the end of the month of *shawwal*. As he walked further from the *qadi*'s villa, he had to grope his way along. He tripped more than once, held on to the bushes and took the grim caress of a weeping willow full in the face.

He had hardly reached his room when he heard a voice of sweet reproach. "I was expecting you earlier."

Had he thought about this woman so much that he now believed he could hear her? As he stood in front of the door, which he slowly closed, he tried to make out a silhouette. In vain, for only the voice broke through again, audible yet hazy.

"You are keeping quiet. You refuse to believe that a woman could dare to force her way into your room like this. In the palace our eyes met and lit up, but the Khan was there as well as the *qadi* and the court and you averted your eyes. Like so many men, you chose not to stop. What good is it to defy fate, what good is it to attract the wrath

29

of a prince just for a woman, a widow who can only bring you as a dowry a sharp tongue and a dubious reputation?"

Omar felt restrained by some mysterious power and could neither move nor loosen his lips.

"You are saying nothing," commented Jahan with gentle irony. "Oh well, I'll go on speaking on my own, and anyway I am the only one who has made the move so far. When you left the court, I asked after you and learned where you live. I gave out that I was going to stay with a cousin who is married to a rich Samarkand merchant. Ordinarily when I move about with the court, I go and sleep with the harem where I have some friends who appreciate my company. They devour the stories I bring them. They do not see me as a rival as they know that I have no desire to be a wife to the Khan. I could have seduced him, but I have spent too much time with kings' spouses for such a fate to tempt me. Life, for me, is so much more important than men! As long as I am someone else's wife, or no one's, the sovereign loves to show me off in his *diwan* with my verses and my laughter. If ever he dreamt of marrying me, he would start by locking me up."

Emerging with difficulty from his torpor, Omar had grasped nothing of Jahan's words, and, when he decided to utter his first words, he was speaking less to her than to himself, or to a shade:

"How often, as an adolescent, or later, have I received a look or a smile. At night I would dream that that look became corporeal, turned into flesh, a woman, a dazzling sight in the dark. Suddenly, in the dark of this night, in this unreal pavilion, in this unreal city, you are here — a beautiful woman, a poetess moreover, and available."

She laughed.

"Available! How do you know? You have not even touched me, you have not seen me, and doubtless you will not see me since I shall depart well before the sun chases me away."

In the dense darkness there was a disorderly rustle of silk and a whiff of perfume. Omar held his breath, his body was aroused. He could not help asking with the naïveté of a schoolboy:

"Are you still wearing your veil?"

"The only veil I am wearing is the night."

6

A woman and a man. The anonymous painter imagined them in profile, stretched out and intertwined. He took away the walls of the pavilion, gave them a bed of grass with a border of roses and made a silvery brook flow at their feet. He gave Jahan the shapely breasts of a Hindu deity. Omar caresses her hair with one hand and holds a goblet in the other.

Every day at the palace their paths would cross, but they avoided looking at each other lest they give themselves away. Every evening Khayyam would dash back to the pavilion to await his beloved. How many nights had fate granted them? Everything depended on the sovereign. When he decamped Jahan would follow. He never announced anything in advance. One morning this nomad's son would jump up onto his charger and set out for Bukhara, Kish, or Panjikent and the court would be thrown into panic trying to catch up with him. Omar and Jahan dreaded this moment and their every kiss carried with it a taste of farewell, their every embrace a breathless flight.

On one of the most oppressive summer nights, Khayyam had gone out to wait on the terrace of the belvedere, when he heard the *qadi's* guards laughing from what seemed very close by and he became uneasy, but for no reason, since Jahan arrived and reassured him that no one had noticed her. They exchanged a first furtive kiss, followed by another more intense. That was how they rounded off a day during which they belonged to others and started off on a night which belonged to them.

"In this city how many lovers do you think there are who at this very moment are being united like us?" Jahan whispered impishly. Omar adjusted his nightcap learnedly and puffed out his cheeks and spoke wistfully:

"Let us consider this carefully: if we exclude bored spouses, obedient slaves, street girls selling or hiring themselves out, and sighing virgins, how many woman are there left, how many women are there being united with the man they have chosen? In the same fashion, how many men will sleep next to a woman they love, a woman who gives herself to them for some reason other than that they have no choice? Who knows, tonight in Samarkand there is perhaps only one such man and one such woman. Why you and why me, you will say? Because God has made us fall in love just as he has made certain flowers poisonous."

He laughed and she let her tears flow.

"Let us go in and shut the door. They will be able to hear our happiness."

Many caresses later, Jahan sat up, half covered herself and gently extricated herself from her lover's embrace.

"I must pass on to you a secret that I have from the Khan's senior wife. Do you know why he is in Samarkand?"

Omar stopped her, thinking it would be some harem tittle-tattle.

"The secrets of princes do not interest me. They burn the ears of those who listen to them."

"Just hear me out. This secret affects us too, since it can disrupt our lives. Nasr Khan has come to inspect the fortifications. At the end of the summer, when the intense heat has subsided, he is expecting an attack by the Seljuk army."

The Seljuks, Khayyam knew them. They peopled his first memories of childhood. Well before they became the masters of Muslim Asia, they had laid into the city of his birth and left behind, for generations, the memory of the Great Fear.

That had taken place ten years before he was born. The people of Nishapur had woken up one morning to find their city completely encircled by the Turkish warriors, headed by two brothers, Tughrul Beg the Falcon and his brother Tchagri Beg the Hawk, sons of Mikhael son of Seljuk, at the time obscure nomadic chieftains who had only recently been converted to Islam. A message came to the city's notables: "It is told that your men are proud and that you have sweet water running in underground canals. If you attempt to resist us, your canals will soon be open to the heavens and your men will be in the ground."

This was the type of bragging that was frequent at the time of a siege. The notables of Nishapur nevertheless made speed to capitulate in return for a promise that the inhabitants' lives would be spared and that their goods, houses, and canals would be safe. But of what value are the promises of a conqueror? When the horde entered the city, Tchagri wanted to loose his men in the streets and the bazaar. Tughrul was of a different opinion, wanting the month of Ramadan to be honored, during which period of fasting a city of Islam could not be pillaged. This argument won the day, but Tchagri was not disarmed and he resigned himself to waiting until the population was no longer in a state of grace.

When the citizens got wind of the dispute between the two brothers and realized that at the beginning of the coming month they would be handed over to be pillaged, raped, and massacred, that was the start of the Great Fear. Worse than rape is the announcement of impending rape, combined with a passive and humiliating wait for the unavoidable. The stalls emptied, men went to ground, and their wives and daughters saw them bewail their impotence. What could they do, how could they flee, by what route? The occupier was everywhere. Soldiers with braided hair lurked in the bazaar of the Grand Square, the various districts of the city and its suburbs, the area around the Burnt Gate. They were constantly drunk and on the lookout for ransom or plunder, and their disorderly hordes infested the neighboring countryside.

Does one not usually desire the fast to come to an end and the feast day to arrive? That year they wanted the fast to go on forever and hoped that the Feast of Breaking would never come. When the crescent moon of the new month was spotted, no one thought to rejoice or to slit the throat of a lamb. The whole city felt like a gigantic lamb fattened for slaughter.

The night before the feast, this night when every wish is granted, was a night of agony, tears, and prayers spent by thousands of families in the precarious shelter of mosques, and the mausoleums of saints.

In the citadel, there was now a stormy discussion raging between the Seljuk brothers. Tchagri shouted that his men had not been paid for months, and that they had only agreed to fight because they had been promised a free hand in this opulent city, that they were on the verge of revolt, and that he, Tchagri, could no longer hold them back.

Tughrul spoke another language:

"We are only at the start of our conquests. There are so many cities to take, Isfahan, Shiraz, Ray, Tabriz, and others further on. If we pillage Nishapur after it has surrendered, after all our promises, no other gate will open for us, no other garrison will show any weakness."

"How will we be able to conquer all those cities of which you are dreaming if we lose our army and our men abandon us? The most loyal are already complaining and threatening."

The two brothers were surrounded by their lieutenants and the elders of the clan who unanimously confirmed Tchagri's words. Encouraged by this, he rose and decided to bring things to a conclusion:

"We have spoken too much. I am going to tell my men to do as they wish with the city. If you wish to restrain your men, do so. To each of us his own troops."

Caught on the horns of a dilemma, Tughrul did not move. Suddenly he sprang away from them and grabbed a dagger.

Tchagri, for his part, had also unsheathed his sword. No one knew whether to intervene or, as was the custom, let the Seljuk brothers settle their difference with blood, when Tughrul called out:

"Brother, I cannot force you to obey me. I cannot restrain your men, but if you set them on the city I will plant this dagger in my heart."

As he said that he clutched the handle of the dagger with both hands and pointed the blade down towards his chest. His brother hesitated little, but walked towards him with his arms open and gave him a long embrace, promising not to go against his will. Nishapur was saved, but it would never forget the Great Fear of Ramadan.

7

"That is how the Seljuks are," Khayyam observed. "Uneducated looters and enlightened sovereigns who are capable of great meanness and sublime gestures. Tughrul Beg above all had the temperament of an empire builder. I was three years old when he took Isfahan and ten years old when he conquered Baghdad, imposing himself as the protector of the Caliph and wheedling out of him the title of 'Sultan, King of the East and West' and at seventy marrying the Prince of the Believers' very own daughter."

Omar recounted in a tone of admiration, perhaps with even a touch of solemnity, but Jahan let out a very irreverent laugh. He was offended and gave her a sharp look, unable to understand this sudden hilarity. She excused herself and explained:

"When you mentioned the marriage, I remembered what they told me in the harem."

Omar vaguely remembered the episode whose every detail Jahan had greedily retained.

When he received the message from Tughrul demanding the hand of his daughter Sayyida, the Caliph had become wild with rage. The emissary of the Sultan had hardly withdrawn before he exploded:

"This Turk who has just stepped out from his yurt! This Turk whose fathers in the very recent past were still worshiping some idol or another and who painted pigs' snouts on their standards! How dare he demand in marriage the daughter of the Prince of the Believers, descendant of the most noble lineage?"

If he was trembling so violently in all his august limbs it was because he knew that he could not deflect the claim. After months of hesitation and two messages of appeal, he ended up by formulating a reply. One of his old counselors was charged with conveying it and he left for the city of Ray, whose ruins are still visible in the area of Tehran. Tughrul's court was there.

The Caliph's emissary was first of all received by the Vizir who confronted him with these words:

"The Sultan's patience is running out and he is harassing me. I am happy that you at last have arrived with a reply."

"You will be less happy when you hear it: the Prince of Believers begs you to excuse him for not being able to accede to the demand that has been put to him."

The Vizir did not seem particularly concerned. He continued to finger his jade worry-beads.

"And so," he said, "you are going to walk down this corridor and go through that tall doorway and announce to the master of Iraq, Fars, Khorassan, and Azerbaijan, to the conqueror of Asia, the sword who defends the true Religion, to the protector of the Abbassid throne: 'No, the Caliph will not give you his daughter!' Very well. This guard will show you the way."

The latter presented himself and the emissary arose to follow him, when the Vizir added innocuously:

"I assume, wise man that you are, that you have paid your debts, shared out your fortune among your sons, and married off all your daughters!"

The emissary sat back down, suddenly exhausted.

"What do you advise me to do?"

37

"Did the Caliph give you no other directive, no other way of settling affairs?"

"He told me that if there was really no way of escaping from this marriage, he wished for three hundred thousand gold dinars as compensation."

"There we have already a better way of proceeding. However, I do not think it is reasonable for him to ask for compensation after all that the Sultan has done for the Caliph, after he had brought him back to the city whence the Shiites had chased him, after he had restored to him his wealth and his territory. We could reach the same result without offending Tughrul Beg. You will tell him that the Caliph offers him his daughter's hand, and I, for my part, will make use of the moment of intense satisfaction to suggest that he gives a gift of dinars commensurate to such a personage."

That was what happened. The Sultan, in a state of excitement, put together a great convoy comprising the Vizir, several princes, dozens of officers and dignitaries, and aged female relatives with hundreds of guards and slaves who carried to Baghdad for him presents of great value — camphor, myrrh, brocade, and boxes full of gems, as well as a hundred thousand pieces of gold.

The Caliph held an audience for the principal members of the delegation and exchanged polite but amorphous greetings. Then, during his talk with the Sultan's Vizir, he told him bluntly that the marriage did not have his consent and that if they tried to coerce him he would leave Baghdad.

"If that is the stance of the Prince of Believers, why did he propose an arrangement in dinars?"

"I could not simply turn him down with a single 'no.' I hoped that the Sultan would understand by my attitude that he could not obtain such a sacrifice from me. I can tell you that no other Sultans, be they Turks or Persians, have ever demanded such a thing from a Caliph. I must defend my honor!"

"Several months ago, when I felt that your response might be negative, I tried to prepare the Sultan. I explained to him that no one before him had ever dared to formulate such a request, that it was untraditional and that people would be surprised. I could never dare to repeat what he replied to me."

"Speak. Fear not!"

"May the Prince of Believers excuse me, for those words can never cross my lips."

The Caliph lost his patience.

"Speak, I order you. Hide nothing!"

"The Sultan started by insulting me and accusing me of siding with the Prince of Believers against him . . . He threatened to have me put in irons . . ."

The Vizir stuttered deliberately.

"Get to the point. Tell me what Tughrul Beg said."

"The Sultan yelled: 'What a strange clan those Abbassids are! Their ancestors conquered the best half of the world, they built the most flourishing cities, and just look at them today! I take their empire and they put up with that. I take their capital and they are happy, they shower me with presents and the Prince of Believers says to me, "I give you all the lands that God has given to me and I place in your hands all the believers whose fate He has entrusted to me." He begs me to put his palace, his person, and his harem under my protection. However, if I ask for his daughter, he rises up and wishes to defend his honor. Is the only territory for which the Sultan is ready to fight the thighs of a virgin?'"

The Caliph choked and could not utter a word. The Vizir made the most of this to conclude the message.

"The Sultan added, 'Go and tell them that I will take that girl the way I took this empire, the way I took Baghdad!'"

8

J ahan recounted in great detail, and with a guilty pleasure, the matrimonial heartbreaks of the great people of the world; having given up
reprimanding her, Omar was now lapping up her stories. When she
mischievously threatened to be quiet, he begged her to continue, backing
this up with caresses, even though he knew perfectly well how the
story ended.

The Prince of Believers therefore resigned himself to saying "yes,"
but he had death in his soul. As soon as he received the Caliph's
response, Tughrul set out for Baghdad, and even before reaching the
city, he sent his Vizir on ahead as a scout, so impatient was he to see
what arrangements had already been planned for the marriage.

Arriving at the Caliph's palace, the emissary heard it plainly stated
that the marriage contract could be signed, but the union of the two
spouses was out of the question, "as the honor of the alliance was the
crucial point and not the match of the couple."

The Vizir was exasperated, but he controlled himself.

"Knowing Tughrul Beg as I do," he explained, "I can assure you beyond all measure of doubt that the importance he gives to the union is in no way secondary."

In fact, in order to emphasize how ardent his desire was, the Sultan did not hesitate to place his troops in a state of alert, to place Baghdad under close control, and to surround the Caliph's palace. The Caliph had to back down and the "union" took place. The Princess sat on a gold-carpeted bed. Tughrul Beg entered the room and kissed the ground in front of her. "Then he honored her," the chronicles confirm, "while she did not remove the veil from her face, say a word, or give heed to his presence." He would come to see her every day with valuable presents and he honored her every day, but not once did she let him see her face. A number of people awaited him as he left after every "meeting," for he was in such good humor that he granted all their requests and gave presents out recklessly.

No child was born of this marriage of decadence and arrogance. Tughrul died six months later. It was generally known that he had been sterile, having repudiated his two first wives and accused them of the ill from which he suffered. With his string of women, wives, and slaves he should have faced up to the fact that if there was any fault it was his. Astrologers, healers, and shamans had been consulted and prescribed that he swallow the foreskin of a newly circumcised infant at full moon. But this had no result and he had to resign himself to the truth. However, in order to prevent this infirmity lowering his prestige amongst his men, he forged himself a solid reputation as an insatiable lover, dragging behind him for even the shortest move of the court an amply furnished harem. His performance was a required subject of conversation amongst his entourage and it was not rare that officers and even foreign visitors would ask after his prowess and, after lauding his nocturnal energy, they would ask him for his recipes and elixirs.

Sayyida thus became a widow. Her golden bed was empty but she did not think to complain. The void in power seemed more serious. The empire had just been born, and, even if it bore the name of its nebulous Seljuk ancestor, its real founder was Tughrul. Was his disappearance without issue now going to plunge the Orient into anarchy? Brothers, nephews, and cousins were legion and the Turks did not recognize any birthright or law of succession.

Very quickly, however, a man managed to impose himself: Alp Arslan, son of Tchagri. Within a few months he came to prevail over the members of the clan, massacring some and buying the allegiance of others. He would soon appear to his subjects as a great sovereign who was firm and just, but he was nevertheless to be dogged by a rumor, nurtured by his rivals. Whereas the sterile Tughrul was accredited with unbounded virility, Alp Arslan, the father of nine children, by reason of his behavior and rumors attached to him, acquired the image of a man for whom the other sex held little attraction. His enemies nick-named him "the Effeminate" and his courtiers avoided mentioning such an embarrassing subject in their conversation. It was this reputa-tion, merited or not, that was to cause his downfall and prematurely interrupt a career that at first had seemed so brilliant.

Jahan and Omar did not yet know this. At the time they were chatting away in the belvedere in Abu Taher's garden, Alp Arslan was at thirty-eight years old the most powerful man on earth. His empire extended from Kabul to the Mediterranean, his power was undivided and his army faithful. As Vizir he had the most able statesman of his time, Nizam al-Mulk. Moreover, in the little village of Manzikart in Anatolia, Alp Arslan had just won a resounding victory over the Byz-antine empire, whose army had been shattered and the Emperor cap-tured. Preachers in all the mosques lauded his exploits and told how, at the hour of battle, he had dressed himself in a white shroud and perfumed himself with embalmer's herbs, how with his own hands he had plaited his horse's tail and surprised Russian scouts sent by the Byzantines who were at the perimeters of his camp and had their noses sliced off, but also how he gave the imprisoned Emperor back his liberty.

Doubtless it was a great moment for Islam, but it was a subject of grave concern for Samarkand. Alp Arslan had always coveted the city and in the past had even sought to seize it. Only his conflict with the Byzantines had constrained him to conclude a truce between the two dynasties which had been sealed by matrimonial alliances: Malikshah, the oldest son of the Sultan, had obtained the hand of Terken Khatun, sister of Nasr Khan; the Khan himself had married the daughter of Alp Arslan.

However, no one was fooled by these arrangements. Ever since he had learnt of his brother-in-law's victory over the Christians, the master of Samarkand had been fearing the worst for his city. He was not wrong and events started to move apace.

Two hundred thousand Seljuk cavalrymen were preparing to cross "the river," which at that time was named the Jayhun, which the ancients had called the Oxus and which was later to become the Amu Darya. It took twenty days until the last soldier had crossed it on a tottery pontoon bridge.

The throne room at Samarkand was often full, but as quiet as the house of a deceased person. The Khan himself seemed subdued by the ordeal and had neither fits of temper nor outbursts of shouting. His courtiers seemed overwhelmed. His haughtiness reassured them even if they were victim to it. His calmness unsettled them and they felt that he had resigned himself to his fate. They judged him to be a defeated man and gave thought to their own safety. Should they flee now, wait around, or pray?

Twice a day the Khan would arise followed by his retinue and would go off to inspect a mulberry patch or be acclaimed by his soldiers or the populace. During one of these rounds some young townspeople attempted to approach the monarch. Held at a distance by the guards, they yelled out that they were ready to fight alongside the soldiers and to die in defense of the city, the Khan, and the dynasty. Far from rejoicing at their initiative, the sovereign was irritated, broke off his visit to retrace his steps and ordered the soldiers to disperse them roughly.

When he was back in the palace, he addressed his soldiers:

"When my grandfather, may God preserve in us the memory of his wisdom, wished to capture the city of Balkh, the inhabitants took up arms in the absence of their sovereign and killed a large number of our soldiers, forcing our army to retreat. My grandfather then wrote a letter to Mahmoud, the master of Balkh, in which he rebuked him: 'I most ardently desire our troops to clash, may God grant victory to whom he wishes, but where will we end up if the common people start meddling in our quarrels?' Mahmoud sided with him and punished his subjects, forbidding them to carry arms. He fined them great amounts of gold to make up for the destruction the clashes had caused. What was true for the people of Balkh is even more so for those of Samarkand who are by nature rebellious. I would rather betake myself to Alp Arslan alone and unarmed than owe my safety to the citizenry."

The officers all fell in with his view. They promised to repress any popular zeal, renewed their oaths of allegiance, and swore to fight like wounded wildcats. These were not just words. The Transoxanian troops were no less brave than those of the Seljuks. Alp Arslan had only the advantage of numbers and age. Not his age, that is, but that of his dynasty. He belonged to the second generation, which was still animated by the ambition of empire-builders. Nasr was the fifth of his line and much more desirous of enjoying his acquisitions than of expansion.

During this whole period of agitation, Khayyam wanted to stay well away from the city. Naturally he could not refrain from putting in a brief appearance at court or at the *qadi's* palace from time to time without seeming to desert them in their ordeal. Hòwever, most often he would stay shut up in his belvedere, immersed in his works or in his secret book whose pages he was furiously blackening as if the war only existed in the detached wisdom that was inspired in him.

Only Jahan brought him back to the reality of the drama happening around them. Every evening she would bring him the latest news from the front and report the moods of the palace to which he would listen without obvious enthusiasm.

On the ground, Alp Arslan's advance was slow. He was weighted down with excess troops, discipline was slipshod, and he had to contend with illness and the swamps as well as occasional outbreaks of fierce resistance. One man in particular was making the Sultan's life hard. He was the commander of a fortress not far from the river. The army could have skirted around it and continued to advance, but its rear would have been less secure, harassments would have continued, and in case of difficulty any retreat would have been turned out to be perilous. Alp Arslan thus had given the order to put the fortress out of action ten days earlier and they had made numerous assaults on it.

The battle was being followed very closely from Samarkand. Every three days a pigeon would arrive, released by the defenders. The message was never an appeal for help. It did not describe the exhaustion of supplies or men, it spoke only of adverse losses and rumors of epidemics rife amongst the besiegers. Overnight the commander of the site, a certain Yussif, originally from Khwarazm, became the hero of Transoxania.

However, eventually the defenders were overwhelmed, the foundations of the fortress were undermined and the walls scaled. Yussif fought to the last before being wounded and captured. He was led off to the Sultan, who was curious to see close up the cause of his troubles. It was a lean little man, hirsute and dusty, who was marched in front of the Sultan. He held himself upright with his head held high, between two giants who gripped him by the arms. Alp Arslan, for his part, was stretched out on a wooden dais covered with cushions. The two men looked at each other defiantly, then the victor ordered:

"Place four posts in the ground, tie him to them, and have him quartered."

Yussif looked at the Sultan condescendingly and scornfully, and shouted, "Is that the way to punish someone who has fought like a man?"

Alp Arslan did not reply. He turned his face away. The prisoner added, "You, the Effeminate. I am talking to you!"

The Sultan jumped up, as if stung by a scorpion. He seized his bow which was lying near him, loaded an arrow, and before firing he ordered the guards to release the prisoner as he could not fire on the man without the risk of wounding his own soldiers. In any case, he had nothing to worry about for he had never missed a target.

Perhaps it was his extreme annoyance, his hurry, or the awkwardness of firing at such a short distance but Yussif was still unharmed and the Sultan did not have time to load a second arrow before the prisoner attacked him. Alp Arslan, who could not defend himself while still perched on his pedestal, tried to extricate himself, tripped on a cushion, stumbled, and fell to the ground. Yussif was upon him straight away, grasping the knife that he had kept hidden in the folds of his clothing. He had time to stab him in the side before he himself was dispatched by a massive blow. The soldiers set upon his lifeless, mutilated body. His lips, however, still kept the sardonic smile that death had frozen on them. He was avenged and the Sultan was not to out-last him for long.

Alp Arslan in fact died after four long nights of agony and bitter meditation. His words were recorded in the chronicles of the time: "The other day I reviewed my troops from high on a promontory and I felt the earth tremble under their step. I told myself, 'I am the master of the world! Who can measure up to me?' For my arrogance and vanity God sent out the most wretched of humans, a prisoner, a condemned man on his way to be executed; he proved himself more powerful than I, he struck me, he knocked me off my throne, he has removed my life."

Was it the day after this drama that Omar Khayyam wrote in his book:

> *Once in a while a man arises boasting;*
> *He shows his wealth and cries out, "It is I!"*
> *A day or two his puny matters flourish;*
> *Then Death appears and cries out, "It is I!"*

9

It was feast-time in Samarkand and a woman dared to cry — the wife of the triumphant Khan, but she was also above all the daughter of the assassinated Sultan. Naturally her husband had gone to present his condolences. He had ordered the whole harem to wear mourning and had a eunuch who had displayed too much good humor flogged in front of her. However, when he was back in his *diwan* he did not hesitate to tell all and sundry that "God has granted the prayers of the people of Samarkand."

It might be supposed that at that time the inhabitants of a city had no reason for preferring one sovereign over the other. However, they said their prayers, for what they really feared was a change of master with his string of massacres and ordeals and the inevitable pillaging and plundering. For the population to wish to be conquered by another, the monarch had to go beyond the limit in submitting them to exorbitant taxes and continuous harassment. This was not the case with Nasr. If he was not the best of princes, he certainly was not the worst. They could live with him and they put their faith in the ability of the Almighty to keep him in check.

Thus in Samarkand they were celebrating being spared from war. The immense square of Ras al-Tak was overflowing with smoke and noise. Itinerant merchants had erected stalls against every wall, and under every street lamp there was a singing girl or a lute player improvising melodies. Myriad groups were forming and dispersing around the storytellers, the palm-readers, and the snake-charmers. In the center of the square, on a hastily constructed and shaky rostrum, they were holding the traditional contest amongst popular poets who sang praise to the incomparability and invincibility of Samarkand. The public's judgment was instant. New stars arose and others waned. There were wood fires almost everywhere, as it was December and the nights had already turned cold. In the palace, jars of wine were being emptied and smashed. The Khan was jovial, boisterous, and swaggering with drink.

The next day he had the prayer for the dead recited in the great mosque and then received condolences over the death of his father-in-law. The same people who had rushed over the day before to congratulate him on his victory came back, wearing expressions of mourning to express their sorrow. The *qadi*, who had recited some appropriate verses and invited Omar to do the same, gave Omar an aside:

"Do not be astonished at anything. Reality has two faces and so do people."

That very evening, Abu Taher was summoned by Nasr Khan, who asked him to join the delegation charged with going to pay Samarkand's homage to the deceased Sultan. Omar had set off too, albeit with a hundred and twenty other people.

The site of the condolences was an old Seljuk army camp, situated just north of the river. Thousands of tents and yurts were pitched all around, a veritable improvised city where the solemn representatives of Transoxania rubbed shoulders distrustfully with the nomad warriors with long plaited hair who had come to renew their clan's allegiance. Malikshah, at seventeen, a giant with the face of a child, was wrapped in a flowing *karakul* coat and sat enthroned on the very dais

48

where his father, Alp Arslan, had fallen. Several steps in front of him stood the Grand Vizir, at fifty-five years old the strongman of the empire, whom Malikshah called "father" as a sign of extreme deference. Nizam al-Mulk, the Order of the Kingdom. Never had a name been more deserved. Every time a visitor of rank approached, the young Sultan gave the Vizir a questioning look. He then gave an imperceptible signal as to whether to receive the visitor warmly or reservedly, serenely or distrustingly, attentively or absently.

The whole delegation from Samarkand prostrated themselves at the feet of Malikshah, who acknowledged them with a condescending nod of the head. Then a number of the notables left the group to make their way towards Nizam. The Vizir was impassive. His colleagues were bustling around him, but he looked at them and listened to them without reacting. He should not be thought of as a master of the palace who shouted out his orders. If his influence was ubiquitous, it was because he worked like a puppeteer, who with a discreet touch impressed on others the movements he desired. His silences were proverbial. It was not rare for a visitor to spend an hour in his presence without any words being exchanged other than the phrases of greeting and parting. He was not visited for his conversation, but so that allegiances could be renewed, suspicions dispelled, and oblivion avoided.

Twelve people from the Samarkand delegation had obtained the privilege of shaking the hand that held the rudder of the empire. Omar followed close behind the *qadi* Abu Taher who muttered a formula. Nizam nodded and kept his hand in the *qadi's* for a few seconds, thereby honoring him. When it was Omar's turn, the Vizir leant over to his ear and murmured:

"On this day next year, be at Isfahan and we shall speak."

Khayyam was not certain that he had heard correctly and he felt a little off-balance. The personage intimidated him, the ceremonies impressed him, the chaos intoxicated him, and the wails of the mourners were deafening him. He could no longer trust his senses. He wanted some confirmation that he had heard correctly but he was already being swept along by the flow of people. The Vizir was looking elsewhere and had started to nod his head in silence again.

On his way back, Khayyam could not stop mulling over the incident.

Was he the only one to whom the Vizir had uttered those words? Had he not confused him for someone else, and why was the meeting so distant, both in terms of time and space?

He decided to take the matter up with the *qadi*. Since he had been just in front of him, he must have heard, felt, seen, or guessed something. Abu Taher let him recount the scene, before admitting mischievously, "I noticed that the Vizir whispered some words to you. I did not hear them, but I can assure you that he did not mistake you for anyone else. Did you see all the people around him. Their job is to obtain information on the composition of each delegation and to whisper him the name and position of those approaching him. They asked me your name, assured themselves that you were the Khayyam of Nishapur, the intellectual and the astrologer. There was no confusion over your identity. Anyway, the only confusion with Nizam al-Mulk is that which he deems fit to create."

The way was flat and stony. To the right in the distance lay a line of high mountains, the foothills of Pamir. Khayyam and Abu Taher rode along side by side with their mounts brushing against each other.

"What can he want of me?"

"In order to find out, you will have to wait a year. Until that time, I advise you not to bog yourself down in conjecture. The wait is too long and you will exhaust yourself. Above all, do not mention this to a soul!"

"Do I usually prattle?"

The tone was that of reproach, but the *qadi* did not allow himself to be flustered:

"I wish to be clear: do not mention this to that woman!"

Omar should have suspected that Jahan's repeated visits could not have gone unnoticed. Abu Taher continued:

"At your first meeting the guards came to inform me. I concocted a complicated story to justify her visits. I ordered them not to see her and forbade them to wake you up every morning. Have not the slightest doubt, that pavilion is your house, I want you to know that today and tomorrow. However, I have to speak to you about that woman."

Omar was embarrassed. He did not appreciate at all the way his friend said "that woman" and he had no desire to discuss his affairs. Although he was saying nothing to his elder, his face tightened.

"I know that what I am saying vexes you, but I shall go on saying it until I have said it all, and if our too-recent friendship does not give me the right, my age and position do. When you saw that woman for the first time in the palace you looked upon her with desire. She is young and beautiful and you liked her poetry and her audaciousness warmed your blood. However, you had differing attitudes towards the gold. She stuffed her mouth with what disgusted you. She behaved like a court poetess and you acted as a sage. Have you spoken to her about it since then?"

The reply was no, and, even though Omar said nothing, Abu Taher heard it clearly. He continued:

"Often, at the beginning of an affair, the sensitive questions are avoided. There is a fear of destroying this fragile edifice which has just been erected with a thousand precautions, but as far as I am concerned what sets you apart from this woman is both serious and fundamental. You do not look at life the same way."

"She is a woman and, what is more, a widow. She is trying to fend for herself without depending on a master, and I can only admire her courage. And how can one reproach her for taking the gold that her verses are worth?"

"I understand," said the *qadi*, satisfied at having finally dragged his friend into that discussion. "But you must admit, at least, that this woman would be unable to envisage any life other than that of the court."

"Perhaps."

"You must also admit that, for you, court life is odious and unbearable and that you will not stay a moment longer than necessary."

An embarrassed silence followed. Abu Taher finished by stating resolutely:

"I have told you that you should listen to a true friend. Henceforth I will not bring up the matter unless you raise it first yourself."

10

By the time they reached Samarkand, they were exhausted by the cold, the jolting of their mounts, and the disquiet that had arisen amongst them. Omar retired to his pavilion straight away without taking the time to dine. During the trip he had composed three quatrains which he started to recite aloud, ten times, twenty times, replacing a word and modifying a turn of phrase before consigning them to the secrecy of his manuscript.

Jahan, who unexpectedly arrived earlier than usual, had slipped in through the half-open door and noiselessly taken off her woolen shawl. She was walking on tip-toe behind Omar. He was still distracted when she suddenly threw her bare arms around his neck, pressed his face to hers, and let her perfumed hair fall into his eyes.

Omar should have been overjoyed. Could a lover hope for more tender aggression? Once the moment of surprise had passed should he not in turn have folded his arms around his beloved, held her and impressed on her body all the pain of absence and all the warmth of reunion? However, Omar was upset by this intrusion. His book still lay open in front of him and he wanted to get it out of sight. His first impulse was to free himself, and even though he repented immediately and his hesitancy had only lasted a second, Jahan, who had felt this wavering and aloofness, very quickly understood the reason. She looked at the book with distrust, as if it were a rival.

"Excuse me! I was so impatient to see you again that I did not think my arrival could unsettle you."

A heavy silence lay between them. Khayyam hastened to break it.

"It's the book, isn't it? It is true that I had not thought of showing it to you. I have always hidden it when you were here, but the person who gave it to me made me promise to keep it a secret."

He held it out to her. She leafed through it for a few moments, pretending to be completely indifferent to the sight of a few pages of writing scattered amongst dozens of blank pages. She handed it back to him with a decided pout.

"Why are you showing it to me? I did not ask you for anything. Anyway, I have never learned to read. I have acquired everything I know from listening to others."

Omar was not surprised. It was not rare at that time for the best poets to be illiterate, just like almost all women of course.

"What is so secret in this book. Does it contain alchemy formulas?"

"They are poems which I write down sometimes."

"Forbidden and heretical poems, subversive poems?"

She looked at him suspiciously, but he defended himself laughingly:

"No, what are you trying to make out? Do I have the soul of a plotter? They are only *rubaiyaat* about wine, beauty, life and its vanity."

"You! You write *rubaiyaat?*"

She let out a cry of incredulity that was almost scorn. *Rubaiyaat* were something of a minor literary genre, they were trite and even coarse and suited only for poets from the popular districts. It could be taken as an amusement, a peccadillo, or even a flirtation for an intellectual like Omar Khayyam to allow himself to compose a *rubai* from time to time, but what astonished and worried a poetess devoted to the norms of eloquence was that he should take such care to consign his verses, and with such extreme gravity, to a book shrouded in mystery. Omar seemed ashamed but Jahan was intrigued:

53

"Could you read some of the verses to me?"

Omar did not want to commit himself further.

"I will be able to read them all to you one day, when I judge them to be ready."

She did not press the point and stopped asking him further questions, but she commented, without stressing the irony:

"When you finish this book, do not offer it to Nasr Khan. He does not think much of the authors of *rubaiyaat*. He will not ask you to join him on his throne any more."

"I have no intention of offering this book to anyone at all. I do not wish to gain anything by it. I do not have the ambitions of a court poet."

She had hurt him and he had wounded her. In the silence that enfolded them, they wondered if they had overstepped the mark and if there was still time to stop and save what could still be saved. At that moment, it was not Jahan whom Khayyam resented, but the *qadi*. He regretted having allowed him to speak and wondered if his words had not damaged irreparably the way he saw his lover. Until then, they had been living a carefree life with neither of them wishing to bring up any potentially divisive subjects. Omar could not decide whether the *qadi* had opened his eyes to the truth, or just clouded his happiness.

"You have changed, Omar. I cannot say how, but there is in the way you are looking at me and talking to me something which I cannot quite put my finger on. It is as if you suspect me of some misdeed, as if you resent me for some reason. I do not understand you, but suddenly I am greatly saddened."

He tried to draw her towards him, but she stepped aside brusquely:

"You cannot reassure me like that! Our bodies can only draw out our words, they cannot take their place or belie them. Tell me what the matter is!"

"Jahan! Let us speak no more of it until tomorrow."

"I shall no longer be here tomorrow. The Khan is leaving Samarkand early in the morning."

"Where is he going?"

"To Kish, Bukhara, Termez, I don't know. The whole court will follow him, along with me."

"Could you not stay in Samarkand with your cousin?"

"If it were only a question of finding excuses! I have my place at court. I had to fight like ten men to gain it and I will not give it up today for a frolic in the belvedere of Abu Taher's garden."

Without really thinking it over, Khayyam said, "It is not a question of a frolic. Would you not share my life?"

"Share your life? There is nothing to share!"

She had said it without spite. It was simply a statement, and not lacking in tenderness. However, when she saw how crestfallen Omar was, she begged him to forgive her and sobbed.

"I knew that I was going to cry this evening, but I did not know I would cry such bitter tears. I knew that we were going to be parted for a long time, perhaps forever, but I did not know we would use such words and glances. I do not want to carry from the most beautiful love affair I have had the memory of those eyes of a stranger. Look at me, Omar. Look at me for the last time! Remember, I am your lover. You loved me and I loved you. Can you still recognize me?"

Khayyam tenderly put his arm around her. He sighed.

"If only we had the time to explain ourselves, I know that this stupid quarrel would be cleared up, but time is rushing us into playing out our future in a few confused minutes."

He could sense a tear sliding down his face. He wanted to hide this tear, but Jahan clutched him savagely to her, pressing his face against hers.

"You can hide your writings, but not your tears. I want to see them, touch them, and mix them with mine. I want to keep their traces on my cheeks and their salty taste on my tongue."

It was as if they were trying to tear each other apart, to suffocate or destroy each other. Their hands ran amok and their clothes were scattered about. There is no night of love comparable to that of two bodies set on fire by burning tears. The fire raged and enveloped them. It wound them up, intoxicated them, inflamed them, and fused them together, skin against skin, taking them to the very extremes of pleasure. On the table an hourglass was running out, grain by grain. The fire died down, smoldered, and went out. They both wore an exhausted smile, and were breathing slowly. Omar murmured, either to her or to the fate that they had just faced:

"Our fight is just beginning."
Jahan clutched him, her eyes closed.
"Do not let me sleep until dawn."

The next day there were two new lines in the manuscript. The calligraphy was scratchy, hesitant, and tortured.

Next to your beloved, Khayyam, how alone you are!
Now that she is gone, you can take refuge in her.

11

Kashan — an oasis of low houses on the silk route, at the end of the Salt Desert. Caravans nestled there, catching their breath before passing by Kargas Kuh, the sinister Vulture Mountain that was the retreat of the bandits who were the scourge of the districts around Isfahan.

Kashan was built of mud and clay. A visitor could search in vain for a gaily decorated wall or an ornamented façade. However, it is in Kashan that the most famous varnished tiles were made to embellish the green and gold of the thousand mosques, palaces, or *madrasas* from Samarkand to Baghdad. Throughout the whole of the Muslim East, faïence was simply called *kashi* or *kashani*, rather as porcelain, in both Persian and English, is named after China.

Outside the city, in the shade of the palm trees, there was a caravansary enclosed by rectangular walls with watch towers, an exterior courtyard for animals and goods and an inside courtyard with small rooms all the way around. Omar wanted to rent a room but the hostelkeeper apologized that he had none left for the night. Some wealthy merchants from Isfahan had just arrived with their sons and servants. He did not need to check the register to verify his claim: the place was swarming with noisy retainers and venerable mounts. In spite of the incipient winter, Omar would have considered sleeping under the stars, but the scorpions of Kashan are hardly less renowned than its faïence.

"Is there really not even a nook for me to spread out my mat until dawn?"

The landlord scratched his forehead. It was dark and he could not refuse shelter to a Muslim.

"I have a small corner room, occupied by a student. Ask him if he will let you share."

They went to the room and found the door closed. The hostelkeeper pushed it open without knocking. A candle flickered and a book was slammed shut.

"This noble traveler left Samarkand three months ago and I wondered if he might share your room."

If the young man was against this idea he avoided showing it. He remained polite, although without appearing eager.

Khayyam entered, greeted him and carefully stated his identity as "Omar of Nishapur."

There was a short, but intense glimmer of interest in the eyes of his companion. He in turn introduced himself:

"Hassan, son of Ali Sabbah, native of Qom, student at Rayy, *en route* to Isfahan."

This detailed listing made Khayyam uneasy. It was an invitation for him to say more about himself, his occupation and the purpose of his voyage. He could not see any point in doing so and was suspicious of such behavior. He thus kept quiet, took the time to sit down against a wall and to take a good look at this dark-skinned young man with such angular features who was so frail and emaciated. Khayyam was disconcerted by his seven-day growth of beard, his tightly-wound black turban, and his bulging eyes.

The student unnerved him with a smile.

"It is not very clever for people called Omar to be out and about in Kashan."

Omar feigned complete surprise. However, he had understood the allusion. His first name was that of the Prophet's second successor, the Caliph Omar who was hated by the Shiites as he had been a fierce rival of their founding father, Ali. Even though, for the time being, the overwhelming majority of Persia's population was Sunni, there were already some pockets of Shiism, namely the oasis cities of Qom and Kashan, where strange traditions were carried on. Every year an absurd carnival celebrated the anniversary of the Caliph Omar's murder. To this end women put on make-up, prepared sweets and grilled pistachio nuts while the children positioned themselves on the terraces and emptied buckets of water on the passers-by as they shouted triumphantly, "God curse Omar!" An effigy of the Caliph was made, holding a string of turds, and this was then paraded through certain districts by people chanting, "Your name is Omar and your abode is Hell. You are the biggest villain ever! You are the infamous usurper!" The cobblers of Qom and Kashan had the custom of writing "Omar" on the soles of the shoes they made, muleteers gave his name to their beasts and liked to utter it as they beat their mules, and hunters, as they flexed their last arrow, would murmur, "This one is for the heart of Omar!"

Hassan had made reference to those practices in a few vague words, avoiding the coarser details, but Omar looked at him unkindly as he stated with finality:

"I will not change my route because of my name, and I will not change my name because of my route."

A long, cold silence ensued during which they avoided each other's sight. Omar took off his shoes and stretched out to try and sleep. It was Hassan who badgered him:

"Perhaps I have offended you by recounting these customs, but I only wanted you to be careful about mentioning your name in this place. Do not be mistaken about my intentions. Naturally, I happened to participate in those festivities during my childhood in Qom, but since my adolescence I have seen them in a different light and have come to understand that such excesses are not worthy of a man of learning. Neither do they conform to the teaching of the Prophet. All the same, when you gaze in awe, in Samarkand or elsewhere, at a mosque wonderfully clad in tiles glazed by the Shiite artisans of Kashan, and when the preacher of that same mosque launches into tirades of invective and curses against 'the accursed heretical sectarians of Ali,' that too is hardly in conformity with the teaching of the Prophet."

Omar raised himself up a little.

"Now those are the words of a sensible man."

"I know how to be sensible, just as I know how to be a fool. I can be likeable or disagreeable. But, how can a man be friendly with someone who comes to share his room but who will not even deign to introduce himself?"

"Telling you my first name was enough for you to unleash a verbal attack on me. What would you have said if I had stated my whole identity?"

"Perhaps I would have said none of what I did. One can hate the Caliph Omar and feel nothing but admiration for Omar the Geometrician, Omar the Algebraist, Omar the Astronomer, or even Omar the Philosopher."

Omar sat upright. Hassan went on triumphantly:

"Do you think that people can only be identified by their name? They can be recognized by the way they look, by their gait and bearing, or the tone they affect. The moment you entered I knew that you were a man of knowledge, accustomed to honors and yet scornful of them, a man who arrives without having to ask the way. The moment you gave out the first part of your name, I understood: my ears can recognize only one Omar of Nishapur."

"If you have been trying to impress me, I have to admit that you have succeeded. Who, then, are you?"

"I have told you my name, but it means nothing to you. I am Hassan Sabbah of Qom. I can boast of nothing save having managed, by the age of seventeen, to read everything there is on science and religion, philosophy, history, and the stars."

"One can never read everything, there is so much new knowledge to acquire every day."

"Put me to the test."

As a jest, Omar started to ask him some questions on Plato, Euclid, Porphyry, Ptolomy, on the medicine of Disocorides, Galen, Razi, and Avicenna, and then on interpretations of Quranic law. His companion's responses were always precise, thorough, and flawless. When dawn arose neither of them had slept or felt the speedy passage of time. Hassan felt a real joy. Omar was fascinated and had to admit:

"I have never met a man who has learnt so many things. What do you plan to do with all this accumulation of knowledge?"

Hassan looked at him distrustingly, as if some secret part of his soul had been violated, but he recovered his composure and lowered his eyes.

"I want to work my way close to Nizam al-Mulk. He may have some position for me."

Omar was so beguiled by his companion that he was on the point of revealing to him that he himself was on his way to see the Grand Vizir. However, at the last moment, he changed his mind. The last trace of distrust had not yet disappeared.

Two days later, when they had joined a caravan of merchants, they rode side by side, quoting from memory in Persian and Arabic large sections of the most beautiful writings of the authors they admired. Sometimes an argument would start up, but then quickly die down. When Hassan spoke of certainties, raised his voice, proclaimed "empirical truths" and enjoined his companion to admit them, Omar remained skeptical. He slowly weighed the merits of certain opinions but seldom settled for any of them, and willingly displayed his ignorance. He found himself repeating untiringly, "What do you want me to say? These things are veiled, and you and I are on the same side of the veil. When it falls, we will no longer be here."

After a week *en route*, they arrived in Isfahan.

12

*E*sfahan, *nesf-é jahan!* is what the Persians of today say. "Isfahan, half of the world!" The expression came into use well after the age of Khayyam, but even in 1074 the city was exalted in words: "Its stones are of galenite, its flies are bees, its grass is saffron," "its air is so pure and healthy that its granaries do not change according to any calendar and flesh does not decompose." It is true that the city lies at an altitude of five thousand feet, but Isfahan also had sixty caravansaries, two hundred bankers and money-changers, and endless covered bazaars. Its workshops produced silk and cotton. Its carpets, cloths, and padlocks were exported to the most distant countries. Its roses blossomed in a thousand varieties and its opulence was proverbial. This city, the most populous in the Persian world, attracted all those who were seeking power, fortune, or knowledge.

I have said "this city," but one can not really speak of a city. They still tell the story there of a young traveler from Rayy, who was in such a hurry to see the wonders of Isfahan that on the last day he galloped ahead of his caravan. After several hours he came to the bank of the Zayandé-Rud, "the life-giving river," and followed it until he reached a wall of earth. The town seemed to him to be of a respectable size, but smaller than his own city of Rayy. When he reached the gate, he asked the guards.

"This is the city of Jay," he was told.

He did not so much as go in but turned and followed his route towards the West. His mount was exhausted, but he did not spare the crop. Soon he found himself, panting, at the gates of another city, more imposing than the first, but scarcely larger than Rayy. He questioned an old passer-by.

"This is Yahoudiyeh, the 'Jews' town.'"

"Are there so many Jews in this country?"

"There are some, but most of the inhabitants are Muslims, like you and I. The town is called Yahoudiyeh because King Nebuchadnezzar is supposed to have settled here the Jews he deported from Jerusalem. Others claim that it was the Jewish spouse of a Persian Shah who, before the age of Islam, had members of her community brought here. God alone knows the truth!"

Our young traveler thus turned away, determined to follow his route even if his horse were to collapse between his legs, when the old man called to him:

"Where are you trying to get to, my son?"

"To Isfahan!"

The old man burst out laughing.

"Has no one ever told you that Isfahan does not exist?"

"What do you mean. Is it not the largest and most beautiful city of Persia? Was it not in the distant past the proud capital of Artaban, King of the Parthians? Have its wonders not been extolled in books?"

"I do not know what the books say, but I was born here sixty years ago and only foreigners have ever spoken to me of the city of Isfahan. I have never seen it."

This was hardly any exaggeration. The name Isfahan had for a long time not designated a city but an oasis where there were the two distant cities Jay and Yahoudiyeh, which were separated from each other by an hour's journey. It was not until the sixteenth century that they, and the surrounding villages, formed a real city. In Khayyam's day, it did not exist yet, but a wall had been built, three *parasangs* or twelve miles long, to protect the whole oasis.

Omar and Hassan arrived late in the evening. They found lodgings in Jay, in a caravansary near the Tirah Gate. There they stretched out and before they could exchange a single word they started to snore in unison.

The next day Khayyam went off to see the Grand Vizir. In the Square of the Money-Changers, Andalusian, Greek, and Chinese travelers and merchants amongst others were milling around the money-changers who, appropriately equipped with their statutory scales, were scratching a Kirman, Nishapur, or Seville *dinar*, sniffing a Delhi *tanka*, feeling the weight of a Bukhara *dirham*, pulling a face at a recently devalued *nomisma* from Constantinople.

The gateway of the *diwan*, the seat of government and the official residence of Nizam al-Mulk, was not far off. The musicians of the *nowba* were stationed there to sound their trumpets three times a day in honor of the Grand Vizir. In spite of all this pomp, everyone, down to the most humble widow, was granted permission to venture into the *diwan*, the huge audience hall, in order to expose their tears and grievances to the strong man of the empire. It was only there that guards and chamberlains made a circle around Nizam, questioned the visitors, and sent away the nuisances.

Omar stopped in the doorway. He examined the room, its bare walls and its three layers of carpet. He greeted those present with a hesitant gesture. They were a mixed but contemplative group who surrounded the Vizir, who was in conversation for the time being with a Turkish officer. Out of the corner of his eye, Nizam had spotted the newcomer; he smiled at him in a friendly manner and signaled to him to be seated. Five minutes later he came over to him, and kissed him on both cheeks and then on the forehead.

"I have been waiting for you. I knew that you would be here on time. I have much to say to you."

He then led him by the hand away from everyone into a small antechamber where they sat down side by side on an enormous leather cushion.

"Some of what I am about to say will surprise you, but I hope that when all is said and done you will not regret having responded to my invitation."

"Could anyone ever regret having entered through Nizam al-Mulk's gateway."

"That has happened," murmured the Vizir with a savage smile. "I have raised men up to the skies, and I have brought others low. Every day I dispense life and death. God will be the judge of my intentions. He is the source of all power. He granted the supreme authority to the Arab Caliph, who ceded it to the Turkish Sultan, who has delivered it into the hands of the Persian Vizir, your servant. Of others I demand that they respect this authority, but of you, *Khawaja* Omar, I demand that you respect my dream. Yes, I dream of making this huge country of mine into the most powerful, prosperous, stable state, into the best policed state in the universe. I dream of an empire where every province and city will be administered by a just and God-fearing man who pays heed to the groans of his weakest subjects. I dream of a state where the wolf and the lamb will drink peacefully together, in complete peace, water from the same brook. However, it is not enough for me merely to dream; I am building. Go and walk about in the districts of Isfahan and you will see regiments of workers digging and building, and artisans going about their work. Hospices, mosques, caravansaries, citadels, and seats of government are being built everywhere. Soon every important city will have its own large school which will carry my name, a "*madrasa Nizamiya*." The one in Baghdad is already in operation. I drew up its plans with my own hands, I established its curriculum, I chose the best teachers for it, and I have allotted a grant for every student. You see, this empire is one large building site. It is rising up, expanding and prospering. Heaven has allowed us to live in a blessed age."

A light-haired servant came in and bowed. He was carrying two goblets of iced rose-syrup on an engraved silver tray. Omar took one. As he raised it his lips felt its icy steam and he decided to sip it slowly. Nizam finished his off in one gulp and continued:

"Your presence here gladdens and honors me!"

Khayyam wanted to reply to this rush of amiability, but Nizam stopped him with a gesture.

"Do not think that I am trying to flatter you. I am so powerful that I need only sing the praises of the Creator. However, you see, *Khawaja* Omar, as far-flung, as populated, or as opulent as an empire may be, there is always a shortage of men. In appearance what a lot of creatures, how teeming the streets are, what dense crowds! But when I chance to look upon the deployment of my army, or a mosque at prayer time, a bazaar, or even my *diwan*, I have to ask myself: if I were to demand some wisdom, knowledge, loyalty, or integrity from these men, would I not, at the mention of each quality, see the throng thin out, then melt and disappear? I find myself alone, *Khawaja* Omar, desperately alone. My *diwan* is empty, as is my palace. This town and this empire are empty. I always feel that I have to clap with one hand behind my back. I am not content with sending for men like you to come from Samarkand, I myself am ready to go on foot to Samarkand to fetch them."

Omar murmured a confused "God forbid!", but the Vizir did not stop.

"Those are my dreams and my worries. I could speak to you of them for days and nights, but I want to listen to you. I am impatient to know if this dream moves you in some way, if you are ready to take your rightful place at my side."

"Your projects are exhilarating and I am honored by your faith in me."

"What do you require in order to work with me? Tell me frankly, the way I have spoken to you. You will obtain everything you desire. Do not be timorous, and do not let my moment of rash prodigality pass by."

He laughed. Khayyam managed to cover his utter confusion with a weak smile.

"My only desire is to be able to carry on my humble works sheltered from need. My greed goes no further than having something to drink, clothing on my back, and shelter for the night."

"By way of shelter, I offer you one of Isfahan's most beautiful houses. I myself resided there while this palace was being built. It will be yours, with its gardens, orchards, carpets, servants, and maidservants. For your expenses, I am allotting you a pension of ten thousand royal dinars. As long as I am alive it will be paid to you at the beginning of every year. Is it sufficient?"

"That is more than I need. I shall not know what to do with such a great sum."

Khayyam was being sincere, but this irritated Nizam.

"When you have bought all the books, had all the jars of wine filled, and all your mistresses covered with jewels, you will distribute alms to the poor, finance the Mecca caravan, and build a mosque in your name!"

Realizing that his detachment and the modesty of his demands had displeased his host, Omar made bold:

"I have always wanted to construct an observatory with a large stone sextant, an astrolabe, and various instruments. I would like to measure the exact length of the solar year."

"Granted! By next week funds will be allotted to you for that end. You will choose the site and your observatory will be erected within a few months. But, tell me, is there nothing else that would give you pleasure?"

"By God, I want nothing more. Your generosity overwhelms me."

"Then perhaps I, in my turn, might formulate a demand for you?"

"After what you have just granted me, I will be only too glad to be able to show you a small part of my immense gratitude."

Nizam did not hesitate.

"I know that you are discreet and little inclined to gossip. I know that you are wise, just, impartial, and in a position to discern the truth from the false in everything. I know that you are trustworthy: I would like to charge you with the most delicate commission of all."

Omar waited for the worst, and indeed it was the worst which was in store for him.

"I name you *sahib-khabar.*"

"*Sahib-khabar*, me! The head spy?"

"Head of the Empire's information. Do not respond in haste, it is not a question of spying on good people or infiltrating the homes of believers, but of looking after the peace for everyone. In a state, the least coercion or injustice must be brought to the attention of the sovereign and quelled in an exemplary fashion, whoever the guilty party may be. We can only learn if some *qadi* or provincial governor is exploiting his office to enrich himself at the expense of the weak by means of our spies, since the victims do not always dare to complain!"

"These spies could still be bought off by the *qadis*, the governors, or the emirs, or become their accomplices!"

"Your role, the role of the *sahib-khabar*, is precisely to find incorruptible men for these assignments."

"If these incorruptible men exist, would it not be simpler to appoint them governors or *qadis!*"

It was a naïve observation, but to Nizam's ears it sounded mocking. He became impatient and arose:

"I have no wish to debate the issue. I have told you what I am offering you and what I expect of you. Go and think over my proposal. Weigh up the arguments on both sides calmly and return tomorrow with your response."

13

That day Khayyam was no longer capable of reflecting, weighing up, or evaluating. After leaving the *diwan*, he disappeared into the narrowest alley of the bazaar, meandered past men and beasts, and made his way under the stucco vaults between mounds of spices. At each step the alley became a little darker and the crowd seemed to be moving sluggishly and speaking in murmurs. Merchants and customers were masked actors and sleepwalking dancers. Omar groped his way along, now to the left, now to the right, afraid of falling down or fainting. Suddenly he came upon a small square that was flooded with light, a clearing in the jungle. The harsh sun beat down on him. He straightened up and breathed. What was happening to him? He was being offered a paradise that was shackled to a hell. How could he say yes, how could he say no? How could he face the Grand Vizir or leave town with any dignity?

To his right, a tavern door was half open. He pushed it and went down a few steps strewn with sand and came out into a dimly lit room with a low ceiling. The floor was damp earth, the benches looked unsteady and the tables unwashed. He ordered a dry wine from Qom. It was brought to him in a chipped jar. He breathed it in for a long while with shut eyes.

> *The blessed time of my youth passes by,*
> *I pour out the wine of my oblivion.*
> *Bitter it is, and thus it pleases me.*
> *For this bitterness is the zest of my life.*

Suddenly, however, an idea occurred to him. He doubtless had had to come to this sordid den to find it; the idea had been waiting for him there, on that table, at the third mouthful of the fourth goblet. He settled his bill, left a generous *baksheesh*, and resurfaced. Night had fallen, the square was already empty, with every alley of the bazaar closed off by a heavy portal, and Omar had to make a detour to get back to his caravansary.

Hassan was already asleep, his face severe and pained, as Khayyam tiptoed into his room. Omar contemplated him for a long while. A thousand questions ran through his mind, but he brushed them aside without trying to find answers. His decision was taken and it was irrevocable.

There is a legend common in the books. It speaks of three friends, three Persians who marked, each in his own fashion, the beginnings of our millenium: Omar Khayym who observed the world, Nizam al-Mulk who governed it, and Hassan Sabbah who terrorized it. They are said to have studied together at Nishapur, which cannot be correct since Nizam was thirty years older than Omar and Hassan carried on his studies at Rayy, and perhaps a little in his native town of Qom, but certainly not at Nishapur.

Is the truth to be found in the *Samarkand Manuscript?* The chronicle that runs along the margins asserts that the three men met for the first time in Isfahan, in the *diwan* of the Grand Vizir, on the initiative of Khayyam — acting as destiny's blind apprentice.

· Nizam had secluded himself in the palace's small hall and was surrounded by papers. As soon as he saw Omar's face in the doorway he understood that his response would be negative.

"So, you are indifferent to my projects."

Khayyam replied, contritely but firmly:

"Your dreams are grandiose and I hope that they will be realized, but my contribution cannot be what you have proposed. When it comes to secrets and those who reveal them, I am on the side of the secrets. The first time an agent came to me to report a conversation, I would order him to be silent, state that it was neither my business nor his, and I would ban him from my house. My curiosity about people and things is expressed in a different way."

"I respect your decision and do not deem it useless for the empire that some men devote themselves completely to science. Naturally, you will still receive everything I promised you — the annual sum of gold, the house, the observatory. I never take back what I have given of my own accord. I would have wished to be able to associate you more closely with my work, but I take consolation in the fact that the chronicles will write for posterity that Omar Khayyam lived in the era of Nizam al-Mulk and that he was honored, sheltered from bad weather, and was able to say no to the Grand Vizir without risking disgrace."

"I do not know if I will ever be able to show the gratitude that your magnanimity deserves."

Omar broke off. He hesitated before continuing:

"Perhaps I may be able to make you forget my refusal by presenting to you a man I have just met. He is a man of great intelligence, his knowledge is immense, and his genius is disarming. He seems just right for the office of *sahib-khabar* and I am sure that your proposal will delight him. He conceded to me that he had come from Rayy to Isfahan with the firm hope of being employed by you."

"An ambitious man," Nazim murmured between his teeth. "But that is my fate. When I find a trustworthy man, he lacks ambition and scorns the apparatus of power; and when a man appears ready to jump at the first office I offer him, his haste unnerves me."

He seemed tired and resigned.

"By what name is this man known?"

71

"Hassan, son of Ali Sabbah. I must warn you, however, that he was born in Qom."

"A Shiite missionary? That does not worry me, even though I am hostile to all heresies and all deviations. Some of my best collaborators are sectarians of Ali, my best soldiers are Armenians and my treasurers are Jews, but that does not mean that I withhold my trust and protection from them. The only ones I distrust are the Ismailis. I do not suppose that your friend belongs to that sect?"

"I do not know. However, Hassan has come here with me. He is waiting outside. With your permission I will summon him and you will be able to question him."

Omar disappeared for a few seconds and came back accompanied by his friend, who did not appear in the least intimidated. However, Khayyam could make out two muscles in Hassan's beard that were flexing and shaking.

"I present Hassan Sabbah. Never has such a tightly-wound turban held such knowledge."

Nizam smiled.

"Here I am surrounded by the learned. Is it not said that the prince who frequents and keeps the company of scholars is the best of princes?"

It was Hassan who retorted:

"It is also said that the scholar who keeps the company of princes is the worst of scholars."

An unaffected but brief laugh drew them together. Nizam was already knitting his brows. He wanted the inevitable series of proverbs that preceded any Persian conversation to be over quickly, in order to make clear to Hassan what he expected of him. Curiously enough, from the very first words they found themselves in collusion. It now only remained for Omar to slip away.

Thus Hassan Sabbah very quickly became the indispensable collaborator of the Grand Vizir. He succeeded in setting up an elaborate network of agents disguised as merchants, dervishes, and pilgrims, who criss-crossed the Seljuk empire, not letting any palace, house, or bazaar out of their earshot. Plots, rumors, and scandals were all reported, exposed, and thwarted in either a discreet or an exemplary manner.

At first, Nizam was overjoyed at having the fearsome machinery under his control. He elicited some satisfaction from the Sultan, who had previously been reticent. Had not his father, Alp Arslan, recommended that he abhor this type of politics? "When you have planted spies everywhere," he had warned, "your true friends will not be on their guard since they know that they are loyal. But the felons will be on the look-out. They will want to bribe the informers. Gradually you will start receiving reports that are unfavorable to your true friends and favorable to your enemies. Good or bad words are like arrows: when you fire many there is always one that hits its target. Your heart will then be hardened against your friends, the felons will take their place at your side, and what will be left of your power?"

It needed a woman from the harem to be caught in the act of poisoning someone to make the Sultan stop doubting the usefulness of his chief of spies and overnight he made him his confidant. However, it was Nizam who took umbrage at the friendship that sprang up between Hassan and Malikshah. The two men were young, and they would happily chat together at the expense of the old Vizir, particularly on Fridays, the day of the *shölen*, the traditional banquet held by the Sultan for his court.

The first part of the festivities was strictly formal and restrained. Nizam was seated to the right of Malikshah. They were encircled by men of letters and intellectuals and discussions took place on the most varied of subjects, from the comparative merits of Indian or Yemenite swords to the various works of Aristotle. The Sultan fleetingly showed a passion for this sort of sparring, then he faded out and his eye started to wander. The Vizir understood that it was time to leave, and the noble guests followed him. They were instantly replaced by musicians and dancers, jugs of wine were tipped and the drinking bout, which would be restrained or wild according to the humor of the prince, would continue into the morning hours. To a couple of chords from the rebec, the lute, or the *târ*, singers improvised on their favorite theme — that of Nizam al-Mulk. The Sultan, who was incapable of doing without his Grand Vizir, avenged himself by laughing freely. One just had to see the infantile frenzy with which he clapped, to know that one day he would manage to hit out at "his father."

Hassan was adept at feeding the sovereign's every sign of resentment towards his Vizir. Upon what did the Vizir pride himself? His wisdom,

73

his learning? But Hassan could make short shrift of both these qualities. The Vizir's capacity to defend the throne and the empire? Hassan very quickly had shown himself equally competent. The Vizir's constancy? There was nothing simpler than to affect loyalty, which anyhow never rings truer than in the mouths of liars.

Above all, Hassan knew how to cultivate Malikshah's proverbial avarice. He constantly spoke to him of the Vizir's expenses, and brought to his attention the new robes of the Vizir and his associates. Nizam liked power and its apparatus, but Hassan liked only power and was rigorous in its pursuit.

When he felt that Malikshah was totally won over and ready for his *éminence grise* to be delivered the death blow, Hassan created the incident. The scene unfolded in the throne room, one Saturday. The Sultan had woken up at midday with an annoying headache. He was in a foul temper, and became exasperated upon learning that sixty thousand golden dinars had just been distributed to the soldiers of the Vizir's Armenian guard. The information had to have come from Hassan and his network. Nizam patiently explained that in order to avoid any hint of insubordination he had to feed the troops and fatten them up a little, and that if the troops reached the point of rebellion the state would have to spend that amount ten times over. Throwing gold around by the armful, retorted Malikshah, meant that they would end up not being able to pay salaries and then the real rebellions would begin. A good government surely had to know how to keep its gold for the difficult times?

One of Nizam's twelve sons, who was present during the scene, thought it clever to intervene:

"During the early days of Islam, when the Caliph Omar was accused of spending all the gold that had been amassed during the conquests, Omar asked his detractors, 'Is this gold not the bounty of the Almighty who lavished it upon us? If you believe God is incapable of granting any more, then spend none of it. As for me, I have faith in the infinite generosity of the Creator and will not keep in my coffer a single coin that I could spend for the welfare of the Muslims.'"

Malikshah, however, had no intention of following this example. He was mulling over an idea of whose merits Hassan had convinced him. He ordered:

"I demand to be presented with a detailed summary of everything that goes into my Treasury and the precise way that it is spent. When can I have it?"

Nizam seemed overwhelmed.

"I can provide this summary, but it will take time."

"How long, *khawaja?*"

He had not said *ata* but *khawaja* — a very respectful title, but in this context so distant that it sounded very much like a repudiation or a prelude to disgrace.

Distraught, Nizam explained:

"An emissary will have to be sent to every emir to carry out long calculations. By the grace of God, the empire is immense, and thus it would be difficult to draw up this report in less than two years."

Hassan, however, approached solemnly:

"I promise our master that if he provides me with the means, if he orders all the papers of the *diwan* to be put into my hands, I will present him a completed report in forty days time."

The Vizir wanted to respond, but Malikshah had already arisen. He strode towards the door and raised his voice:

"Very well, Hassan will be installed in the *diwan*. The whole secretariat will be under his orders. No one will enter without his permission. In forty days time I will conclude the matter."

14

Soon the whole empire was in an upheaval, the administration was paralyzed, troop movements were reported, and people spoke of civil war. It was said that Nizam had distributed arms in certain districts of Isfahan. In the bazaar, the merchandise had been stored away. The gates of the principal souks, notably that of the jewelers, were closed at the beginning of the afternoon. In the neighborhood of the *diwan* the tension was at its greatest. The Grand Vizir had had to hand over his offices to Hassan, but his residence adjoined them and only a small garden separated him from what had become the territory of his rival. Now the garden had been transformed into a veritable barracks, and Nizam's personal guard patrolled it nervously, armed to the teeth.

No one was more embarrassed than Omar. He wanted to intervene to calm spirits down and to find a way for the two adversaries to compromise. Even though Nizam continued to receive him, he missed no occasion to reproach him for the "poisoned gift" that he had made him. Hassan, on the other hand, spent his time locked up with his papers, busy preparing the report he had to present to the Sultan. Only at night did he allow himself to stretch out on the large carpet of the *diwan*, surrounded by a handful of his trusty men.

Three days before the fateful day, Khayyam still wanted to attempt a final mediation. He went to Hassan's apartments and insisted upon seeing him, but he was asked to come back one hour later as the *sahib-khabar* was holding a meeting with the treasurers. Omar decided that he would take a few steps outside, and had just passed through the doorway when one of the royal eunuchs, dressed all in red, addressed him:

"If *Khawaja* Omar would be so kind as to follow me, he is expected."

After the man led him through a labyrinth of tunnels and staircases, Khayyam found himself in a garden of whose existence he had had no suspicion. Peacocks strutted around free, apricot trees were in blossom, and a fountain murmured. Behind the fountain they came to a low door encrusted with mother-of-pearl. The eunuch opened it and invited Omar to proceed.

It was a vast room with brocade-lined walls, and at one end it had a sort of vaulted niche protected by a curtain, which fluttered indicating someone's presence behind it. Khayyam had hardly entered before the door was shut with a muffled sound. Another minute of waiting and confusion ensued before a woman's voice was heard. He did not recognize it, but he thought he could identify a certain Turkish dialect. However, the voice was low and the speech was rapid, with only a few words emerging like rocks in a flood. The gist of the discourse escaped him and he wanted to interrupt her and ask her to speak in Persian or Arabic, or just more slowly, but it was not so easy to address a woman through a curtain. Suddenly another voice took over:

"My mistress, Terken Khatun, the wife of the Sultan, thanks you for having come to this meeting."

This time the language was Persian, and the voice was one that Khayyam would recognize in a bazaar on the Day of Judgment. He was going to shout, but his shout quickly turned into a happy but plaintive murmur:

"Jahan!"

She pulled aside the edge of the curtain, raised her veil and smiled, but with a gesture prevented him from drawing close to her.

"The Sultana," she said, "is worried about the struggle unfolding within the *diwan*. Disquiet is spreading and blood is going to be spilled. The Sultan himself is very concerned about this and has become irritable. The harem resounds with his bursts of anger. This situation cannot last. The Sultana knows that you are attempting to do the impossible and reconcile the two protagonists, and she desires to see you succeed, but such success seems distant."

Khayyam concurred with a resigned nod of his head. Jahan continued:

"Things having come so far, Terken Khatun considers that it would be preferable to dismiss the two adversaries and to confer the vizirate upon a decent man who can calm spirits down. Her spouse, our master, is surrounded, according to her, with schemers, but he just needs a wise man who is devoid of base ambition, a man of sound judgment and excellent counsel. As the Sultan holds you in high esteem, she would like to suggest to him that he name you Grand Vizir. Your nomination would relieve the whole court. Nevertheless, before putting forward such a suggestion, she would like to be assured of your agreement."

Omar took some time to digest what was being asked of him, but he called out:

"By God, Jahan! Are you after my downfall? Can you see me commanding the armies of the empire, decapitating people, or quelling a slave revolt? Leave me to my stars!"

"Listen to me, Omar. I know that you have no desire to conduct affairs of state, your role will be simply to be there! The decisions will be taken and carried out by others!"

"In other words, you will be the real Vizir, and your mistress the real Sultan. Isn't that what you are after?"

"And how would that upset you? You would have the honors with none of the worries. What better could you wish for?"

Terken Khatun intervened to qualify her proposal. Jahan translated:

"My mistress says it is because men like you turn away from politics that we are so badly governed. She considers you to have all the qualities of an excellent vizir."

"Tell her that the qualities needed to govern are not those which are needed in order to accede to power. In order to run things smoothly, one must forget oneself and only be interested in others — particularly the most unfortunate; to get into power, one must be the greediest of men, think only of oneself, and be ready to crush one's closest friends. I, however, will not crush anyone!"

For the moment, the two women's projects were at a standstill. Omar refused to bend to their demands. Anyway, it would have served no use, as the confrontation between Nizam and Hassan had become unavoidable.

That same day, the audience hall was a peaceful arena, and the fifteen people there were content to watch in silence. Malikshah himself, usually so exuberant, was conversing in hushed tones with his chamberlain while idiosyncratically twiddling with the ends of his mustache. From time to time he shot a glance at the two gladiators. Hassan was standing up, wearing a creased black robe and a black turban and wearing his beard lower than usual. His face was furrowed and his searing eyes were ready to meet those of Nizam, although they were red with fatigue and lack of sleep. Behind him a secretary carried a bundle of papers tied up with a wide band of cordovan.

As a privilege that comes with age, the Grand Vizir was seated, or more correctly slumped, in a chair. His robe was gray, his beard flecked with white, and his forehead wizened. Only his glance was young and alert, one might even say sparkling. Two of his sons accompanied him, flashing looks of hatred or defiance.

Right next to the Sultan was Omar, as dour as he was overwhelmed. He was drawing up in his mind various conciliatory words that he would doubtless not have occasion to utter.

"Today is the day that we were promised a detailed report on the state of our Treasury. Is it ready?" asked Malikshah.

Hassan leaned over.

"My promise has been kept. Here is the report."

He turned towards his secretary who came forward to meet him and carefully untied the leather band holding together the pile of papers. Sabbah started to read them out. The first pages were, as custom would have it, expressions of thanks, pious discourses, erudite quotations, and well-turned eloquent pages, but the audience was waiting for more. Then it came:

"I have been able to calculate precisely," he declared, "what the tax office of every province and known town has sent in to the royal Treasury. In the same way, I have evaluated the booty won from the enemy and I now know how this gold has been spent . . ."

With great ceremony, he cleared his throat, handed to his secretary the page he had just read, and fixed his eyes on the next one. His lips opened a little and then shut tight. Silence fell again. He threw aside the leaf of paper and then set that one aside with a furious gesture. There was still silence.

The Sultan was becoming a little anxious and impatient:

"What is going on? We are listening to you."

"Master, I cannot find the continuation. I had arranged my papers in order. The sheet I am looking for must have fallen out. I shall find it."

He leafed through them again, rather pathetically. Nizam made the most of the situation by intervening, in a tone that tried to sound magnanimous:

"Anyone can lose a piece of paper. We should not hold that against our young friend. Instead of waiting around, I propose that we go on with the rest of the report."

"You are right, *ata*, let us go on with the report."

Everyone noticed that the Sultan had called his Vizir "father" anew. Did this mean that he was back in favor? While Hassan was still caught up in the most pathetic state of confusion, the Vizir pushed his advantage:

"Let us forget this lost page. Instead of making the Sultan wait, I suggest that our brother Hassan presents to us the figures on some important cities or provinces."

The Sultan was eager to agree. Nizam carried on:

"Let us take the city of Nishapur, for example, the birthplace of Omar Khayyam, who is here with us. Could we be informed how much that city and its province have contributed to the Treasury?"

"Immediately," responded Hassan, who had been trying to land on his feet.

He had ploughed expertly through his pile of papers, trying to extract page thirty-four, where he had written everything about Nishapur, but it was in vain.

"The page is not there," he said. "It has disappeared, I have been robbed of it . . . Someone has messed up my papers . . ."

Nizam stood up. He went up to Malikshah and whispered in his ear, "If our master cannot have confidence in his most competent servants, who are aware of the difficulty of projects and can tell the difference between the possible and the impossible, there will be no end to his being thus insulted, held up to ridicule, and fair game for the ignorant, the foolish, and charlatans."

Malikshah did not doubt for a moment that Hassan had just been the victim of some practical joke. As the chroniclers reported, Nizam al-Mulk had succeeded in bribing Hassan's secretary and ordered him to filch some pages and to misfile others, reducing to nought the patient work carried out by his rival. Hassan tried in vain to claim that he was the victim of a plot, but his voice could not be heard over the tumult, and the Sultan, disappointed to have been duped, but even more so to realize that his attempt to shake his Vizir's tutelage had failed, directed the whole blame onto Hassan. Having ordered his guards to seize him, he there and then sentenced him to death.

For the first time, Omar spoke up: "May our Master be merciful. Hassan Sabbah may have made mistakes, he may have sinned through an excess of zeal or enthusiasm, and he should be dismissed for these misdemeanors, but he is in no way guilty of a serious misdeed against your person."

"Then let him be blinded! Bring the galenite and heat up the iron."

Hassan stayed silent and it was Omar who spoke up again. He could not allow a man, whom he had had engaged, to be silenced or blinded.

"Master," he begged, "do not inflict such a punishment on a young man who could only find solace in his disgrace by reading and writing."

Malikshah then stated:

"It is for your sake, *Khawaja* Omar, the wisest and purest of men, that I agree to retract a decision of mine yet again. Hassan Sabbah is thus condemned to be banished and will be exiled to a distant country until the end of his life. He will never be able to tread anew upon the soil of the empire."

But the man from Qom was to return and carry out an exceptional act of vengeance.

BOOK TWO

The Assassins' Paradise

Both Paradise and Hell are in you

OMAR KHAYYAM

15

Seven years had past, seven years of plenty both for Khayyam and the empire, the last years of peace.

On a table under an awning of vine stood a long-necked carafe for the best Shiraz white wine with just the right hint of muskiness and all around a hundred bowls burst into a riotous feast. Such was the ritual of a June evening on Omar's terrace. He recommended starting with the lightest, first of all the wine and fruit, then the cooked dishes such as rice with vine-leaves and stuffed quince.

A soft wind from the Yellow Mountains blew through the orchards in flower. Jahan picked up a lute and plucked one string and then another. The drawn-out slow music accompanied the wind. Omar raised his goblet and inhaled deeply. Jahan was watching him. She chose from the table the largest, reddest, and softest jujube and offered it to her man, which, in the language of fruit, signified "a kiss, straight away." He leant over to her and their lips brushed against each other, separated, touched again, parted, and joined. Their fingers intertwined, a serving girl arrived, and without undue haste they separated and both picked up their goblets. Jahan smiled and murmured:

"If I had seven lives, I would spend one coming here to stretch out every evening on this terrace; I would lounge on this divan drinking this wine and dangling my fingers in this bowl, for in monotony lurks happiness."

Omar retorted:

"One lifetime, three, or seven, I would pass them all just like this one, stretched out on this terrace with my hand in your hair."

Together, and different. Lovers for nine years, married for four years and their dreams still did not live under the same roof. Jahan devoured time, Omar sipped it. She wanted to rule the world and had the ear of the Sultana who had the ear of the Sultan. By day she intrigued in the royal harem, intercepting incoming and outgoing messages, alcove rumours, promises of jewels, and the stench of poison— all of which excited, agitated, and inflamed her. In the evening she would give herself up to the happiness of being loved. For Omar, life was different. It was the pleasure of science and the science of pleasure. He would arise late, take the traditional "morning glass" on an empty stomach, then settle down at his work table to write, calculate, draw lines and figures, write more, and transcribe a poem in his secret book.

At night, he would go off to the observatory built on a hillock near his house. He only had to cross a garden in order to be in the midst of the instruments that he cherished and caressed, oiled and polished with his own hand. Often he was accompanied by some astronomer who was passing through. The first three years of his stay had been devoted to the Isfahan observatory. He had supervised its construction and the manufacture of the equipment. Most importantly he had instituted the new calendar, ceremonially inaugurated on the first day of *Favardin* 458, March 21, 1079. What Persian could forget that year, when due to Khayyam's calculation the sacrosanct festival of Nowruz had been displaced, and the new year which ought to have fallen in the middle of the sign of Pisces had been held off until the first day of Aries, and that since that reform the Persian months have conformed to the signs of the zodiac, with *Favardin* thus becoming the month of Aries and *Esfand* that of Pisces? In June 1081 the inhabitants of Isfahan and the whole empire were living out the third year of the new era. This officially carried the name of the Sultan, but in the street, and even in certain documents, it was enough to mention "such and such year in the era of Omar Khayyam." What other man has known such honor in his lifetime? While Khayyam, at the age of thirty-three, was a renowned and respected personage, he was doubtless feared by those who did not know of his profound aversion to violence and domination.

What was it that kept him close to Jahan in spite of everything? A detail, but a gigantic detail: neither of them wanted children. Jahan had decided, once and for all, not to burden herself with offspring. Khayyam had made his the maxim of Abu al-Ala, a Syrian poet he venerated: "My suffering is the fault of my progenitor, let no one else's suffering be my fault."

Let us not be mistaken about this attitude; Khayyam had none of the makings of a misanthropist. Was it not he who had written: "When unhappiness overwhelms you, when you end up wishing for an eternal night to fall on the world, think of the greenery that springs up after the rain, think of the awakening of a child"? If he refused to father children, it was because existence seemed to him to be too heavy to bear. "Happy is he who has never come into the world," he never ceased proclaiming.

It was clear that the reasons both of them had for refusing to give life to a child were not one and the same. She acted out of an excess of ambition, he out of an excess of detachment. However, for a man and a woman to be closely drawn together by an attitude condemned by all the men and women of Persia, and to give free reign to rumors that one or the other was sterile without even deigning to respond was what, at that time, forged an imperative complicity.

However, it was a complicity that had its limits. With Omar, Jahan generally came to learn the valuable opinion of a man who coveted nought, but she rarely took the trouble of informing him of her activities. She knew that he disapproved of them. What good would it do to feed endless quarrels? Of course, Khayyam was never far from the court. Even though he avoided becoming embroiled in it, despised and fled from all the intrigues, particularly those that had always worked against the palace doctors and astrologers, he nevertheless had some inescapable obligations, such as being present sometimes at the Friday banquet, examining a sick Emir, and above all providing Malikshah with his *taqvim*, his monthly horoscope — the Sultan being, just like everyone else, constrained to consult it to know what he should do or should not do every day. "On the 5th, a star is lying in wait for you, do not leave the palace. On the 7th, neither be bled nor take any sort of potion. On the 10th, wind your turban the other way. On the 13th, do not approach any of your wives . . ." The Sultan never thought to transgress these directives, and nor did Nizam, who received his *taqvim* from Omar's hand before the end of the month, read it greedily and followed it to the letter. Gradually, other personages acquired this privilege, the chamberlain, the Grand Qadi of Isfahan, the treasurers, certain emirs of the army, and some rich merchants, which ended up meaning considerable work for Omar and took up the ten last nights of every month. People were so partial to predictions! The luckiest consulted Omar. The others found themselves a less prestigious astrologer, unless they went to a man of religion for every decision. Closing his eyes, and opening the Quran at random, he would place his finger on a verse, which he would read aloud to them so that they could find therein the answer to their worries. Some poor women, in a great hurry to make a decision, would go out into a public square and would interpret the first phrase they heard as a directive from Providence.

"Terken Khatoun asked me today if her *taqvim* for the month of *Tir* is ready," Jahan said that evening.

Omar looked out into the distance:

"I am going to prepare it for her during the night. The sky is clear and none of the stars are hidden. It is time for me to go to the observatory."

He readied himself to stand up, without hurry, when a servant came to announce:

"There is a dervish at the door. He is asking for hospitality for the night."

"Let him come in," said Omar. "Give him the small room under the stairway and tell him to join us for the meal."

Jahan covered her face ready for the entrance of the stranger, but the servant came back alone.

"He prefers to stay and pray in his room. Here is the message he gave me."

Omar read it and blushed. He arose like an automaton. Jahan was worried:

"Who is this man?"

"I shall return."

He tore the message into a thousand pieces, strode towards the little room and shut the door behind him. There was a moment of waiting and then of incredulity, an accolade followed by a reproach:

"What have you come to Isfahan for? All Nizam al-Mulk's agents are after you."

"I have come to convert you."

Omar stared at him. He wanted to make sure that Hassan still had all his wits about him, but Hassan laughed, the same muffled laugh that Khayyam had recognized in the caravansary in Kashan.

"You can be reassured that you are the last person I would think of converting, but I need shelter. What better protector could there be than Omar Khayyam, companion to the Sultan, friend to the Grand Vizir?"

"Their hatred for you is greater than their friendship for me. You are welcome under my roof, but do not think for a moment that my relations with them could save you if your presence were suspected."

"Tomorrow I shall be far away."

Omar appeared distrusting:

"Have you come back for revenge?"

Hassan reacted as if his dignity had just been held up to ridicule.

"I do not seek to avenge my miserable person, I desire to destroy Turkish power."

Omar looked at his friend: he had exchanged his black turban for another, white but covered in sand, and his clothing was of coarse and threadbare wool.

"You appear so sure of yourself! I can only see before me an outlaw, a hunted man, hiding from house to house, whose whole equipment consists of this bundle and this turban while yet thinking yourself the equal of an empire that extends over all the Orient from Damascus to Herat!"

"You are speaking of what is. I speak of what will be. The new

89

order will soon position itself against the Seljuk empire. It will be intricately organized, powerful, and fearsome and will cause Sultan and vizirs to quake. Not so long ago, when you and I were born, Isfahan belonged to a Persian Shiite dynasty that imposed its law on the Caliph of Baghdad. Today the Persians are no more than the servants of the Turks, and your friend Nizam al-Mulk is the vilest servant of these intruders. How can you establish that what was true yesterday is unthinkable for tomorrow?"

"Times have changed, Hassan. The Turks are in power and the Persians have been vanquished. Some, like Nizam, seek a compromise with the victors, and others, like me, take refuge in books."

"And yet others fight. They are only a handful today, but tomorrow they will be thousands, a great decisive and invincible army. I am the apostle of the New Prediction. I will travel the country without respite. I will use persuasion as well as force and, with the aid of the Almighty, I shall fight against corrupt power. I am telling you, Omar, since you saved my life one day: the world will soon witness events whose import will be understood by few men, but you will understand. You will know what is happening, what is shaking this earth and how the tumult will end."

"I do not wish to cast any doubt upon your convictions or your enthusiasm, but I remember having seen you fight at the court of Malikshah with Nizam al-Mulk over the favors of the Turkish Sultan."

"You are mistaken to suggest that I am such an ignoble person."

"I am not suggesting anything. I am simply mentioning some unpalatable facts."

"They are due to your ignorance of my past. I cannot take offense at you for judging things by their appearance, but you will see me differently when I have told you my real history. I come from a traditional Shiite family. I was always taught that the Ismailis were simply heretics until I met a missionary, who, through a long discussion with me, shook my faith. When I decided not to speak to him any more for fear of giving in to him, I fell so seriously ill that I thought it was my last hour. I saw a sign, a sign from the Almighty, and I made an oath that if I survived I would convert to the faith of the Ismailis. I recovered overnight. None of my family could believe my sudden recovery.

"Naturally I kept my word and took the oath and at the end of two years I was assigned a mission to get close to Nizam al-Mulk, to infiltrate his *diwan* in order to protect our Ismaili brothers in difficulty. Thus I left Rayy for Isfahan and stopped *en route* at a caravansary in Kashan. Finding myself alone in my small room, I was in the middle of wondering how I could get close to the Grand Vizir when the door opened and who should enter but Khayyam, the great Khayyam whom heaven sent to me there to facilitate my mission."

Omar was dumbstruck.

"To think that Nizam al-Mulk asked me whether you were an Ismaili and I replied that I did not think so!"

"You did not lie. You did not know. Now you do."

He broke off.

"You have not offered me anything to eat?"

Omar opened the door, called the servant, ordered her to bring some dishes and then continued his questioning:

"And you have been wandering about for seven years dressed as a Sufi?"

"I have wandered about much. When I left Isfahan I was pursued by agents of Nizam who were after my life. I shook them off at Qom where some friends hid me and then I continued my journey to Rayy where I met an Ismaili who suggested that I go to Egypt, to the missionary school where he had studied. I made a detour through Azerbaijan before going on to Damascus. I was planning to travel to Cairo on the land route, but there was fighting between the Turks and the Maghrebis around Jerusalem and I had to turn back and take the coastal route through Beirut, Sidon, Tyre, and Acre, where I found a place on a boat. Upon my arrival in Alexandria I was received as a high-ranking emir. A reception committee was waiting for me, headed by Abu Daud, the paramount chief of the missionaries."

The servant had come in and placed some bowls on the carpet. Hassan started a prayer which he broke off when she left the room.

"I spent two years in Cairo. There were several dozen of us at the missionary school, but only a handful of us were destined to be active outside Fatimid territory."

He avoided giving out too many details. It is known, however, from various sources, that courses were held in two different places: the principles of the faith were revealed by the *ulema* in the university of Al-Azhar, and missionary propaganda was taught within the Caliphal palace. It was the chief missionary himself, a high ranking official of the Fatimid court, who revealed to the students the methods of persuasion, the art of developing a line of argument and of addressing reason instead of aiming for the heart. It was also he who made them memorize the secret code they had to use in their communications. At the end of every session, the students came to kneel before the chief missionary, who passed over their heads a document bearing the signature of the Imam. Then another, shorter, session would be held for the women.

"In Egypt I received all the instruction I needed."

"Did you not tell me, one day, that you already knew everything at the age of seventeen?" Khayyam said mockingly.

"By the age of seventeen I had accumulated information, then I learnt how to believe. In Cairo I learnt how to convert."

"What do you say to those whom you are trying to convert?"

"I tell them that faith is nothing without a master to teach it. When we proclaim, 'There is no God but God,' we immediately add, 'And Muhammad is his Messenger.' Why? Because it would make no sense to state that there is only one God if we do not quote the source, that is to say the name of the man who brought us this truth. But this man, this Messenger, this Prophet, has been dead a long time and how can we know that he existed and that he spoke as was reported. I, who like you have read Plato and Aristotle, need proof."

"What sort of proof? Can one find proof for those things?"

"For you Sunnites there is effectively no proof. You think that Muhammad died without appointing an heir, that he just left the Muslims to their own devices to be governed by the strongest and wiliest. That is absurd. We think that the Messenger of God named a successor as a depository for his secrets: the Imam Ali, his son-in-law, his cousin, and almost his brother. In his turn, Ali designated a successor. The line of legitimate Imams was thus perpetuated, and through them, the proof of the message of Muhammad and of the existence of a single God was passed down."

"I cannot see, in what you say, how you differ from other Shiites."

"The difference between my faith and that of my parents is great.

They always taught me that we must submit patiently to the power of our enemies while waiting for the hidden Imam to return and establish the rule of justice on earth and reward the true believers. My own conviction is that we must act immediately to prepare by any means for the advent of our Imam in this country. I am the Precursor, he who will smooth the way in preparation for the Mahdi. You surely are aware that the Prophet spoke of me?"

"Of you, Hassan, son of Ali Sabbah, native of Qom?"

"Did he not say: 'A man will come from Qom. He will call upon the people to follow the straight path. Men will gather around him, like spearheads. Tempestuous winds will not be able to scatter them, nor will they tire of war or become weakened but they will rely upon God.'"

"I do not know that quote, even though I have read the certified collections of tradition."

"You have read the collections which you want. The Shiites have other collections."

"And they speak of you?"

"Soon you will have no doubt about it."

16

The man with the bulging eyes went back to his life of wandering. A tireless missionary, he criss-crossed the Muslim East — Balkh, Merv, Kashgar, and Samarkand — always preaching, arguing, converting, and organizing. He never left a town or a village until he had designated a representative whom he left surrounded by a circle of followers, Shiites who were tired of waiting and submitting, Persian or Arab Sunnites exasperated by Turkish domination, young men in a state of agitation, or believers in search of rigor. Hassan's army was growing every day. Its members were called "Batinites," the people of the secret, and they were treated as heretics or atheists. The *ulema* pronounced anathema after anathema upon them: "Woe betide him who joins them, woe betide him who eats at their table, woe betide him who joins them through marriage, it is as legitimate to spill their blood as to water one's garden."

The pitch mounted and violence did not remain long restricted to words. In the town of Savah, the preacher of a mosque denounced certain people, who, at the time of prayer, were assembling away from the other Muslims. He invited the police to deal ruthlessly with them and eighteen heretics were arrested. A few days later, the man who had denounced them was found stabbed. Nizam al-Mulk ordered the punishment to set an example: an Ismaili carpenter was accused of murder. He was tortured and crucified. Then his body was dragged through the alleys of the bazaar.

A chronicler considered that "That preacher was the Ismailis' first victim and that carpenter was their first martyr." He added that their first great victory was won near the city of Kain, south of Nishapur. A caravan was arriving from Kirman, consisting of more than six hundred merchants and pilgrims as well as an important cargo of antimony. A half-day from Kain, masked and armed men barred their way. The senior man of the caravan thought that they were bandits and wanted to negotiate a ransom as he was used to doing. That, however, was not what they were after. The travelers were led towards a fortified village where they were held for several days, preached to and invited to convert. Some accepted and others were released but most of them were ultimately massacred.

However, the kidnaping of a caravan was soon going to seem a very minor affair in the huge, but underhand, test of strength that was building up. Killings and counter-killings followed each other. No town, province, or route was spared and the peace of the Seljuk empire started to crumble.

That was when the memorable crisis in Samarkand broke out. A chronicler attested categorically that "the *qadi* Abu Taher was at the basis of the event." However, things were not quite so simple.

It is true that one November afternoon Khayyam's former protector arrived unexpectedly in Isfahan with wives and luggage, reeling off curses and oaths. Once through the gate of Tirah, he had taken himself to his friend, who lodged him, happy at last to have an occasion to show him his gratitude. Customary expressions of emotion were quickly disposed of. Abu Taher, on the edge of tears, asked:

"I must speak to Nizam al-Mulk as soon as possible."

Khayyam had never seen the *qadi* in such a state. He tried to reassure him:

"We are going to see the Vizir tonight. Is it so serious?"

"I have had to flee Samarkand."

He could not go on. His voice was stifled and his tears flowed. He had aged since their last meeting. His skin was withered, his beard was white, and only his bushy eyebrows retained their black hue. Omar uttered some words of consolation. The *qadi* pulled himself together, straightened his turban and then declared:

"Do you remember the man who was nicknamed 'Scar-Face'?"

"How could I forget that he debated my own death in front of my eyes?"

"You remember how he lost his temper at the slightest suspicion of a smell of heresy? Well, three years ago he joined the Ismailis and today he is proclaiming their beliefs with the same zeal with which he used to defend the True Faith. Hundreds and thousands of citizens are following him. He is master of the street and imposes his law on the merchants in the bazaar. On several occasions I have been to see the Khan. You knew Nasr Khan and his sudden outbursts of anger that subsided just as quickly, his fits of violence or prodigality, may God save his soul. I mention his name in every prayer. Today power is in the hands of his nephew, Ahmed, a smooth-chinned young man who is irresolute and unpredictable. I never know how to approach him. On many occasions I have complained to him about the machinations of the heretics. I have explained to him the dangers of the situation but he was distracted and bored and only half listened to me. Seeing that he had not taken any decision to act, I gathered the commanders of the militia as well as several officials whose loyalty I had acquired and I requested them to place the Ismailis' meetings under surveillance. Three trusty men took turns to follow Scar-Face, my aim being to present to the Khan a detailed report in order to open his eyes to their activities, until my men informed me that the chief of the heretics had arrived in Samarkand."

"Hassan Sabbah?"

"In person. My men had positioned themselves at both ends of Abdack Street, in the district of Ghatfar, where an Ismaili meeting was being held. When Sabbah came out, disguised as a Sufi, they jumped him, placed a sack over his head, and brought him to me.

"Immediately I led him to the palace to announce news of his capture to the sovereign. Then, for the first time, he appeared interested and asked to see the man. Except that when Sabbah was brought before him, he ordered his cords to be untied and for them to be left alone together. In vain I tried to warn him against this dangerous heretic, recalling the misdeeds of which he was guilty, but to no avail. He wanted, he claimed, to convince the man to return to the straight path. Their conversation went on and on. From time to time one of his courtiers would half-open the door, but the two men were still talking. At first dawn they were both seen suddenly prostrating themselves in prayer, murmuring the same words. The counselors jostled with each other to try and observe them."

After taking a mouthful of orgeat syrup, Abu Taher uttered a formula of gratitude before carrying on:

"Going by the evidence, it was certain that the master of Samarkand, the sovereign of Transoxania and heir to the dynasty of the Black Khans, had gone over to the heresy. Naturally he avoided proclaiming this fact and continued to affect attachment to the True Faith, but nothing was the same any more. The Prince's counselors were replaced by Ismailis. The chiefs of the militia, who had effected Sabbah's capture, died brutally one after another. My own guard was replaced by Scar-Face's men. What choice did I have left except to leave with the first pilgrim caravan and to come and make the situation known to those who carry the sword of Islam, Nizam al-Mulk and Malikshah."

That evening Khayyam took Abu Taher to the Vizir. He introduced him and then left them to talk in private. As Nizam listened reverently to his visitor his face took on a worried expression. When the *qadi* stopped speaking, he spoke up:

"Do you know who is really responsible for Samarkand's misfortunes, and for all of ours too? It is the man who brought you here!"

"Omar Khayyam?"

"Who else? It was *Khawaja* Omar who interceded for Hassan Sabbah on the day I could have obtained his death. He prevented us from killing him. Can he now prevent him from killing us?"

The *qadi* did not know what to say. Nizam sighed. A short embarrassed silence ensued.

"What do you suggest doing?"

It was Nizam who was asking the question. Abu Taher already had his idea formulated and he spoke it in the tones of a solemn proclamation:

"It is time for the Seljuk flag to fly over Samarkand."

The Vizir's face lit up and then darkened again.

"Your words are worth their weight in gold. I have been telling the Sultan for years that the empire should extend to Transoxania and that cities as prestigious and prosperous as Samarkand and Bukhara cannot remain outside the realm of our authority, but it was wasted effort. Malikshah would not listen."

"The Khan's army, mind you, is greatly weakened. Its emirs are no longer paid and its forts are falling into ruin."

"We are aware of that."

"Is Malikshah afraid of undergoing the same fate as his father Alp Arslan if, as his father did, he crosses the river?"

"Not at all."

The *qadi* asked no more questions, but awaited further elucidation.

"The Sultan is afraid neither of the river nor of the enemy army," stated Nizam. "He is afraid of a woman!"

"Terken Khatun?"

"She has sworn that, if Malikshah crosses the river, she will ban him from her couch and transform her harem into Gehenna. Let us not forget that Samarkand is her city. Nasr Khan was her brother and Ahmed Khan is her nephew. It is to her family that Transoxania belongs. If the kingdom built up by her ancestors were to collapse she would lose the position she occupies amongst the palace women and the chances of her son one day succeeding Malikshah would be compromised."

"But her son is only two years old!"

"Precisely. The younger he is, the more his mother must fight to keep his trump cards."

"If I have understood correctly," concluded the *qadi*, "the Sultan will never agree to take Samarkand."

"I have not said that, but we must make him change his mind and it will not be easy to find more persuasive arms than those of Khatun."

The *qadi* blushed. He smiled politely, without letting himself be deflected from his mission.

"Would it not suffice for me to repeat to the Sultan what I have just told you and to inform him of the plot hatched by Hassan Sabbah?"

"No," Nizam replied drily.

For a moment he was too absorbed to argue. He was formulating a plan. His visitor waited for him to make up his mind.

"Now," the Vizir pronounced with authority, "you will go tomorrow morning and present yourself at the door of the Sultan's harem and ask to see the chief of the eunuchs. You will tell him that you have come from Samarkand and that you wish to convey news of her family to Terken Khatun. As you are the *qadi* of her city and an old servant of her dynasty, she will have to receive you."

The *qadi* had only to nod his head for Nizam to continue:

"Once in the tentwork room, you will tell her about the misery Samarkand is in because of the heretics, but you will omit to mention Ahmed's conversion. On the contrary, you will make sure to tell her that Hassan Sabbah covets her throne, that her life is in danger, and that only providence can still save her. You will add that you have been to see me but that I was hardly inclined to listen to you, nay I even dissuaded you from speaking about it to the Sultan."

The next day the plan worked without the slightest hitch. While Terken Khatun took it upon herself to convince the Sultan of the need to save the Khan of Samarkand, Nizam al-Mulk, who was pretending to be against this, threw himself into making preparations for the expedition. By this make-believe war Nizam was not just trying to annex Transoxania, and even less was he trying to save Samarkand, but above all to re-establish his prestige which had been slighted by Ismaili subversion. For that, he needed a clear and stunning victory. For years his spies had been swearing to him, every day, that Hassan had been pinned down, and that he was on the point of being apprehended, but the rebel was not up for capture and his troops vanished at the first contact. Nizam was thus seeking a chance to confront him face to face, army to army. Samarkand was just the perfect place.

In the spring of 1089 an army of two hundred thousand men was on the march, with elephants and instruments of siege. The intrigues and lies that instigated its march are insignificant, for it was to accomplish what every army must. It began by taking possession of Bukhara without the least resistance and then it headed on towards Samarkand. Arriving at the gates of the city, Malikshah announced to Ahmed Khan in a pitiful message that he had come at last to deliver him from the yoke of the heretics. "I have asked nothing of my august brother," the Khan replied coldly. Malikshah was astonished, whereas Nizam was not at all disturbed. "The Khan is no longer a free agent. We must act as if he did not exist." In any case, the army could not retrace its steps. The emirs wanted their share of the booty and would not return empty-handed.

In the first days, the treachery of a tower guard permitted the assailants to sweep into the city. They took up position to the west, near the Monastery Gate. The defenders fell back to the souks in the south, around the Kish Gate. According to their faith, one section of the population decided to provide for the Sultan's troops, feeding them and giving them encouragement, and another section embraced the cause of Ahmed Khan. Fighting raged for two weeks, but there was never a second's doubt of the outcome. The Khan, who had taken refuge with a friend in the district of the domes, was quickly taken prisoner along with all the Ismaili chiefs. Only Hassan managed to escape through a subterranean canal at night.

Nizam had won, it is true, but by dint of playing the Sultan off against the Sultana he had poisoned irreparably his relations with the court. Even if Malikshah did not regret having conquered the most prestigious cities of Transoxania so easily, his self-respect suffered at having allowed himself to be abused. He went so far as to refuse to organize the traditional victory banquet for his troops. "It's out of avarice," Nizam whispered spitefully to all and sundry.

As for Hassan Sabbah, he learnt a valuable lesson from his defeat. Rather than try and convert princes, he would forge a fearsome instrument of war that would bear no resemblance to anything mankind had known until then: the order of the Assassins.

17

Alamut. A fortress on a rock six thousand feet high in a country-side of bare mountains, forgotten lakes, sheer cliffs, and narrow passes. The greatest army could only reach it in single file and the most powerful catapults could not graze its walls.

The Shahrud River, nicknamed the "mad river," dominated the mountains, swelling up in springtime with the melted snow of the Elburz mountains and snatching up trees and stones as it sped down its course. Woe to him who dared approach it! Woe to the army that dared pitch camp on its banks!

Every evening a thick, wooly mist rose from the river and the lakes, stopping halfway up the cliffs. To those who were there, the castle of Alamut was at such times an isle in an ocean of clouds. Seen from below, it was the abode of the jinns.

In the local dialect, Alamut means "the eagle's lesson." It was told that a prince who wanted to build a fortress to control these moun-tains released a trained bird of prey. The bird, after flying around in the sky, came to land on this rock. The master understood that no other site would be better.

Hassan Sabbah had imitated the eagle. He had searched the length and breadth of Persia for somewhere to gather, teach, and organize his faithful. He had learnt from his misadventure in Samarkand that it would be unrealistic to try and seize a large city, for confrontation with the Seljuks would be immediate and would inevitably turn out to the empire's advantage. He thus needed something else, a mountain redoubt that was inaccessible and impregnable, a sanctuary from which he could develop his activity in all directions.

Just as the flags captured in Transoxania were being unfurled in the streets of Isfahan, Hassan was in the vicinity of Alamut. The site had been a revelation for him. From the moment he first saw it from in the distance, he understood that it was here, and nowhere else, that his task would be accomplished and that his kingdom would arise. Alamut was at that time one fortified village among so many others, where a few soldiers lived with their families along with some artisans, farmers, and a governor, named by Nizam al-Mulk, who was a courageous nobleman called Mahdi the Alawite, whose only concerns were his irrigation water and his harvest of nuts, raisins, and pomegranates. The turmoil taking place in the empire did not disturb his slumber.

Hassan started by sending out some companions, local men, to join the garrison, to preach and convert. Some months later they were ready to announce to the master that the ground was prepared and that he could come. Hassan turned up disguised as a Sufi dervish as was his practice. He strolled around, inspecting and checking everything. The governor received the holy man and asked him what would please him.

"I need this fortress," said Hassan.

The governor smiled, thinking that the dervish certainly did not lack humor. His guest, however, was not smiling.

"I have come to take possession of this place. I have won over all the men of the garrison."

The outcome of this exchange was, admittedly, as extraordinary as it was incredible. Orientalists, who have consulted the chronicles of the time, particularly the accounts set down by the Ismailis, needed

102

to read and re-read them in order to reassure themselves that they were not the victims of a hoax.

Indeed, let us take another look at the scene.

It was the end of the eleventh century, or to be exact September 6, 1090. Hassan Sabbah, the brilliant founder of the Order of the Assassins, was about to take over the fortress that was to be, for 166 years, the seat of the most fearsome sect in all history. Now, there he was, seated cross-legged in front of the governor, to whom he was saying, without raising his voice:

"I have come to take possession of Alamut."

"This fortress has been given to me in the Sultan's name," the governor replied. "I have paid to obtain it."

"How much?"

"Three thousand gold dinars!"

Hassan Sabbah took a piece of paper and wrote: "Pay the sum of three thousand gold dinars to Mahdi the Alawite for the fortress of Alamut. May God meet our needs, for He is the best of protectors." The governor was unsettled and did not think that the signature of a man dressed in homespun might be honored for such a sum. However, when he arrived in the city of Damghan, he was able to cash his gold without any delay.

18

When news of the taking of Alamut reached Isfahan it aroused little concern. The city was much more interested in the conflict then currently raging between Nizam and the palace. Terken Khatun had not pardoned the Vizir for the operation he had conducted against her family's preserve. She urged Malikshah to rid himself of his overpowerful Vizir with no further ado. For the Sultan to have had a tutor upon his father's death she pronounced absolutely normal as he was then only seventeen years old; today he was thirty-five, an accomplished man, and he could not leave the management of affairs indefinitely in the hands of his *ata*; it was time for people to know who the real master of the empire was! Had the Samarkand business not proved that Nizam was trying to impose his will, that he was tricking his master and treating him as a minor before the whole world?

Malikshah was still hesitant about taking this step when something happened to push him into it. Nizam had named his own grandson governor of the city of Merv. This conceited adolescent held too much store by his grandfather's omnipotence, and had gone so far as to insult an old Turkish emir in public. The emir then came in tears to complain to Malikshah, who beside himself with rage had the following letter written to Nizam there and then: "If you are my aide, you must obey me and forbid your relatives to malign my men; if you deem yourself my equal, my associate in power, I will make the necessary decisions."

Nizam sent back his response to the message, which had been conveyed by a delegation of the empire's high dignitaries: "Tell the Sultan, if he was not aware of it until now, that I am indeed his associate and that without me he would never have been able to build up his power! Has he forgotten that it was I who took charge of his affairs upon his father's death, that it was I who eliminated the other aspirants and crushed all rebels? That it is thanks to me that he is obeyed and respected to the ends of the earth? Yes, go and tell him that the fate of his head is tied to that of my inkwell!"

The emissaries were dumbfounded. How could a man as wise as Nizam al-Mulk address the Sultan with words that would cause his downfall, and without doubt his death? Could his arrogance have gone over into madness?

That day, only one man knew with precision how to explain such determination, and that was Khayyam. For weeks Nizam had been complaining to him of dreadful pains that had been keeping him awake at night and preventing him from concentrating on his work by day. After examining him, probing his body with his fingers, and questioning him, Omar diagnosed a phlegmonic tumor that would not leave him long to live.

It was a truly unpleasant night when Khayyam had to announce to his friend his true condition.

"How much time do I have left to live?"

"A few months."

"Will I go on suffering?"

"I could prescribe you opium to reduce the suffering, but you will feel constantly dizzy and unable to work any more."

"Will I not be able to write?"

"Nor hold a long conversation."

"Then I prefer to suffer."

Between one retort and the next there were long moments of silence and suffering contained with dignity.

"Are you afraid of the hereafter, Khayyam?"

"Why should one be afraid? After death there is either nothing or forgiveness."

"And the evil that I have wrought?"

"However great your faults, God's mercy is greater."

Nizam seemed somewhat reassured.

"I have also done good. I have built mosques and schools and have fought against heresy."

As Khayyam did not contradict him, he went on:

"Will I be remembered in a hundred years' time, in a thousand years?"

"There is no knowing."

Nizam stared at him hard with distrust, and then continued:

"Was it not you who said one day: 'Life is like a fire. Flames which the passer-by forgets. Ashes which the wind scatters. A man lived.' Do you think that will be the fate of Nizam al-Mulk?"

He gasped for breath. Omar had still not said anything.

"Your friend Hassan Sabbah has gone throughout the country broadcasting that I am no more than a vile servant of the Turks. Do you think that is what they will say about me tomorrow, that they will make me into the scourge of the Aryans? Will they have forgotten that I was the only person to have stood up to sultans for thirty years and to have imposed my will upon them? What else could I do after their armies' victory? But you are not saying anything."

He had a vacant look about him.

"Seventy-four years. Seventy-four years which have passed before my eyes. So much deceit, so many regrets, and so many things I would have experienced differently!"

His eyes were half-closed, his lips contorted:

"Woe betide you, Khayyam! You are to blame for Hassan Sabbah being able to perpetrate his misdeeds."

Omar had wanted to reply: "How much you and Hassan have in common! If you are seduced by a cause such as building an empire or preparing for the reign of the Imam, you do not think twice about

106

killing in order to make your scheme triumph. In my opinion, any cause that involves killing no longer attracts me. It becomes unattractive to me, it becomes sordid and debased, no matter how beautiful it may have been. No cause can be just when it allies itself to death."

He wanted to shout it out, but he got the better of himself and remained silent. He had decided to allow his friend to slide peacefully towards his fate.

In spite of this trying night, Nizam ended up by resigning himself to his fate. He became used to the idea of not existing any more. However, from one day to the next he turned aside from affairs of state and determined that he ought to devote what time remained to him to completing a book, *Siyasset-Nameh*, the Treatise of Government. This was a remarkable work, the Muslim world's equivalent of Machiavelli's *The Prince*, which was to appear in the West four centuries later with one crucial difference. *The Prince* is the work of a man disappointed by politics and thwarted from having any power, while the *Siyasset-Nameh* is the fruit of the irreplaceable experience of an empire builder.

Thus, at the very moment when Hassan Sabbah had just conquered the unassailable sanctuary of which he had long dreamt, the empire's strongman was concerned only with his own place in History. He preferred words of truth over pleasantries and was prepared to defy the Sultan to the very end. It could be said that he wanted a spectacular death, a death that befitted him.

He was to obtain it.

When Malikshah received the delegation that had come from meeting Nizam, he could not believe what he was told.

"Did he really say that he was my associate, my equal?"

When the emissaries dolefully confirmed this, the Sultan let his anger come pouring out. He spoke of having his tutor impaled, dismembered alive, or crucified on the battlements of the citadel. Then he rushed off to announce to Terken Khatun that he had finally decided to discharge Nizam al-Mulk from all his duties and that he wished to see his death. It only remained to work out how he could be executed without provoking any reaction from the numerous regiments who were still loyal to him. However, Terken and Jahan had their own idea: since Hassan also wanted to see Nizam's death, why not facilitate the matter for him, while leaving Malikshah free from suspicion? An army corps was thus sent out to Alamut, under the command of a man loyal to the Sultan. The ostensible objective was to lay siege to the Ismailis' fortress but in reality it was a smoke-screen so that negotiations could take place without rousing suspicions and the course of events was planned down to the very details. The Sultan would lure Nizam to Nahavand, a city equidistant from Isfahan and Alamut. Once there, the Assassins would take over.

Texts from the time report that Hassan Sabbah gathered his men together and addressed them as follows: "Which man amongst you will rid this country of the evil Nizam al-Mulk?" A man named Arrani placed his hand on his chest as a sign of acceptance, the master of Alamut charged him with the mission, and added, "The murder of this demon is the gateway to happiness."

During this period Nizam stayed shut up in his residence. Those who had previously visited his *diwan* had deserted him upon learning of his disgrace, and only Khayyam and officers of the *nizamiya* guard frequented his residence. He spent most of his time at his desk. He scribbled away furiously and sometimes asked Omar to read it over.

As he read through the text, Omar gave off a smile or a grimace here and there. In the evening of his life, Nizam could not resist shooting off a few arrows and settling some accounts — for example, with Terken Khatun. The forty-third chapter was titled "On women who live behind the tent-work." "In ancient times," Nizam wrote, "the spouse of a king had great influence over him and there resulted therefrom nothing but discord and troubles. I shall say no more about it, for anyone can observe such things in other epochs." He added, "For an undertaking to succeed, it must be carried out the opposite way to what women say."

The following six chapters were devoted to the Ismailis and ended as follows: "I have spoken of this sect so that people can be on their guard ... My words will be remembered when these infidels manage to annihilate people close to the Sultan as well as statesmen, when their drums sound everywhere and their designs are unveiled. In the midst of the resultant tumult the Prince will surely know that everything I have said is the truth. May the Almighty preserve our master and the empire from an evil fate!"

The day when a messenger arrived from the Sultan to see him and invite him to join him on a trip to Baghdad, the Vizir had not a moment's doubt of what was in store for him. He called Khayyam to take his leave of him.

"In your condition, you should not cover such distances," Khayyam told him.

"In my condition nothing matters any more, and it is not the journey that will kill me."

Omar was lost for words. Nizam kissed him and dismissed him amicably, before going to bow before the man who had condemned him. With supreme elegance, recklessness, and perversity, the Sultan and the Vizir were both playing with death.

When they were *en route* for the place of trial, Malikshah questioned his "father":

"How long do you think you will yet live?"

Nizam replied without a hint of hesitation:

"A long time, a very long time."

The Sultan was distraught:

"You can still get away with being arrogant with me, but with God! How can you be so sure. You ought to call upon His will to be done for He is the arbiter of life!"

"I replied thus because I had a dream last night. I saw our Prophet, God bless and preserve him. I asked him when I was going to die and I received a reassuring response."

Malikshah grew impatient:

"What reply?"

"The Prophet told me, 'You are a pillar of Islam. You behave properly towards those around you, your existence is of value to the believers, and I thus am giving you the privilege of choosing when you will die.' I replied, 'God forbid. What man could choose such a day! One would always want more, and even if I determined the most distant date possible, I would live on obsessed by its approach. On the eve of that day, whether it were in a month or a hundred years time, I would shake with fear. I do not wish to choose the date. The only favor I ask, beloved Prophet, is not to outlive my master, Sultan

Malikshah. I have seen him grow up and have heard him call me "father," and I would not wish to undergo the humiliation and the suffering of seeing him dead.' 'Granted!' the Prophet said to me. 'You will die forty days before the Sultan.'"

Malikshah's face was pale and he was trembling so much that he almost gave himself away. Nizam smiled:

"You see, I am not showing any arrogance. I am now sure that I will live a long time."

Was the Sultan tempted, at that moment, to forgo having his Vizir killed? He would have been well advised to do so. Even if the dream was only a parable, Nizam in fact took formidable precautions. On the eve of his departure, the officers of his guard, assembled at his side, had sworn one after another with their hands placed on the Book that, should he be killed, not a single one of his enemies would live on!

19

I n the Seljuk empire, at a time when it was the most powerful
empire in the world, a woman dared to take power with her bare
hands. Seated behind her tenting, she arrayed armies from one end of
Asia to the other, named kings and viziers, governors and *qadis*, dic-
tated letters to the Caliph and sent emissaries off to the master of
Alamut. To emirs who grumbled upon hearing her give orders to the
troops, she responded, "Here it is the men who make war, but it is
the women who tell them against whom to fight."

In the Sultan's harem, she was nicknamed "the Chinese woman." She
had been born in Samarkand, to a family originally from Kashgar,
and, like her elder brother Nasr Khan, her face showed no intermin-
gling of blood — neither the Semitic features of the Arabs, nor the
Aryan features of the Persians.
    She was Malikshah's oldest wife by far. When she married him he

was only nine years old and she was eleven. She waited patiently for him to mature. She had felt the first down of his beard, surprised the first spring of desire in his body, and seen his limbs grow out and his muscles swell up as he turned into the majestic windbag whom she soon learnt to tame. She had never ceased being the favorite wife — adulated, wooed, honored, and above all listened to and obeyed. At the end of a day, or upon his return from a lion hunt, a tournament, a bloody clash, a stormy assembly of the emirs, or, worse, a tedious work session with Nizam, Malikshah would find peace in the arms of Terken. He would peel off her diaphanous silk covering, snuggle up to her bare skin, play about, bellow, and tell her about his exploits and what was tiring him. The Chinese woman would throw her arms around the excited lion, cocoon him, give him a hero's welcome in the folds of her body, and hold on to him long and tight, only letting go so that she could pull him back again; he stretched himself out with all his weight, conquering, breathless, panting, submissive, and bewitched. She knew how to take him to the very limits of pleasure.

Then, gently his thin fingers would start to trace her eyebrows, her eyelashes, her lips, her earlobes, and the lines of her moist neck; the lion was subdued, he was purring, growing sluggish, smiling. Terken's words would then flow into the hollows of his soul. She would speak of him, of herself and their children. She would tell him anecdotes, recite poems for him, whisper parables laden with teachings. He was never bored for a second in her arms and he resolved to stay with her every evening. In his own rough, childish, and animal way he loved her and was to love her until his last breath. She knew that he could refuse her nothing and it was she who planned his conquests of the moment, his mistresses or provinces. In the whole empire she had no rival other than Nizam, and in this year of 1092 she was on the verge of felling him.

Was the Chinese woman exultant at this? How could she be? The moment she was alone, or with Jahan her confidante, she would cry the tears of a mother and Sultana. She could curse her unjust fate and no one thought to blame her for it. Her eldest son had been chosen by Malikshah as his heir and was with him on all his trips and at all his ceremonies. His father was so proud of him that he displayed him everywhere, showing him his provinces one by one, telling him of the day when he would succeed him. "No Sultan ever left such a large empire to his son!" he would tell him. At that time Terken was indeed overjoyed and no unhappiness soured her smile.

Then the heir died from a sudden, shattering, and merciless fever. In vain the doctors prescribed bleedings and poultices but within two nights he passed away. It was said to be the work of the evil eye or even an undetectable poison. Terken managed to control her tears and pull herself together. When the period of mourning was over, she had her second son designated as heir to the throne. Malikshah took to him very quickly and showered him with surprising titles for a nine-year-old, but it was an era of pomp and ceremony: "King of Kings, Pillar of the State, Protector of the Prince of the Believers . . ."

The curse of the evil eye did not tarry in doing away with the new heir. He died as suddenly as his brother of a fever that was just as suspect.

The Chinese woman had a last son whom she asked the Sultan to designate as heir. The affair was trickier this time, since the child was only a year-and-a-half old and Malikshah was the father of three other boys who were all older. Two of them were born to a slave girl, but the eldest, named Barkiyaruk, was the son of the Sultan's own cousin. What pretext could she use to brush them aside? Who better than this prince, who was doubly Seljuk, to be elevated to the rank of heir to the throne? Such was the view of Nizam, who wanted to interject some order into the Turkish squabbles, who had always been eager to institute some form of hereditary dynasty and who had insisted, with the best arguments in the world, that Malikshah's eldest son should be designated heir, but with no success.

Malikshah dared not go against Terken, and as he could not nominate his son by her, he nominated no one, preferring to risk dying without an heir, like his father and all his clan.

Terken was not satisfied and would not be until her lineage was duly assured — that is to say that more than anything in the world she desired to see Nizam, the obstacle to her ambitions, fall into disgrace. In order to obtain his death warrant, she was ready to use intrigue or issue threats, and day after day she followed the negotiations with the Assassins. She had accompanied the Sultan and his vizir on their journey to Baghdad. She was keen to be there for the execution.

113

It was Nizam's last meal. The supper was an *iftar*, the banquet which marks the break of the fast of the tenth day of Ramadan. Dignitaries, courtiers, and emirs of the army were all unusually abstemious out of respect for the holy month. The table was laid inside a huge yurt. Slaves carried torches to enable people to choose their food. Sixty ravenous hands stretched towards the huge silver platters, the best piece of camel or lamb, and the choicest legs of partridge, skimming off flesh and sauce. They divided the food, ripped it apart, and devoured it. If someone found himself in possession of a particularly toothsome item, he would offer it to a neighbor he wished to honor. Nizam was eating little. That evening he was suffering more than usual. His chest was on fire and his insides felt as if they were being churned by the hand of an invisible giant. He was making an effort to hold himself upright. Malikshah was at his side, munching everything his neighbors passed to him. From time to time he was seen to look at his vizir out of the corner of his eye, thinking that he must be afraid. Suddenly he stretched his hand towards a plate of black figs, selected the plumpest and offered it to Nizam, who accepted it politely and bit into it. What savor could figs have when one was three times condemned, by God, the Sultan, and the Assassins?

By the time the *iftar* was over, it was already night. Malikshah jumped up, in a hurry to go and join his Chinese woman and tell her about the vizir's grimaces. Nizam leant on his elbows and hoisted himself up with some effort. His harem's tents were not far off and his old female cousin would have prepared a concoction of myrobalan to provide him some ease. He only had to take a hundred steps to be there. Around him was the inevitable confusion of royal camps with its soldiers, servants, and wandering tradesmen. Now and then he could hear the stifled laugh of a courtesan. How long the path seemed, and he was dragging himself along it alone. Usually he was surrounded by a group of courtiers, but who now wished to be seen with an outlaw? Even the beggars had fled — what could they hope to obtain from a disgraced old man?

However, someone was approaching him, a decent-looking man clothed in a patched coat. He muttered some pious words and Nizam felt for his purse and retrieved three pieces of gold. This unknown man who would still approach him ought to be rewarded.

114

There was a flash, the flash of a sword, and everything happened very quickly. Hardly had Nizam seen the hand move before the dagger pierced his clothing and skin and the point worked its way between his ribs. He had not even shouted out, but just made a dazed movement and gasped a last breath. As he was dying, he may have seen again, in slow motion, the blade, the arm stretching out and withdrawing and the nervous mouth which spat out: "This present comes to you from Alamut!"

Then cries went up. The Assassin had run off but had been tracked from tent to tent and found. Hurriedly they slit his throat and dragged him barefoot to be thrown on to a fire.

In the years and decades to come, innumerable messengers from Alamut would meet the same death, the only difference being that they would not attempt to flee. "It is not enough to kill our enemies," Hassan taught them. "We are not murderers but executioners. We must act in public as an example. By killing one man we terrorize a hundred thousand. However, it is not enough to execute and terrorize, we must also know how to die, for if, by killing, we discourage our enemies from undertaking any action against us, by dying in the most courageous fashion, we force the masses to admire us, and from their midst men will come to join us. Dying is more important than killing. We kill to defend ourselves, but we die to convert, and to conquer. Conquering is the aim we are seeking; defending ourselves is only a means thereto."

Assassinations generally took place on Friday in the mosque, at the moment of solemn prayer and in front of the assembled people. The victim, be he vizir, prince, or religious dignitary, would arrive surrounded by an imposing guard. The crowd would be impressed, submissive, and admiring. The emissary from Alamut would be there somewhere in the most unexpected of disguises — as a member of the guard, for example. At the moment when everyone's gaze was on the victim, he would strike. The victim would die and the executioner would not move, but would yell out a formula he had learnt and with a smile of defiance would wait to be set upon by the furious guards and then ripped limb from limb by the frightened crowd. The message had been delivered; the successor to the person who had been assassinated would make himself more conciliatory towards Alamut, and there would be a score, or two score conversions amongst those present.

So unreal were these scenes that it was often said that Hassan's men were drugged. How otherwise could it be explained that they went to their deaths with a smile? Some credence was given to the assertion that they were acting under the influence of hashish, and it was Marco Polo who popularized this idea in the West. Their enemies in the Muslim world would contemptuously call them *hash-ishiyun*, "hashish-smokers"; some Orientalists thought that this was the origin of the word "assassin," which in many European languages has become synonymous with murderer. The myth of the "Assassins" was more terrifying yet.

The truth is different. According to texts that have come down to us from Alamut, Hassan liked to call his disciples *Assassiyun*, meaning people who are faithful to the *Assass*, the "foundation" of the faith. This is the word, misunderstood by foreign travelers, that seemed similar to "hashish."

Hassan Sabbah indeed had a passion for plants and he had a miraculous knowledge of their curative, sedative, or stimulative characteristics. He himself grew all sorts of herbs and looked after his adepts when they were ill, knowing what potions to prescribe for them to revive their constitution. Thus we know of one of his recipes, which was intended to stimulate his disciples' minds and render them more adept at their studies. It was a mixture of honey, pounded nuts, and coriander and was considered a very agreeable medicine. However, we must go by the evidence, in spite of the tenacity and allure of tradition: the Assassins had no drug other than straightforward faith, which was constantly reinforced by the intense instruction, the most efficient organization, and the strictest apportionment of tasks.

At the top of the hierarchy sat Hassan, the Grand Master, the Supreme Preacher, the possessor of all the secrets. He was surrounded by a handful of missionaries, the *da'is*, amongst whom there were three commissioners: one for eastern Persia, Khorassan and Kuhistan, and Transoxania: one for western Persia and Iraq; and one for Syria. Immediately under them were the companions, the *rafiks*, the cadres of the

116

movement. After receiving adequate instruction, they were entitled to command a fortress and to lead the organization at the city or province level. The brightest would one day be missionaries.

Lower down the hierarchy were the *lassek*, literally those who were attached to the organization. They were the rank and file believers, with no particular predisposition to studies or violent action. They included many shepherds from the Alamut region and a number of women and old men.

Then came the *mujibs*, the "answerers," who were in fact the novices. They received some preliminary teaching and then, according to their capability, they were directed towards deeper studies in order to become companions, towards the body of the believers or towards the category that symbolized in the eyes of the Muslims of the time the real power of Hassan Sabbah, the class of the *fida'iyeen*, "those who sacrifice themselves." The Grand Master chose them from among the disciples who had huge reserves of faith, skill, and endurance, but little aptitude for study. He never sent to his death a man who could become a missionary.

The training of a *fida'i* was a delicate task to which Hassan devoted himself with a passion. The *fida'i* would learn how to keep his dagger hidden, how to unsheathe it with stealth and plunge it into the victim's heart, or into his neck if he was wearing a coat of mail; how to handle homing pigeons and memorize codes to be used for rapid and secret communication with Alamut; sometimes the *fida'i* would have to learn a ·dialect or regional accent, or how to infiltrate a foreign environment and be part of it for weeks or months, lulling all distrust while awaiting the most propitious moment to strike; he would learn how to stalk his prey like a hunter, making a careful study of his behavior, his clothing, his habits, and at what time he went out and returned; sometimes, when the victim was an exceptionally well-protected personage, he would have to find a means to be employed by him, to get near to him and form a bond with some of his circle. It was told that in order to execute one of their victims, two *fida'iyeen* lived for two months in a Christian convent, passing themselves off as monks. Such a remarkable talent for disguise and dissimulation could in no way have gone hand in hand with the use of hashish! Most importantly, the disciple had to acquire the necessary faith to confront

117

death and a faith in a paradise that the martyr would earn at the very moment when his life was taken from him by the raging crowd.

No one could stand up to Hassan Sabbah. He had succeeded in building up the most feared killing machine in history. Nonetheless, another arose, at the bloody turn-of-the-century — that of the Nizamiya, which out of loyalty to the assassinated Vizir went on to sow death with different methods which were perhaps more insidious, certainly less spectacular, but whose effects were to be no less devastating.

20

While the crowd was attacking the remains of the Assassin, five officers gathered around the still warm body of Nizam. They were in tears and stretched out their right hands as they mouthed in unison, "Rest in peace, master. None of your enemies will live!"

But where would they begin? The list of outlaws was long, but Nizam's orders were clear. The five men almost had no need to consult each other. They muttered a name and stretched out their hands anew. Then they kneeled down and together raised up the body which had been emaciated by illness but was now weighed down by death, and carried it in a cortège to his quarters. The women had already assembled to wail and the sight of the cadaver renewed their ululations, arousing the ire of one of the officers: "Do not cry while he is still unavenged!" The women were afraid and broke off their crying to look at the man who was already making his way off. Then they started up their noisy lamentations again.

The Sultan arrived. He had been with Terken when the first cries reached him. A eunuch who had been sent out for the news came back trembling. "It's Nizam al-Mulk, master! A killer jumped on him. He has given you the rest of his life!" The Sultan and Sultana exchanged a glance and then Malikshah arose. He put on his long cloak of *karakul*, patted his face in front of his spouse's mirror, and then ran off to see the deceased, feigning surprise and a state of the gravest affliction.

The women stepped aside to allow him to approach the body of his *ata*. He leant over, uttered a prayer and some appropriate phrases, before returning to Terken for some discrete celebrations.

How curiously Malikshah behaved. One would have thought that he would have profited from his tutor's disappearance to take complete control over the affairs of his empire, but not so. He was so happy at finally being rid of the man who checked his passions that he frolicked — and there can be no other word for it. Every meeting was canceled as a matter of course, as was every reception for an ambassador, and the Sultan's days were given over to polo and hunting while his nights were spent in bouts of drinking.

Yet more serious was the fact that upon his arrival in Baghdad he had sent a message to the Caliph, saying, "I intend to make this city my winter capital. The Prince of Believers must decamp post haste and find another residence." The successor of the Prophet, whose ancestors had been living in Baghdad for three and a half centuries, requested a month's grace in order to put his affairs in order.

Terken was worried by this frivolity, which was little worthy of a thirty-seven-year-old sovereign who was master of half of the world, but her Malikshah was what he was so she let him fool around and took the opportunity this gave her to establish her own authority. It was to her that emirs and dignitaries had recourse and it was her trusted men who replaced Nizam's acolytes. Between trips and drunken binges the Sultan gave his agreement.

On November 18, 1092 Malikshah was in the north of Baghdad hunting wild ass in a woody and swampy area. Only one of his previous twelve arrows had missed its target. His companions were singing his praises and none of them dreamed of matching his feats. The trip had made him hungry — a feeling he expressed in oaths. The slaves set to it. There were a dozen of them brought along to dismember, skewer, and gut the wild beasts, which were to be roasted in a clearing. The meatiest leg was for the sovereign, who took hold of it and ripped it to pieces hungrily while treating himself liberally to some fermented liquor. From time to time he munched on fruit preserved in vinegar, which was his favorite dish and huge vessels of which were carried everywhere Malikshah went by his cook so that he would never have to do without.

Suddenly he was beset with violent stomach cramps. Malikshah screamed in pain and his companions trembled. He threw down his goblet and spat out what he had in his mouth. He was bent double, he threw up everything he had eaten, became delirious, and then fainted. Around him dozens of courtiers, soldiers, and servants trembled as they watched him with disbelief. No one would ever know whose hand slipped the poison into his liquor, or was it in the vinegar, or the game? Nonetheless everyone made their calculations: thirty-five days had passed since Nizam's death. He had said "less than forty" and his avengers were on time.

Terken Khatun was in the royal camp, an hour away from the scene of the drama. The Sultan was carried in to her inanimate but still alive. She hurriedly sent away all onlookers, keeping by her only Jahan and two or three other trusted courtiers as well as the court doctor who was holding Malikshah's hand.

"Might the master recover?" the Chinese woman inquired.

"His pulse is weakening. God has blown on the candle and it is flickering before going out. Our only hope is prayer."

"If such is the will of the Almighty, then listen to what I am going to say."

This was not the tone of a widow-to-be, but of the mistress of an empire.

"No one outside this yurt must know that the Sultan is no longer with us. Merely say that he is recovering slowly, that he needs to rest, and that no one may see him."

What a fleeting and bloody epic was that of Terken Khatun. Even before Malikshah's heart had ceased beating, she demanded her handful of faithful courtiers to swear loyalty to Sultan Mahmoud, whose age was four years and a few months. Then she sent a messenger to the Caliph to announce the death of her spouse and to ask him to confirm her son's succession; in exchange the Prince of Believers would no longer have cause for concern in his capital and his name would be glorified in the sermons of mosques throughout the empire.

When the Sultan's court set off again for Isfahan, Malikshah had been dead for some days but the Chinese woman continued to keep the news from the troops. The cadaver was laid out on a large chariot pulled by six horses and covered by a tent. However, the charade could not last indefinitely for a corpse that has not been embalmed cannot linger amongst the living without its decomposition betraying its presence. Terken chose to be rid of it and thus Malikshah, "the revered Sultan, the great Shahinshah, the King of the Orient and the Occident, the Pillar of Islam and of the Muslims, the Pride of the World and of the Religion, the Father of Conquests, the Steadfast Support of the Caliph of God," was hastily interred by night at the side of the road in a place that no one has ever been able to find. "Never," said the chroniclers, "has there been told of such a powerful sovereign dying without anyone to pray or weep over his corpse."

News of the Sultan's disappearance finally got out, but Terken had no trouble justifying her actions: her first concern had been to hide the news from the enemy since the army and the court were far from the capital. In fact the Chinese woman had won the time she needed to place her son on the throne and to take up the reins of power herself.

The chronicles of the time make no mistake. When speaking of the imperial troops, they henceforth say "the armies of Terken Khatun." When speaking of Isfahan, they point out that it is Terken's capital city. As for the name of the child-Sultan, it would be as good as forgotten, and he would only be remembered as the "son of the Chinese woman."

The officers of the Nizamiya were nevertheless opposed to the Sultana. Terken Khatun was second on their list of outlaws, just after Malikshah, to whose eldest son, Barkiyaruk, aged eleven, they gave their support. They surrounded him, advised him, and led him off to battle. The first skirmishes left them with the advantage and the Sultana had to fall back on Isfahan, which was soon under siege. Terken, however, was not a woman to admit defeat and to defend herself she was willing to use tricks that would long be famous.

For example, to several provincial governors she wrote letters worded as follows: "I am a widow with the care of a minor who needs a father to guide his steps and to steer the empire in his name. Who better than you could fill this role? Come as quickly as possible at the head of your troops, lift the siege, and you will enter Isfahan triumphant; I shall marry you and you will wield complete power." The argument carried weight and emirs rushed from Azerbaijan and from Syria, and even though they did not manage to break the siege on the capital they did provide long months of respite for the Sultana.

Terken also re-established contact with Hassan Sabbah. "Did I not promise you Nizam al-Mulk's head? I offered it to you. Today I am offering you Isfahan, the capital of the empire. I know that you have many men in this city. Why do they live in the shadows? Tell them to show themselves and they will obtain gold and arms and will be able to preach in the open." In fact, after so many years of persecution, hundreds of Ismailis revealed themselves. The number of conversions increased and in certain quarters they formed armed militias on behalf of the Sultana.

However, Terken's last ruse was probably the most ingenious and the most audacious: emirs from her entourage presented themselves one day at the enemy camp, announcing to Barkiyaruk that they had decided to abandon the Sultana, that their troops were on the verge of revolt, and that, if he would agree to accompany them and infiltrate the city with them, they could give the signal for an uprising: Terken and her son would be massacred, and Barkiyaruk would be able to establish himself firmly on the throne. The year was 1094, the pretender was thirteen years old and the proposition took him in — to win control of the city in person when his emirs had been besieging it for over a year! He jumped at the chance. The following night, he slipped out of his camp unbeknown to his men, presented himself with Terken's emissaries at the gate of Kahab, which opened for him as if by magic. He walked in decisively, surrounded by an escort that was a little too jolly for his taste, but whose mood he ascribed to the unmitigated success of his exploit. If the men laughed too loud, he ordered them to calm down and they responded respectfully before bursting out laughing even more.

Alas — when he started to suspect their cheerfulness, it was too late. They pinned him down, bound his hands and feet, gagged and blindfolded him, and led him amid much scoffing to the gate of the harem. The chief eunuch, woken from his sleep, ran off to warn Terken of their arrival. It was up to her to decide the fate of her own son's rival — whether she should have him strangled or just blinded. The eunuch had disappeared in the long dark corridor when suddenly shouts, cries, and sobs broke out. Intrigued and worried, the officers, who could not hold back from penetrating the forbidden zone, came upon a talkative old servant: Terken Khatun had just been discovered dead in her bed with the instrument of the crime at her side — a large soft cushion with which she had been smothered. A eunuch with sturdy arms had disappeared and a servant-girl remembered that he had been introduced into the harem some years earlier upon Nizam al-Mulk's recommendation.

21

What a strange dilemma for Terken's followers: their Sultana was dead, but their principal adversary was at their mercy; their capital was surrounded but the very person laying the siege was now their prisoner. What should they do with him? Jahan had taken over Terken's place as guardian of the child-Sultan, and it was to her that the discussion was brought so that she might settle it. Until then she had shown herself to be extremely resourceful, but her mistress's death had shaken the ground under her feet. To whom could she turn, whom could she consult if not Omar!

Omar arrived to find her seated on Terken's divan at the foot of the drawn curtain with her head lowered and her tresses spread carelessly over her shoulders. The Sultan was next to her, dressed all in silk with a turban on his little head. He was sitting on his cushion; his face was red and spotty, and his eyes half-closed. He looked bored.

Omar went up to Jahan. He took her hand tenderly, stroked her face with his palm, and whispered:

"I have just been told about Terken Khatun. You have done well to call me to your side."

When he caressed her hair, Jahan pushed him away.

"If I have summoned you, it is not so that you can console me, but to consult you on a serious matter."

Omar took a step backwards, crossed his arms, and listened.

"Barkiyaruk has been caught in a trap and is a prisoner in the palace. The men are divided over the fate that should be meted out to him. Some demand his death, notably those who set the trap. They want to be certain of never having to answer to him for their actions. Others prefer to come to an understanding with him, place him on the throne, and win his favors, hoping that he will forget his misadventure. Still others have suggested keeping him hostage in order to negotiate with the besiegers. Which path do you advise me to follow?"

"You snatched me away from my books to ask me that?"

Jahan stood up. She was furious.

"Does the matter not appear sufficiently serious? My life depends on it. The fate of thousands of people, this city, and this empire may depend on your decision. Yet you, Omar Khayyam, you do not wish to be disturbed for such a trifle!"

He went towards the door, and just as he was about to open it he came back over to Jahan.

"I am consulted after the crime has been committed. What do you want me to tell your friends now? If I counsel them to release the youth, how could I guarantee that he will not wish to slit their throats tomorrow? If I counsel them to keep him as a hostage, or to kill him, I become their accomplice. Leave me out of these quarrels, Jahan, and you too should leave yourself out."

He looked at her with compassion.

"One son of a Turkish Sultan replaces another son, a Vizir dismisses a Vizir. By God, Jahan, how can you spend the best years of your life in this cage of wild animals? Let them rip each other's throats out, kill and die. Will the sun be any less bright or wine any less smooth?"

"Lower your voice, Omar. You are frightening the child. And we can be overheard in the adjoining rooms."

Omar persevered:

"Did you not call me to ask my opinion? Well I shall not beat around the bush: leave this room, abandon this palace, do not look back, do not say goodbye, do not even collect your belongings. Come, give me your hand and let us go home. You will compose your poems and I shall observe my stars. Every evening you will come and curl up naked next to me. Wine with the aroma of musk will make us sing and the world will cease to exist for us. We shall cross it without seeing or hearing it. Neither its mud nor its blood will cleave to the soles of our feet."

Jahan's eyes were misty.

"If I could return to that age of innocence, do you think that I would hesitate? However, it is too late, I have gone too far. If Nizam al-Mulk's men take Isfahan tomorrow they will not spare me. I am on their list of outlaws."

"I was Nizam's best friend and I shall protect you. They will not come into my house to make off with my wife."

"Open your eyes, Omar. You do not know these men. They think only of vengeance. Yesterday they rebuked you for having saved Hassan Sabbah's head. Tomorrow they will reproach you for having hidden Jahan and they will kill you at the same time as me."

"So we will stay together at home, and if my fate is to die with you, I will resign myself to it."

She straightened herself up.

"I will not resign myself! I am here in this palace, surrounded by troops who are faithful to me, in a city that is now mine, and I shall fight to the end. If I die, it will be as a Sultana."

"And how do Sultanas die? Poisoned, smothered, strangled! Or in childbirth! Pomp will not help you to escape human misery."

They looked at each other in silence for a long while. Jahan drew close to Omar and placed on his lips a kiss that she wanted to be impassioned and sank into his arms, but he pushed her aside, not able to bear farewells. He begged her one last time:

"If you still attach the least value to our love, come with me, Jahan. The table is laid on the terrace, a light wind from the Yellow Mountains will blow over us and within two hours we will be drunk and we will go to lie down. I shall tell the servants not to wake us until Isfahan changes master."

22

That evening the wind from Isfahan carried a sharp perfume of apricot. But how lifeless were the streets! Khayyam took refuge in his observatory. Usually he only had to enter it, look at the sky, and feel in his fingers the graduated disks of the astrolobe in order for the worries of the world to vanish. Not this time. The stars were taciturn, there was no music, not a sound, no secrets. Omar did not rush them for they had to have good reason for remaining silent. He decided to go home and walked slowly holding a reed which sometimes hit against a tuft of grass or an unruly branch.

He was now stretched out in his bedroom with the lights out; his arms desperately held an imaginary Jahan, his eyes were red from tears and wine. On the floor to his left were a carafe and a silver goblet which he seized from time to time with a weary hand in order to take long pensive drafts of disillusion. His lips held a dialogue with himself, with Jahan, with Nizam, but above all with God. Who else could hold together this universe that was crumbling?

It was not until dawn that an exhausted Omar, his head clouded, finally gave himself over to sleep. How many hours did he sleep? The sound of footsteps woke him up. The sun was already high and, pouring through a slit in the tenting, forced him to shield his eyes. He was able to make out in the doorway the man whose noisy arrival had disturbed him. He was big and wore a mustache. His hand was tapping the sheath of his sword with a maternal gesture. His head was bound in a bright green turban and on his shoulders was the short velvet cape of the officers of the Nizamiya.

"Who are you?" Khayyam asked with a yawn. "Who gave you rights over my sleep?"

"Has the master never seen me with Nizam al-Mulk? I was his bodyguard, his shadow. They call me Vartan the Armenian."

Omar remembered now and it hardly reassured him. He felt as if a cord were being knotted from his neck to his gut. However, if he was afraid, he did not want to show it.

"His bodyguard and shadow, you say. So it was up to you to protect him from the assassin?"

"He had ordered me to stay away. Everyone knows that he wanted to die like that. I could have killed one murderer and another would have sprung up. Who am I to intercede between my master and his fate?"

"And what do you want?"

"Last night, our troops slipped into Isfahan. The garrison rallied to us. Sultan Barkiyaruk has been rescued and this city belongs to him from now on."

Khayyam sat bolt upright.

"Jahan!"

It was a shout and an anguished question. Vartan said nothing. His worried air jarred with his martial bearing. Omar thought he could read in his eyes a monstrous admission. The officer muttered:

"I really wanted to try and save her. I would have been so proud to present myself to the illustrious Khayyam, bringing to him his spouse, unharmed! But I arrived too late. All the people of the palace had been massacred by the soldiers."

Omar went towards the officer and punched him as hard as he could without even succeeding in shaking him.

"And you have come here to tell me that!"

The officer kept his hand on the sheath of his sword but had not drawn it. He spoke calmly.

"I came for something else completely. The officers of the Nizamiya have decided that you must die. When you wound the lion, they say, it is wise to finish him off. I took on myself the task of putting you to death."

Khayyam suddenly became calmer. He would keep his bearing up to the end. How many sages had devoted their whole life to reach this peak of the human condition! He did not plead for his life, but on the contrary, he felt his fear wane by the second and he thought above all of Jahan. He had no doubt that she too had kept her bearing.

"I would never have pardoned those who killed my wife. My whole life I would have been their enemy, and my whole life I would have dreamed of seeing them impaled! You are absolutely right to rid yourselves of me!"

"It is not my opinion, master. It was up to five officers to decide your fate. My companions all wanted your death and I was the only one to oppose it."

"You were wrong. Your companions seem to be wiser."

"I often saw you with Nizam al-Mulk. You were sitting down conversing like father and son. He never stopped loving you in spite of your wife's schemes. If he were here with us, he would not have condemned you. He would also have forgiven her, for your sake."

Khayyam took a close, hard look at his visitor, as if he had just now discovered his presence.

"If you were against my death, why did they choose you to come and execute me?"

"It was I who offered myself. The others would have killed you, but I planned to leave you alive — otherwise why would I have stayed talking with you?"

"And how will you explain this to your companions?"

"I will not explain anything. I shall go away. I shall follow you."

"You announce it so calmly, as if it were a long-standing decision."

"It is the very truth. I do not act impulsively. I was the most faithful servant of Nizam al-Mulk — I believed in him. If God had allowed it, I would have died to protect him. However, long ago I decided that, if the master should disappear, I would serve neither his sons nor his successors and I would forever give up the profession of the sword. The circumstances of his death have forced me to use it one last time. I was involved in the murder of Malikshah and I do not regret it: he had betrayed his tutor, his father, the man who raised him up to the summit; he thus deserved to die. I had to kill, but that has not made me a killer. I would never have shed the blood of a woman, and when my companions outlawed Khayyam, I understood that the time had come for me to leave, to change my life and to became a hermit or a wandering poet. If you want, master, collect some belongings and we shall leave this city as soon as possible."

"To go where?"

"We shall take whatever path you wish. I shall follow you everywhere, as a disciple, and my sword will protect you. We will be able to return when the tumult has died down."

While the officer was readying the mounts, Omar hurriedly gathered up his manuscript, his writing case, his flask, and a purse bulging with gold. They rode right through the oasis of Isfahan to the suburb of Marbine towards the west without being troubled by the numerous soldiers. One word from Vartan was enough for the gates to be opened and the guards to stand aside respectfully. The servility shown to Vartan did not fail to intrigue Omar, who nevertheless avoided questioning his companion. For the moment he had no choice other than to trust in him.

They had been gone less than an hour before a seething crowd came to pillage Khayyam's house and set it on fire. By the end of the afternoon the observatory had been laid waste. At the same moment, the lifeless body of Jahan was interred at the foot of the mulberry tree that bordered the palace garden.

There would be no tombstone to show posterity her place of burial.

A parable from the *Samarkand Manuscript:*

"Three friends were taking a walk on the high plateaus of Persia. A panther sprang out at them with all the fierceness in the world.

"The panther looked at the three men for a long while and then ran towards them.

"The first was the oldest, the richest, and the most powerful. He cried out, 'I am the master of these districts. I shall never allow a beast to ravage the lands that belong to me.' He had with him two hunting dogs and set them on to the panther. They managed to bite it but the panther only became stronger, overwhelmed them, jumped on their master, and ripped out his intestines.

"Thus was the fate of Nizam al-Mulk.

"The second man wondered, 'I am a man of knowledge, everyone honors and respects me. Why should my fate be decided by dogs and a panther?' He turned tail and fled without waiting for the outcome of the fight. Since then he has wandered from cave to cave, from hut to hut, convinced that the wild beast was always at his heels.

"Thus was the fate of Omar Khayyam.

"The third was a man of belief. He walked towards the panther with his hands open, with a dominating demeanor and eloquent words. 'You are welcome to these lands,' he said to the panther. 'My companions were richer than I and you despoiled them. They were prouder than I and you have laid them low.' The beast listened, seduced and subdued. The man had the advantage over the panther, and managed to train it. Since then no panther has dared to approach him and men keep away."

The *Manuscript* concludes, "When the time of upheavals arrived, no one could stop its course, no one could flee it but some managed to use it. Hassan Sabbah, more than anyone, knew how to tame the ferocity of the world. He sowed fear all around him in order to make a tiny piece of calm for himself in his redoubt of Alamut."

No sooner had he gained control of the fortress than Hassan Sabbah undertook actions to assure that he was sealed off from any contact with the outside world. His first priority was to render impossible any enemy penetration. With the help of some clever building he thus improved the already exceptional quality of the site by blocking off the slightest passageway between two hills.

However, these fortifications were not enough for Hassan. Even if an assault was impossible, the besiegers would still hope to starve him out or cut off his water. It is thus that most sieges end. And it was on this point that Alamut was particularly vulnerable, having only meager stocks of drinking water. The Grand Master found the answer. Instead of drawing his water from the neighboring rivers, he had an impressive network of cisterns and canals dug in the mountain to collect rainwater and the melting snows. The visitor to the ruins of the castle today can still admire, in the large room where Hassan lived, a "magic basin" that filled itself up with as much water as was taken out from it, and that, by a stroke of ingenuity, never overflowed.

For provisions, the Grand Master had storage shafts fitted out for oil, vinegar, and honey; he also stockpiled barley, sheep fat, and dried fruit in sufficient quantities to get them through an almost total blockade — which, at that time, was far beyond the capacity of any besiegers, particularly in a region that had a harsh winter.

Hassan thus had an infallible shield. He had, one could say, the ultimate defensive weapon. With his devoted killers, he also possessed the ultimate offensive weapon. How can precautions be taken against a man intent on dying? All protection is based upon dissuasion, and we know that important personages are surrounded by an imposing guard whose role is to make any potential attacker fear inevitable death. But what if the attacker is not afraid of dying, and has been convinced that martyrdom is a short-cut to paradise? What if he has imprinted in his mind the words of the Preacher: "You are not made for this world, but for the next. Can a fish be afraid if someone threatens to throw it into the sea?" If, moreover, the assassin had succeeded in infiltrating the victim's entourage? Nothing could be done to stop him. "I am less powerful than the Sultan but I can harm you more than he can," Hassan wrote one day to a provincial governor.

Thus, having forged the most perfect tools of war imaginable, Hassan Sabbah installed himself in his fortress and never left it again; his biographers even say that during the last thirty years of his life he only went out of his house twice, and both times it was to go up on the roof! Morning and evening he was there, sitting cross-legged on a mat that his body had worn out but which he never wished to change or have repaired. He taught, he wrote, he set his killers on to his enemies, and, five times a day, he prayed on the same mat along with whoever was visiting him at the time.

For the benefit of those who have never had the opportunity to visit the ruins of Alamut, it is worth pointing out that this site would not have acquired such historical importance if its only advantage had been its inaccessibility and if the plateau at the mountain's summit had not been large enough to support a town, or at least a very large village. At the time of the Assassins it was reached by a narrow tunnel to the east which emerged into the lower fortress with its tanglé of alleys and little mud houses in the shadow of the walls; the upper fortress was reached by crossing the *maydan,* the large square, the only meeting area for the whole community. This was shaped like a bottle lying on its side, with its wide base in the east and its neck towards the west. The bottleneck itself was a heavily guarded corridor at the end of which lay Hassan's house whose single window looked out on to a precipice. It was a fortress within a fortress.

By means of the spectacular murders that he ordered, and the legends that grew up around him, his sect, and his castle, the Grand Master of the Assassins terrorized the Orient and the Occident over a long period. In every Muslim town high officials fell and even the Crusaders had two or three eminent victims to lament. However, it is all too often forgotten that it was primarily at Alamut that terror reigned.

What reign is worse than that of militant virtue? The Supreme Preacher wanted to regulate every second of his adherents' lives. He proscribed all musical instruments; if he discovered the smallest flute he would break it in public and throw it into the flames; the transgressor was put in irons and given a good whipping before being expelled from the community. The use of alcoholic drinks was even more severely punished. Hassan's own son, found intoxicated one evening by his father, was condemned to death on the spot; in spite of his mother's pleadings he was decapitated at dawn the next day as an example. No one ever dared to swallow a mouthful of wine.

The justice of Alamut was, to say the least, speedy. It was said that a crime had been committed one day within the fortress and that a witness had accused Hassan's second son. Without attempting to verify the fact, Hassan had his last son's head cut off. A few days later, the real culprit confessed; he in turn was decapitated.

Biographers of the Grand Master mention the slaughter of his sons in order to illustrate his strictness and impartiality; they point out that the community of Alamut became a haven of virtue and morality through the blessing of such exemplary discipline, and this can very easily be believed; however, we know from various sources that the day after these executions Hassan's only wife as well as his daughters rose up against his authority, and that he ordered them thrown out of Alamut and recommended that his successors do the same in the future in order to avoid the womenfolk having any influence over their correct judgment.

To loose himself from the world, create a void around his person, surround himself with walls of stone and fear — such seems to have been Hassan Sabbah's demented dream.

However, this void started to stifle him. The most powerful kings have jesters or jovial companions to lighten the oppressive atmosphere that surrounds them. The man with the bulging eyes was incurably alone, walled up in his fortress, shut up in his house, closed to himself. He had no one to talk to, only docile subjects, dumb servants, and awestruck disciples.

Of all the people he had known, there was only one to whom he could still talk, if not as friend to friend then at least as man to man, and that was Khayyam. He had thus written him a letter in which despair disguised itself behind a thick façade of pride:

"Instead of living as a fugitive, why do you not come to Alamut? Like you, I have been persecuted but now it is I who persecute. Here you will be protected, looked after, and respected. No emir on earth will be able to harm a hair of your head. I have founded a huge library where you will find the rarest works and will be able to read and write at leisure. In this place you will find peace."

23

Since he had left Isfahan, Khayyam had been leading effectively the existence of a fugitive and a pariah. When he betook himself to Baghdad, the Caliph forbade him to speak in public or to receive his numerous admirers who presented themselves at his door. When he visited Mecca, his detractors sniggered, "A pilgrimage of servility!" When, on his return, he passed through Basra, the sons of the *qadi* of the city came to ask him, in the politest of terms, to cut short his stay.

His fate then was unsettling in the extreme. No one contested his genius or his erudition; wherever he went large groups of intellectuals gathered around him. He was questioned on astrology, algebra, medicine, and even religious problems and he was listened to warmly. However, without fail, a few days or weeks after his arrival, a clique would emerge and would disseminate all sorts of lies. He would be called an infidel or a heretic, and his friendship with Hassan Sabbah would-be recalled. Sometimes the accusations of being an alchemist, raised against him of old in Samarkand, were dredged up. Ardent opponents were sent to break up his discussions and those who dared shelter him were threatened with reprisals. Usually, he put up no opposition. As soon as he felt the atmosphere become uncomfortable he would feign illness in order not to appear in public again, and he would then not linger, but would go away to somewhere new where his stay would be just as short and precarious.

Honored and cursed, with no companion other than Vartan, he was constantly in search of a roof, a protector, and a patron too; the generous pension that Nizam had allotted to him was no longer being paid out since his death and he was forced to visit princes and governors and prepare their monthly horoscopes. However, even though he was often in need, he managed to get himself paid without bowing his head.

It was told that a vizir, astonished to hear Omar demand a sum of five thousand golden dinars, remarked:

"Do you know that I myself am not paid that much?"

"That is quite normal," retorted Khayyam.

"And how so?"

"Because there are only a handful of intellectuals like me every century, while one could name five hundred vizirs like you every year."

The chroniclers state that the man found this extremely amusing and went on to satisfy Khayyam's demands, courteously recognizing the correctness of such a haughty equation.

"No Sultan is happier than I, no beggar sadder," Omar wrote during this period.

The years passed and we find him again in 1114 in the city of Merv, the old capital of Khorassan, still famous for its silks and its ten libraries, but deprived for some time now of any political role. To restore some luster to its tarnished court, the local sovereign was trying to attract the celebrities of the time. He knew just how to seduce Khayyam — by offering to build him an observatory identical to that of Isfahan. At sixty-six years of age, Omar no longer dreamt of anything else and he accepted with adolescent enthusiasm and set right down to work on the project. Soon the building was rising up on a hilltop in the district of Bab Senjan in the middle of a garden of daffodils and white mulberries.

Omar was happy for two years and he worked feverishly. We are told that he carried out astonishing experiments in weather forecasting, his knowledge of the sky allowing him to note exactly the changes of climate over five successive days. He also developed his mathematical theories, which were way ahead of his time. It was not until the nineteenth century that European researchers recognized him to be the brilliant precursor of non-Euclidean geometry. He also wrote *rubaiyaat*, stimulated, we must believe, by the outstanding quality of Merv's vineyards.

For all that, there was evidently a negative side. Omar was obliged to be present at endless palace ceremonies and to pay homage solemnly to the sovereign at each feast, whenever a prince was circumcised, upon the sovereign's return from the hunt or the country, and to be in frequent attendance at the *diwan*, ready to utter a witticism, a quotation, or a fitting verse. These sessions exhausted Omar. As well as the impression of having put on the skin of a performing bear, he was always aware of losing precious time at the palace that he could have turned to better use at his work table, not to mention the risk of unpleasant encounters.

Like the one that took place that cold February day, when someone picked a memorable quarrel with him over a youthful quatrain that had fallen into jealous ears. That day the *diwan* was packed with beturbaned intellectuals and the monarch was overjoyed as he blissfully contemplated his court.

When Omar arrived, debate was already raging on a subject that fascinated the men of religion: "Could the universe have been created better?" Those who replied "yes" laid themselves open to accusations of impiety since they implied that God had not taken sufficient care over his work. Those who replied "no" were also open to accusations of impiety, as they were giving to understand that the Almighty was incapable of doing better.

They were in hot discussion, with much gesticulating. Khayyam was happy absent-mindedly to watch everyone's expressions. However, a speaker called him, heaped praise upon his erudition, and asked for his opinion. Omar cleared his throat. He had not yet uttered a single syllable when the grand *qadi* of Merv, who had never appreciated Khayyam's presence in his city, nor the considerations constantly shown to him, jumped up from his place and pointed an accusing finger at him.

"I did not know that an atheist could express opinions on the questions of our faith!"

Omar gave a tired but worried smile.

"Who gives you permission to treat me as an atheist? At least wait until you have heard me out!"

"I have no need to hear you. Is it not to you that this verse has been attributed: 'If You punish with evil the evil I have done, tell, what is the difference between You and me?' Is not the man who puts forward such words an atheist?"

Omar shrugged.

"If I did not believe that God existed, I would not address Him!"

"But you would address Him in that tone?" sniggered the *qadi*.

"It is to Sultans and *qadis* that one must speak with circumlocution — not to the Creator. God is great, He has nothing to do with our airs and graces. He made me a thinker and so I think, and I give over to Him the undiluted fruits of my thought."

To murmurs of approval from those present, the *qadi* withdrew, uttering dire threats. When he had stopped laughing, the sovereign was beset with worry, fearing the consequences in certain quarters. As his expression became gloomy his visitors hurried to take their leave.

As he returned home accompanied by Vartan, Omar inveighed against court life with its snares and time-wasting, promising himself that he would leave Merv as soon as possible; his disciple was not too concerned as it was the seventh time that his master had threatened to leave; as a rule, he was much calmer the next day having taken up his research again, and that was the appropriate time to console him.

That evening, back in his room, Omar wrote in his book a vexed quatrain which ended as follows:

> *Swap your turban for some wine*
> *And without regrets, put on a woolen hat!*

Then he slipped the manuscript into its usual hiding place, between the bed and the wall. When he woke up, he wanted to re-read his *rubai* since one word seemed to him out of place. He groped about and grasped the book. It was as he opened it that he discovered the letter from Hassan Sabbah that had been slipped between the two pages as he slept.

In an instant Omar recognized the writing and the nomenclature agreed upon between them forty years earlier: "The friend from the caravansary at Kashan." As he read it he could not help bursting out laughing. Vartan, who was just waking up in his adjoining room, came in to see what was amusing his master so much after his ill feelings of the night before.

"We have just received a generous invitation. We can be lodged, protected, and have all our expenses looked after until the end of our lives."

"By which great prince?"

"The prince of Alamut."

Vartan jumped. He felt guilty.

"How could the letter have got here? I checked all the doors and windows before I went to lie down!"

"Do not try to find out. Sultans and Caliphs themselves have given up protecting themselves. When Hassan decides to send you a message or a dagger's blade, you can be certain of receiving it whether your doors are wide open or padlocked."

The disciple held the letter to his mustache, sniffed it noisily, and then read and re-read it.

"That demon may well have a point," he concluded. "It is indeed at Alamut that your safety would be best assured. After all, Hassan is your oldest friend."

"For the moment, my oldest friend is the new wine of Merv!"

With childish glee, Omar set to tearing up the sheet of paper into a multitude of little pieces which he threw up in the air. As he watched them flutter down, he started to speak again:

"What do we have in common, this man and I? I worship life and he worships death. I write, 'If you cannot love, what use is the rising and the setting of the sun?' Hassan demands his men to give no heed to love, music, poetry, wine, or the sun. He despises the most beau-

'tiful things in all creation, yet he dares pronounce the name of the Creator — and to promise people paradise! Believe you me, if his fortress were the gateway of paradise, I would renounce paradise! I shall never set foot in that den of pious shams."

Vartan sat down and had a good scratch of his neck before saying, in the most exhausted of voices:

"If that is your response then the time has come for me to reveal to you a secret which has been kept too long. Have you never wondered why the soldiers let us pass through so easily when we fled from Isfahan?"

"It has always intrigued me, but since I have seen nothing but loyalty, devotion, and filial affection from you for years, I have not wished to stir up the past."

"That day, the officers of the Nizamiya knew that I was going to save you and leave with you. That was part of a strategy I had drawn up."

Before carrying on, he served his master, and himself, a useful glass of grenadine wine.

"You do know that the list of outlaws set up by Nizam al-Mulk contained the name of one man whom we had never managed to reach — Hassan Sabbah. Was he not the man principally responsible for the assassination? My plan was simple: to leave with you in the hope that you would take refuge in Alamut. I would have accompanied you, asking you not to reveal my identity, and I would have found an occasion to rid the Muslims and the entire world of that demon. However, you have stubbornly refused to set foot in the dark fortress."

"Yet you stayed by my side all this time."

"At the beginning I thought I would just have to be patient and that when you had been chased out of fifteen cities in succession you would resign yourself to taking the road to Alamut. Then, as the years passed, I grew attached to you, my companions have been dispersed to the four corners of the empire and my determination has wavered. See now how Omar Khayyam has saved Hassan Sabbah's life a second time."

"Do not bewail it — it may well be your life that I have saved."

"In truth he must be very well protected in his hideout."

Vartan could not suppress all traces of bitterness, which amused Khayyam.

141

"Having said that, if you had revealed your plan to me, doubtless I would have led you to Alamut."

The disciple jumped out of his seat.

"Is that the truth?"

"No. Sit yourself down! I only said that to give you cause for regret! In spite of all the evil Hassan has managed to commit, if I were to see him drowning in the Murghab River I would offer him my hand in help."

"Well I would shove his head down under the water! However, your attitude gives me some comfort, and it is just because you are capable of such words and acts that I chose to stay in your company. And I do not regret that."

Khayyam gave his disciple a long hug.

"I am happy that my doubts about you have been dispelled. I am old now and need to know that I have a trusty man at my side — because of the manuscript. That it is the most precious thing I possess. In order to take on the world Hassan Sabbah has built Alamut, whereas I have only constructed this minuscule paper castle, but I choose to believe that it will outlive Alamut. Nothing frightens me more than to think that upon my death my manuscript could fall into careless or malevolent hands."

In an almost offhand manner he held the secret book out to Vartan:

"You may open it, since you will be its guardian."

The disciple was moved.

"Would anyone else have had this privilege before me?"

"Two people. Jahan, after a quarrel in Samarkand, and Hassan when we were living in the same room upon our arrival in Isfahan."

"You trusted him to that extent?"

"To tell you the truth, I did not. However, I often wanted to write and he ended up noticing the manuscript. I preferred to show it to him myself since, anyhow, he could have read it behind my back. Moreover, I deemed him capable of keeping a secret."

"He really does know how to keep a secret — the better to use it against you."

Henceforth the manuscript would spend its night in Vartan's room.

At the slightest noise the former officer would be bolt upright, brandishing his sword, his ears pricked up; he would check every room in the house and then go out to make a round of the garden. Upon his return he would not always be able to fall asleep again and so would light a lamp on his table and read a quatrain, which he would memorize and then indefatigably go over in his head to draw out its most profound meanings and to try and guess under what circumstances his master had been able to write it.

At the end of a string of disturbed nights, an idea took shape in his thoughts that received Omar's hearty approval: to write the manuscript's history in the margins of the *Rubaiyaat* and through this device the history of Khayyam himself, his childhood in Nishapur, his youth in Samarkand, his fame in Isfahan, his meetings with Abu Taher, Jahan, Hassan, Nizam, and many others. Thus it was, under Khayyam's supervision, and sometimes with him dictating the words, that the first pages of the chronicle were written. Vartan threw himself into it, writing each phrase down ten or fifteen times on a loose sheet before transcribing it, in a thin, angular, and laborious hand — which, one day, was brutally interrupted in the middle of a phrase.

Omar had woken up early that morning. He called Vartan, who did not reply. Another night spent writing, Khayyam said to himself in a fatherly way. He let him rest a while longer, poured himself a morning drink, just a drop at the bottom of the glass which he swallowed in one gulp followed by a whole glassful which he carried with him as he went for a walk in the garden. He walked around it, diverting himself by blowing on the dew which was still on the flowers, then he went off to gather some juicy white mulberries which he placed on his tongue and squashed against his palate with every sip of wine.

He was enjoying himself so much that a good hour had passed before he decided to go back in. It was time for Vartan to get up. He did not call him again, but went straight into his room to find him stretched out on the ground, his throat black with blood, his mouth and eyes open and set rigid as if in a last suffocated cry.

On his table between the lamp and the writing desk was the dagger with which the crime had been committed. It was planted in a curled up sheet of paper that Omar unrolled to read:

"Your manuscript has gone on ahead of you to Alamut."

24

O mar Khayyam mourned his disciple with the same dignity, the same resignation, and the same discreet agony as he had mourned other friends. "We were drinking the same wine, but they got drunk two or three rounds before me." Anyway, how could he deny that it was the loss of the manuscript that affected him most grievously? He was certainly able to reproduce it; he remembered its every letter, but apparently he did not want to, for there is no trace of a rewritten version. It seems that Khayyam learnt a wise lesson from the theft of his manuscript; he would never more try to have control over either his future or that of his poems.

He soon left Merv, not for Alamut — not once did he envisage going there! — but for his home town. "It is time," he told himself, "to put an end to my peregrinations. Nishapur was the first port of call in my life. Is it not within the order of things that it should also be the last?" It is there that he was going to live, surrounded by relatives, a younger sister, a considerate brother-in-law, nephews, and above all a niece who was to be the recipient of most of the tenderness of his autumn years. He was also surrounded by his books. He did not write any more, but untiringly re-read the works of his masters.

One day, as he was seated in his room as usual with Avicenna's *Book of Healing* on his knees, open at the chapter entitled "The One and the Multiple," Omar felt a dull pain start up. He placed his golden tooth-pick, which he had been holding in his hand, between the leaves to mark the page, closed the book, and summoned his family in order to dictate to them his last testament. Then he uttered a prayer which finished with the words: "My God, You know that I have sought to perceive You as much as I could. Forgive me if my knowledge of You has been my only path towards You!"

He opened his eyes no more. It was December 4, 1131. Omar Khayyam was in his eighty-fourth year, having been born on June 18, 1048 at daybreak. The fact that the date of birth of a person from that era is known with such precision is indeed extraordinary, but Khayyam showed an astrologer's obsession with the subject. He had most probably questioned his mother to find out his ascendant, Gemini, and to determine the position of the sun, Mercury, and Jupiter at the hour of his coming into the world. Thus he drew up his birth chart and took care to pass it on to the chronicler Beihaki.

Another of his contemporaries, the writer Nizami Aruzi, recounted, "I met Omar Khayyam twenty years before his death in the city of Balkh. He had come to stay with one of the notables on the Slave-Traders' Road, and, knowing of his fame, I shadowed him in order to hear every one of his words. That is how I heard him say: 'My tomb will be in a place where the north wind scatters flowers every spring.' His words at first seemed absurd to me; however, I knew that a man like him would not speak in an unconsidered manner."

The witness continued, "I passed through Nishapur four years after Khayyam's death. As I venerated him as one should a master of science, I made a pilgrimage to his last home. A guide led me to the cemetery. Upon turning to the left after entering, I saw the tomb adjoining the wall of a garden. Pear and peach trees spread out their branches and had dropped so much blossom on to his sepulcher that it was hidden under a carpet of petals."

A drop of water fell into the sea.
A speck of dust came floating down to earth.
What signifies your passage through this world?
A tiny gnat appears — and disappears.

Omar Khayyam was wrong. Far from being as transitory as he said, his existence, or at least that of his quatrains, had just begun. But, was it not for them that the poet, who dared not wish it for himself, wished immortality?

Those who had the terrifying privilege at Alamut of being allowed in to see Hassan Sabbah did not fail to notice the silhouette of a book in a hollow niche in the wall, behind a thick wire grate. No one knew what it was, nor dared to question the Supreme Preacher. It was assumed that he had his reasons for not depositing it in the great library where there were great works that contained the most unspeakable truths.

When Hassan died, at almost eighty years old, the lieutenant he had designated to succeed him did not dare install himself in the master's den and even less did he dare open the mysterious grate. For a long time after the disappearance of the founder, the inhabitants of Alamut were terrified by the mere sight of the walls that had sheltered him; they avoided venturing towards this previously inhabited quarter lest they come across his shade. The order was still subjected to the rules Hassan had decreed; the community members' permanent lot was one of the strictest asceticism. There was no deviation, no pleasure, and only more violence against the outside world, more assassinations than ever, most probably to prove that the leader's death had in no way weakened his adherents' resolve.

And did these adherents accept this strictness good-naturedly? Less and less. Murmurs started to be heard. Not so much amongst the veterans who had won Alamut while Hassan was alive; they still lived with the memory of the persecutions they had undergone in their countries of origin and feared lest the slightest relaxation make them more vulnerable. However, these men were becoming less numerous every day and the fortress was more and more inhabited by their sons and grandsons. From the cradle, all of them had been accorded the most rigorous indoctrination that forced them to learn and respect Hassan's onerous directives as if they were divine revelation. But most of them were becoming more resistant. Life was staking its claim on them again.

Some dared one day to ask why they were forced to spend their whole youth in that barracks-type convent from which all joy had been banished. They were so thoroughly repressed that henceforth they guarded against uttering the slightest discordant opinion. That is, in public, for meetings started to be held secretly indoors. The young conspirators were encouraged by all those women who had seen a son, a brother, or a husband depart on a secret mission from which he had not returned.

One man made himself the spokesman for this stifled and suppressed longing. No one else would allow himself to be put forward: he was the grandson of the man Hassan had designated as his successor and he himself was named to become the fourth Grand Master of the order upon the death of his father.

He had a distinct advantage over his predecessors. Having been born a little after the death of the founder, he had never had to live under his terror. He observed his home with curiosity, and naturally with a certain amount of apprehension, but without that morbid fascination that paralyzed all the others.

He had even gone into the forbidden room once, at the age of seventeen, had walked around it, gone up to the magic basin and dipped his hand into the icy water, then stopped in front of the niche that enclosed the manuscript. He almost opened it, but changed his mind, took a step back, and then walked backwards out of the room. He did not want to go any further on his first visit.

When the heir wandered, in pensive mood, through the alleyways of Alamut, people gathered around while not getting too close and uttered curious formulae in blessing. He was also called Hassan, like Sabbah, but another name was already being whispered around him: "The Redeemer! The Long-Awaited!" Only one thing was feared: that the old guard of the Assassins, who knew his feelings and who had already heard him rashly censure the prevailing atmosphere of severity, would prevent him from acceding to power. In fact his father did try to impose silence upon him, even accusing him of being an atheist and of betraying the teachings of the Founder. It was even said that he had two hundred and fifty of his son's partisans put to death and expelled two hundred and fifty others, forcing them to carry the corpses of their executed friends on their backs down to the foot of the mountain. However, due to a trace of paternal feeling, the Grand Master did not dare follow Hassan Sabbah's tradition of infanticide.

When the father died, in 1162, the rebellious son succeeded him without the slightest hitch. For the first time in a long while real joy broke out in the gray alleyways of Alamut.

But was it really a question of a long-awaited Redeemer, the adherents asked themselves. Was it really this man who was to put an end to their suffering? He himself said nothing. He continued to walk around distractedly in the alleyways of Alamut or he spent long hours in the library under the protective eye of the copyist who was in charge of it, a man originally from Kirman.

One day he was seen walking decisively towards Hassan Sabbah's former residence. He threw the door open, walked up to the niche, and shook the grate with such violence that it came away from the wall letting a stream of sand and bits of stone pour on to the floor. He lifted out Khayyam's manuscript, tapped the dust off it, and carried it away with him under his arms.

It was then said that he shut himself up to read, to read and to meditate, until the seventh day, when he gave the order that everyone in Alamut, men, women, and children, should assemble in the *maydan*, the only place large enough to hold them all.

It was August 8, 1164. The sun of Alamut was beating down on their heads and faces but no one thought of protecting himself. Towards the west there rose a wooden dais, decked out with a huge standard, one red, one green, one yellow, and one white, at each of the four corners. It was in this direction that everyone's gaze was directed.

Suddenly he appeared, dressed all in dazzling white, with his slight young wife behind him, her face unveiled, her eyes cast to the ground, and her cheeks flushed with confusion. In the crowd it seemed that this apparition dispelled the last doubts; people were boldly murmuring, "It is He. It is the Redeemer!"

Solemnly he climbed the few steps to the platform, and gave his faithful a warm gesture of welcome, intended to silence the murmurings. Then he went on to pronounce one of the most astonishing speeches ever heard on our planet:

"To all the inhabitants of the world, jinns, men, and angels!" he said. "The Mahdi offers you his blessing and pardons all your sins, both past and future.

"He announces to you that the sacred Law is abolished, for the hour of the Resurrection has sounded. God imposed on you his Law to make you earn Paradise and indeed you now deserve it. From today on, Paradise is yours. You are thus free of the yoke of the Law.

"Everything that was forbidden is permitted, and everything that was obligatory is forbidden!

"The five daily prayers are forbidden," the Redeemer continued. "Since we are now in Paradise and in permanent contact with the Creator, we no longer have any need to address Him at fixed times; those who persist in making the five prayers show thereby how little they believe in the Resurrection. Prayer has become an act of unbelief."

On the other hand, wine, considered by the Quran to be the drink of Paradise, was from now on authorized; not to drink it was considered to be a manifest sign of a lack of faith.

"When this was proclaimed," a Persian historian of the time related, "the assembly started to rejoice on the harp and the flute and to drink wine conspicuously on the very steps of the dais."

It was an excessive reaction, in proportion to the excesses practiced by Hassan Sabbah in the name of Quranic Law. Soon the successors of the Redeemer would set themselves to diminishing his messianic ardor, but Alamut would never again be this reservoir of martyrs desired by the Supreme Preacher. Life would henceforth be sweet and the long series of murders which had terrorized the cities of Islam would be interrupted. The Ismailis, as radical a sect as there ever was, would change into a community of exemplary tolerance.

In fact, after having announced the good news to the people of Alamut and its surroundings, the Redeemer sent emissaries off to the other Ismaili communities of Asia and Egypt. They were provided

149

with documents signed by his hand, and asked everyone to celebrate the day of redemption whose date they gave according to three different calenders; that of the Hijra of the Prophet, that of Alexander the Greek, and that of the "most eminent man of both worlds, Omar Khayyam of Nishapur."

At Alamut the Redeemer gave orders that the *Samarkand Manuscript* be venerated as a great book of wisdom. Artists were commissioned to ornament it with pictures, to illuminate it, and to make for it a casket of chased gold encrusted with precious stones. No one had the right to copy its contents but it was placed permanently on a low cedar table in the small inner room where the librarian worked. There, under his suspicious surveillance, some privileged members would come to consult it.

Until then, people knew only a few of Khayyam's quatrains, which had been composed in his impetuous youth; now many others were learnt, quoted, and repeated — some with serious alterations. This period also saw one of the strangest phenomena: whenever a poet composed a quatrain that might cause trouble for him, he would attribute it to Omar; hundreds of false *rubaiyaat* came to be intermixed with those of Khayyam, to the extent that, in the absence of the manuscript, it was impossible to discern which were truly his.

Was it at the Redeemer's request that the librarians of Alamut, from father to son, took up the chronicle of the manuscript at the point where Vartan left it? In any case, it is from this single source that we know Khayyam's posthumous influence on the metamorphosis the Assassins underwent. The concise yet irreplaceable account of history was carried on in the same way for almost a century until a new brutal interruption — the Mongol invasions.

The first wave, led by Genghis Khan, was, beyond a shadow of doubt, the most devastating scourge ever to cross the Orient. Important cities were razed and their populations exterminated. Such was the case with Peking, Bukhara, and Samarkand, whose inhabitants were treated like cattle with the young women handed around the officers of the victorious horde, the artisans reduced to slavery, and the rest massacred, with the sole exception of a minority who, regrouping around the grand *qadi* of the time, very quickly proclaimed their allegiance to Genghis Khan.

In spite of this apocalypse, Samarkand appeared to be almost favored, since it would one day be reborn from its rubble to become the capital of a worldwide empire — that of Tamerlane — in contrast to so many cities which were never to rise again, namely the three great metropolises of Khorassan where all this world's intellectual activity had long been concentrated: Merv, Balkh, and Nishapur — to which list must be added Rayy, the cradle of oriental medicine, whose very name would be forgotten. The world would have to wait several centuries in order to see the rebirth, on a neighboring site, of the city of Tehran.

It was the second wave of Mongol invasions that swept over Alamut. It was a little less bloody, but more far-reaching. How can we not share the terror of the people alive at the time, knowing that the Mongol troops were able, over a period of a few months, to lay waste to Baghdad, Damascus, Cracow in Poland, and the Chinese province of Szechuan?

The Assassins' fortress thus opted to surrender, the fortress that had resisted so many invaders over a hundred and sixty-six years! Prince Hulagu, grandson of Genghis Khan, came in person to admire this masterpiece of military construction; legend says that he found provisions that had been conserved intact from the days of Hassan Sabbah.

After inspecting the place with his lieutenants, he ordered the soldiers to destroy everything, not to leave a stone untouched, not to spare even the library. However, before setting fire to it, he permitted a thirty-year-old historian, a certain Juvayni, to go inside. He had been in the process of writing a *History of the Conqueror of the World* at Hulagu's request, which book is still today our most valuable source on the Mongol invasions. He thus was able to go into this mysterious place where tens of thousands of manuscripts were kept in rows, stacked up or rolled up; outside he was awaited by a Mongol officer and a soldier with a wheelbarrow. What the wheelbarrow could hold would be saved, the rest was to be victim to the flames. There was no question of reading the texts or cataloguing the titles.

A fervent Sunni, Juvayni told himself that his first task was to save the Word of God from the fire. He started to pile up as quickly as he could any copies of the Quran, recognizable by their thick binding and stored in the same place. He had a good score of them and made three trips to carry them out to the wheelbarrow, which was already almost full. Now, what to chose? Heading towards one of the walls, against which the volumes seemed to be better ordered than elsewhere, he came across innumerable works written by Hassan Sabbah during his thirty years of voluntary reclusion. He chose to save one of them, an autobiography of which he would quote some fragments in his own work. He also found a chronicle of Alamut that was recent and apparently well documented and which related in detail the history of the Redeemer. He hurried to take it away with him, since that episode was totally unknown outside the Ismaili community.

Did the historian know of the existence of the *Samarkand Manuscript?* It seemed not. Would he have looked for it if he had heard it spoken of, and having thumbed through it, would he have saved it? We do not know. What is told is that he stopped in front of a group of works devoted to the occult science and that he delved into them, forgetting the time. The Mongol officer who came to remind him with a few words had his body covered with thick red-framed armor and had as head protection a helmet that broadened out like long hair towards the neck. He was carrying a torch in his hand and to show just how much in a hurry he was, he placed it next to a pile of dusty scrolls. The historian gave in and gathered into his hands and up to his armpits as many as he could grab, and when the manuscript entitled *Eternal Secrets of Stars and Numbers* fell to the ground, he did not bend over to pick it up again.

Thus it was that the Assassins' library burnt for seven days and seven nights, causing the loss of innumerable works, of which there was no copy remaining, and which are supposed to have contained the best-guarded secrets in the universe.

For a long time it was believed that the *Samarkand Manuscript* had also been consumed in the inferno of Alamut.

BOOK THREE

The End of the Millennium

Arise, we have eternity for sleeping!

OMAR KHAYYAM

25

Until now I have spoken little of myself. I have been trying to expose, as faithfully as possible, what the *Samarkand Manuscript* reveals of Khayyam and of those he knew and some of the events he witnessed. It remains to be told just how this work, spared at the time of the Mongols, has come down to our time, and through what adventures I managed to gain possession of it, and, to start with, through what stroke of luck I learnt of its existence.

I have already mentioned my name, Benjamin O. Lesage. In spite of its French sound, the heritage of a Huguenot forebear who emigrated in Louis XIV's century, I am an American citizen and a native of Annapolis in Maryland on the Chesapeake Bay, a modest inlet of the Atlantic. My connection with France is not limited, however, to that distant forefather, and my father applied himself to renewing the link. He had always had an obsession about his origins — even noting in his school book, "Was my genealogical tree felled in order to construct a get-away boat!" — and he set about learning French. Then,

155

with pomp and circumstance, he crossed the Atlantic in the opposite direction to the hands of time.

His year of pilgrimage was either extremely badly or well chosen. He left New York on July 9, 1870, on board the *Scotia*; he reached Cherbourg on the 18th and was in Paris on the evening of the 19th, with war having been declared at midday. There followed retreat, calamity, invasion, famine, the Commune, and massacres. My father was never to live a more intense year. It would remain his finest memory, why should it be denied? There is a perverse joy in finding oneself in a besieged city where barricades fall as others arise and men and women rediscover the joys of primitive bonding. How many times in Annapolis, around the inevitable holiday turkey, would father and mother recall with emotion the piece of elephant trunk they had shared on New Year's Eve in Paris and which they had bought for forty francs a pound at Roos', the English butcher on Boulevard Haussmann!

They had just become engaged, they were to be married a year later, and the war christened their happiness. "Upon my arrival in Paris," my father would recall, "I took up the habit of going to Café Riche in the morning, on the Boulevard des Italiens. With a pile of newspapers, *Le Temps, Le Gaulois, Le Figaro, La Presse*, I would settle down at a table, reading every line and listing discreetly in a note-book the words I could not understand — words such as *'gaiter'* or *'moblot'* — so that I would be able, upon my return to my hotel, to ask the erudite concierge.

"The third day a man with a gray mustache came and sat at the next table. He had his own stack of newspapers, but he abandoned them soon in order to observe me; he had a question on the tip of his tongue. Unable to restrain himself any longer, he spoke out with his hoarse voice, keeping one hand on the handle of his cane while the other tapped nervously on the wet marble. He wanted to be certain that this young man, apparently in sound health, had good reasons for not being at the front in order to defend the fatherland. His tone was polite, although very suspicious, and accompanied by sidelong glances at the notebook in which he had seen me hurriedly scribbling. I had no need to argue as my accent proved to be an eloquent defense. The man gallantly apologized, invited me to his table, and mentioned Lafayette, Benjamin Franklin, de Tocqueville, and Pierre L'Enfant, before explaining in detail what I had just read in the press — how this war would be 'just an excursion to Berlin for our troops.'"

My father wanted to contradict him. Although he knew nothing of the comparable strengths of the French and the Prussians, he had just taken part in the Civil War and had been wounded in the siege of Atlanta. "I could testify that no war was a picnic," he told us. "But nations are so forgetful and gunpowder so intoxicating that I held back from being drawn into an argument. It was not the time for discussions and the man did not ask my opinion. From time to time he would utter a 'Don't you think so?' which hardly required an answer; I replied with a knowing nod.

"He was friendly. Besides, we met every morning after that. I still spoke very little and he stated that he was happy that an American could share his views so thoroughly. At the end of his fourth monologue, which was just as spirited, this august gentleman invited me to dine with him at his home; he was so certain of obtaining my agreement yet again that he hailed a coach before I could even formulate a reply. I must admit that I have never regretted it. He was called Charles-Hubert de Luçay and lived in a mansion on Boulevard Poissonière. He was a widower. His two sons were in the army and his daughter was going to become your mother."

She was eighteen and my father was ten years older. They observed each other in silence throughout long patriotic harangues. From August 7, when it became clear, after three defeats in a row, that the war was lost and that the national territory was under threat, my grandfather became less verbose. As his daughter and future son-in-law busied themselves trying to temper his melancholy a complicity sprang up between them. From then on, a glance was enough to decide which of them was going to intervene and with the medicine of which argument.

"The first time we were alone, she and I in the huge salon, there was a deathly silence — followed by a burst of laughter. We had just discovered that, after numerous meals taken together, we had never addressed a word to each other directly. It was sweet, knowing, and uncontrolled laughter, but it would have been unbecoming to prolong it. I was supposed to speak first. Your mother was clutching a book to her blouse, and I asked her what she was reading."

At that very moment, Omar Khayyam entered into my life. I should almost say that it gave birth to me. My mother had just acquired *Les Quatrains de Khéyam*, translated from the Persian by J.B. Nicolas, formerly chief dragoman of the French Embassy to Persia, published in 1867 by the Imperial Press. My father had in his luggage the 1868 edition of Edward Fitzgerald's *The Rubáiyát of Omar Khayyám*.

"Your mother's rapture was no better hidden than mine. We were both sure that our lifelines were going to join. At no moment did we think that it could just be a simple coincidence that we were reading the same book. Omar appeared to us instantly like fate's password — to ignore it would have been almost sacrilegious. Naturally, we had said nothing of what was going on inside us, the conversation centered on the poems. She informed me that Napoleon III in person had ordered the publication of the work."

At that time, Europe had just discovered Omar. Some specialists, in truth, had spoken of him earlier in the century, his algebra had been published in Paris in 1851, and articles had appeared in specialized reviews. But the Western public was still unaware of him, and, in the East itself, what was left of Khayyam? A name, two or three legends, some quatrains of indefinite authorship, and a hazy reputation as an astrologer.

When an obscure British poet, Fitzgerald, decided to publish a translation of seventy-five quatrains in 1859 there was indifference. The book was published in an edition of two hundred and fifty copies; the author offered some to his friends and the rest were selling very slowly at the bookshop of Bernard Quaritch. "Poor old Omar, he apparently was of interest to no one," so Fitzgerald wrote to his Persian teacher. After two years the publisher decided to sell off the stock: from an initial price of five shillings, the *Rubaiyaat* went down to a penny, sixty times less. Even at this price, few were sold until the moment when two literary critics discovered it. They read it and were amazed by it. They came back the next day and bought up six copies to give out. Feeling that some interest was about to be aroused, the editor raised the price to two pence.

And to think that on my last trip to England I had to pay the same Quaritch, now finely established in Piccadilly, four hundred pounds sterling for a copy that he had kept from that first edition!

However, success was not immediate in London. It had to come from Paris where M. Nicolas published his translation, where Théophile Gautier had to write, in the pages of the *Moniteur Universel*, a resounding "Have you read the Quatrains of Kéyam?" and welcome "this absolute freedom of spirit which the boldest modern thinkers can hardly equal," and Ernest Renan had to add, "Khayyam is perhaps the most curious man to study in order to understand what the unfettered genius of Persia managed to become within the bounds of Muslim dogmatism" — in order for Fitzgerald and his "poor old Omar" to come out of their anonymity. The awakening was thunderous. Overnight all the images of the Orient were assembled around the sole name of Khayyam. Translation followed translation, editions of the work multiplied in England and then in several American cities "Omar" societies were formed.

To reiterate, in 1870 the Khayyam vogue was just starting. The circle of fans of Omar was growing every day, without yet having transcended the circle of intellectuals. After this shared reading matter brought my father and mother together, they started to recite the quatrains of Omar and to discuss their meaning: were wine and the tavern, in Omar's pen, purely mystical symbols, as Nicolas stated? Or were they, on the other hand, the expression of a life of pleasure, indeed of debauchery, as Fitzgerald and Renan claimed? These debates took on a new taste in their mouths. When my father evoked Omar, as he caressed the perfumed hair of his beautiful girl, my mother blushed. It was between two amorous quatrains that they exchanged their first kiss. The day they spoke of marriage, they made a vow to call their first son Omar.

During the 1890s, hundreds of little Americans were also given that name: when I was born on March 1, 1873 it was not yet common. Not wishing to encumber me too much with this exotic first name, my parents relegated it to second place, in order that I might, if I so desired, replace it with a discrete O; my school friends supposed that it stood for Oliver, Oswald, Osborne, or Orville and I did not disabuse anyone.

The inheritance that was thus handed down to me could·not fail to arouse my curiosity about this remote godfather. At fifteen I started to read everything about him. I had made a plan to study the language and literature of Persia and to make a long visit there. However, after a bout of enthusiasm I cooled down. Indeed, in the opinion of all the critics, Fitzgerald's verses constituted a masterpiece of English poetry, but they had only a remote connection with what Khayyam could have composed. When it came to the quatrains themselves, some authors quoted almost a thousand, Nicolas had translated more than four hundred, while some thorough specialists only recognized a hundred of them as being "probably authentic." Eminent Orientalists went as far as to deny that a single one could be attributed to Omar with certainty.

It was believed that there could have existed an original book that once and for all would have allowed the real to be distinguished from the false, but there was nothing to lead one to believe that such a manuscript could be found.

Finally I turned away from the person, as I did from the work. I came to see my middle initial O as the permanent residue of parental childishness — until a meeting took me back to my first love and directed my life resolutely in the footsteps of Khayyam.

26

I t was at the end of the summer of 1895 that I embarked for the old world. My grandfather had just celebrated his seventy-sixth birthday and had written tearful letters to me and my mother. He was eager to see me, even if it were only once, before his death. Having finished my studies, I rushed off, and on the ship I readied myself for the role I would have to play — to kneel down at his bedside, to hold his frozen hand bravely while listening to him murmur his last orders.

That was all absolutely wasted. Grandfather was waiting for me at Cherbourg. I can still see him, on the Quai de Caligny, straighter than his cane with his perfumed mustache, his lively gait, and his top hat tipping automatically when a lady passed by. When we were seated in the Admiralty restaurant, he took me firmly by the arm. "My friend," he said, deliberately theatrical, "a young man has just been reborn in me, and he needs a companion."

I was wrong to take his words lightly. Our time there was a whirl.

We would hardly have finished eating at the Brébant, at Foyot, or at Chez le Père Lathuile before we would have to run to the Cigale where Eugénie Buffet was appearing, to the Mirliton where Aristide Bruant reigned, or to the Scala where Yvette Guilbert would sing *Les Vierges*, *Le Foetus*, and *Le Fiacre*. We were two brothers, one with a white mustache, the other with a brown one. We had the same gait, the same hat, and he was the one the women looked at first. With every champagne cork that popped I studied his gestures and his behavior, and I could not even once find fault with them. He arose with a bound, walked as quickly as I did, his cane being hardly more than an ornament. He wanted to gather every rose of this late spring. I am happy to say that he would live to be ninety-three — another seventeen years, a whole new youth.

One evening he took me to dine at Durand in the Place de la Madeleine. In an aisle of the restaurant, around several tables that had been placed together, there was a group of actors, actresses, journalists, and politicians whose names Grandfather audibly reeled off for me one by one. In the middle of these celebrities there was an empty chair, but soon a man arrived and I realized that the place had been saved for him. He was immediately surrounded and adulated. Every last word of his gave rise to exclamations and laughs. My grandfather stood up and made a sign to me to follow him.

"Come on, I must present you to my cousin Henri!"

As he said that, he dragged me over to him.

The two cousins greeted each other before returning to me.

"My American grandson. He wanted to meet you so much!"

I did not hide my surprise too well, and the man looked at me with some skepticism before stating:

"Let him come and see me tomorrow morning, after I have had my tricycle ride."

It was only upon sitting back at my table that I realized to whom I had been presented. My grandfather was very eager for me to know him, and had spoken of him often with an irritating pride of clan.

It is true that the aforementioned cousin, who was little known on my side of the Atlantic, was more famous in France than Sarah Bernhardt, as he was Victor-Henri de Rochefort-Luçay, now known in democratic France as Henri Rochefort, a marquis and a communard, former

162

deputy, minister, and convict. He had been deported to New Caledonia by the regular troops. In 1874 he effected a swashbuckling escape that inflamed his contemporaries' imagination, and which Eduard Manet depicted in his painting *The Flight of Rochefort*. However, in 1889 he was sent off into exile again for having plotted against the Republic with General Boulanger, and it was from London that he managed his influential newspaper *L'Intransigeant*. Returning in 1895 thanks to an amnesty, he had been welcomed back by two hundred thousand delirious Parisians — both Blanquistes and Boulangistes, revolutionaries of the left and the right, idealists and demagogues. He had been made the spokesman of a hundred different and contradictory causes. I knew all of that, but I was unaware of the most important thing.

On the appointed day I went off to his residence on Rue Pergolèse, incapable of imagining at the time that this visit to my grandfather's favorite cousin would be the first step of my never-ending trip in the universe of the Orient.

"So," he said accosting me, "you are sweet Geneviève's son. Are you not the one to whom she gave the name of Omar?"

"Yes. Benjamin Omar."

"Do you know that I have held you in my arms?"

As this was the case, he was now obliged to address me familiarly. The same, however, did not apply to me when addressing him.

"My mother has actually told me that after your escape you landed at San Francisco and took the train for the East Coast. We went to New York to meet you at the station. I was two."

"I remember perfectly. We spoke of you, of Khayyam, and of Persia, and I even predicted that you would be a great Orientalist."

I shammed a little embarrassment in admitting to him that I had side-stepped his vision and that my interests were elsewhere — I was more oriented towards financial studies, foreseeing myself one day taking over the maritime construction business started by my father. Appearing to be sincerely disappointed by my choice, Rochefort set off on a lengthy plea, intermixed with the *Persian Letters* of Montesquieu and his famous "How can one be Persian?", the adventure of the gambling-addict Marie Petit who had been received by the Shah of Persia by passing herself off as Louis XIV's ambassador, and the story of Jean-Jacques Rousseau's cousin who ended his days as a watchmaker in Isfahan. I was only listening to the half of it. Above all I was watching him, with his voluminous and immoderate head, his protruding forehead topped by a tuft of thick wavy hair.

He spoke with passion, but without emphasis and without the gesticulations that one might have expected from him having read his intense writings.

"I am mad about Persia, although I have never set foot there," Rochefort declared. "I do not have the soul of a traveler. Had I not been banished or deported those few times I should never have left France. But times change, and the events taking place at the other end of the planet are affecting our lives. If I were twenty today, instead of being sixty, I should have been very tempted by an adventure in the Orient — particularly if I were called Omar!"

I felt constrained to justify my lack of interest in Khayyam. In order to do so, I had to mention the dubious nature of the *Rubaiyaat*, the absence of a copy that could prove their authenticity once and for all. For all that, as I was speaking, an intense glimmer came into his eyes, an exuberance I failed to understand. Nothing in my words was supposed to provoke such excitement. Intrigued and irritated, I ended up compressing what I had to say and then falling silent quite abruptly. Rochefort questioned me enthusiastically:

"If you were certain that such a manuscript existed, would your interest in Omar Khayyam be reborn?"

"Naturally," I admitted.

"And if I were to tell you that I have seen this manuscript of Khayyam with my own eyes, in Paris what's more, and that I have leafed through it?"

27

To say that this revelation immediately turned my life upside down would be inexact. I do not believe that I reacted the way Rochefort had presumed I would. I was both abundantly surprised and intrigued, but I was still skeptical. The man did not inspire me with unlimited confidence. How could he know that the manuscript he had leafed through was the authentic work of Khayyam? He did not know Persian and the wool might have been pulled over his eyes. For what incongruous reason would this book have been in Paris without a single Orientalist reporting the fact? I did no more than utter a polite but sincere "Incredible!", since it showed both the enthusiasm of the man I was speaking to and my own doubts, for I was not yet ready to believe in it.

Rochefort went on:

"I had the chance to meet an extraordinary personality, one of those beings who cross History determined to leave their imprint on the generations to come. The Sultan of Turkey fears and courts him, the

165

Shah of Persia trembles at the mere mention of his name. He is a descendant of Muhammad, but was nonetheless chased out of Constantinople for having said, at a public conference in the presence of the greatest religious dignitaries, that the profession of the philosopher was as indispensable to humanity as that of the prophet. He is called Jamaladin. Have you heard of him?"

I could only confess my total ignorance.

"When Egypt rose up against the English," Rochefort continued, "it was at this man's call. All the intellectuals of the Nile Valley take their inspiration from him. They call him 'Master' and revere his name. However, he is not an Egyptian and has only made a short stay in that country. He was exiled to India where he managed to arouse a considerable movement of opinion. Under his influence newspapers were established and associations were formed. The Viceroy became alarmed and had Jamaladin expelled, whence he decided to settle down in Europe and he continued his incredible activity in London and then in France.

"He worked regularly on *L'Intransigeant* and we used to meet often. He presented his disciples to me — Muslims from India, Jews from Egypt, and Maronites from Syria. I believe that I was his closest French friend, but certainly not the only one. Ernest Renan and Georges Clemenceau knew him well, and in England his friends were people like Lord Salisbury, Randolph Churchill, and Wilfred Blunt. A little before his death, Victor Hugo met him too.

"This very morning, I was in the middle of going over some notes about him that I am thinking of inserting in my memoirs."

Rochefort took some sheets covered in minuscule writing out of a drawer and read: "I was introduced to an outlaw, a man famous throughout all of Islam as a reformer and a revolutionary — Sheikh Jamaladin, a man with the head of a saint. His beautiful black eyes, so gentle and yet fiery and his deep tawny beard which reached his chest gave him a particularly majestic air. He looked like a born leader. He understood French more or less although he could hardly speak it, but his ever alert intelligence easily made up for what he lacked of our language. Behind his calm and serene appearance his activity was frenetic. We soon became good friends for my spirit is instinctively that of a revolutionary and I am attracted to all freedom fighters . . ."

He quickly put the sheets of paper away and then continued:

"Jamaladin had rented a small room on the top floor of a hotel in Rue de Sèze near the Madeleine. That modest space was enough for him to edit a newspaper which went off by the bundle to India and Arabia. I only managed to wheedle my way into his den once, being curious to see what it could look like. I had invited Jamaladin to dine *chez* Durand and promised to go by and pick him up. I went straight up to his room. It was difficult to move around in it because of all the newspapers and books piled up to the ceiling there, some of them even covering the bed. There was a suffocating smell of cigar smoke."

In spite of his admiration for him, he had pronounced this last phrase with a hint of distaste, which induced me to extinguish on the spot my own cigar, which was an elegant Havana I had just lit. Rochefort thanked me for that with a smile and carried on:

"After apologizing for the mess in which he was receiving me, and which, he said, was unbefitting for someone of my rank, Jamaladin showed me that day some books he was fond of — particularly that of Khayyam which was full of exquisite miniatures. He explained to me that this work was called the *Samarkand Manuscript*, and that it contained the quatrains that had been written in the poet's own hand, together with a chronicle running in the margins. Above all, he told me through what tortuous route the *Manuscript* had reached him."

"Good Lord!"

My pious English interjection draw a triumphal laugh out of cousin Henri. It was the proof that my cold skepticism had been swept away and that I would henceforth hang on to his every word and he lost no time in taking advantage of this.

"Of course, I do not remember everything that Jamaladin must have said to me," he added cruelly. "That evening we spoke mainly of the Sudan. After that I never saw the *Manuscript* again but I can testify that it existed; but I am truly afraid that by now it has been lost. Everything my friend possessed was burned, destroyed, or scattered around."

"Even the Khayyam *Manuscript?*"

By way of reply, Rochefort made a discouraging pout, before throwing himself into an impassioned explanation during which he made close reference to his notes:

AMIN MAALOUF

"When the Shah came to Europe to go to the World Fair in 1889, he suggested to Jamaladin that he return to Persia, 'instead of passing the rest of his life in the midst of infidels,' giving him to understand that he would install him in high office. The exile set some conditions: that a constitution be promulgated, that elections be organized, that equality be recognized by law 'as in civilized countries,' and that the huge concessions granted to the foreign powers be abolished. It must be stated that in this area the situation of Persia had for years been the butt of our cartoonists: the Russians, who already had a monopoly on road-building, had just taken over military training. He had formed a brigade of Cossacks, the best equipped in the Persian army, which was directly commanded by officers of the Czar; by way of compensation, the English had obtained, for a song, the right to exploit all the country's mineral and forest resources as well as to manage the banking system; as for the Austrians — they had control of the postal services. In demanding that the monarch put an end to royal absolutism and to the foreign concessions, Jamaladin was convinced that he would receive a rebuff. However, to his great surprise, the Shah accepted all his conditions and promised to open up the country to modernization.

"Jamaladin thus went and settled in Persia, as part of the sovereign's entourage. The sovereign, at the start, showed him all due respect and went as far as to introduce him with great ceremony to the women of his harem. However, the reforms were put off. As for a constitution, the religious chiefs persuaded the Shah that it would be against the Law of God, and courtiers foresaw that elections would allow their absolute authority to be challenged and that they would end up like Louis XVI. The foreign concessions? Far from abolishing those that existed, the monarch, ever short of money, was to contract new ones: for the modest sum of fifteen thousand pounds sterling he granted an English company the monopoly of Persian tobacco — not only its export but also domestic consumption. In a country where every man, every woman, and a good number of children were addicted to the pleasures of the cigarette or the pipe, this was a most profitable business.

"Before news of this last renunciation of Persian rights was announced in Tehran, pamphlets were distributed in secret advising the Shah to rescind his decision. A copy was even placed in the monarch's bedroom, and he suspected Jamaladin of being the author. The reformer, who was by now worried, decided to go into a state of passive rebellion. This is a custom practiced in Persia: when a person fears for his liberty or his life, he withdraws to an old sanctuary near Tehran, locks himself in there, and receives visitors to whom he lists his grievances. No one is allowed to cross through the doorway to lay hold of him. That is what Jamaladin did and thereby provoked a surge of people. Thousands of men streaming from all corners of Persia to hear him.

"In a state of vexation the Shah gave orders for him to be dislodged. It was reported that he hesitated a long time before committing this felony, but his vizir, who was educated in Europe moreover, convinced him that Jamaladin had no right to claim sanctuary since he was only a philosopher and a notorious infidel. Armed soldiers broke into the holy place, cleared a passage through the numerous visitors and seized Jamaladin, whom they stripped of everything he possessed before dragging him half-naked to the border.

"That day, in the sanctuary, the *Samarkand Manuscript* was lost under the boots of the Shah's soldiers."

Without breaking his flow, Rochefort stood up, leant against the wall, and crossed his arms in his favorite pose.

"Jamaladin was alive but he was ill and above all shocked that so many visitors, who had been listening to him enthusiastically, could have stood meekly by while he was publicly humiliated. He drew some curious conclusions from this — the man who had spent his life denouncing the obscurantism of certain clerics, who had been a regular visitor at the masonic lodges of Egypt, France, and Turkey — he made up his mind to exploit the last weapon he had to make the Shah bend no matter what the consequences.

"So he wrote a long letter to the chief of the Persian clerics, asking him to use his authority to prevent the monarch from selling off the property of the Muslims to the infidels. What happened then, you know from the newspapers."

I remember that the American press indeed reported that the great pontiff of the Shiites had circulated an astounding proclamation: "Any person who consumes tobacco places himself thereby in a state of rebellion against the Mahdi, may God speed his arrival." Overnight no Persian lit a single cigarette. The pipes, the famous *kalyans*, were shelved or smashed and tobacco merchants closed up shop. Amongst the wives of the Shah the ban was strictly observed. The monarch panicked, and wrote a letter to the religious chief accusing him of irresponsibility "since he was not concerned with the grave consequences that being deprived of tobacco could have on the health of Muslims." However, the boycott lasted and was accompanied by stormy demonstrations in Tehran, Tabriz, and Isfahan. The concession had to be annulled.

"Meanwhile," Rochefort carried on, "Jamaladin had left for England. I met him there and had long talks with him; he seemed to be distraught and could only say, time and again, 'We must bring the Shah down.' He was a wounded and humiliated man who could think of nothing but avenging himself — all the more so since the monarch, the target of his hatred, had written an angry letter to Lord Salisbury: 'We expelled this man because he was working against the interests of England, and where should he take refuge? In London.' Officially the Shah was informed that Great Britain was a free country and that no law could be invoked to suppress a person's freedom of expression. In private, the Shah was promised that they would seek legal means of restraining Jamaladin's activity and he found himself being asked to cut short his stay — which made him decide to leave for Constantinople, but with death in his heart."

"Is that where he is now?"

"Yes. I am told that he is deeply dejected. The Sultan has allotted him fine quarters where he can receive friends and disciples, but he is forbidden to leave the country and lives under constant and tight surveillance."

28

I t was a sumptuous prison with wide open doors: a palace of wood
and marble on the hill of Yildiz, near the residence of the Grand
Vizir; hot meals were delivered straight from the Sultan's kitchens;
visitors came one after another, crossing through a metal gate and
walking down an alley before leaving their shoes outside the door.
The Master's voice boomed from above with its grating syllables and
closed vowels; he could be heard castigating Persia and the Shah and
announcing the evils that would come to pass.

I tried to make myself unobtrusive, being the foreigner — an American
with a small foreign hat, small foreign footsteps, and my foreign concerns who made the trip from Paris to Constantinople, a trip of seventy hours by train across three empires, in order to ask after a
manuscript, an old poetry book, a pathetic bundle of papers in a tu-
multuous Orient.

A servant came up to me. He made an Ottoman bow, spoke a few
words of greeting in French but asked not the slightest question. Everyone

came here for the same reasons, to meet the Master, to hear the Master, or to spy on the Master. I was invited to wait in the huge sitting room.

As I entered, I noticed the silhouette of a woman. This induced me to lower my eyes; I had been told too much about the country's customs to walk forward beaming and cheery with my hand outstretched. I simply mumbled a few words and touched my hat. I had already repaired to the other side of the room from where she was sitting to settle myself into an English-style armchair. I looked along the carpet and my glance came up against the visitors shoes, then traveled up her blue and gold dress to her knees, her bust, her neck, and her veil. Strangely, however, it was not the barrier of a veil that I came across but that of an unveiled face, of eyes that met mine, and a smile. I looked quickly down at the ground, over the carpet again, swept over the edge of the tiling, and then went over inexorably towards her again, like a cork coming up to the surface of the water. Over her hair she wore a fine silk kerchief which could be pulled down over her face should a stranger appear. However, the stranger was there and her veil was still drawn back.

This time she was looking into the distance, offering me her profile to contemplate and her skin of such pure complexion. If sweetness had a color, it would be hers. My temples were throbbing with happiness. My cheeks were damp and my hands cold. God, she was beautiful — my first image of the Orient — a woman such as only the desert poet knew how to praise: her face was the sun, they would have said, her hair the protecting shadow, her eyes fountains of cool water, her body the most slender of palm-trees, and her smile a mirage.

Could I speak to her? In what way? Could I cup my hands to my mouth so that she would hear me on the other side of the room? Should I stand up and walk over to her? Sit down in an armchair closer to her and risk seeing her smile evaporate and her veil drop like a blade? Our eyes met again, and then parted as if in jest when the servant came and interrupted us — which he did a first time to offer me tea and cigarettes. A moment later he bowed to the ground to speak to her in Turkish. I watched her stand up, veil herself, and give him a small leather bag to carry. He went quickly towards the exit and she followed him.

However, as she reached the door of the sitting room she slowed down, leaving the man to distance himself from her. Then she turned towards me and stated, in a loud voice and in a French purer than mine:

"You never know, our paths might meet!"

Whether it was said in politeness or as a promise, her words were accompanied by a mischievous smile which I saw as much as defiance as sweet reproach. Then, as I was getting up out of my seat with the utmost awkwardness, and while I was stumbling about trying to regain both my balance and my composure, she remained immobile, her look enveloping me with amused benevolence. I could not manage to utter a single word. She disappeared.

I was still standing by the window, trying to make out amongst the trees the coach carrying her off, when a voice brought me back to reality.

"Forgive me for having kept you waiting."

It was Jamaladin. His left hand held an extinguished cigar; he held out his right hand and shook mine with warmth and friendship.

"My name is Benjamin Lesage. I have come on the recommendation of Henri Rochefort."

I handed him my letter of introduction, but he slipped it into his pocket without looking at it. He opened his arms, gave me a hug and a kiss on the forehead.

"Rochefort's friends are my friends. I speak to them with an open heart."

Putting his arm around my shoulder, he escorted me towards a wooden staircase that led upstairs.

"I hope that my friend Henri is keeping well. I heard that his return from exile was a real triumph. With all those Parisians lining the streets and shouting his name, he must have felt great happiness! I read the account in *L'Intransigeant*. He sends it to me regularly although it reaches me late. Reading it brings back to my ears the sounds of Paris."

Jamaladin spoke labored but correct French. Sometimes I prompted the word he seemed to be looking for. When I was right, he thanked me and if not, he continued to rack his brains, contorting his lips and chin slightly. He carried on:

173

"I lived in Paris in a room that was dark but that opened up on to a vast world. It was a hundred times smaller than this house but I was less cramped there. I was thousands of miles from my people but I worked for their advancement more efficiently than I can do here or in Persia. My voice was heard from Algiers to Kabul. Today only those who honor me with their visits can hear me. Of course, they are always welcome, particularly if they come from Paris."

"I do not actually live in Paris. My mother is French and my name sounds French, but I am an American. I live in Maryland."

This seemed to amuse him.

"When I was expelled from India in 1882 I stopped off in the United States. Can you imagine that I even envisaged asking for American citizenship. You are smiling! Many of my fellow Muslims would be scandalized. The Sayyid Jamaladin, apostle of the Islamic renaissance, descendant of the Prophet, taking the citizenship of a Christian country? However, I was not ashamed of it and moreover I have told this story to my friend Wilfred Blunt and authorized him to quote it in his memoirs. My justification is quite simple: there is no single corner of the whole of the Muslim world where I can live free from tyranny. In Persia I tried to take refuge in a sanctuary that traditionally benefits from full immunity, but the monarch's soldiers came in and dragged me away from the hundreds of visitors who were listening to me, and with one unfortunate exception, almost no one moved or dared to protest. There is no religious site, university, or shed where one can be protected from the reign of the arbitrary!"

He feverishly stroked a painted wooden globe resting on a low table before adding:

"It is worse in Turkey. Am I not an official guest of Abdul-Hamid, the Sultan and Caliph? Did he not send me letter after letter, reproaching me, as the Shah did, for spending my life amongst infidels? I should have just replied: if you had not transformed our beautiful countries into prisons, we would have no need to find refuge with the Europeans! But I weakened and let myself be tricked. I came to Constantinople and you can see the result. In spite of the rules of hospitality, that half-mad man holds me prisoner. Lately I sent a message to him, saying, 'If I am your guest, give me permission to depart! If I am your prisoner, put shackles on my feet and throw me into a dungeon!' However, he did not deign to respond. If I had the citizenship of the United States, France, or Austria-Hungary, never mind that of Russia or England, my consul would have marched straight into the Grand Vizir's office without knocking and he would have obtained my freedom within a half-hour. I tell you, we, the Muslims of this century, are orphans."

He was breathless but made an effort to add:

"You may write up everything that I have just said except that I called Sultan Abdul-Hamid half-mad. I do not wish to lose every last chance of flying out of this cage one day. Besides, it would be a lie since that man is almost completely mad, a dangerous criminal, pathologically suspicious and completely under the sway of his Alepine astrologer."

"Have no fear, I shall write nothing of all this."

I took advantage of his request to clear up a misunderstanding.

"I must tell you that I am not a journalist. Monsieur Rochefort, who is my grandfather's cousin, recommended that I come and see you, but the aim of my visit is not to write an article about Persia nor about yourself."

I revealed to him my interest in the Khayyam manuscript and my intense desire to be able to leaf through it one day and to study its contents closely. He listened to me with unflagging attention and evident joy.

"I am obliged to you for snatching me away from my woes for some moments. The subject that you mention has always gripped me. Have you read in Monsieur Nicholas' introduction to the *Rubaiyaat*, the story of the three friends, Nizam al-Mulk, Hassan Sabbah, and Omar Khayyam? They were radically different men, each of whom represented an eternal aspect of the Persian soul. Sometimes I have the impression that I am all three of them at the same time. Like Nizam al-Mulk I dream of establishing a great Muslim state, even if it were led by an unbearable Turkish Sultan. Like Hassan Sabbah, I sow subversion over all the lands of Islam, I have disciples who would follow me to the death . . ."

He broke off, worried, then pulled himself together, smiled, and carried on:

"Like Khayyam, I am on the lookout for the rare joys of the present

175

moment and I compose verses about wine, the cupbearer, the tavern, and the beloved; like him, I mistrust false zealots. When, in certain quatrains, Omar speaks about himself, I sometimes believe that he is depicting me: 'On our gaudy Earth there walks a man, neither rich nor poor, neither believer nor infidel, he courts no truth, venerates no law . . . On our gaudy Earth, who is this brave and sad man?'"

Having said that, he relit his cigar and became pensive. A small piece of glowing ash landed on his beard. He brushed if off with a practiced gesture, and started speaking again:

"Since my childhood I have had an immense admiration for Khayyam the poet, but above all the philosopher, the free-thinker. I am amazed that it took him so long to conquer Europe and America. You can imagine how happy I was to have in my possession the original book of the *Rubaiyaat* written in Khayyam's own hand."

"When did you have it?"

"It was offered to me fourteen years ago in India by a young Persian who had made the trip with the sole aim of meeting me. He introduced himself to me with the following words: 'Mirza Reza, a native of Kirman, formerly a merchant in the Tehran bazaar. Your obedient servant.' I smiled and asked him what he meant by saying 'formerly a merchant,' and that is what led him to tell me his story. He had just opened a used clothing business when one of the Shah's sons came to buy some merchandise, shawls and furs, to the value of eleven hundred toumans — about one thousand dollars. However, when Mirza Reza presented himself the next day to the Prince to be paid, he was insulted, beaten, and even threatened with death if he took it into his head to collect what he was owed. It was then that he decided to come and see me. I was teaching in Calcutta. 'I have just understood,' he told me, 'that in a country run in an arbitrary fashion one cannot earn an honest living. Was it not you who wrote that Persia needs a Constitution and a Parliament? Consider me, from this day on, your most devoted disciple. I have shut my business and left my wife in order to follow you. Order and I shall obey!'"

In mentioning this man Jamaladin seemed to be suffering.

"I was moved but embarrassed. I am a roving philosopher, I have neither house nor homeland and have avoided marrying in order that I would have no one in my charge. I did not want this man to follow me as if I were the Messiah or the Redeemer, the Mahdi. To dissuade him I said, 'Is it really worth leaving everything, your business and your family, over a wretched question of money?' His face closed up, he did not respond, but went out.

"He returned only six months later. From an inside pocket he took out a small golden box, inlaid with precious stones, which he held out to me, open."

"'Look at this manuscript. How much do you think it could be worth?'

"'I leafed through it, then discovered its contents as I trembled with emotion.

"'The authentic text of Khayyam; those pictures, the embellishment! It is priceless!'

"'More than eleven hundred *tomans?*'

"'Infinitely more!'

"'I give it to you. Keep it. It was to remind you that Mirza Reza did not come to you to recover his money, but to regain his pride.'

"That was how," Jamaladin continued, "the manuscript fell into my possession and that I could not be separated from it. It came with me to the United States, England, France, Germany, Russia, and then to Persia. I had it with me when I withdrew into the sanctuary of Shah Abdul-Azim. That is where I lost it."

"Do you know where it could be at this moment?"

"I told you, when I was apprehended only one man dared to stand up to the Shah's soldiers and that was Mirza Reza. He stood up, shouted, cried, and called the soldiers and all present cowards. He was arrested and tortured and spent more than four years in the dungeons. When he was released he came to see me in Constantinople. He was so ill that I made him go to the French hospital in town where he stayed until last November. I tried to keep him longer, lest he be detained again on his return, but he refused. He said he wanted to retrieve the Khayyam *Manuscript* and that nothing else interested him. There are some people who drift from one obsession to the next."

"What is your feeling? Does the *Manuscript* still exist?"

"Only Mirza Reza can give you that information. He believes he can find that soldier who spirited it away when I was arrested. He hoped to take it back from him. In any case, he was determined to go and see him and spoke of buying it back with God knows what money."

"If it is a question of retrieving the *Manuscript*, money is no problem!" I had spoken with fervor. Jamaladin stared at me and frowned. He leant towards me as if he were about to listen to my heart.

"I have the impression that you are no less fixated on this *Manuscript* than the unfortunate Mirza. In that case, there is only one path for you to follow. Go to Tehran! I cannot guarantee that you will uncover the book there, but, if you know how to look, perhaps you will find other traces of Khayyam."

My spontaneous response seemed to confirm his diagnosis:

"If I obtain a visa, I'll be ready to go tomorrow."

"That is not an obstacle. I shall give you a note for the Persian consul in Baku. He will look after all the necessary formalities and even provide you with transport as far as Enzeli."

My expression must have betrayed some worry. Jamaladin was amused by that.

"Doubtless you are wondering: how can I give a recommendation from an outlaw to a representative of the Persian government? You should know that I have disciples everywhere, in every town, in all circles, even in the monarch's close entourage. Four years ago, when I was in London, I and an American friend published a newspaper which was sent off to Persia in discreet little bundles. The Shah was alarmed by that. He summoned the Minister of Post and ordered him to put an end to this newspaper's circulation, no matter what it took. The minister ordered the customs officers to intercept all the subversive packages at the frontier and send them on to his house."

He drew on his cigar and the smoke was scattered by a burst of laughter.

"What the Shah did not know," Jamaladin continued, "was that his Minister of Post was one of my most faithful disciples and that I had entrusted him with distributing the newspaper as best he could."

Jamaladin was chuckling as three visitors sporting blood-red felt fezzes arrived. He arose, greeted and kissed them and invited them to be seated, and exchanged a few words with them in Arabic. I guessed that he was explaining to them who I was, and begging their forgiveness for a few moments more. He came back towards me.

"If you are determined to set off for Tehran, I will give you some

letters of introduction. Come tomorrow, they will be ready. Above
all, do not be afraid. No one will think of searching an American."

The next day three brown envelopes were waiting for me. He laid
them in my hand, open. The first was for the consul in Baku and the
second for Mirza Reza. As he gave me that one, he made a comment:
"I must warn you that this man is unbalanced and obsessive. Do
not spend more time with him than you must. I have much affection
for him, he is more sincere, more faithful, and doubtless purer than
all my disciples, but he is capable of the worst blunders."

He sighed and dug his hand into the pocket of the wide pantaloons
he was wearing under his white tunic.

"Here are ten gold pounds. Give them to him from me; he no longer
has anything and perhaps he is hungry, but he is too proud to beg."

"Where will I find him?"

"I have not the slightest idea. He no longer has a house or a family
and he roams from place to place. That is why I am giving you this
third letter addressed to another quite different young man. He is the
son of the richest trader in Tehran, and although he is only twenty
and burns with the same fire as we all do, he is still even-tempered
and ready to debate the most revolutionary ideas with the smile of a
satisfied child. I sometimes reproach him for not being very Oriental.
You will see, beneath his Persian clothing there is English cool, French
ideas, and a more anti-clerical spirit than that of Monsieur Clemenceau.
His name is Fazel. It is he who will take you to Mirza Reza. I have
charged Fazel with keeping an eye on him, as much as possible. I do
not think that he can stop him committing his acts of folly, but he
will know where to find him."

I stood up to leave. He bade me a fond farewell and kept hold of
my hand in his own.

"Rochefort tells me in his letter that you are called Benjamin Omar.
In Persia only use the name Benjamin. Never say the word Omar."

"But it is Khayyam's name!"

"Since the sixteenth century, when Persia converted to Shiism, that
name has been banned. It could cause you much trouble. If you try to
identify with the Orient, you could find yourself caught up in its quarrels."

I made an expression of regret and consolation, a sign of impotence. I thanked him for his advice and made to leave, but he caught hold of me:

"One last thing. Yesterday you met a young person here as she was getting ready to leave. Did you speak to her?"

"No. I had no occasion to."

"She is the Shah's granddaughter, Princess Shireen. If, for whatever reason, you find all the doors shut, get a message to her and remind her that you saw her here. One word from her will be enough to overcome many obstacles."

29

On board a ship to Trebizond, the Black Sea was calm, too calm. The wind blew only lightly and for hours on end one could contemplate only the same piece of coast, the same rock, or the same Anatolian copse. It would have been wrong of me to complain, I needed some peace and quiet given the arduous task that I had to accomplish: to memorize the whole book of Persian-French dialogue written by Monsieur Nicolas, Khayyam's translator. I had resolved to speak to my hosts in their own language. I was not unaware of the fact that in Persia, as in Turkey, many of the intellectuals, the merchants, and the high officials spoke French. Some even knew English. However, if one wanted to move outside the restricted circle of the palaces and the legations, and travel outside the main cities or in their seedier districts, it had to be done in Persian.

The challenge stimulated and amused me. I delighted in discovering affinities with my own language, as well as with various Romance languages. Father, mother, brother, daughter in Persian were "*pedar*,"

AMIN MAALOUF

"madar," *"baradar,"* and *"dokhtar,"* and the common Indo-European roots can hardly be better illustrated. Even in naming God, the Muslims of Persia say *"Khoda,"* a term much closer to the English "God" or the German *"Gott"* than to *"Allah."* In spite of this example, the predominate influence is that of Arabic, which is exercised in a curious way: many Persian words can be replaced arbitrarily by their Arabic equivalent. It is even a form of cultural snobbery, much appreciated by intellectuals, to pepper their speech with terms, or with whole phrases, in Arabic — a practice of which Jamaladin was particularly fond.

I resolved myself to apply myself to Arabic later, but for the moment I had enough on my plate trying to understand Monsieur Nicholas' text, which apart from a knowledge of Persian were providing me with useful information about the country. It was full of conversations such as:

"Which products could one export from Persia?"

"Shawls from Kirman, fine pearls, turquoise, carpets, tobacco from Shiraz, silks from Mazanderan, leeches, and cherrywood pipes."

"When traveling, should a cook be taken along?"

"Yes, in Persia one cannot move without a cook, a bed, carpets, and servants."

"What foreign coins are used in Persia?"

"Russian Imperials, Dutch *carbovans* and ducats; English and French coins are very rare."

"What is the current king called?"

"Nasser ed-din Shah."

"It is said that he is an excellent king."

"Yes. He is extremely benevolent to foreigners and extremely generous. He is highly educated, with a knowledge of history, geography, and drawing; he speaks French and is fluent in the Oriental languages — Arabic, Turkish, and Persian."

Once at Trebizond I took a room in the Hotel d'Italie, the only hotel in town, which was comfortable if one could but forget the swarms of flies that transformed every meal into an uninterrupted and exasperating gesticulation. I resigned myself to imitating the other visitors by employing for a few meager coins a young adolescent whose job was

182

to fan me and keep the insects away. The most difficult thing was convincing him to get them away from my table without squashing them before my eyes, in between the dolmas and the kebabs. He obeyed me for some time, but as soon as he saw a fly within reach of his fearsome instrument, the temptation was too great and he would swat.

On the fourth day I found a place on board a freight steamer running the Marseille-Constantinople-Trebizond line. It look me as far as Batum, the Russian port on the east of the Black Sea, where I took the Transcaucasian Railway to Baku on the Caspian Sea. The Persian consul there received me so warmly that I hesitated to show him Jamaladin's letter. Would it not be better to remain an anonymous traveler and not arouse any suspicions? However, I was beset by some scruples. Perhaps the letter contained a message concerning something other than myself and I therefore did not have the right to keep it to myself. Abruptly I thus resolved to say, in any enigmatic way:

"We have perhaps a friend in common."

I took out the envelope. The consul opened it carefully; he had taken his gold-rimmed glasses from his desk and was reading, when I suddenly noticed that his fingers were trembling. He stood up, went over to lock the door to the room, placed his lips to the paper, and remained so for a few seconds as if in contemplation. Then he came over to me and held me as if I were a brother who had survived a shipwreck.

As soon as he had managed to recompose his expression, he called his servants and ordered them to fetch my trunk, to show me to the best room and prepare a feast for the evening. He kept me there for two days, neglecting all his work in order to stay with me and question me ceaselessly about the Master, his health, his mood, and particularly what he was saying about the situation in Persia. When it was time for me to leave, he rented a cabin for me on a steamer of the Russian Caucaset-Mercure Line. Then he entrusted me with his coachman to whom he gave the task of accompanying me to Kazvin and to stay at my side as long as I had need of his services.

The coachman immediately proved to be extremely resourceful, and often even irreplaceable. It was not I who would have known to slip some coins into the hand of that proudly mustached customs officer so that he would deign to leave his *kalyan* pipe for a moment to come

and inspect my huge Wolseley. It was the coachman again who nego-
tiated with the Roads Administration for the immediate provision of
a four-horse carriage, although the official was imperiously inviting us
to come back the next day and a seedy innkeeper, who was most
apparently his accomplice, was offering us his services.

I consoled myself for all these difficulties of the route by thinking
of the suffering of the travelers who had preceded me. Thirteen years
earlier, the only way to Persia had been the old caravan route that
started at Trebizond and led towards Tabriz through Erzerum, with
its forty staging points taking six exhausting and expensive weeks and
which was sometimes truly dangerous owing to the incessant tribal
warfare. The Transcaucasian had revolutionized matters. It had opened
Persia to the world and one could reach that empire with neither risk
nor major discomfort by taking a steamer from Baku to the port of
Enzeli, then it only took one more week, on a road suitable for motor
vehicles, to reach Tehran.

In the West, the cannon is an instrument for war or ceremonial occasions; in Persia it is also an instrument of torture. If I speak of it, it
is because I was confronted by the spectacle of a cannon that served
the most horrific purpose as I reached the town limits of Tehran — a
man, who was tied and whose head was the only part of him visible,
had been placed in the large barrel. He had to stay there, under the
sun and without food or water, until death came to him; even then, I
was told, the custom was to leave his body exposed for a long time in
order to make the punishment an example, to inspire silence and dread
in all those who passed through the city gates.

Was it because of this first image that the capital of Persia exerted
such little magic on me? In the cities of the Orient, one always looks
for the colors of the present and the shades of the past. In Tehran I
came up against none of that. What did I see there? Thoroughfares
that were too wide, linking the rich of the northern districts to the
poor of the southern districts, a bazaar absolutely swarming with camels,
mules, and gaudy materials, but which could hardly bear comparison
with the souks of Cairo, Constantinople, Isfahan, or Tabriz. And wherever
one's gaze alighted there were innumerable gray buildings.

It was too new. Tehran had too short a history! For a long time it had only been an obscure dependency of Rayy, the prestigious city of the scholars that was demolished at the time of the Mongols. It was not until the end of the eighteenth century that a Turkoman tribe, the Qajars, took possession of the area. Having succeeded in subduing the whole of Persia by the sword, the dynasty elevated its modest abode to the rank of capital. Until then, the political center of the country had been in the south, at Isfahan, Kirman, or Shiraz. That is to say that the inhabitants of these cities had nothing good to say about the "brutish northerners" who governed them and whose lack of knowledge included even that of their language. The reigning Shah, upon his accession to power, needed an interpreter to address his subjects. Anyway, it seems that after that he acquired a better knowledge of Persian.

It must be pointed out that he had plenty of time to do so. When I arrived in Tehran, in April 1896, the monarch was preparing to celebrate his jubilee, his fiftieth year in power. In honor of this the city was decked with the national emblem bearing the sign of the lion and the sun. Notables had come from all the provinces, numerous foreign delegations had turned up, and even though most of the official guests were lodged in villas, the two hotels for Europeans, the Albert and the Prévost, were unusually full. It was in the latter-named hotel that I finally found a room.

I had thought of going straight to Fazel, to deliver the letter to him and ask him how I could find Mirza Reza, but I was able to overcome my impatience. Not being unaware of the customs of Orientals, I knew that Jamaladin's disciple would invite me to stay with him; I did not want to offend him by refusing but nor did I want to take the risk of being caught up in his political activity, and still less in that of his Master.

I therefore checked into the Hotel Prévost, which was run by a Swiss man from Geneva. In the morning I rented an old mare so I could go to the American legation — a practical act of courtesy — on the Boulevard des Ambassadeurs. Then I went to see Jamaladin's favorite disciple. With his slender mustache, his long white tunic, the majestic way he held his head, and a hint of coldness, Fazel corresponded on the whole to the image that the exile in Constantinople had drawn for me.

We were going to become best friends in the world, but the contact was distant and his direct language disturbed and upset me. Such as when we spoke of Mirza Reza:

"I will do what I can to help you, but I do not wish to have anything to do with that madman. The Master told me that he is a living martyr. I replied, 'Then it would be better if he were to die!' Do not look at me like that, I am not a monster, but that man has suffered so much that his spirit is completely deformed; every time he opens his mouth he harms our cause."

"Where is he today?"

"For weeks he has been living in the mausoleum of Shah Abdul-Azim, prowling around the gardens or in the corridors, between the buildings, speaking to people about Jamaladin's arrest and entreating them to turn against the monarch, telling them of his own suffering, shouting and gesticulating. He never stops avowing that Sayyid Jamaladin is the Mahdi, even though he himself has forbidden him to mouth such crazed utterings. I really have no wish to be seen in his company."

"He is the only person who can give me information about the manuscript."

"I know. I shall take you to him, but I shall not stay with the two of you for a second."

That evening a dinner was held in my honor by Fazel's father, one of the richest men in Tehran. He was a close friend of Jamaladin and even though he kept out of any political activity he was keen to honor the Master through me; he had invited almost a hundred people. The conversation centered on Khayyam. Everyone was spouting forth quatrains and anecdotes, and there were animated discussions which sometimes veered off into politics; everyone seemed perfectly at ease in Persian, Arabic, and French, and most of them could speak some Turkish, Russian, and English. I felt all the more ignorant as they all considered me a great Orientalist and specialist in the *Rubaiyaat*, which was a very great, or, I would even say, an extreme overstatement, but I had to stop contradicting it since my protests were taken as a sign of humility, which as everyone knows, is the mark of a true intellectual.

The evening began at sunset, but my host had insisted that I arrive earlier; he wanted to show me the splendors of his garden. Even if he possessed a palace, as was the case with Fazel's father, a Persian rarely showed people around it. He would neglect it in favor of his garden, his only subject of pride.

As they arrived, the guests picked up a goblet and went off to find a place near the streams, both natural and made-made, that wound among the poplars. According to whether they preferred to sit on a carpet or a cushion, the servants would rush to place one in the chosen spot, but some perched on a rock or sat on the bare ground; the gardens of Persia do not have lawns, which in American eyes gives them a slightly barren aspect.

That night we drank within reason. The more pious stuck to tea, and to that end a gigantic samovar was carried about by three servants, two to hold it and a third to serve the tea. Many people preferred araq, vodka, or wine, but I did not observe any misbehavior, the tipsiest being happy to hum along with the musicians who had been engaged by the master of the house — a *târ* player, a virtuoso on the *zarb*, and a flautist. Later there were dancers, who were mostly young boys. No woman was to be seen during the reception.

Dinner was served towards midnight. The whole evening we had been plied with pistachios, almonds, salted seeds, and sweetmeats, the dinner being only the final point of the ceremony. The host had the duty to delay it as long as possible, for when the main dish arrived — that evening it was a *javaher pilau*, a "jeweled rice" — the guests ate it all up in ten minutes, washed their hands, and went off. Coachmen and lamp-bearers clustered around the door as we left, to collect their respective masters.

At dawn the next day, Fazel accompanied me in a coach to the gate of the sanctuary of Shah Abdul-Azim. He went in alone, to return with a man who had a disturbing appearance: he was tall but terribly thin, with a shaggy beard, and his hands trembled incessantly. He was clothed in a long narrow white robe with patches on it and he was carrying a colorless and shapeless bag that contained everything he possessed in the world. In his eyes could be read all the distress of the Orient.

When he learnt that I came from Jamaladin, he fell to his knees and clutched my hand, covering it with kisses. Fazel, ill at ease, stuttered an excuse and went off.

187

I held out the letter from the Master to Mirza Reza. He almost snatched it from my hands, and although it comprised several pages, he read it all the way through without hurrying, forgetting completely that I was there.

I waited for him to finish before speaking to him about what interested me. But he spoke to me in a mixture of Persian and French that I had some difficulty in understanding.

"The book is with a soldier who comes from Kirman, which is also my town. He promised to come and see me here the day after tomorrow — on Friday. I will have to give him some money. Not to buy the book back but to thank the man for returning it. Unfortunately I do not have a single coin."

Without hesitating I took out of my pocket the gold that Jamaladin had sent for him and I added an equal sum of my own. He seemed to be satisfied by that.

"Come back on Saturday. If God wishes, I will have the manuscript and I will hand it over to you to give to the Master in Constantinople."

30

The sounds of laziness rose from the sleepy city. The dust was hot and glistened in the sunlight. It was a wholly languorous Persian day, with a meal of chicken with apricots, a cool Shiraz wine, and a siesta flat-out on the balcony of my hotel room underneath a faded sun-shade, my face covered with a damp towel.

However, on this May 1, 1896, someone's life was going to be ended at dusk and another would begin thereafter.

There was some furious and repeated banging on my door. I finally heard it and stretched out and jumped up barefoot, my hair stuck together and my mustache unwaxed, wearing a loose white shirt which I had bought in town. My limp fingers fumbled with the latch. Fazel pushed the door open, pushed me out of the way to close it again, and shook me by the shoulders.

"Wake up! In quarter of an hour you be dead man!"

What Fazel informed me in a few broken phrases was the news that the whole world would know the next day by the magic of the telegraph.

189

The monarch had gone at midday to the Shah Abdul-Azim sanctuary for the Friday prayer. He was wearing the ceremonial suit he had had made up for his jubilee with gold threads, cornices of turquoise and emerald, and a feather cap. In the great hall of the sanctuary he chose his prayer space and a carpet was unrolled at his feet. Before kneeling down, his eyes sought out his wives and signaled them to stand behind him and he smoothed out his long tapering mustache which was white with bluish highlights, while the crowd of the faithful and the mullahs was pushing against the guards who were trying to contain them. Shouts were still coming from the outer courtyard. The royal wives came forward. A man had infiltrated amongst them, clothed in wool in the manner of a dervish. He was holding a sheet of paper in his outstretched arm. The Shah looked through his binoculars to read it. Suddenly there was a shot. A pistol had been hidden by the sheet of paper. The sovereign was hit right in the heart, but he still managed to murmur, "Hold me up," before he tottered and fell.

In the general tumult it was the Grand Vizir who was the first to gather his wits about him and shout, "It is nothing. It is a superficial wound!" He had the hall evacuated and the Shah carried to the royal carriage. He fanned the cadaver on the back seat all the way to Tehran as if the Shah were still breathing. Meanwhile he had the Crown Prince summoned from Tabriz, where he was governor.

In the sanctuary the murderer was attacked by the Shah's wives who insulted and thrashed him. The crowd ripped his clothing off him and he was about to be torn limb from limb when Colonel Kassakovsky, the commander of the Cossack brigade, intervened to save him — or rather to submit him to a first interrogation. Curiously the murder weapon had disappeared. It was said that a woman picked it up and hid it under her veil — she was never found. On the other hand, the sheet of paper that had been used to camouflage the pistol was retrieved.

Naturally Fazel spared me all those details. His account was terse:

"That idiot Mirza Reza has killed the Shah. They found a letter from Jamaladin on him. Your name was written on it. Keep your Persian clothing, take your money and your passport. Nothing else. Run and take refuge in the American legation."

My first thought was for the manuscript. Had Mirza Reza got it back that morning? In truth I was not yet aware of the gravity of my situation. An accomplice to the assassination of a head of state, I — who had come to the Orient of poets! Nevertheless, appearances were against me. They were deceptive, misleading, and absurd, but damning. What judge or commissar would not suspect me?

Fazel was watching from the balcony; suddenly he ducked and shouted out hoarsely:

"The Cossacks are here. They are setting up roadblocks all around the hotel!"

We hurtled down the stairs. When we reached the foyer we took up a more dignified and less suspect pace. An officer with a blond beard had just made his entrance, his hat pulled tight down and eyes that were sweeping all the room's nooks and crannies. Fazel just had time to whisper to me, "To the legation!" Then he separated from me and went over towards the officer. I heard him say "Palkovnik! Colonel!" and saw him ceremoniously shake hands and exchange a few words of condolence. Kassakovsky had often dined with my friend's father and that awarded me a few seconds of respite. I took advantage of it by speeding up my pace towards the exit, wrapped up in my *aba*, and turning into the garden, which the Cossacks were busy turning into a fortified camp. They did not give me any trouble. As I was coming from inside the hotel they must have assumed that their commander had let me through. I went through the gate and headed towards the little alley to my right which led to the Boulevard des Ambassadeurs and in ten minutes to my legation.

Three soldiers were posted at the entrance to my alley. Would they let me through? To the left I could make out another alley. I thought it would be better to follow that one even if it meant having to come back later down the right alley. I walked on, avoiding looking in the direction of the soldiers. A few more steps and I would not be able to be see them any more, nor they me.

"Stop!"

What should I do? Stop? With the very first question they asked me they would discover that I could hardly speak Persian, they would ask to see my papers and arrest me. Should I run off? They would not have much difficulty catching up with me, I would have been acting in a guilty fashion and would not even be able to plead in innocence. I had only a split second to make a choice.

I decided to carry on my way without hurrying, as if I had heard nothing. However there was a new commotion, the sound of rifles being loaded and footsteps. I did not give it a second thought but ran through the alleys without looking back and threw myself into the narrowest and darkest passageways. The sun had already set and in half an hour it would be pitch dark.

I was searching my memory for a prayer to recite, but could only manage to repeat "God! God! God!" in an insistent pleading, as if I had already died and was drumming on the gate of Paradise.

And the gate opened. The gate of Paradise. A little hidden gate in the mud-stained wall at the corner of the street. It opened. A hand touched mine and I grasped on to it. It pulled me towards it and shut the gate behind me. I kept my eyes shut out of fear. I was breathless with disbelief and happiness. Outside the procession went on and on.

Three pairs of laughing eyes were watching me — three women whose hair was covered but whose faces were unveiled and who were looking at me lovingly, as if I were a newborn babe. The oldest, in her forties, gave me a sign to follow her. At the end of the garden I had landed up in there was a small cabin where she seated me on a wicker chair, assuring me with a gesture that she would come to rescue me. She reassured me with a pout and with the magic word: *andaroun*, "inner house." The soldier would not come to search where the women lived!

In fact the noise of the soldiers had come closer only to get more distant again, before fading away altogether. How could they have known into which of the alleys I had vanished? The district was a maze, made up of dozens of passages, hundreds of houses and gardens — and it was almost night.

After an hour I was brought some black tea, cigarettes were rolled for me, and a conversation struck up. In slow Persian phrases with a few French words they explained to me to whom I owed my safety. The rumor had run through the district that an accomplice of the assassin was at the foreigners' hotel. Seeing me flee they understood that I was the guilty hero and they had wanted to protect me. What were their reasons for this? Their husband and father had been executed fifteen years earlier, unjustly accused of belonging to a dissident sect, the *Babis*, who advocated the abolition of polygamy, complete equality between men and women, and the establishment of a democratic regime. Led by the Shah and the clergy, repression had been bloody and, aside from the scores of thousands of *Babis*, many completely innocent people had also been massacred upon a simple denunciation by a neighbor. Then, left alone with two young girls, my benefactress had been waiting for the hour of revenge. The three women said that they were honored that the heroic avenger had landed in their humble garden.

When one is viewed as a hero by women, does one really wish to disabuse them? I persuaded myself that it would be unseemly, even foolish, to disillusion them. In my difficult battle for survival, I needed these allies, I needed their enthusiasm and courage — and their unjustified admiration. I therefore took refuge in an enigmatic silence which, for them, lifted their last doubts.

Three women, a garden, and a salutary misunderstanding — I could recount forever those forty unreal days of a sweltering Persian spring. It was difficult being a foreigner; I found it doubly awkward in the world of Oriental women where I did not belong at all. My benefactress was well aware of the difficulties into which she had been thrown. I am certain that the whole of the first night, while I was sleeping stretched out on all three mats laid on top of each other in the cabin at the bottom of the garden, she was the victim of the most intractable insomnia, for at dawn she summoned me, had me sit cross-legged to her right, sat her two daughters to her left, and gave us a carefully prepared speech.

She started by hailing my courage and restated her joy at taking me in. Then, having observed some moments of silence, she suddenly started to unhook her bodice before my startled eyes. I blushed and turned my eyes away but she pulled me towards her. Her shoulders were bare and so were her breasts. With word and gesture she invited me to suckle. The two daughters giggled under their cloaks but the mother had all the solemnity of a ritual sacrifice. I complied, placing my lips, as modestly as possible, on the tip of one breast and then on the other. Then she covered herself up, without haste, adding in the most formal tones:

"By this act you have become my son, as if you were born of my flesh."

Then, turning towards her daughters, who had stopped laughing, she declared that henceforth they had to treat me as if I was their own brother.

At the time the ceremony seemed both moving and grotesque to me. Thinking back over it, however, I can see in it all the subtlety of the Orient. In fact my situation was embarrassing for that woman. She had not hesitated to hold out a helping hand to me at great peril to herself, and she had offered me the most unconditional hospitality. At the same time, the presence of a stranger, a young man, near her daughters night and day, could only lead to some incident at some point in the future. How better to diffuse the difficulty than by this ritual gesture of symbolic adoption. Then I could move around the house as I pleased, sleep in the same room, place a kiss on my "sisters'" foreheads and we were all protected and kept strictly in check by the fiction of adoption.

People other than me would have felt trapped by this performance. I, on the contrary, was comforted by it. Having landed up on a women's planet and then to form a hasty attachment, through idleness or lack of privacy, with one of the three hostesses; to try bit by bit to edge away from the other two, to outwit and exclude them; to bring upon myself their inevitable hostility and to find myself excluded — sheepish and contrite at having embarrassed, saddened, or disappointed the women who had been nothing less than providential — that would have been a turn of affairs that would not have suited my nature at all. Having said that, I, being a Westerner, would never have been able to come up with the solution which that woman found in the never-ending arsenal of her religious commandments.

As if by a miracle, everything became simple, clear, and pure. To say that desire was dead would be telling a lie, everything about our relationships was eminently carnal; yet, I reiterate, eminently pure. Thus I experienced moments of carefree peace in the intimacy of these women who were neither veiled nor excessively modest, in the middle of a city where I was probably the most wanted man.

With the passage of time, I see my stay with those women as a moment of privilege without which my attachment to the Orient would have remained short-lived or superficial. It is to them I owe the immense steps I made in understanding and speaking idiomatic Persian. Although my hostesses had made the praiseworthy effort to put together some words in French on the first day, all our conversations were henceforth carried on in the country's vernacular. Our conversations might be animated or casual, subtle or crude, often even flirtatious, since in my capacity as elder brother anything was allowed as long as I stayed beyond the bounds of incest. Anything that was playful was permitted, including the most theatrical shows of affection.

Would the experience have kept its allure had it gone on for longer? I shall never know. I do not wish to know. An event that was unfortunately only too foreseeable put an end to all that. It was a visit, a routine visit, by the grandparents.

Ordinarily I stayed far away from the entrance gates, the *birouni* gate, which led to the men's abode and was the main doorway, and the garden gate through which I had entered. At the first sound I would slip away. This time, through recklessness or overconfidence, I did not hear the old couple arrive. I was sitting cross-legged in the women's room and for the last two hours had been peacefully smoking a *kalyan* pipe prepared by my "sisters" and had fallen asleep there with the pipe still in my mouth and my head leaning against the wall, when a man's cough woke me up with a start.

31

For my adoptive mother, who arrived a few seconds too late, the presence of a European male in the interior of her apartments had to be promptly explained. Rather than tarnish her reputation or that of her daughters, she chose to tell the truth in the most patriotic and triumphant way she could. Who was this stranger? None less than the *farangi* the police were looking for, the accomplice of the man who had cut down the tyrant and avenged her martyred husband!

There was a moment of indecision and then the verdict came. They congratulated me and praised my courage as well as that of my protectress. It is true that confronted with such an incongruous situation her explanation was the only plausible one. Even though the fact that I had been slumped out right in the middle of the *andaroun* was somewhat compromising, she could easily have explained it away by speaking of the necessity of shielding me from sight.

Honor had been safeguarded, but it was now clear that I had to leave. There were two paths open to me. The most obvious was to leave disguised as a woman and to walk over to the American legation; in short, to complete the interrupted walk of a few weeks earlier. However, my "mother" dissuaded me. Having carried out a scouting expedition she had discerned that all the alleys leading to the legation were being watched. Moreover, being rather tall at just over six feet, my disguise as a Persian woman would not fool even the most unobservant soldier.

The other solution was, following Jamaladin's advice, to send a distress message to Princess Shireen. I spoke of her to my "mother" who gave her approval; she had heard of the assassinated Shah's granddaughter who was said to be sensitive to the suffering of the poor, and she offered to carry a letter to her. The problem was finding the words with which to address her — words which, while being sufficiently explicit, would not give me away were they to fall into other hands. I could not mention my name, nor that of the Master. I made do with writing on a sheet of paper the only phrase she had ever said to me: "You never know, our paths might meet!"

My "mother" had decided to go up to the Princess at the ceremonies on the fortieth day of the death of the old Shah, the last stage of the funeral ceremonies. In the inevitable general confusion of the onlookers and the professional weepers smeared with soot, she had no difficulty in slipping the paper from her hand into the Princess's, who then read it and with dread looked about her for the man who had written it. The messenger whispered to her, "He is at my house!" Immediately Shireen left the ceremony, summoned her coachman, and placed my "mother" at her side. In order not to attract any suspicion, the coach with the royal insignia stopped in front of the Hotel Prévost from which spot the two heavily veiled and anonymous women continued their route on foot.

Our second meeting was hardly more wordy than our first. The Princess looked me up and down with a smile on the corner her lips. Suddenly she gave an order:

"Tomorrow at dawn my coachman will come to fetch you. Be ready. Wear a veil and walk with your head down!"

I was convinced that she was going to drive me to my legation. It was at the moment when her carriage went out through the city gate that I realized my mistake. She explained:

"I could easily have taken you to the American minister's. You would have been safe, but no one would have had any trouble guessing how you got there. Even if I do have some influence, being a member of the Qajar family, I cannot use it to protect the apparent accomplice to the assassination of the Shah. I would have been placed in an awkward predicament and then they would have found the brave women who looked after you. Your legation, moreover, would not have been too delighted to have to protect a man accused of such a crime. Believe me, it is better for everyone if you leave Persia. I will take you to one of my maternal uncles, one of the Bakhtiari chiefs. He has come down with his tribe's warriors for the fortieth day ceremonies. I have told him who you are and stated your innocence, but his men know nothing. He has undertaken to escort you to the Ottoman frontier by routes unknown to the caravans. He is waiting for us in Shah Abdul-Azim's village. Do you have any money?"

"Yes. I gave two hundred *tomans* to the women who saved me, but I still have almost four hundred."

"That is not enough. You must distribute half of what you have to the men accompanying you and keep a decent amount behind for the rest of the trip. Here are some Turkish coins, they will not be too much. Here also is a text that I would like the Master to have. You will be passing through Constantinople?"

It was difficult to say no. She continued, as she slipped some folded papers into the slit of my cloak:

"They contain a transcript of Mirza Reza's first cross-examination. I spent the night writing it out. You can read it, in fact you should read it. You will learn a lot. Besides, it will keep you busy during the long trip. But do not let anyone else see it."

We were already on the outskirts of the village. The police were everywhere and searching everything down to the packs on the mules, but who would have dared hold up a royal convoy? We followed our route as far as the courtyard of a hugh saffron-colored building. In its center was an immense and ancient oak tree around which warriors, with two bandoliers crossed across their chests, were bustling. The Princess could only look with disdain upon these virile ornaments which complemented their thick mustaches.

"I am leaving you in good hands, as you see; they will protect you better than the weak women who have looked after you so far."

"I doubt it."

My eyes worriedly followed the rifle barrels that were pointing in all directions.

"I doubt it too," she laughed. "But all the same they will take you over to Turkey."

As the moment came to say goodbye, I decided not to:

"I know that the time is hardly right to speak about it, but perhaps you know by some chance if an old manuscript was found in Mirza Reza's luggage."

Her eyes avoided mine and her voice took on a grating tone.

"The time is indeed badly chosen. Do not utter that madman's name again until you get to Constantinople!"

"It is a manuscript by Khayyam!"

I was right to insist. After all, it was because of that book that I had allowed myself to be dragged into this Persian adventure. However, Shireen gave a sigh of impatience.

"I know nothing of it. I will make inquiries. Leave me your address and I will write to you. However, please do not reply to me."

As I scribbled down "Annapolis, Maryland" I had the impression that I was already far away and I had started feeling sorry that my foray into Persia had been so short and that it had gone so wrong from the start. I held the paper out to the Princess. As she was about to take it, I took hold of her hand — briefly but firmly. She also squeezed my hand, digging a fingernail into my palm, without scratching me but leaving behind its distinct outline for a few minutes. Smiles came to both our lips and we uttered the same phrase in unison:

"You never know, our paths might meet!"

For two months I saw nothing that resembled what I was used to calling a road. Upon leaving Shah Abdul-Azim we headed southwest in the direction of the Bakhtiaris' tribal territory. After we had skirted the salt lake of Qom we followed its eponymous river but did not go into the city itself. My guides, who brandished their rifles permanently for battle, took care to avoid built-up areas and although Shireen's uncle often took the trouble to inform me that we were at Amouk, Vertcha, or Khomein, it was only a turn of phrase by which he meant that we were on a level with those localities whose minarets we could make out in the distance and whose contours I was happy to leave to my imagination.

In the mountains of Luristan, beyond the sources of the Qom River, my guides became less vigilant — we were in Bakhtiari territory. A feast was organized in my honor. I was given an opium pipe to smoke and I fell asleep on the spot amid general hilarity. I then had to wait two days before starting off again on the route which was still long: Shuster, Ahvaz, and finally the perilous swamp crossing to Basra, the city of Ottoman Iraq that lay on the Shatt al-Arab.

At last, out of Persia and safe! There was still a long month at sea to get by sailboat from Fao to Bahrain, then I had to sail down the Pirate coast to Aden and come back up the Red Sea and the Suez Canal to Alexandria in order finally to cross the Mediterranean in an old Turkish steamer to Constantinople.

Throughout this interminable escape, which was tiring but went without a hitch, the only leisure activity I had was to read and reread the ten manuscript pages of Mirza Reza's cross-examination. Doubtless I would have tired of it had I any other distractions, but this forced meeting with a man condemned to death exercised an undeniable fascination over me, in that I could easily imagine him, with his gaunt limbs, his eyes racked with pain, and his unlikely clothing of a devout. Sometimes I thought I could even hear his tortured voice:

"What were the reasons that induced you to kill our beloved Shah?"

"Those who have eyes to see with will have no difficulty in noticing that the Shah was struck down in the very same place where Jamaladin was abused. What had that saintly man done, that true descendant of the Prophet, to deserve to be dragged out of the sanctuary the way he was?"

"Who induced you to kill the Shah, who are you accomplices?"

"I swear by almighty and omnipotent God, by God who created Jamaladin and all other humans, that no one apart from me and the Sayyid knew anything of my plan to kill the Shah. The Sayyid is in Constantinople. Try and reach him!"

"What instructions did Jamaladin give you?"

"When I went to Constantinople, I told him of the tortures to which the Shah's son had submitted me. The Sayyid ordered me to be silent, saying, 'Stop whining as if you were leading a funeral service! Can you do nothing other than cry? If the Shah's son tortured you, kill him!'"

"Why kill the Shah rather than his son, since he is the one who wronged you and it is upon the son that Jamaladin advised you to take your revenge?"

"I said to myself, 'If I kill the son, the Shah with his vast power will kill thousands of people in reprisal.' Instead of cutting off a branch, I preferred to pull out the whole tree of tyranny by its roots in the hope that a different tree would spring up in its place. Besides, the Sultan of Turkey said to Sayyid Jamaladin in private that in order to bring about the union of all Muslims we had to get rid of this Shah."

"How do you know what the Sultan might have said to Jamaladin in private?"

"Sayyid Jamaladin himself told me. He trusted me and hid nothing from me. When I was in Constantinople he treated me like his own son."

"If you were so well treated there why did you come back to Persia where you feared being arrested and tortured?"

"I am one of those who believe that no leaf falls from a tree unless that has been planned and inscribed, since the beginning of time, in the Book of Destiny. It was written that I would come to Persia and would be the tool for the act that has just been carried out."

32

I f those men who strolled about on Yildiz Hill, all around Jamaladin's house, had written on their fezzes "Sultan's spy," they would not have given away any more than what the most artless of visitors took in at first glance. Perhaps, however, that was their real purpose in being there: to discourage visitors. In fact, the residence, which usually swarmed with disciples, foreign correspondents, and various personages who were in town, was totally deserted on that close September day. Only the servant was there, as discreet as ever. He led me to the first floor where the Master was to be found, pensive and distant and slumped deep in a cretonne and velvet armchair.

When he saw me arrive his face lit up. He came towards me with great strides and held me to him, apologizing for the trouble he had caused and saying that he was happy that I had been able to extricate myself. I described to him my escape in the smallest detail, and how the Princess had intervened, before returning to tell him of my too brief meeting with Fazel and then with Mirza Reza. The very mention of the latter's name irritated Jamaladin.

"I have just been informed that he was hanged last month. May God forgive him! Naturally he knew what his fate would be and could only have been surprised by the length of time it took to execute him — more than a hundred days after the Shah's death! Doubtless they tortured him to extract a confession."

Jamaladin spoke slowly. He seemed to have grown weak and thin; his face, which was usually so serene, was beset with twitches that at times disfigured him without detracting from his magnetism. One had the impression that he was suffering, particularly when he spoke of Mirza Reza.

"I can hardly believe it of that poor boy, whom I had looked after there in Constantinople, whose hand never stopped shaking, and who seemed incapable of holding a cup of tea — that he could hold a pistol and fell the Shah with one shot. Do you not think that they might be exploiting his unbalanced mind to pin someone else's crime on him?"

I replied by handing him the cross-examination the Princess had copied out. He put on a slim pair of pince-nez and read and re-read it with fervor, or was it terror, or, it seemed to me from time to time, a sort of inner joy. Then he folded it up, slipped it into his pocket, and proceeded to pace up and down the room. There were ten minutes of silence before he uttered this curious prayer:

"Mirza Reza, lost child of Persia! Would that you had simply been mad, would that you had just been wise! If only you had been content to betray me or to remain faithful to me, to inspire tenderness or revulsion! How can we love or hate you? And God Himself, what will He do with you? Will He raise you up to the victims' Paradise or relegate you to hangman's hell?"

He came and sat down again, exhausted, with his face buried in his hands. I remained silent, and even made myself breathe more quietly. Jamaladin sat up. His voice seemed calmer and his mood more lucid.

"The words I read are indeed Mirza Reza's. Until now I still had my doubts, but I do not any more. He is definitely the assassin. He probably thought he was acting to avenge me. Perhaps he thought he was obeying me. However, contrary to what he believes, I never gave him an order to murder. When he came to Constantinople to tell me how he had been tortured by the Shah's son and his cohorts his tears were flowing. Wanting to shake him out of it, I told him, 'Now stop whining! People will say that you just want them to feel sorry for you, that you would even mutilate yourself so that they will feel sorry for you!' I told him an old legend: when the armies of Darius confronted those of Alexander the Great, the Greek's counselors brought to his attention that the troops of the Persians were much more numerous than his. Alexander kept his poise and shrugged. 'My men,' he said, 'fight to win. The men of Darius fight to die!'"

Jamaladin seemed to be racking his memory.

"That is when I told Mirza Reza, 'If the Shah's son is persecuting you, destroy him, instead of destroying yourself!' Was that really a call to murder? Do you, who know Mirza Reza, really think that I could have entrusted such a mission to a madman whom a thousand people may have met here in this very house?"

I wanted to be honest.

"You are not capable of the crime they are attributing to you, but your moral responsibility cannot be denied."

He was touched by my frankness.

"That I admit. Just as I admit that daily I wished that the Shah would die. But what use is it for me to defend myself. I am a condemned man."

He went over to a small chest and took out a sheet with some fine calligraphy on it.

"This morning I wrote my will."

He placed the text in my hands and I read it with emotion:

"I do not suffer from being kept prisoner. I have no fear of death being near. My only source of sorrow is having to state that I have not seen blossom the seeds I have sown. Tyranny continues to oppress the peoples of the Orient and obscurantism still stifles their freedom cry. Perhaps I would have been more successful if I had planted my seeds in the fertile soil of the people rather than in the arid soil of royal courts. And you, people of Persia, in whom I placed my greatest hopes, do not think that by eliminating a man you can win your freedom. It is the weight of secular tradition that you must dare to shake."

"Keep a copy of it and translate it for Henri Rochefort. *L'Intransigeant* is the only newspaper that still holds me innocent. The others treat me as an assassin. The whole world wants my death. Let them be reassured — I have cancer. Cancer of the jaw."

As with every time that his resolve weakened and he complained, he tried to make up for it on the spot by giving a forced laugh of unconcern and making a learned jest.

"Cancer, cancer, cancer," he repeated as if in warning. "In the past doctors attributed illnesses to the conjunctions of the stars, but only cancer has kept its astrological name, in all languages. The fear is still there."

He remained pensive and melancholy for a few moments, but then hurried to carry on, in a happier vein that was blatantly affected but, for all that, more poignant.

"I curse this cancer. Yet nothing says that it is the cancer that will kill me. The Shah is demanding my extradition: the Sultan cannot hand me over since I am still his guest, but he cannot let a regicide go unpunished. He has hated the Shah and his dynasty to no avail, plotted against him every day, but members of the brotherhood of the great of this world bolster each other against an intruder like Jamaladin. What is the solution? The Sultan will have me kill myself, and the new Shah will be comforted, since, in spite of his repeated requests for my extradition, he has no wish to stain his hands with my blood at the outset of his reign. Who will kill me? The cancer? The Shah? The Sultan? Perhaps I will never have the time to know. But you, my friend, you will know."

He then had the gall to laugh!

In fact I never knew. The circumstances surrounding the death of the great reformer of the Orient remained a mystery. I heard the news a few months after my return to Annapolis. A notice in the March 12, 1897 edition of *L'Intransigeant* informed me of his death three days earlier. It was only towards the end of the summer, when the promised letter from Shireen arrived, that I heard the version of Jamaladin's death that was current among his disciples. "For some months he had been suffering from raging toothache," she wrote, "no doubt caused by his cancer. That day, as the pain had become unbearable, he sent his servant to the Sultan who sent over his own dentist who listened to Jamaladin's chest, unwrapped a syringe he had already prepared, and gave him an injection in the gums while explaining that the pain would soon die down. Hardly a few seconds passed before the Master's jaw swelled up. Seeing him suffocating, the servant ran off to bring back the dentist, who had not yet left the house, but instead of coming back the man started to run as fast as he could towards the carriage that was waiting for him. Sayyid Jamaladin died a few minutes later. In the evening, agents of the Sultan came to take away his body, which was hurriedly washed and buried." The Princess's account finished, without any transition, by quoting words from Khayyam which she had carefully translated: "Those who have amassed so much information, who have guided us towards knowledge, are they themselves not swamped by doubt? They tell a story and then go to bed."

As to the fate of the *Manuscript*, which was her purpose in writing to me, Shireen informed me in rather terse terms, "It was in fact amongst the murderer's belongings. It is now with me. You may consult it at your leisure when you return to Persia."

Return to Persia, where I had aroused so many suspicions?

33

I had retained from my Persian adventure nothing but cravings. It had taken me one month to get to Tehran and three months to get out. I had spent a few days, which were both brief and numb, in its streets, having hardly had the time to breathe in the smells, or to get to know or see anything. Too many images were still calling me towards the forbidden land: my proud *kalyan* smoker's sluggishness, lording it over the whisps of smoke rising from the charcoal in the copper holders; my hand closing around Shireen's, a promise; my lips on breasts chastely offered by my mother of an evening; and, more than anything else, the *Manuscript* that awaited me lying in its guardian's arms with its pages open.

To those who may never have contracted the obsession with the Orient, I scarcely dare mention that on Saturday at dusk I took myself out for a walk on a stretch of the Annapolis beach that I knew would be deserted, wearing a pair of Turkish slippers, my Persian robe, and a lambskin *kulah* hat. There was no one on the beach, and immersed in my daydreams on my way back I made a detour via Compromise Road, which was not at all quiet. "Good evening Mr. Lesage," "Have a nice walk, Mr. Lesage." "Good evening Mrs. Baymaster, Miss Highchurch," the greetings rang out, "Good evening Reverend." It was the pastor's raised eyebrows that brought me back to myself. I stopped dead in order to look contritely at myself from my chest to my feet, to feel my headgear and hurry on my way. I think I even ran, draped in my *aba* as if to cover my nakedness. Once home I tore off my attire, rolled it up with a gesture of finality, and then tossed it angrily to the back of a broom cupboard.

I was on my guard not to do the same again, but that one walk had labeled me an eccentric — a label that doubtless would be with me for life. In England eccentrics have always been viewed sympathetically or even admiringly, as long as they had the excuse of being rich. America, in those years, was hardly ready for such behavior; the country was approaching the turn of the century with a certain prudish reticence — perhaps not in New York or San Francisco, but certainly in my town. A French mother and a Persian hat — that was far too exotic for Annapolis.

That was the dark side, but my moment of folly also had its bright moments. It won me, on the spot, an undeserved reputation as a great explorer of the Orient. The director of the local newspaper, Matthias Webb, who had got wind of my walk, suggested that I write an article about my experience in Persia.

The last time that the name of Persia had been printed on the pages of the *Annapolis Gazette and Herald* was back in 1856, I believe, when a transatlantic liner, which was the pride of Cunard and the first ever metal-framed paddle-boat, collided with an iceberg. Seven sailors from our county perished. The unfortunate ship was called the *Persia.*

Seafaring people do not play games with the signs of destiny. I also thought it necessary to remark in the introduction to my article that the term "Persia" was incorrect, and that the Persians themselves called their country "Iran," which was an abbreviation of a very ancient expression "Aïrania Vaedja," meaning "Land of the Aryans."

I then mentioned Omar Khayyam, the only Persian that most of my readers might have heard of, quoting one of his quatrains that was imbued with a deep skepticism. "Paradise and Hell. Might someone have visited these unique regions?" It provided a useful preamble before I expounded over the course of some dense paragraphs on the numerous religions that, since the dawn of time, have prospered on Persian soil, such as Zoroastrianism, Manicheism, Sunni and Shiite Islam, Hassan Sabbah's Ismaili variant, and, nearer our time, the *Babis*, the *Sheikhis*, and the *Bahais*. I did not omit to mentioned that our word "paradise" comes originally from the Persian word "*paradaeza*," which means "garden."

Matthias Webb congratulated me on my apparent erudition, but when I became encouraged by his praise and suggested making a more regular contribution he seemed embarrassed and suddenly irritated.

"I really would like to put you to the test, if you will promise to drop this annoying habit of peppering your text with barbarian words!"

My face betrayed my surprise and incredulity. Webb had his reasons.

"The *Gazette* does not have the means to take on, permanently, a Persian specialist. However, if you agree to take charge of all the foreign news, and if you think you are capable of making distant countries accessible to our compatriots, there is a place for you on this newspaper. What your articles lose in profundity they will gain in range."

We both managed to smile again; he offered me a peace cigar before continuing:

"Just yesterday, abroad did not exist for us. The Orient stopped at Cape Cod. Now suddenly, under the pretext of the end of one century and the start of another, our peaceful city has been laid hold of by the world's troubles."

I must point out that our discussion was taking place in 1899, a little after the Spanish-American War, which took our troops not only to Cuba and Puerto Rico but also the Philippines. Never before had the United States exercised its authority so far from its shores. Our victory over the dilapidated Spanish empire had cost us only two thousand four hundred dead, but in Annapolis, seat of the Naval Academy, every loss could have been that of a relative, a friend, or an actual or potential fiancé; the most conservative of my fellow citizens saw in President MacKinley a dangerous adventurer.

That was not Webb's opinion at all, but he had to pander to his readers' phobias. To get the point over to me, this serious and graying paterfamilias stood up, uttered a roar, pulled a hilarious face, and curled his fingers up as if they were the claws of a monster.

"The tough world outside is striding towards Annapolis, and your mission, Benjamin Lesage, is to reassure your compatriots."

It was a heavy responsibility, of which I acquitted myself without too much ado. My sources of information were articles in newspapers from Paris, London, and of course New York, Washington, and Baltimore. Out of everything I wrote about the Boer War, the 1904–5 conflict between the Czar and the Mikado, or the troubles in Russia, I am afraid that not a single line deserves to go down in history.

It was only on the subject of Persia that my career as a journalist can be mentioned. I am proud to say that the *Gazette* was the first American newspaper to foresee the explosion that was going to take place and news of which was going to occupy much column space in the last months of 1906 in all the world's newspapers. For the first, and probably the last, time articles from the *Annapolis Gazette and Herald* were quoted, often even reproduced verbatim, in more than sixty newspapers in the South and on the East Coast.

My town and newspaper owe that much to me. And I owe it to Shireen. It was in fact thanks to her, and not to my meager experience in Persia that I was able to understand the full extent of the events that were brewing.

I had not received anything from my princess for over seven years. If she owed me a response on the matter of the *Manuscript*, she had supplied me with one that was frustrating but precise. I did not expect to hear anything more from her, which does not mean that I was not hoping to. With every mail delivery the idea ran through my mind and I looked over the envelopes for her handwriting, for a stamp with Persian writing, a number five shaped like a heart. I did not dread my daily disappointment, but experienced it as a homage to dreams that were still haunting me.

I have to say that at that time my family had just left Annapolis and settled in Baltimore, where my father's most important business was to be concentrated. He envisaged founding his own bank along with two of his young brothers. As for me, I had decided to stay in the house where I was born, with our old half-deaf cook, in a city where I had few good friends. I do not doubt that my solitude amplified the fervor of my waiting.

Then, one day, Shireen finally wrote to me. There was not a word about the *Samarkand Manuscript* and nothing personal in the long letter, except perhaps the fact that she began it with "Dear distant friend." There followed a day-by-day report of the events unfolding around her. Her account abounded in painstaking details, none of which was superfluous, even when they seemed so to my vulgar eyes. I was in love with her wonderful intellect and flattered that she had chosen to direct the fruit of her thoughts to me of all men.

From that moment I lived to the rhythm of her monthly letters, which were a vibrant chronicle and which I would have published as they were if she had not demanded absolute discretion from me. She did authorize me, however, to use the information contained in them, which I did shamelessly, drawing on them and sometimes translating and using whole passages with neither italics nor quotation marks.

My way of presenting the facts to my readers, however, differed greatly from hers. For example, the Princess never would have thought of writing:

"The Persian revolution was triggered when a Belgian minister had the disastrous idea of disguising himself as a mullah."

That, however, was not so far from the truth, although for Shireen the beginnings of the revolt were discernible at the time of the Shah's course of treatment at Contrexéville in 1900. Wanting to go there with his retinue, the Shah needed money. His treasury was empty as usual and he had asked the Czar for a loan and was granted 22.5 million roubles.

There was almost never such a poisoned gift. In order to make sure that their neighbor to the south, who was permanently on the brink of bankruptcy, would be able to pay back such a large sum, the St. Petersburg authorities demanded and succeeded in gaining control of the Persian customs whose receipts were now to be paid directly to them. For a period of seventy-five years! Aware of the enormity of this privilege and fearing lest the other European powers take umbrage at this complete control over the foreign trade of Persia, the Czar avoided entrusting the customs to his own subjects and preferred to have King Leopold II take charge of them on his behalf.

That is how thirty or so Belgian functionaries came to the Shah's court and their influence was to grow to dizzy heights. The most eminent of them, namely a certain Monsieur Naus, managed to haul himself up to the highest spheres of power. On the eve of the revolution, he was a member of the Supreme Council of the Kingdom, Minister of Post and Telegraph, General Treasurer of Persia, Head of the Passport Department, and Director General of the Customs. Amongst other things, his job was to reorganize the whole fiscal system and it was to him that the new tax on freight carried by mule was attributed.

It goes without saying that by that time Monsieur Naus had become the most hated man in Persia, the symbol of foreign control. From time to time a voice would arise to demand his recall, a demand that seemed the more justified as he had neither a reputation for incorruptibility nor the alibi of competence. However, he stayed in place, supported by the Czar, or rather by the retrograde and fearsome cabal who surrounded the latter and whose political objectives were now being expressed aloud in the official press of St. Petersburg — the exercise of undivided tutelage over Persia and the Persian Gulf.

Monsieur Naus's position seemed unshakeable and it remained so until the moment his protector was shaken. That happened more quickly than anyone in Persia had dreamt and it was precipitated by two major events. First, the war with Japan, which to the whole world's surprise ended with the defeat of the Czar and the destruction of his fleet. Then the anger of the Russians, which was fueled by the humiliation inflicted upon them because of incompetent leaders, the *Potemkin* rebellion, the Cronstadt mutiny, the Sebastopol uprising, and the events in Moscow. I shall not discuss in detail these facts, which no one has yet forgotten, but I shall content myself by emphasizing the devastating effect that they had on Persia, in particularly in April 1906 when Nicholas II was forced to convene a parliament, the Duma.

It was in this atmosphere that the most banal event occurred. A masked ball was held at the residence of a Belgian functionary which Monsieur Naus decided to attend dressed up as a mullah. There were chuckles, laughs, and applause; people gathered around him to congratulate him and posed for photographs with him. A few days later hundreds of copies of this picture were being distributed in the Tehran bazaar.

212

34

S hireen had sent me a copy of this document. I still have it and
sometimes I still cast a nostalgic and amused glance at it. It shows,
seated on a carpet spread out amongst the trees of a garden, about
forty men and women dressed in Turkish, Japanese, or Austrian garb.
In the center foreground appears Monsieur Naus, so well disguised
that with his white beard and salt-and-pepper mustache he could easily be taken for a pious patriarch. Shireen had written on the back of
the photograph, "Unpunished for so many crimes, penalized for a trifle."

It assuredly was not Monsieur Naus's intention to mock the religious. On that occasion he could only be found guilty of naïveté, of
a lack of tact and a touch of bad taste. His real mistake, since he was
acting as the Czar's Trojan horse, was not understanding that, for a
while, he should allow himself to lie low.

The distribution of the picture caused some angry gatherings and
some incidents. The bazaar shut its gates. First of all Naus's departure
was demanded, then that of the whole government. Tracts were handed

out demanding the institution of a parliament, as in Russia. For years secret societies had been at work amongst the population, invoking the name of Jamaladin and sometimes even that of Mirza Reza, and were now transformed by circumstances into a symbol of the struggle against absolutism.

The Cossacks surrounded the districts in the center of the city. Certain rumors, propagated by the authorities, gave out that unprecedented repression was about to fall upon the protesters and that the bazaar would be opened by the armed forces and left for the troops to pillage — a menace that had terrified the merchants for centuries.

That is why, on July 19, 1906, a delegation of tradesmen and moneychangers from the bazaar went to see the British chargé d'affaires on a matter of urgency: if people in danger of being arrested were to come and take refuge in the legation, would they be afforded protection? The response was positive. The visitors retired, showing expressions of gratitude and making solemn bows.

That very evening, my friend Fazel presented himself at the legation with a group of friends and was enthusiastically received. Although he was hardly thirty years old, he was, as his father's heir, already one of the richest merchants in the bazaar. However, his rank was even more elevated by his vast culture and his influence was great amongst his peers. To a man of his status, the British diplomats had to offer one of the rooms reserved for visitors of distinction. However, he turned down the offer and, mentioning the heat, expressed his desire to install himself in the legation's vast garden. He said that he had brought with him a tent for that purpose, along with a small carpet and a few books. Tight-lipped and frowning, his hosts watched as all these items were unpacked.

The next day thirty other merchants came in the same way to profit from the right of asylum. Three days later, on July 23, there were eight hundred and sixty. By July 26 there were five thousand — and twelve thousand by August 1.

This Persian town planted in an English garden was a strange sight. There were tents all around, clustered together by guild. Life there had been speedily organized, with a kitchen being set up behind the guards pavilion from which enormous cauldrons were sent around to the different "districts," each sitting lasting three hours.

214

There was no disorder and very little noise. Taking refuge, or taking *bast* as the Persians say, means giving oneself over to a strictly passive resistance in the shelter of a sanctuary of which there were several in the area of Tehran: the mausoleum of Shah Adbul-Azim, the royal stables, and the smallest *bast* of all, the wheeled cannon in Topkhane Square — if a fugitive clung to it, the forces of order no longer had any right to lay hands on him. However, Jamaladin's experience had shown that the powers that be would not tolerate this form of protest for long. The only immunity that they recognized was that of the foreign legations.

To the English, every refugee had brought his *kalyan* and his dreams. From tent to tent there was a world of difference. Around Fazel was the modernist elite; they were not just a handful but hundreds of young and old men, organized into *anjuman* — which were more or less secret societies. Their debates raged ceaselessly around the topics of Japan, Russia, and particularly France, whose language they spoke and whose books and newspapers they assiduously read — the France of Saint-Simon, Robespierre, Rousseau, and Waldeck-Rousseau. Fazel had carefully cut out the section of the law on the separation of church and state that had been voted on a year earlier in Paris. He had translated it and handed it out to his friends and they were now debating it heatedly albeit in hushed tones, for not far from their circle there was a gathering of mullahs.

The clergy itself was divided. One party rejected everything that came from Europe, including the very idea of democracy, parliament, and modernity. "How," they said, "could we need a constitution when we have the Quran?" To which the modernists replied that the Book had left to men the task of governing themselves democratically since it declared, "Let your affairs be a matter of mutual consent." Cunningly they added that if, upon the death of the Prophet, the Muslims had had a constitution organizing the institutions of their embryonic state, they would not have seen the bloody struggles for succession that led to the ousting of the Imam Ali.

Beyond the debate on doctrine, the majority of the mullahs nevertheless accepted the idea of a constitution to put an end to the arbitrary nature of royal rule. Having come in their hundreds to take *bast*, they delighted in comparing their act to the Prophet's migration to Medina and the sufferings of the people to those of Hussein, the son of Imam Ali, whose passion is the closest Muslim equivalent to that of Christ. In the legation's gardens, professional mourners, the *rozeh-khwan*, recounted to their audience the sufferings of Hussein. People cried, flagellated themselves, and grieved unrestrainedly for Hussein, for themselves, and for a Persia that was astray in a hostile world and had sunk over the centuries into unending decadence. Fazel's friends distanced themselves from these displays. Jamaladin had taught them to feel disdain for the *rozeh-khwan*. They could only listen to them with worried condescension.

I was struck by a cold reflection written by Shireen in one of her letters. "Persia is ill," she wrote. "There are several doctors at her bedside, some modern and some traditional, and each one offers his own remedies. The future belongs to him who can effect a cure. If this revolution triumphs, the mullahs will have to turn themselves into democrats; if it fails, the democrats will have to turn themselves into mullahs."

For the moment they were all in the same trench, in the same garden. On August 7, the legation counted sixteen thousand *bastis*, the streets of the city were empty, and any merchant of renown had "emigrated." The Shah had to give in. On August 15, less than a month from the start of the *bast*, he announced that elections would be organized to elect a national consultative assembly by direct suffrage in Tehran and indirect suffrage in the provinces.

The first parliament in the history of Persia met on October 7. To read out the Shah's speech, he judiciously sent a veteran opponent, Prince Malkom Khan, an Armenian from Isfahan and a companion of Jamaladin, the very same man who had put him up during his stay in London. He was a magnificent old man in the British mold who had dreamt throughout his whole life of standing in front of Parliament as he read out the speech of a constitutional sovereign to the representatives of the people.

Those who wish to examine this page of history more closely should not look for the name of Malkom Khan in documents of the time. Today, as in the time of Khayyam, Persia does not remember its leaders by their names, but by their titles, such as "Sun of the Kingdom," "Pillar of the Religion," or "Shadow of the Sultan." To the man who had the honor of inaugurating the era of democracy the most prestigious title of all was given: Nizam al-Mulk. Disconcerting Persia, so immutable in its convulsions but how unchanged after so many metamorphoses!

35

It was a privilege to be present at the awakening of the Orient. It was a moment of intense emotion, enthusiasm, and doubt. What ideas, both brilliant and monstrous, had been able to sprout in its sleeping brain? What would it do as it woke up? Was it going to pounce blindly upon those who had shaken it? I was receiving letters from readers with anguished requests that I look into the future. They still remembered the Boxer Revolt in Peking in 1900, the foreign diplomats who were taken hostage, the troubles the expeditionary force came up against with the old Empress, the fearsome Daughter of Heaven, and they were afraid of Asia. Would Persia be any different? I replied with a definite "yes," putting my trust in the emerging democracy. A constitution had just been promulgated in fact, as well as a charter of rights for the citizens. Clubs were coming into being every day, as well as newspapers: ninety dailies and weeklies in the space of a few months. They were entitled *Civilization, Equality, Liberty,* or more pompously, *Trumpets of the Resurrection.* They were frequently quoted in the British press or the opposition Russian newspapers such as the liberal *Ryesh* and *Sovremenny Mir*, which was close to the social democrats. A satirical newspaper met with overwhelming success from its very first issue. Its cartoonists' favorite targets were the shady courtiers, agents of the Czar, and, above all, the false zealots.

Shireen was jubilant. "Last Friday," she wrote, "some young mullahs tried to raise a mob in the bazaar. They called the constitution a heretical innovation and tried to incite the crowd to march on Baharistan, the seat of the Parliament — but without success. They shouted themselves hoarse, but to no avail since the townspeople remained indifferent. From time to time a man would stop, listen to the end of some piece of invective, and then walk off shrugging his shoulders. Finally three of the city's most respected *ulema* arrived and with no further ado invited the preachers to go home by the shortest route and to keep their eyes cast below knee level. I can hardly believe it — fanaticism is dead in Persia."

I used this last phrase as the title of my best article. I was so imbued with the Princess's enthusiasm that what I wrote was a real act of faith. The director of the *Gazette* suggested that I make it more balanced, but the readers approved of my ardor, judging by the ever-increasing number of letters I was receiving.

One of them bore the signature of a certain Howard C. Baskerville, a student at Princeton University in New Jersey. He had just received his B.A. and wanted to go to Persia to observe the events I was describing. One of his expressions had stopped me in my tracks: "I bear the deep conviction that if, at the beginning of this century, the Orient does not manage to wake up, the West soon will not be able to sleep any more." In my reply I encouraged him to make this trip and promised to provide him, when he had made his decision, with the names of some friends who would be able to receive him.

A few weeks later, Baskerville came to Annapolis to tell me in person that he had obtained the position of teacher in Tabriz at the Memorial Boys' School, which was run by the American Presbyterian Mission; he was to teach young boys English and science. He was leaving immediately and requested advice and letters of recommendation. I eagerly congratulated him and promised, without thinking too much about it, to stop by and see him should I be in Persia.

I was not thinking of going there so soon. It was not that I lacked the desire to do so, but I was still hesitant about making the trip because of the spurious accusations hanging over me. Was I not considered an accomplice to a regicide? In spite of the rapid changes that had taken place in Tehran, I feared being arrested at the border because of some dusty warrant and not being able to notify my friends or my legation.

Baskerville's departure nevertheless prodded me into taking some steps to straighten out my position. I had promised never to write to Shireen, and not wishing to risk the loss of her letters, I wrote to Fazel, whose influence I knew to be growing daily. In the National Assembly where the big decisions were made he was the most sought-after deputy.

His answer reached me three months later. It was warm and friendly and most importantly it was accompanied by an official paper bearing the seal of the Ministry of Justice and stating that I had been cleared of all suspicion of complicity in the assassination of the old Shah and accordingly I was authorized to travel freely throughout all the provinces of Persia.

Without waiting a second longer I set off for Marseille and from there to Salonika and Constantinople and then Trebizond. Riding a mule, I skirted around Mount Ararat and finally reached Tabriz.

I arrived there a on a hot June day. I settled myself into the caravansary in the Armenian quarter as the sun was level with the rooftops. However, I was eager to see Baskerville as soon as I could, and with this intention I went off to the Presbyterian Mission, which was a low sprawling building freshly painted brilliant white and set amongst a forest of apricot trees. There were two discreet crosses on the gate, and on the roof above the main doorway there was a banner studded with stars.

A Persian gardener came to meet me and take me to the office of the pastor, who was a large red-haired man with a beard and the looks of a sailor. He gave me a firm and welcoming handshake. Before even asking me to take a seat he offered me a bed for the duration of my stay.

"We have rooms that we keep prepared for our countrymen who surprise us and honor us with their visits. You are not being accorded any special treatment. I am just happy to be able to follow a custom which has been practiced as long as this mission has been in existence."

I expressed my sincere regrets.

"I have already placed my baggage at the caravansary and I am planning to move on the day after tomorrow to Tehran."

"Tabriz deserves more than one hurried day. How can you come this far without agreeing to spend an idle day or two in the labyrinths of the largest bazaar in the Orient or without going to see the ruins of the Blue Mosque which was mentioned in the *Thousand and One Nights*? Travelers are in too great a rush these days, in a rush to arrive — whatever it takes. But you do not arrive only at your destination. At every stage of the journey you arrive somewhere and with every step you can discover a hidden facet of our planet. All you have to do is look, wish, believe, and love."

He seemed sincerely upset that I was such a bad traveler and I felt obliged to justify myself.

"In fact I have some urgent work to do in Tehran. I only made a detour via Tabriz in order to see a friend of mine who is teaching at your mission, Howard Baskerville."

At the mere mention of this name the atmosphere became heavy. There was no more joviality, animation, or paternal reproach. Only an embarrassed look that I took to be evasive and utter silence. Then he spoke:

"Are you a friend of Howard's?"

"In a manner of speaking, I am responsible for his coming to Persia."

"What a heavy responsibility!"

In vain I tried to make out a smile on his lips. He seemed suddenly old and worn. His shoulders drooped and he seemed almost to be entreating me.

"I have been running this mission for fifteen years. Our school is the best in the city and I go so far as to believe that our work is useful and Christian. Those who take part in our activities have at heart this country's progress, otherwise, believe you me, nothing would force them to come so far in order to take on an environment that is often hostile."

I had no reason to doubt him, but this man's eagerness to defend himself put me off him. I had only been in his office for a few minutes, I had not accused him of anything and had not asked him for anything. I merely nodded politely. He continued:

"When a missionary displays indifference towards the difficulties facing the Persians or when a teacher no longer derives any joy from his students' progress, I strongly advise him to go back to the United States. Sometimes enthusiasm sags, above all with the younger teachers. What could be more human?"

Having spoken this preamble, the Reverend sat silent and his stubby hands nervously fingered his pipe. He seemed to be having diffiiculty in finding his words. I thought it my duty to make the task easier for him. I adopted my most detached tone:

"Are you trying to say that Howard has become discouraged after these few months and that his love of the East has turned out to be a passing fancy?"

He jumped up.

"Good Lord, no. Not Baskerville! I was trying to explain what happens occasionally with some of our recruits. With your friend it is the opposite and I am infinitely more worried by that. In one sense, he is the best teacher we have ever employed. His students are making wonderful progress, their parents swear by him, and the mission has never received so many presents — sheep, chicken, halva — all in honor of Baskerville. The problem with him is that he refuses to behave like a foreigner. If he were just happy to dress like the people here, to live on *pilau* and to greet me in the vernacular of the country, I would have been happy to smile at all that. But Baskerville is not the sort of man who stops at appearances and he has thrown himself wholeheartedly into the political battle. In class he praises the constitution and encourages his students to criticize the Russians, the English, and the Shah and the backward-looking mullahs. I even suspect him of being what they call here a 'son of Adam,' that is to say a member of the secret societies."

He sighed.

"Yesterday morning a demonstration took place in front of our gate, led by two of the most eminent religious chiefs, demanding that Baskerville leave or, failing that, purely and simply that the mission close down. Three hours later another demonstration broke out in the same spot in support of Howard demanding that he be kept on. You must understand that if a conflict like this goes on we will not be able to stay in this city much longer."

"I suppose that you have already spoken of this with Howard."

"A hundred times, and a hundred different ways. He invariably replies that the reawakening of the Orient is more important than the mission's fate and that if the constitutional revolution fails we will be obliged to leave in any case. Naturally I can always end his contract, but such an act will not be understood and will only arouse hostility amongst that section of the population that has always supported us. The only solution is for Baskerville to cool his ardor. Perhaps you can reason with him?"

While not formally agreeing to the undertaking, I asked to see Howard. A glimmer of triumph suddenly lit up the Reverend's ginger beard. He jumped up from his seat.

"Follow me," he said. "I shall show you Baskerville. I believe I know where he is. Watch him in silence — you will understand my reasons and share my feelings of helplessness."

BOOK FOUR

A Poet at Sea

We are the pawns, and Heaven is the player;
This is plain truth, and not a mode of speech.
We move about the chessboard of the world.
Then drop into the casket of the void.

OMAR KHAYYAM

36

I n the ocher dusk of a walled garden there was a groaning crowd.
How was I going to recognize Baskerville? Everyone's face was so
brown! I leant against a tree, waiting and watching. The doorway of a
lighted cabin had been made into an improvised theater. The *rozeh-
khawan*, storyteller and mourner, was drawing out the tears of the
faithful along with their shouts and their blood.

A man stepped out of the shadows, a volunteer for pain. His feet
were bare, his torso naked, and he had a chain wound around each
hand: he threw the chains up in the air and let them fall behind his
shoulders on to his back: the chains were smooth, bruising and
pummeling his flesh, but it did not give — it took thirty to fifty
strokes for the first blood to appear as a black spot which then started
pouring out in fascinating spurts. It was the theater of suffering, the
age-old game of the passion.

The beating became more vigorous as his noisy breathing was ech-
oed by the crowd. The blows went on and the storyteller spoke louder

to make his voice carry over the sound of the flagellation. Then an actor sprang up and threatened the audience with his saber. His grimaces first attracted curses and then volleys of stones. He did not stay on the scene for long. Soon his victim appeared and the crowd gave out a roar. I myself could not hold back a shout, for the man dragging himself along the ground had been decapitated.

I turned horrified to the Reverend; he reassured me with a cold smile and whispered:

"It is an old trick. They get a child, or a very small man, and on his head they place a sheep's head which is turned upside-down so that its bloody neck points upward. Then they wrap a white cloth around it with a hole in the appropriate place. As you can see the effect is transfixing."

He drew on his pipe. The headless man hopped and wheeled around the stage for minutes on end, until he gave up his place to a strange person in tears.

"Baskerville!"

I gave the Reverend another questioning look. He did no more than raise his eyebrows enigmatically.

The strangest thing was that Howard was dressed as an American, even sporting a top hat, which struck me as irresistibly amusing in spite of the pervading atmosphere of tragedy.

The crowd was still yelling and lamenting, and, as far as I could see, no one else's face showed the least hint of amusement except the pastor's. Finally he deigned to enlighten me:

"There is always a European in these funeral rites, and curiously, he is one of the 'goodies.' Tradition has it that a Frankish ambassador at the Omayyad court was moved by the death of Hussein, the supreme martyr of the Shiites, and that he showed his disapproval of the crime so noisily that he himself was put to death. Naturally, there is not always a European to hand who can appear in the spectacle, so they use a Turk or a light-skinned Persian. However, since Baskerville has been at Tabriz they always call upon him to play this role. He plays it splendidly — and he really cries!"

At that moment the man with the sword came back and pranced boisterously around Baskerville, who stood still and then flicked his hat off, revealing his blond hair which was carefully parted to the left.

Then, with the slowness of a zombie, he fell to his knees and stretched out on the ground. A beam of light lit up his clean-shaven child's face and his cheekbones, which were puffed up with tears, and a nearby hand threw a cluster of petals on to his black suit.

I could not hear the crowd any longer. My eyes were riveted to my friend and I was waiting anxiously for him to get up again. The ceremony seemed to go on forever and I was impatient to retrieve him.

An hour later we met around bowls of pomegranate soup at the mission. The pastor left us alone and we ate amid an embarrassed silence. Baskerville's eyes were still red.

"It takes me a while to become a Westerner again," he apologized with a broken smile.

"Take your time, the century has just begun."

He coughed, brought the hot bowl to his lips, and became lost again in silent thought.

Then haltingly he said:

"When I arrived in this country, I could not understand how grown and bearded men could sob and work themselves up over a murder committed twelve hundred years ago. Now I have understood. If the Persians live in the past it is because the past is their homeland and the present is a foreign country where nothing belongs to them. Everything that is a symbol of modern life and greater freedom for us, for them is a symbol of foreign domination: the roads — Russia; the railways, telegraph, and banking system — England; the postal service — Austria-Hungary . . ."

"And the teaching of science, that's Mr. Baskerville from the American Presbyterian Mission."

"Exactly. What choice do the people of Tabriz have? To send their children to a traditional school where they learn by rote the same misshapen phrases that their ancestors were repeating back in the twelfth century; or to send them to my class where they receive an education that is the same as that of young Americans, but in the shadow of a cross and a star-spangled banner? My students will be the better, the more adept, and the more useful for their country, but how can we prevent the others from seeing them as renegades? In the very first week of my stay I asked myself that question, and it was during a ceremony like the one you have just been watching that I found the solution.

"I had mingled with the crowd and groans were being emitted all around me. Watching those devastated faces, bathed in tears, and gazing at those haggard, worried, and entreating eyes, the whole misery of Persia appeared to me — they were tattered souls besieged by never-ending mourning. Without realizing it, my tears started to flow. Someone in the crowd noticed, they looked at me and were moved, and then they pushed me towards the stage where they made me act out the role of the Frankish ambassador. The next day my students' parents came to see me; they were happy that they could now answer the people who had been reproaching them for sending their children to the Presbyterian Mission: 'I have entrusted my son to the teacher who cried for the Imam Hussein.' Some religious chiefs were irritated, but their hostility towards me can be attributed to my success. They prefer foreigners to behave like foreigners."

I understood his behavior better, but I was still skeptical:

"So, for yóu, the solution to Persia's problem is to join in with the crowds of mourners!"

"I did not say that. Crying is not a recipe for anything. Nor is it a skill. It is simply a naked, naive, and pathetic gesture. No one should be forced to shed tears. The only important thing is not to scorn other people's tragedy. When they saw me crying, when they saw that I had thrown off the sovereign indifference of a foreigner, they came to tell me confidentially that crying serves no purpose and that Persia does not need any extra mourners and that the best thing I could do would be to provide the children of Tabriz with an adequate education."

"Wise words. I was going to tell you the same thing."

"Except that if I had not cried, they never would have come to talk to me. If they had not seen me crying, they would never have let me tell the pupils that this Shah was rotten and that the religious chiefs of Tabriz were hardly any better!"

"Did you say that in class?"

"Yes, I said that. This young beardless American, this young teacher at the Presbyterian Mission denounced both the crown and the turban and my students agreed with him. So did their parents. Only the Reverend was outraged."

Seeing that I was perplexed he added:

"I have also spoken to the boys about Khayyam. I told them that millions of Americans and Europeans had made his *Rubaiyaat* their bedside book and I made them learn Fitzgerald's verses by heart. The next day, a grandfather came to see me. He was very moved by what his grandson had told him and he said, 'We too have great respect for the American poets!' Naturally he was completely unable to name a single one, but that makes no difference. It was his way of expressing his pride and gratitude. Unfortunately, not all the parents reacted in the same way. One of them came to complain to me. In the pastor's presence he yelled at me, 'Khayyam was a drunkard and an impious man!' I replied, 'By saying that you are not insulting Khayyam but praising drunkenness and ungodliness!' The Reverend almost choked on the spot."

Howard laughed like a child. He was incorrigible and disarming.

"So you hail everything they accuse you of! Might you also be a 'son of Adam'?"

"Did the Reverend tell you that too? I have the impression that you both spoke a great deal about me."

"We have no one else in common."

"I will not hide anything from you. My conscience is as pure as that of a new-born babe. About two months ago a man came to see me. He was a huge man with a mustache, but quite timid. He asked if I could give a talk at the *anjuman* — the club of which he was a member, and you will never guess on what subject! On Darwin's theory! I found the matter amusing and touching, given the atmosphere of political upheaval that reigns in this country, and I accepted. I gathered together everything I could lay my hands on about Darwin. I set out the theories of his detractors. I think that my performance must have been boring, but the room was crowded and they listened to me religiously. After that I went to other meetings on more diverse subjects. There is an immense thirst for knowledge among these people. They are also the most determined Constitutionalists. Sometimes I would pass by their meeting hall to hear the latest news from Tehran. You ought to meet them; they dream of the same world as you and I."

37

In the evening few stalls stayed open in the Tabriz bazaar, but the streets were alive and men were sitting around talking at the crossroads, setting up circles of wicker chairs and of *kalyan* pipes, whose smoke was gradually displacing the thousand smells of the day. I followed close on Howard's heels as he turned from one alley into another without a second glance; from time to time he would stop to greet the parent of one of his students, and the street urchins everywhere stopped their games and scattered as he passed.

We finally arrived in front of a gate that was almost eaten away by rust. My companion pushed it open and we went through a small overgrown garden and up to a mud-brick house whose door, after seven raps, opened creaking on to a huge room lit up by a row of storm lamps hung from the ceiling that a draught of air was swaying ceaselessly. The people present must have been used to it, but I very quickly felt as if I was on board a flimsy raft. I could no longer focus on anyone's face and felt the need to lie down as soon as possible and close my eyes for a few moments. Baskerville was not unknown at the "sons of Adam" meeting — he caused quite a stir when he walked in, and as I had accompanied him I also had the right to some fraternal embraces, which were duly redoubled when Howard revealed that his arrival in Persia was partly due to me.

When I thought it was time for me to sit down against a wall, a large man stood up at the end of the room. He had a long white cape draped over his shoulders which set him apart from the others as the most eminent person in the meeting. He took a step towards me: "Benjamin!"

I stood up again, took two steps, and rubbed my eyes. "Fazel!" We fell into each other's arms with an oath of surprise.

"Mr. Lesage was a friend of Sayyid Jamaladin!"

Immediately I stopped being a distinguished visitor and became an historic monument, or even a religious relic. People came up to me with awe, which was quite embarrassing.

I presented Howard to Fazel. They knew each other only by reputation. Fazel had not been to Tabriz for more than a year, even though it was his birthplace. Moreover, there was something unusual and unsettling about the whole evening, together with Fazel being there within those flaking walls and under those dancing lights. Was he not one of the leaders of the democratic party in Parliament, a pillar of the Constitutional Revolution? Was this the moment for him to be away from the capital? These were the questions I put to him. He appeared embarrassed. However, I had spoken quietly in French. He looked furtively at the men next to him, and then by way of an answer he said, "Where are you staying?"

"In the caravansary in the Armenian quarter."

"I shall come to see you during the night."

Towards midnight we met again, six of us, in my room. There were Baskerville, myself, Fazel, and three of his companions whom he introduced hurriedly for reasons of secrecy only by their first names.

"You asked at the *anjuman* why I was here and not in Tehran. Well, it is because the capital is already lost as far as the constitution goes. I could not state it in these terms to thirty people, I would have caused panic. But that is the truth."

We were all too stunned to react. He explained:

"Two weeks ago a journalist from St. Petersberg came to see me. He was the correspondent of *Ryesh*. His name is Panoff but he writes under the pseudonym 'Tane.'"

I had heard about him and his articles were often quoted in the London press.

"He is a social democrat," Fazel continued, "and an enemy of Czarism, but when he arrived in Tehran some months ago he managed to hide his beliefs, worked his way into the Russian legation, and by some chance or other or even by some plan, he managed to lay his hands on some compromising documents including a project for a coup d'état that the Cossacks would carry out in order to re-impose an absolute monarchy. It was all written down in black and white. The underworld was to be given free rein in the bazaar in order to sap the merchants' confidence in the new regime, and some religious chiefs were to address petitions to the Shah asking him to invalidate the constitution by reason of its being against Islam. Naturally, Panoff was taking a risk in bringing me those documents. I thanked him for them and immediately asked for an extraordinary meeting of Parliament. Having exposed the facts in detail, I demanded that the Shah be dismissed and replaced by one of his young sons, that the Cossack brigade be broken up, and the clerics incriminated in the documents be arrested. Several speakers came up to the dais to express their indignation and to support my proposals.

"Suddenly an usher came to inform us that the ministers plenipotentiary of Russia and England were in the building and that they had an urgent note to convey to us. The session was suspended and the president of the *Majlis* and the Prime Minister went out; when they returned they looked like death. The diplomats had come to warn them that if the Shah were deposed, the two Powers would consider themselves regrettably obliged to intervene militarily. Not only were they getting ready to strangle us, but we were being forbidden to defend ourselves!"

"Why such resolve?" Baskerville asked, appalled.

"The Czar does not want a democracy within his borders. The very word 'parliament' makes him tremble with rage."

"But even so, that is not the case with Britain!"

"No. Except that if the Persians managed to govern themselves in an adult manner, that could give ideas to the Indians! And England would then just have to pack its bags. Then there is oil. In 1901 a British subject, Mr. Knox d'Arcy, obtained for the sum of twenty thousand pounds sterling the right to exploit oil reserves throughout the Persian empire. So far production has been insignificant, but a few months ago immense reserves were found in the Bakhtiari tribal areas; doubtless you have heard talk of this already. These reserves could represent an important source of revenue for the country. I therefore asked Parliament to revise the agreement with London so that we might obtain more equitable conditions. Most of the deputies agreed with me. Since then the English minister has no longer invited me to the legation."

"But it is in the legation's gardens that the *bast* is taking place," I said pensively.

"The English consider that Russian influence is currently too great, and that Russia is only leaving them the congruent portion of the Persian cake, so they encouraged us to protest and opened their gardens to us. It is even said that they were the ones who printed the photograph that compromised Monsieur Naus. When our movement triumphed, London managed to obtain an agreement from the Czar to share the country. The north of Persia would be the Russian zone of influence and the south would be the private property of England. Once the British got what they wanted, our democracy suddenly ceased to interest them. Like the Czar they can only see it as an inconvenience and would prefer to see it disappear."

"By what right!" Baskerville exploded.

Fazel gave him a paternal smile before carrying on with his account:

"After the visit of the two diplomats, the deputies were disheartened. They were unable to confront so many enemies at the same time and could do no better than to lay the blame on the unfortunate Panoff. Several speakers accused him of being a forger and an anarchist whose sole aim was to provoke a war between Persia and Russia. The journalist had come with me to Parliament and I had left him in an office near the door to the great hall so that he could give his testimony should it be necessary. Now the deputies were asking for him to be arrested and delivered to the Czar's legation and a motion had been put forward to that effect.

"This man who had helped us against his own government was going to be handed over to the executioners! I who am so calm by nature could no longer hold myself back. I jumped up on to a chair and shouted like one possessed, 'I swear, by the soil which covers my father, that if this man is arrested I will call the "sons of Adam" to arms and set this parliament awash in blood. No one who votes for this motion will leave here alive!' They could have lifted my immunity and arrested me too, but they did not dare. They suspended the session until the next day. That very night I left the capital for my birthplace, where I arrived today. Panoff came with me and is now hiding somewhere in Tabriz while waiting to leave the country."

We talked and talked and soon dawn surprised us. The first calls to prayer sounded and the light became brighter. We debated and constructed a thousand gloomy futures and then debated again, too exhausted to stop. Baskerville stretched out, stopped in full flight, consulted his watch, and stood up again like a sleep-walker and gave his neck a thorough scratch:

"My God, it's already six o'clock, a night with no sleep, how can I face my pupils? And what will the Reverend say seeing me come back at this hour?"

"You can always pretend that you spent the night with a woman!"

Howard, however, was no longer in the mood to smile.

I do not want to speak of coincidence, since chance did not play a large role in the affair, but I am duty bound to point out that, just as Fazel finished his description of the plot being hatched against the young Persian democracy based on the documents that had been spirited away by Panoff, the coup d'état had already begun.

In fact, as I later learnt, it was towards four o'clock in the morning of that Wednesday, June 23, 1908, that a contingent of one thousand Cossacks, commanded by Colonel Liakhov, set off toward the Baharistan, the seat of the parliament, in the heart of Tehran. The building was surrounded and its exits under guard. Members of a local *anjuman*, who had noticed the troop movements, ran over to a neighboring college, where a telephone had recently been installed, in order to call some deputies and certain religious democrats such as Ayatollah Behbahani and Ayatollah Tabatabai. They all came there before dawn to indicate by their presence their attachment to the constitution. Curiously, the Cossacks let them through. Their orders had been to prevent anyone leaving, not entering.

The crowd of protesters kept swelling and at daybreak there were several hundreds of them, including numerous "sons of Adam." They had rifles, but not much ammunition — about sixty cartridges each, certainly not enough to enable them to withstand a siege. Moreover, they were hesitant about using their arms and ammunition. They effectively took up position on rooftops and behind windows but they did not know whether they should fire the first shots, thereby giving the signal for an inevitable massacre, or whether they should wait passively while the preparations for the coup were carried out.

It was precisely that which delayed the Cossacks' assault even longer. Liakhov, surrounded by Russian and Persian officers, was busy stationing his troops as well as his cannons, of which six were counted that day, the most lethal one being installed in Topkhaneh Square. On several occasions the Colonel rode within the defenders' line of sight, but the personalities present prevented the "sons of Adam" from opening fire lest the Czar use such an incident as a pretext for invading Persia.

It was towards the middle of the afternoon that the order to attack was given. Although the sides were unequal, the fighting raged for six or seven hours. By a series of bold strokes, the resisters managed to put three cannons out of action.

However, this was the heroism of despair. By nightfall the white flag of defeat was raised over the first parliament in Persian history, but several minutes after the last shot Liakhov ordered his artillery to fire again. The Czar's directives were clear; it was not enough to abolish the parliament, they also had orders to destroy the building that had accommodated it, so the inhabitants of Tehran would see its ruins and it would be forever a lesson to all.

237

38

Fighting had not yet come to an end in the capital when the first shooting broke out in Tabriz. I had gone to collect Howard as he came out of class and we were to meet Fazel at the *anjuman* to go and have dinner with one of his relatives. We had not yet stepped into the labyrinth of the bazaar when we heard shots that sounded as if they came from nearby.

With a curiosity marked by recklessness, we headed down towards the source of the noise, only to see, at about a hundred yards distance, a vociferous crowd marching forward. There was dust, smoke, a forest of clubs, rifles, and glowing torches, as well as shouts that I could not understand as they were in Azeri, the Turkish language of the people of Tabriz. Baskerville did his best to translate: "Death to the constitution," "Death to Parliament," "Death to atheists," "Long live the Shah." Dozens of townspeople were running about in all directions. An old man was dragging a stupefied goat at the end of a rope. A woman stumbled and her son, hardly six years old, helped her to get up and supported her as she fled limping with him.

We ourselves hurried towards our meeting place. On the way a group of young men were erecting a barricade made of two tree trunks upon which they were piling up in completely random fashion tables, bricks, chairs, boxes, and barrels. We were recognized and allowed to pass, but we were advised to go quickly with the words "they are coming here," "they want to burn down the quarter," "they have sworn to massacre the sons of Adam."

In the *anjuman* building Fazel was surrounded by forty or fifty men and he was the only one not carrying a rifle. He only had an Austrian Mannlicher pistol whose sole use was to point out to all around him the positions they should take up. He was calm, less anxious than the evening before, in the state of calm a man of action feels when the unbearable waiting is over.

"You see!" he told us with an imperceptibly triumphant tone of voice. "Everything Panoff stated was true. Colonel Liakhov has carried out his coup d'état. He has declared himself military governor of Tehran and has imposed a curfew there. Since this morning supporters of the constitution have become fair game in the capital and all other cities, starting with Tabriz."

"It has all happened so quickly!" Howard marveled.

"It was the Russian consul who was notified of the launch of the coup by telegram and he then informed the religious chiefs of Tabriz this morning. They in turn summoned their supporters to assemble at midday in the Deveshi, the Quarter of the Camel-Drivers, whence they spread out through the city, first heading for the home of one of my journalist friends, Ali Meshedi. They dragged him out of his house accompanied by the screams of his wife and mother, cut his throat and severed his right hand, and then left him in a pool of blood. But have no fear — Ali will be avenged before nightfall."

His voice betrayed him. He managed a respite of a second and drew a deep breath before continuing:

"If I have come to Tabriz, it is because I know this city will resist. The ground we are standing on is still ruled by the constitution. This is now the seat of parliament, the seat of the legitimate government. It will be a fine battle but we will end up winning. Follow me!"

We followed him, along with a half-dozen of his supporters. He led us towards the garden, and walked around the house to a wooden staircase whose extremities disappeared in thick foliage. We went up to the roof, through a passageway, up a few more steps, and then came to a room with thick walls and small yet potentially deadly windows. Fazel invited us to take a look: we were overhanging the most vulnerable entrance to the quarter, which at present was blocked by a barricade. Behind it there were about twenty men, kneeling to the ground with their rifles aimed.

"There are others," Fazel explained, "just as determined. They are blocking all the entrances to the quarter. If the pack comes, they will be given the welcome they deserve."

The pack, as he called them, was not far off. They must have stopped on the way to set fire to two or three houses belonging to sons of Adam, but they were relentless and the noise and shots grew closer.

Suddenly we were seized by a kind of shudder. However much we expected them and were sheltered by a wall, the spectacle of a wild crowd calling out death and coming straight at one is probably the most frightening experience one can have.

Instinctively I whispered:

"How many are they?"

"A thousand, a thousand five hundred at the most," Fazel replied in a loud voice that was clear and reassuring.

Then he added, like an order:

"Now it is up to us to frighten them."

He asked his aides to give us rifles. Howard and I exchanged a quasi-amused glance. We felt the weight of those cold objects with both fascination and distaste.

"Position yourselves at the windows," Fazel yelled. "And shoot at anyone who approaches. I have to leave you. I have a surprise up my sleeve for these barbarians."

He had hardly gone out before the battle started, although to speak of it as such is most probably an exaggeration. The rioters arrived. They were a vociferous and bird-brained mob and their forward ranks threw themselves against the barricade as if it were an obstacle course. The sons of Adam fired one salvo and then another. A dozen of the assailants were downed and the rest fell back. Only one managed to scale the barricade, but that was only to be run through by a bayonet.

He gave out a horrible cry of agony and I turned my eyes away.

Most of the demonstrators wisely stayed back, making do with shouting out hoarsely the same slogan: "Death!" Then a squad was thrown anew into an assault on the barricade — this time with a little more method, that is to say that they were firing on the defenders and the windows from which the shots had come. A son of Adam hit on the forehead was the only loss in his camp. His companions' salvoes were already starting to mow down the first lines of the assailants.

The offensive tailed off, they fell back and discussed a new strategy noisily. They were regrouping for a new attempt when a rumbling sound shook the quarter. A shell had just landed in the middle of the rioters, causing carnage followed by headlong flight. The defenders then raised their rifles and shouted, "*Mashrouteh! Mashrouteh!*" — Constitution! From the other side of the barricade we could make out dozens of corpses stretched out on the ground. Howard whispered:

"My weapon is still cold. I have not fired a single cartridge. What about you?"

"Nor have I."

"To have someone's head in my sights, and to press the trigger to kill him . . ."

Fazel arrived a few moments later in jovial mood.

"What did you think of my surprise? It was an old French cannon, a de Bange, which was sold to us by an officer in the imperial army. It is on the roof — come and take a look at it! One day soon we shall place it in the middle of the largest square in Tabriz and write underneath it, 'This cannon saved the constitution!'"

I found his words too optimistic, even though I could not contest the fact that he had won a significant victory in a few minutes. His objective was clear — to maintain a zone where the last Constitutionalists could assemble and find protection, but above all where they could all plan out the steps they were to take.

If someone had told us on that troubled June day that from just a few tangled alleys in the Tabriz bazaar and with our two loads of Lebel rifles and our single de Bange cannon we were going to win back for Persia its stolen freedom, who would have believed it?

Yet that is what happened, but not without the purest of us paying for it with his life.

39

They were dark days in the history of Khayyam's country. Was this the promised dawn of the Orient? From Isfahan to Kazvin, from Shiraz to Hamand, the same shouts issued blindly from thousands upon thousands of people: "Death! Death!" Now one had to go into hiding in order to say the words liberty, democracy, and justice. The future was no more than a forbidden dream and the Constitutionalists were hunted down on the streets, the meeting rooms of the sons of Adam were laid to waste, and their books were thrown into a pile and burnt. Nowhere, throughout the whole of Persia, could the odious spread of violence be checked.

Nowhere apart from Tabriz. And when the interminable day of the coup came to an end, out of the thirty main quarters of the heroic city only one was holding out — the district called Amir-Khiz at the extreme northwest of the bazaar. That night a few dozen young partisans took turns to guard the approaches, while Fazel was sketching ambitious arrows on a crumpled map in the *anjuman* building in the general quarter.

There were about a dozen of us fervently following the smallest mark of his pencil which the swinging storm lamps accentuated. The deputy stood up straight.

"The enemy is still suffering the shock of the losses we inflicted on them. They think that we are stronger than we actually are. They have no cannons and do not know how many we have. We must profit from this without delay to extend our territory. It will not take the Shah long to send troops and they will be in Tabriz within a few weeks. By then we must have liberated the whole city. Tonight we shall attack."

He bent over and every head — bare or turbaned — bent over too.

"We cross the river by surprise," he explained. "We charge in the direction of the citadel and attack it from two sides, the bazaar and from the cemetery. It will be ours before evening."

The citadel was not taken for ten days. Lethal battles raged in every street but the resisters advanced and all the clashes turned to their advantage. Some sons of Adam occupied the bureau of the Indo-European Telegraph on the Saturday, thanks to which they were able to keep in contact with Tehran as well as with London and Bombay. The same day a police barracks went over to their side, bringing with it as a dowry a Maxim machine gun and thirty cases of ammunition. These successes gave the population its confidence back. Young and old became emboldened and flocked to the liberated quarters in their hundreds, sometimes with their weapons. Within a few weeks the enemy had been pushed back to the outskirts. It was only holding on to a thinly populated area in the northeast of the city stretching from the Quarter of the Camel-Drivers to the camp of Sahib-Divan.

Towards mid-July an army of irregulars was formed, as well as a provisional administration in which Howard found himself made quartermaster. He now passed most of his time scouring the bazaar and compiling a list of food stocks. The merchants showed themselves more than willing to cooperate. He himself found his way perfectly through the Persian system of weights and measures.

"You have to forget liters, kilos, ounces, and pints," he told me. "Here they speak of *jaw, miskal, syr,* and *kharvar,* which is the load of an ass."

He tried to teach me.

243

"The basic unit is the *jaw*, which is a medium-sized grain of barley which still has its husk but which has had the little tuft of hair at each end cut off."

"That's quite tortuous," I guffawed.

My teacher threw his student a look of rebuke. To make amends I thought I had better prove that I had been taking it in.

"So the *jaw* is the smallest unit of measure."

"Not at all, said Howard indignantly.

Unruffled, he referred to his notes:

"The weight of a grain of barley equals that of seventy grains of *seneveh*, or if you like, six hairs of a mule's tail."

In comparison, my own mission was light! Given my complete ignorance of the local dialect, my only job was to keep in contact with the foreign nationals in order to reassure them of Fazel's intentions and to watch over their safety.

It should be mentioned that Tabriz, until the construction of the Transcaucasian Railway twenty years earlier, had been the gateway to Persia, the entrance point for all travelers, goods, and ideas. Several European establishments had branches there, such as the German company of MMO Mossig and Schünemann, and the Eastern Trading Company, an important Austrian firm. There were also consulates, the American Presbyterian Mission, and various other institutions, and I am happy to say that at no moment during the long and difficult months of the siege did the foreign nationals become targets.

Not only were they in no danger, but there was some moving fraternization. I do not wish to speak of Baskerville, myself, nor of Panoff, who quickly joined the movement, but I wish to salute other people, such as Mr. Moore, the correspondent of the *Manchester Guardian*, who, not hesitating to take up arms at the side of Fazel, was wounded in combat, or Captain Anginieur, who helped us to resolve numerous logistical problems and who, through his articles in *L'Asie Française*, helped produce the surge of solidarity in Paris and throughout the world that saved Tabriz from the dreadful fate threatening it. For some of the city's clergy, the active presence of the foreigners was, I quote, "a motley crowd of Europeans, Armenians, Babis, and infidels of all sorts." However, the population remained impervious to this propaganda and showered us with grateful affection. Every man was a brother for us and every woman a sister or a mother.

I hardly need to point out that it was the Persians themselves who gave the Resistance the most spontaneous and enormous help from the first day. First the free inhabitants of Tabriz and then the refugees who had had to flee their towns and villages for their beliefs and seek protection in the last bastion of the constitution. This was the case with hundreds of sons of Adam who had rushed from all corners of the empire and who asked nothing more than that they be allowed to bear arms. This was also the case with several deputies, ministers, and journalists from Tehran who had managed to escape the dragnet ordered by Colonel Liakhov and who often arrived in small groups, exhausted, haggard, and distraught.

However, the most precious recruit beyond a shadow of a doubt was Shireen, who had defied the curfew to leave the capital by car without the Cossacks daring to impede her. Her landaulet was greeted enthusiastically by the populace, the more so as her chauffeur came from Tabriz and was one of the rare Persians to drive such a vehicle.

The Princess set up home in an abandoned palace that had been built by her grandfather, the old Shah who had been assassinated. He had envisaged spending a month there every year, but after the first night, as legend goes, he felt faint and his astrologers advised him never to set foot again in a place of such ill omen. For thirty years no one had lived there. It was referred to, not without a little fear, as the Empty Palace.

Shireen did not hesitate to defy bad luck and her residence became the heart of the city. Resistance leaders liked to meet in her vast gardens, which were a cool oasis during those summer nights, and I was often in their company.

The Princess always seemed happy to see me. Our correspondence had caused a bond to spring up between us to which no one could become privy. Of course, we were never alone, there being dozens of other people present whenever we met or dined. We debated indefatigably and sometimes we just joked but not excessively. Familiarity is never tolerated in Persia and one must be punctilious and flamboyant about being polite. In Persian there is often the tendency to say "I am the slave of the shadow of the greatness" of the individual to whom one is talking, and when it is matter of female highnesses, one starts if not actually kissing the ground at least doing so in the import of the most grandiose phrases.

Then came that disturbing Thursday evening. September 17 to be exact. How could I ever forget it?

For a hundred different reasons our companions had all left the palace and I was among the last to leave. Just as I went through the outer gate of the property, I realized that I had left next to my chair a briefcase into which I had the habit of placing some important papers. So I retraced my steps, but not at all with the intention of seeing the Princess; I was under the impression that she had retired after seeing off the last of her visitors.

Not so. She was still sitting alone in the middle of twenty empty chairs. She seemed worried and distant. Never taking my gaze from her, I picked up the briefcase as slowly as I could. Shireen was still sitting with her profile towards me, motionless and deaf to my presence. I sat down in contemplative silence and watched her for a little while. Imagining that it was twelve years earlier, I could see the two of us in Jamaladin's sitting room in Constantinople. She looked just the same then, sitting in profile, with a blue scarf crowning her hair and trailing down to the leg of the chair. How old had she been? Seventeen? Eighteen? Today at thirty she was a mature, regal, and serene woman, and just as slender as on that first day. She obviously had been able to resist the temptation of women of her rank who lay around eating and lazed their lives away on an opulent divan. Had she married? Was she a divorcee or a widow? We had never spoken of it.

I wanted to say in an unquavering voice, "I have loved you ever since Constantinople." My lips trembled and tightened but without emitting the slightest sound.

However, Shireen had turned gently towards me. She observed me without surprise, as if I had neither left nor returned. Her look wavered and she spoke to me with familiarity:

"What are you thinking about?"

The answer shot from my lips:

"Of you. From Constantinople to Tabriz."

A smile, which was perhaps one of embarrassment, but which resolutely did not wish to be a barrier, spread over her face. As for me, I could do no more than quote her own phrase that had become almost a code between us:

"You never know, our paths might meet!"

We were both taken up by a few seconds of silent memories. Then Shireen said:

"I did not leave Tehran without the book."

"The *Samarkand Manuscript*?"

"It is always on the chest of drawers near my bed. I never tire of reading it. I know the *Rubaiyaat* and the chronicle written in the margin by heart."

"I would willingly give a decade of my life for one night with that book."

"I would willingly give a night of my life."

Within an instant I was bent over Shireen's face, our eyes were shut and the only thing that existed around us was the monotony of the cicadas' song amplified in our numbed minds, and our lips touched in a long ardent kiss which transcended and broke down the barriers of years.

Lest other visitors arrive or the servants should come, we rose and I followed her down a covered path, through a small hidden door and up a broken staircase into the former Shah's apartment that his granddaughter had taken over. Shireen closed two heavy shutters with a huge bolt and we were alone, together. Tabriz was no longer a city isolated from the world — it was the world that languished isolated from Tabriz.

By dawn I had still not opened the manuscript. I could see it on the chest of drawers on the other side of the bed, but Shireen was sleeping naked with her head on my neck and her breasts falling against my ribs and nothing in the world would have made me move. I was breathing in her breath, her smell, and her night, and contemplating her eyelashes, trying desperately to guess what dream of happiness or anguish was making them quiver. When she awoke the first sounds of the city were already to be heard. I had to slip away quickly and promised myself that I would dedicate my next night of love to Khayyam's book.

40

When I came out of the palace I walked along with my shoulders hunched — dawn in Tabriz is never warm — and in this manner I made my way towards the caravansary without trying to take any short cuts. I was not in a hurry to get there. I needed some time to think things over as I had not calmed down from the exhilaration of the night and my mind was still full of images, gestures, and whispered words. I could no longer tell whether I was happy. In a way I felt complete, but this feeling was tinged with the inevitable guilt that comes with clandestine affairs. Thoughts kept on coming back to me, as haunting as thoughts can be during sleepless nights. "After I left, did she go back to sleep with a smile? Does she have any regret? When I see her again and if we are not alone will she treat me as an accomplice or a stranger? I shall return tonight and try and look for some faith in her eyes."

Suddenly a cannon shot rang out. I stopped and listened. Was it our brave and solitary de Bange? It was followed by a silence, then a prolonged fusillade, and finally a lull. I ventured a few more steps and kept my ears peeled. There was a new roar, immediately followed by a third. By this time I was starting to be worried; a single cannon cannot fire at that rate, there had to be two or even more. Two shells exploded a few streets away from me and I started to run towards the citadel.

Fazel quickly confirmed the news that I feared; the first of the Shah's forces had arrived during the night. They had taken up position in the districts held by the religious chiefs. Other troops were on their way and were converging from all directions. The siege of Tabriz had begun.

The tirade given by Colonel Liakhov, the military governor of Tehran and the architect of the coup d'état, before his troops set off for Tabriz went along the following lines:

"Brave Cossacks! The Shah is in danger. The people of Tabriz have rejected his authority and have declared war in an attempt to force him to recognize the constitution. The constitution would abolish your privileges and dissolve your brigade. If it triumphs, it is your women and children who will go hungry. The constitution is your worst enemy and you must fight like the furies against it. The way you destroyed the parliament has aroused the greatest admiration throughout the world. Follow this salutary action by crushing the rebel city and, on behalf of the sovereigns of Russia and Persia, I promise you money and honors. All the riches of Tabriz are yours, you only have to help yourselves!"

The command that was shouted out in Tehran and St. Petersburg and murmured in London was the same: Tabriz must be destroyed, it deserves the most exemplary punishment. If it is defeated no one will dare speak of a constitution, parliament, or democracy; once again the Orient will be able to sink comfortably into death.

That is how the whole world came to witness a strange and heartrending race over the following months: while the example set by Tabriz started to revive the flame of resistance in various corners of Persia, the city itself was undergoing a more and more rigorous siege. Would the Constitutionalists have enough time to pick themselves up, organize, and take up arms before their bastion gave out?

In January they won their first big success: in answer to an appeal by the Bakhtiari chiefs who were Shireen's maternal uncles, Isfahan, the former capital, rebelled and affirmed its attachment to the constitution and its solidarity with Tabriz. When the news reached the besieged city an explosion of joy erupted on the spot. The whole night long people chanted indefatigably, "Tabriz-Isfahan, the country is waking up!" However, the very next day a massive attack forced the defenders to abandon several positions in the south and west. There was only one road left connecting Tabriz to the outside world and that was the one that led north, towards the Russian border.

Three weeks later the city of Rashd rebelled in turn. Like Isfahan, it rejected the tutelage of the Shah and extolled the constitution and Fazel's resistance. There was a new eruption of joy in Tabriz, but immediately the besieging troops launched a new attack and the last road was cut: Tabriz was completely surrounded. The post could no longer get through, and nor could any food. They had to organize very strict rationing to be able to keep on feeding the two hundred thousand or so inhabitants of the city.

In February and March 1909 more towns rallied. The territory of the constitution now extended to Shiraz, Hamadan, Meshed, Astarabad, Bandar-Abbas, and Bushir. In Paris the Committee for the Defense of Tabriz was formed, headed by a certain Monsieur Dieulafoy, who was a distinguished Orientalist; there was the same drive in London, under the presidency of Lord Lamington, and more important still, the principal Shiite clergymen who were based in Karbala in Ottoman Iraq pronounced themselves solemnly and unambiguously in favor of the constitution and disavowed the backward-looking mullahs.

Tabriz was triumphant. But it was also dying.

Unable to confront so many rebellions and so much disaffection, the Shah became utterly single-minded: Tabriz, the source of the evil, had to be brought down. When it fell the others would yield. Since he had failed to take it by assault, he decided to starve it into submission.

In spite of rationing, bread was scarce. By the end of March there were already several deaths, mostly among the old and very young.

The press in London, Paris, and St. Petersburg was shocked and started to criticize the Powers, who, it was stated, still had in the besieged city many of their nationals whose lives were now in danger. Echoes of this stance reached us by way of telegraph.

Fazel summoned me one day to tell me:

"The Russians and the English are going to evacuate their nationals soon so that Tabriz can be crushed without it provoking too much commotion in the rest of the world. That will be a hard blow for us, but I want you to know that I will not oppose the evacuation. I shall not hold anyone here against his will."

He charged me to inform the people involved that everything would be done to facilitate their departure. Then the most extraordinary event of all came to pass. Having been there as a privileged witness allows me to overlook much human pettiness.

I had started my round, intending my first visit to be to the Presbyterian Mission where I felt some trepidation about seeing the Reverend Director again and having to suffer his reprimands. He who had been counting on me to reason with Howard, was he not going to reproach me for having taken an identical path? Indeed, he was quite distant with me and showed the minimum of courtesy.

However, when I had explained the reason for my visit he responded without a moment's hesitation:

"I shall not leave. If they can organize a convoy to evacuate the foreigners, they can just as well organize similar convoys to bring supplies to the hungry city."

I thanked him for his viewpoint, which seemed to me to conform to the religious and humanitarian ideal that drove him. Then I went off to visit three businesses that were in the vicinity and to my great surprise their response was identical. The businessmen did not wish to leave any more than the pastor. As one of them, an Italian, explained to me:

"If I left Tabriz at this difficult moment, I would be ashamed to return later and carry on my business here. So I shall stay. Perhaps my presence will help make my government act."

Everywhere it was as if word had gone round. I received the same immediate, clear, and irrevocable reply. Mr. Wratislaw, the British consul, and the staff of the Russian Consulate, with the notable exception of the consul, Mr. Pokhitanoff, all gave the same reply to me and to their shattered governments: "We will not leave!"

In the city, the foreigners' admirable solidarity lifted people's spirits, but the situation was still precarious. On April 18 Wratislaw telegraphed London: "Bread is hard to find today, tomorrow it will be even harder." On the nineteenth he sent a new message: "The situation is desperate, there is talk here of a last attempt to break the stranglehold."

In fact, a meeting was being held that day at the citadel at which Fazel announced that Constitutionalist troops were advancing from Rashd towards Tehran, that the authorities there were on the verge of collapse, and that it would not take much to make them fall and our cause triumph. But Howard spoke after him to mention that the bazaars were at present devoid of all foodstuffs.

"People have already slaughtered domestic animals and street cats. Whole families wander around the streets, night and day, in search of a shriveled pomegranate or a piece of Barbary bread dropped in a gutter. Soon we run the risk of seeing people turn to cannibalism."

"Two weeks. We only need to hold out two weeks!"

Fazel's voice was pleading. But Howard could do nothing about it:

"Our reserves have allowed us to survive up until now. But there is no longer anything left to distribute. Nothing. In two weeks the population will have been decimated and Tabriz will be a ghost town. In recent days there have been eight hundred deaths — from starvation and the numerous diseases that go with it."

"Two weeks. Just two weeks!" Fazel repeated. "Even if we have to fast!"

"We have all been fasting for several days!"

"What else can we do? Capitulate? Let go of the huge wave of support that we have so patiently built up? Is there no means of lasting out?"

Last out. Last out. These twelve men were haggard and dizzy with hunger and exhaustion, but also drunk on the thought that victory was within grasp. They had no thought in mind other than holding out.

"There might be a solution," Howard said. "Perhaps . . ."

All eyes turned towards Baskerville.

"If we attempt to break out, by surprise. If we manage to take this position," he pointed to a spot on the map, "our forces will be able to sweep into the breach and re-establish contact with the outside world. By the time the enemy recovers, help will perhaps be in sight."

I immediately stated my opposition to the plan; the military chiefs were of the same opinion. Everyone, without exception, considered it suicidal. The enemy was situated on a promontory at some five hundred yards from our lines. It meant having to cross that distance over flat ground and scaling a massive wall of dried mud to dislodge the defenders and then getting enough men into position to be able to resist the inevitable counter-attack.

Fazel hesitated. He was not even looking at the map, but was pondering over the political outcome of the operation. Would it allow him to gain a few days? The debate went on and became animated. Baskerville insisted and argued, often supported by Moore. The *Guardian* correspondent laid out his own military experience and stated that the surprise element could turn out to be decisive. Fazel brought the debate to a conclusion.

"I am still not convinced, but, as no other action can be envisaged I will not oppose Howard's plan."

The attack was launched the next day, April 20, at three in the morning. It was agreed that if by five o'clock the position had been won, operations would take place at multiple points along the front in order to prevent the enemy pulling troops back for a counter-attack. However, within the first minutes the attempt seemed in jeopardy: a barrage of fire met the first sortie, led by Moore, Baskerville, and some sixty other volunteers. Apparently the enemy was not at all taken by surprise. Could a spy have informed them of our preparations? We will never know, but the sector was guarded, Liakhov having entrusted it to one of his most adept officers.

Fazel sensibly ordered the operation to be halted without delay and had the signal for a withdrawal given — a lengthy bird-call. The fighters rushed back. Several of them, including Moore, were wounded.

Baskerville was the only one who did not return. He had been felled by the first salvo.

For three days Tabriz would live to the rhythm of condolences. There were discreet condolences at the Presbyterian Mission and noisy, impassioned, incensed condolences in the districts held by the sons of Adam. My eyes were red as I shook hands with people whom I mostly did not know, and I listened to endless tributes.

Among the throng of visitors was the English consul. He took me aside.

"It will perhaps be of some consolation to you to learn that six hours after your friend's death I received a message from London informing me that the Powers had reached agreement on the question of Tabriz. Mr. Baskerville will not have died in vain. An expeditionary force has already set out to relieve the city by bringing in provisions, as well as to evacuate the foreign community."

"A Russian expeditionary force?"

"Of course," Wratislaw admitted. "They are the only ones who have an army in the area. However we have obtained guarantees. Constitutionalists will not be troubled and the Czar's troops will withdraw when their mission is completed. I am counting on you to convince Fazel to lay down his arms."

Why did I accept? Perhaps I was overwhelmed or exhausted, or maybe a Persian sense of fatalism had worked its way into me. Whatever the reason, I did not protest and let myself be persuaded that I was the one who had to carry out this loathsome mission. However, I decided not to go to Fazel's straight away. I preferred to escape for a few hours — to Shireen.

Since our night of love I had only met her again in public. The siege had created a new atmosphere in Tabriz. People were always speaking of enemy infiltration. They thought that they saw spies or sappers everywhere. Armed men patrolled the streets and guarded the access of the main buildings. There were often five, six, or sometimes more men at the gates of the empty palace. Although they were always ready to greet me with beaming smiles, their presence effectively prevented a visit being discreet.

That evening everyone's vigilance was relaxed, and I managed to wend my way as far as the Princess's bedroom. The door was ajar and I pushed it noiselessly.

Shireen was sitting up in bed with the manuscript open on her knees. I slipped to her side, shoulder to shoulder and hip to hip. Neither of us had any thought for caresses, but that night we loved in a different fashion, immersed in the same book. She guided my eyes and lips. She knew every word, every painting; for me it was the first time.

She would often translate into French in her own way the ends of poems that dealt with a wisdom so accurate or a beauty so timeless that one forgot that they had been uttered for the first time eight centuries earlier in some garden in Nishapur, Isfahan, or Samarkand.

The wounded birds hide so they may die.

There were words of heartache and consolation, the touching monologue of a defeated and dignified poet:

Peace to man in the black silence of the beyond.

But there were also words of joy and sublime unconcern:

Some wine! Let it be as pink as your cheeks
And my regrets as light as your locks.

After we had read aloud the very last quatrain and gazed admiringly at each miniature, we turned back to the beginning of the book to go through the chronicles written in the margins. First of all we read the one by Vartan the Armenian, which covered a good half of the work, and thanks to which that night I learnt the history of Khayyam, Jahan, and the three friends. There followed the chronicles written by the librarians of Alamut — father, son, and grandson — each chronicle being thirty pages long and telling the manuscript's extraordinary fate after it was stolen from Merv and its influence on the Assassins, as well as a concise history of the Assassins up until the invasion of the Mongol hordes.

Shireen read out the last lines as I could not make out the handwriting very easily: "I had to flee Alamut on the eve of its destruction, towards Kirman, my place of birth, carrying the manuscript of the incomparable Khayyam of Nishapur, which I have decided to hide this very day in the hope that it will not be found until there are men fit to hold it and for that I put my trust in the Almighty. He guides whom He wishes and leads astray whom He wishes." There followed a date, which according to my reckoning corresponds to March 14, 1257.

This set me thinking.

"The manuscript ends at the thirteenth century," I said. "Jamaladin was given it in the nineteenth. What happened to it in the meantime?"

"A long sleep," said Shireen. "An interminable Oriental siesta. Then it was jolted awake in the arms of that madman, Mirza Reza. Wasn't he from Kirman, like the librarians from Alamut? Are you so shocked to find that he had an ancestor who was an Assassin?"

She had got up and gone to sit on a stool in front of her oval mirror with a comb in her hand. I could have stayed hours just watching the gracious movements of her bare arms, but she brought me back to the prosaic reality of things:

"You must get ready if you do not wish to be caught in my bed."

In fact daylight was already flooding into the room, as the curtains were too light.

"It is true," I said wearily. "I almost forgot your reputation."

She turning towards me, laughing:

"Exactly. I have my reputation to maintain. I do not want it told in all the harems of Persia that a handsome stranger was able to pass a whole night at my side without even thinking of taking his clothes off. No one would ever desire me again!"

After placing the manuscript back in its box, I placed a kiss upon my beloved's lips, and then I ran down the corridor and through two secret doors to dive back into the turmoil of the besieged city.

41

Of all those who died during those months of hardship, why have I singled out Baskerville? Because he was my friend and compatriot? Most probably. But also because his only ambition was to see liberty and democracy triumph in the rebirth of the Orient, which for all that was foreign to him. Had he given his life for nothing? In ten, twenty, or a hundred years would the West remember his example, or would Persia remember his action? I chose not to think about it lest I fall into the inescapable melancholy of those who live between two worlds that are equally promising and disappointing.

However, if I limit myself to the events immediately after Baskerville's death, I can make myself believe that he did not die in vain.

Foreign intervention, the lifting of the blockade, and a food convoy all happened. Was it thanks to Howard? Perhaps the decision had already been taken, but my friend's death quickened the rescue effort and thousands of gaunt townspeople owed their survival to him.

It can be imagined that the prospect of the Czar's soldiers arriving in the besieged city did not thrill Fazel. I did my best to talk him into accepting the situation.

"The population is no longer in a state to resist. The only gift that you can still give them is to save them from famine and you owe them that after all the hardship they have put up with."

"To have fought for six months only to end up under the thumb of Czar Nicholas, the Shah's protector!"

"The Russians are not acting alone, they have the mandate of the whole international community. Our friends throughout the world will applaud this operation. To resist it or to fight it would be to lose the benefit of the enormous support that has been lavished upon us so far."

"But to submit and lay down our weapons now that victory is in sight!"

"Is it me that you are talking to, or are you just inveighing against fate?"

Fazel recoiled and gave me a look of deep reproach.

"Tabriz does not deserve to be so humiliated!"

"I can do nothing about it, and neither can you. There are some times when any decision is a bad one and we must choose the one we will regret least!"

He seemed to calm down and gave the matter serious thought.

"What fate is in store for my friends?"

"The British are guaranteeing their safety."

"Our weapons?"

"Everyone will be able to keep his rifle. The houses will not be searched with the exception of those from which there was shooting. However, heavy weapons must be handed over."

He did not seem in any way reassured.

"And tomorrow who will force the Czar to withdraw his troops?"

"For that we have to trust Providence!"

"Suddenly I find you extremely Oriental."

Those who knew Fazel knew that he hardly ever meant the word "Oriental" to be a compliment — and particularly when he had a suspicious scowl on his face. I felt obliged to try a different tactic, so I stood up with a resounding sigh.

"No doubt you are right. I was wrong to argue. I am going to tell the British Consul that I have not been able to convince you. Then I shall come back and stay with you until the end."

Fazel took me by the shoulder to hold me back.

"I have not accused you of anything. I have not even turned down your suggestion."

"My suggestion? I have only passed on a suggestion from the English, and made sure to tell you its provenance."

"Calm down and listen to me! I know very well that I do not have the means to prevent the Russians entering Tabriz. I also know that if I offer them the slightest resistance the whole world will condemn me, starting with my compatriots who want now to be rescued, no matter by whom. I am even aware of the fact that the end of the siege will constitute a defeat for the Shah."

"Was that not what you were fighting for?"

"Not at all! You see, I may condemn the Shah, but it is not against him that I am fighting. To triumph over a despot cannot be one's ultimate goal; I have been fighting so that Persians might be aware of being free, being sons of Adam as we say we are, so that they might have faith in themselves and their strength and be able to take their place in today's world. That is what I wanted to see come to pass here. This city has thrown off the tutelage of the Shah and the religious chiefs, it has defied the Powers and aroused the support and admiration of well-intentioned men everywhere. The people of Tabriz are on the verge of winning, but they are not allowed to. It is feared that they would set a precedent and they must therefore be humiliated. The proud population of this city will have to bow to the Czar's soldiers for bread. You who were born free in a free country ought to understand."

I remained silent for a few strained seconds and then brought the matter to a conclusion:

"So what do you want me to reply to the English Consul?"

Fazel forced his face to smile.

"Tell him that I will be delighted to seek asylum once again in His Majesty's Consulate."

I needed some time in order to understand just how much Fazel's bitterness was justified, for in the short term events seemed to contradict his fears. He only stayed a few days at the British Consulate before Mr. Wratislaw drove him in his car across the Russian lines to the outskirts of Kazvin. There he could join the Constitutionalist troops, who, after a long wait, were preparing themselves to march towards Tehran.

In fact, while Tabriz was in danger of being strangled, the Shah had a powerful means of dissuasion against his enemies and he could still manage to frighten and contain them. Once the siege was lifted, Fazel's friends felt free to move and with no further delay they set off to march on to the capital, which they did with two armies, one coming from Kazvin in the north and the other from Isfahan in the south. The latter, mostly made up of men from Bakhtiari tribes, seized Qom on June 23. A few days later a joint Anglo-Russian communiqué was broadcast demanding the Constitutionalists to cease their offensive immediately in order to come to an arrangement with the Shah. If not, the two Powers would find themselves obliged to intervene. However, Fazel and his friends turned a deaf ear and hurried on: on July 9 their troops joined up below the walls of Tehran; on the 13th, two thousand men made their entrance into the capital by an unguarded gate in the northwest near the French legation, watched with astonishment by the correspondent of *Le Temps*.

Only Liakhov tried to resist. With three hundred men, some old cannons, and two Creusot machine guns he managed to keep control over several districts in the center of the city. Heavy fighting went on unabated until July 16.

On that day, at eight-thirty in the morning, the Shah went to take refuge in the Russian Legation, formally accompanied by five hundred soldiers and courtiers. His action was tantamount to an act of abdication.

The commander of the Cossacks had no choice other than to lay down his arms. He swore henceforth to respect the constitution and to place himself in the service of the victors on condition that his brigade was not dissolved, which reassurance he was duly given.

A new Shah was appointed: the youngest son of the fallen Shah, who was just twelve years old. According to Shireen, who had known him since the cradle, he was a gentle and sensitive adolescent, with neither cruelty nor perversity. When he crossed the capital the day after the fighting to go to the palace in the company of his tutor, Mr. Smirnoff, he was greeted with shouts of "Long live the Shah!", coming from the same people who a day earlier had been yelling, "Death to the Shah!"

42

I n public the young Shah cut a fine figure. He appeared royal, did
not smile to excess, and waved his pale hand in greeting to his
subjects. However, once back at the palace he caused great concern to
his courtiers. Having been brutally separated from his parents, he cried
and cried. He even tried to run away that summer in order to join his
father and mother. When he was caught he tried to hang himself
from the palace ceiling, but when he started to choke he took fright,
called for help, and was rescued in time. That misadventure had a
beneficial effect on him. He was now cured of his anxieties and would
act his role of constitutional monarch in a dignified and good-natured
manner.

Real power, however, was in the hands of Fazel and his friends.
They inaugurated the new era with a purge: six supporters of the old
régime were executed, including the two main religious chiefs of Tabriz
who had led the struggle against the sons of Adam, as well as Sheikh
Fazlullah Nouri. He was accused of having given his backing to the
massacres that followed the coup d'état the previous year; he therefore

was convicted on a charge of collusion to murder and his death warrant was ratified by the Shiite hierarchy. However, there was hardly
any doubt that the sentence had symbolic value: Nouri had been responsible for decreeing that the constitution was a heresy. He was
hanged in public in the Topkhaneh Square on July 31, 1909. Before
he died he murmured, "I am not a reactionary," only to follow this
by stating to his supporters who were dotted throughout the crowd
that the constitution was contrary to their religion and that religion
would have the last word.

The first task of the new leaders, however, was to rebuild the Parliament: the building rose out of its ruins and elections were organized. On November 15, the young Shah formally inaugurated the second
Majlis in Persian history with these words:

*In the name of God who has given us Freedom, and with the protec-
tion of his Holiness the hidden Imam, the National Consultative Assembly is hereby opened in joy and with the best omens.*

*Intellectual progress and the evolution of our way of thinking have
rendered change inevitable. It has come about after a dreadful ordeal,
but Persia has known, down the centuries, how to survive many crises,
and today its people see their desires accomplished. We are happy to state
that the new progressive government enjoys the support of the people, and
that it is bringing peace and confidence back to the country.*

*In order to be able to carry out the necessary reform, it must be a
priority of the government and the Parliament to bring the state, particularly its public finances, into line with the accepted norms for civilized
nations.*

*We beseech God to guide the representatives of the nation and to assure
honor, independence, and happiness for Persia.*

Tehran was jubilant that day. Everyone was out in the street, singing at the crossroads, reciting improvised poems whose words all either rhymed or were made to rhyme with "Constitution," "Democracy,"
or "Liberty." Merchants offered the passers-by drinks and sweetmeats,
and dozens of newspapers that had been silenced after the coup d'état
brought out special editions announcing their resurrection.

At nightfall fireworks lit up the city. Seating had been erected in

263

the gardens of the Baharistan. The diplomatic corps sat on the grand-stand together with members of the new government, deputies, religious dignitaries, and the bazaar guilds. As a friend of Baskerville, I was entitled to sit near the front and my chair was just behind Fazel's. There was a stream of explosions and bangs, the sky was lit up at times, and people turned their heads and leaned to and fro smiling like overjoyed children. Outside, sons of Adam tirelessly chanted the same slogans for hours.

I do not know what noise or shout brought Howard back into my thoughts. He so deserved to be at the celebration! At that very moment, Fazel turned to me:

"You seem sad."

"Sad. Certainly not! I have always wanted to hear the word 'freedom' ringing out on the soil of the Orient, but some memories are bothering me."

"Cast them aside. Smile and rejoice. Make the most of the last moments of exhilaration."

Worrying words which divested me of any wish to celebrate that evening. Was Fazel, after an interval of seven months, about to take up the difficult discussion that set us against each other in Tabriz? Did he have new cause for worry? I made up my mind to go and see him the following day for an explanation, but in the end I decided against it. I avoided seeing him for a whole year.

What were the reasons? I believe that after the arduous adventure I had just been through, I had some nagging doubts about the wisdom of the role I had played in Tabriz. I had come to the Orient in search of a manuscript; had it been right for me to become so involved in a struggle that was not mine? To begin with, by what right had I advised Howard to come to Persia?

In the language of Fazel and his friends, Baskerville was a martyr; in my eyes he was a dead friend, a friend who had died in a foreign country for a foreign cause, a friend whose parents would one day write to me to ask me in the most poignantly polite of terms why I had led their son astray.

Was it remorse I was feeling over Howard? It was, to be more correct, a certain feeling of decency. I do not know if that is the right word, but I am trying to say that after my friends' victory I had no desire to strut around Tehran listening to people laud my supposed exploits during the siege of Tabriz. I had played a minimal and quite fortuitous role. Above all, I had had a friend who was a heroic compatriot and I had no intention of exploiting his memory to obtain privileges and respect for myself.

To tell the whole truth, I felt a great need to disappear from view, to be forgotten and not to visit politicians, *anjuman*-members, and diplomats. The only person I saw every day, and with a pleasure that never diminished, was Shireen. I had talked her into going to live in one of the numerous residences belonging to her family in the heights of Zarganda, a holiday resort outside the capital. I myself had rented a small house in the neighborhood, but that was for the sake of appearances, and I spent my days and nights at Shireen's, with the collusion of her servants.

That winter we managed to spend whole weeks without leaving her huge bedroom. We were warmed by a magnificent copper brazier, we read the manuscript and some other books, lazed around for hours smoking the *kalyan*, drinking Shiraz wine and sometimes even champagne, munching Kirmani pistachios and Isfahani nougat; my Princess could be a great lady or a little girl at one and the same time and we felt great tenderness for each other the whole time.

With the onset of the first warm days, Zarganda started to liven up. Foreigners and the richest Persians had sumptuous houses there and would move in for long months of idleness surrounded by luxuriant vegetation. It is a matter beyond dispute that only the proximity of this paradise made the gray dullness of Tehran bearable for innumerable diplomats. However, Zarganda became a ghost-town in the winter, with only the gardeners, some caretakers, and the rare survivors of its indigenous population staying behind. Shireen and I were badly in need of just such a desert.

However, from April on, alas, the visitors took up their summer lodgings. There were people strolling in front of all the entrance-gates and people walking down all the paths. After every night and every siesta, Shireen offered tea to female visitors with roving eyes. I was always having to hide or flee down the corridors. The gentle months of hibernation had been used up, and it was time for me to leave.

When I informed her, my princess was sad but resigned.

"I thought you were happy."

"I have experienced a rare moment of happiness. I want to put it in suspended animation so that it will still be intact when I come back to it. I never tire of watching you, with both astonishment and love. I do not want the invading crowd to change the way I see you. I am going away in the summer so that I may find you again in the winter."

"Summer, winter. You go away, you come back. You think that you can dispose of the seasons, the years, your life and mine with impunity. Have you learnt nothing from Khayyam?

"'*Suddenly Heaven robs you of even the moment you need to moisten your lips.*'"

She looked deep into my eyes, as if she were reading an open book. She had understood everything and sighed.

"Where are you thinking of going?"

I did not know yet. I had come to Persia twice and twice I had led a besieged existence. I still had the whole of the Orient to discover, from the Bosphorus to the China Sea: Turkey, which had just risen up at the same time as Persia, which had deposed its Sultan-Caliph and which now prided itself upon its deputies, senators, clubs, and opposition newspapers; proud Afghanistan, which the British managed to subdue, but at what cost! And of course there was all of Persia to explore. I knew only Tabriz and Tehran. But what of Isfahan, Shiraz, Kashan, and Kirman? Nishapur and Khayyam's tomb, a gray stone watched over for centuries by untiring generations of petals.

Out of all the roads that lay before me, which should I take? It was the manuscript that chose for me. I took the train to Krasnovodsk, crossed Ashkabad and old Merv, and hence to Bukhara.

Most importantly, I went to Samarkand.

43

I was curious to see what was left of the city where Khayyam spent the flower of his youth.

What had become of the district of Asfizar and of that belevedere in the garden where Omar had loved Jahan? Was there still some trace of the suburb of Maturid, where in the eleventh century that Jewish paper-maker was still turning white mulberry branches into pulp according to an old Chinese recipe. For weeks I went about on foot, and then on a mule; I questioned the merchants, the passers-by, and the imams of the mosques, but they only replied with blank unknowing looks, amused smiles, and generous invitations for me to squat on their sky-blue divans and take tea with them.

It was my luck to be in the Registan Square one morning. A caravan was passing. It was a short caravan, consisting of just six or seven thick-haired and heavy-hoofed Bactrian camels. The old camel-driver had stopped not far from me in front of a potter's stall, holding a new-born lamb to his chest; he proposed a barter and the craftsman discussed it; without taking his hands off the jar or the wheel, he pointed with his chin towards a pile of varnished vessels. I watched the two men with their black-bordered woolen hats, their striped robes, reddish beards, and their ancient gestures. Was there any detail of this scene that had not come down unchanged from the time of Khayyam?

There was a slight breeze and the sand started to swirl, their clothing billowed, and the whole square was covered with an unreal haze. I cast my eyes around. At the edge of the square rose three monuments, three gigantic complexes of towers, domes, gateways, and high walls completely covered with minute mosaics, arabesques studded with gold, amethyst, and turquoise, and intricate calligraphy. It all retained its majesty, but the towers were leaning, the domes had gaping holes, the facades were crumbling, ravaged by time, wind, and centuries of neglect; people no longer looked at these monuments, these haughty, proud, and forgotten giants which provided an imposing backdrop for a derisory play.

I was retreating backwards and stepped on someone's foot. When I turned round to apologize I was face to face with a man dressed like me in European clothing, a man who had set sail from the same distant planet. We struck up a conversation. He was Russian, an archaeologist. He also had come with a thousand questions, but he already had some answers.

"In Samarkand, time moves from one cataclysm to the next and from one *tabula rasa* to the next. When the Mongols destroyed the city in the thirteenth century, its various districts were left a mass of ruins and corpses. It had to be abandoned; the survivors went to rebuild their dwellings on another site, further to the south, with the result that the whole of the old city, the Samarkand of the Seljuks, was gradually covered by layers of sand and became a raised field. There are treasures and secrets under the ground, but the surface is a pasture. One day it will all have to be opened up, the houses and the street dug up. Once freed, Samarkand will be able to tell us its history."

He broke off.

"Are you an archaeologist?"

"No. This city attracts me for other reasons."

"Would it be impolite of me to ask what they are?"

I told him of the manuscript, the poems, the chronicle, and the paintings that evoked the lovers of Samarkand.

"I would love to see that book! Do you know that everything from that time has been destroyed — as if by a curse. Walls, palaces, orchards, gardens, water-pipes, religious sites, books, and the principal *objets d'art*. The monuments we admire today were all built later by Tamerlane and his descendants. They are less than five hundred years old. From Khayyam's era we only have potsherds and, as you have just informed me, this manuscript that has miraculously survived. It is a privilege for you to be able to hold it in your hands and read it at your leisure. It is a privilege and also a heavy responsibility."

"Believe me, I am quite aware of that. For years, ever since I learnt that this book existed, I have lived for nothing else. It has led me from adventure to adventure, its world has become mine and its guardian my beloved."

"And have you made this trip to Samarkand to discover the places it describes?"

"I was hoping that the townspeople would be able at least to give me some indication of where the old districts lay."

"I am sorry to have to disappoint you," the Russian continued, "but if you are searching for something from the period for which you have a fascination, you will only gather legends, stories of jinns and *divs*. This city cultivates them with delight."

"More than other cities in Asia?"

"I am afraid so. I wonder if the proximity of these ruins does not naturally inflame the imagination of our miserable contemporaries. Then there is the city buried under the ground. Over the centuries how many children have fallen down cracks never to reappear, what strange sounds people have heard or thought that they heard, apparently coming out of the entrails of the earth! That is how Samarkand's most famous legend was born — the legend that had a lot to do with the mystery that envelops the name of the city."

I let him tell the story.

"It was told that a king of Samarkand wanted to make everyone's dream come true: to escape death. He was convinced that death came from the sky and he wanted to do something so that it could never reach him, so he built an immense underground palace of iron which he made inaccessible.

"Being fabulously rich, he also had fashioned an artificial sun, which rose in the morning and set in the evening, to warm him and indicate the passing of days.

"Alas, the God of Death managed to foil the monarch's vigilance and he slipped inside the palace to accomplish his job. He had to show all humans that no creature could escape death, no matter how powerful, skillful, or arrogant he was. Samarkand thus became the symbol of the inescapable meeting between man and his destiny."

And after Samarkand, where to? For me it was the furthest extremity of the Orient, the place of all wonders and unfathomable nostalgia. The moment I left the city I decided to go back home; my desire was to be back in Annapolis and to spend some sedentary years there resting from my travels and only then to set off again.

I thus drew up the most insane plan — that of going back to Persia to fetch Shireen and the Khayyam manuscript, and then to go off and disappear in some great metropolis, such as Paris, Vienna, or New York. For the two of us to live in the West but to an Oriental rhythm; would that not be paradise?

On my way back, I was continually alone and distracted, preoccupied solely with the arguments that I was going to present to Shireen. "Leave? Leave . . .?" she would say wearily. "Is it not enough for you to be happy?" However, I did not despair of being able to overcome her reservations.

When the convertible I had rented at the edge of the Caspian set me down at Zarganda in front of my closed door, there was a car there already, a Jewel-40 sporting a star-spangled banner right in the middle of its hood.

The chauffeur stepped out and enquired as to my identity. I had the idiotic impression that he had been waiting for me ever since I left. He reassured me that he had only been there since the morning.

"My master told me to stay here until you came back."

"I might have come back in a month, a year, or perhaps never."

My astonishment hardly upset him.

"But you are here now!"

He handed me a note scribbled by Charles W. Russell, minister plenipotentiary of the United States.

Dear Mr. Lesage,

I would be most honored if you could come to the Legation this afternoon at four o'clock. It is a matter of great importance and urgency. I have asked my chauffeur to remain at your disposal.

44

Two men were waiting for me at the legation, with the same suppressed impatience. Russell, in a gray suit, a moiré bow-tie, and with a drooping mustache like Theodore Roosevelt's but more carefully shaped; and Fazel, in his undeviating white tunic, black cape, and blue turban. Naturally, it was the diplomat who opened the session in hesitant but correct French.

"The meeting taking place today is one of those that change the course of history. In our persons, two nations are meeting, defying distances and differences: the United States, which is a young nation but already an old democracy, and Persia, which is an old nation, several thousand years old, but a brand-new democracy."

He said all this with a touch of mystery, a whiff of formality, and a glance towards Fazel to make sure that his words were not upsetting him. He continued:

"Some days ago I was a guest of the Democratic Club of Tehran. I expressed to my audience the great sympathy I feel for the Constitutional Revolution. This feeling is shared by President Taft and Mr. Knox, our Secretary of State. I must add that the latter is aware of our meeting today and he is waiting for me to apprise him, by telegraph, of the conclusions we reach."

He left it to Fazel to explain to me:

"Do you remember the day when you tried to convince me not to resist the Czar's troops?"

"What a job that was!"

"I have never held it against you. You did what you had to do and in one sense you were correct. However, what I feared has unfortunately not died away. The Russians still have not left Tabriz, and the populace is subjected to daily torments. The Cossacks snatch the veils off women in the street, and sons of Adam are imprisoned upon the least pretext.

"Yet there is something more serious. More serious than the occupation of Tabriz and more serious than the fate of my companions. It is our democracy that is at risk of floundering. When Mr. Russell said 'young,' he should have added 'fragile' and 'under threat.' To all appearances everything is going well, the people are happier, the bazaar is prospering, and the religious appear to be conciliatory. However, it would need a miracle to stop the edifice from crumbling. Why? Because our coffers are empty, as in the past. The old régime had a very strange way of collecting taxes. It farmed each province out to some money-grubber who bled the population and kept the money for himself, deducting a small part to buy the court's protection. That is what has caused all our difficulties. As the Treasury was bare, they borrowed from the Russians and the English, who, in order to be reimbursed, obtained concessions and privileges. That is how the Czar became involved in our affairs and how we sold off all our wealth. The new government finds itself with the same dilemma as the old leaders: if it cannot manage to collect taxes the way modern countries do, it will have to accept the tutelage of the Powers. Our most urgent priority is to get our finances into order. The modernization of Persia will follow on from that: such is the cost of Persia's freedom."

"If the remedy is so obvious, why the delay in implementing it?"

"There is no Persian today who is up to undertaking such a task. It is sad to say, for a nation of ten million, but the weight of ignorance should not be underestimated. Only a handful of us here have received a modern education similar to that of the top-ranking civil servants in the advanced nations. The only area in which we have numerous competent people is the field of diplomacy. As for the rest, by which I mean the army, communications, and above all finance, there is nothing. If our régime can last twenty or thirty years, doubtless it will produce a generation capable of looking after all these sectors, but while we wait, the best solution available to us is to call upon honest and competent foreigners for help. It is not easy to find them, I know. In the past, we have had the worst experiences with Naus, Liakhov, and many others, but I do not despair. I have spoken on this subject with some of my colleagues in Parliament and the government, and we think that the United States might help."

"I am flattered," I said spontaneously, "but why my country?"

Charles Russell reacted to my remark with a movement of surprise and worry. Fazel's response quickly calmed him down.

"We have reviewed all the Powers, one by one. The Russians and the British are only too happy to push us towards bankruptcy so they can have more control over us. The French are too preoccupied with their relations with the Czar to be worried about our fate. On a more general level, the whole of Europe is beset by a game of alliances and counter-alliances in which Persia is only small change — a pawn on the chessboard. Only the United States could take an interest without trying to invade us. I therefore turned to Mr. Russell and asked him if he knew an American capable of taking on such a heavy task. I must acknowledge that it is he who mentioned your name. I had completely forgotten that you had studied finance."

"I am flattered by your faith," I replied, "but I am certainly not the man you need. In spite of my degree, I have only middling skill in finance and I have never had the opportunity to put my knowledge to the test. It is my father who is to blame, since he built so many ships that I have not had to work. I have only ever busied myself with the essential — that is to say, the futile: traveling and reading, loving and believing, doubting and fighting, and sometimes writing."

There were embarrassed laughs and an exchange of perplexed looks. I carried on:

"When you find your man, I can be at his side, give him unlimited advice and provide him with small services, but it is from him that you must demand competence and hard work. I am brimming over with good will but I am ignorant and lazy."

Fazel chose not to insist, but replied to me in the same tone: "It is true, I can testify to it. But you also have other faults that are even greater. You are my friend as the whole world knows, and my political adversaries would have only one aim: to stop you succeeding."

Russell listened in silence with a rigid smile on his face, as if he had been left out. Our banter was certainly not to his taste, but he did not lose his composure. Fazel turned to him:

"I am sorry about Benjamin's defection, but it does not change anything as far as we are concerned. Perhaps it is better to entrust this type of responsibility to a man who has never been mixed up in Persian affairs, neither from near nor afar."

"Are you thinking of someone in particular?"

"I have no one's name in mind. I would like him to be someone rigorous, honest, and with an independent spirit. There are some of that race amongst you, I know. I can see the person clearly and can almost tell you that I can see him before me; an elegant, neat man who holds himself upright and looks straight ahead, and who speaks to the point. A man like Baskerville."

The message of the Persian government to its legation in Washington on December 25, 1910, a Sunday and Christmas Day, was cabled in these terms:

Request the Secretary of State immediately to put you in contact with the American financial authorities with a view to engaging a disinterested American expert for the post of Treasurer General on the basis of a preliminary contract for three years, subject to ratification by the Parliament. He will be charged with reorganizing the state's resources and the collection of revenues and their disbursement with the help of an independent auditor who will supervise tax collection in the provinces.

The Minister of the United States in Tehran informs us that the Secretary of State is in agreement. Contact him directly and avoid using intermediaries. Transmit the whole text of this message to him and act according to the suggestions he makes to you.

On the following February 2, the Majlis approved the nomination of the American experts with an overwhelming majority and to thunderous applause.

A few days later, the Minister of Finance, who had presented the plan to the deputies, was assassinated in broad daylight by two Georgians. That very evening, the dragoman of the Russian legation went to the Persian Ministry of Foreign Affairs to demand that the murderers, subjects of the Czar, be handed over to him with no further ado. In Tehran everyone knew that this act was St. Petersburg's response to the vote in Parliament, but the authorities preferred to give in so as not to poison their relations with their powerful neighbor. The assassins therefore were led off to the legation and thence to the border; once over it they were free.

In protest, the bazaar closed its doors, sons of Adam called for a boycott of Russian goods, and there were even reports of acts of vengeance against the numerous Georgian nationals, the Gordji, in the country. However, the government, backed up by the press, preached patience; the real reforms were going to begin, they said, experts were going to arrive and soon the state's coffers would be full, they would pay off their debts and throw off all tutelage, they would have schools and hospitals as well as a modern army — which would force the Czar to leave Tabriz and stop him threatening them.

Persia was waiting for miracles, and, in fact, miracles were going to come to pass.

45

It was Fazel who announced the first miracle to me, triumphantly, albeit in a whisper:

"Look at him! I told you that he would look like Baskerville!"

"He" was Morgan Shuster, the new Treasurer General of Persia, who was coming over to greet us. We had gone to meet him on the Kazvin road. He arrived, with his men, in dilapidated poste-chaises pulled by feeble horses. It was strange how much he looked like Howard: the same eyes, the same nose, the same clean-shaven face, which was perhaps a little rounder, the same light hair parted the same way, the same polite but firm handshake. The way we looked at him must have irritated him, but he did not show it; it is true that he must have expected to be the object of sustained curiosity, coming to a foreign country in this way and in such exceptional circumstances. Throughout his stay, he would be watched, examined, and followed — sometimes with malice. Each of his actions, and every one of his omissions, would be reported and commented on, praised or damned.

A week after his arrival the first crisis broke out. Amongst the hundreds of people who came every day to welcome the Americans, some asked Shuster when he was planning to visit the English and Russian legations. His response was evasive, but the questions became insistent and the affair leaked out and gave rise to animated discussions in the bazaar: should the American pay courtesy calls to the legations or not? The legations let it be known that they had been belittled and the climate became strained. Given the role that he had played in bringing Shuster, Fazel was particularly embarrassed by this diplomatic hitch, which was threatening to put his whole mission at stake. He asked me to intervene.

I therefore went to see my compatriot at the Atabak Palace, a white stone building, the fine columns of which were reflected in a pond and which consisted of thirty huge rooms, some furnished in the Oriental and some in the European manner, filled with carpets and *objets d'art.* All around was an immense park crossed by streams and peppered with man-made lakes — a real Persian paradise where the noises of the city were filtered out by the song of the cicadas. It was one of the most beautiful residences in Tehran. It had belonged to a former prime minister before being bought up by a rich Zoroastrian merchant who was a fervent supporter of the constitution and who had graciously placed it at the American's disposal.

Shuster received me on the steps. Having recovered from the exhaustion of the journey, he seemed to me quite young. He was only thirty-four years old and did not look it. And I had thought that Washington would send over someone who looked like Father Time!

"I have come to speak to you about this business with the legations."

"You too!"

He pretended to be amused.

"I do not know," I stated, "whether you are aware of just how serious this question of protocol has become. Don't forget, we are in the country of intrigue!"

"No one enjoys intrigue more than I do!"

He laughed again but stopped suddenly and became as serious as his position demanded of him.

"Mr. Lesage, it is not just a question of protocol. It is a question of

278

principles. Before I accepted this post, I briefed myself thoroughly on the dozens of foreign experts who came to this country before me. Some of them lacked neither competence nor goodwill, but they all failed. Do you know why? Because they fell into the trap I am being asked to fall into today. I have been named Treasurer General of Persia by the Parliament of Persia. It is thus normal for me to signal my arrival to the Shah, the Regent, and the government. I am an American and can thus also go to visit the charming Mr. Russell. But why am I being demanded to make courtesy calls to the Russians, the English, the Belgians, and Austrians?

"I will tell you: because they want to show to everyone, to the Persian people who expect so much from the Americans, to the Parliament which took us on in spite of all pressure put on it, that Morgan Shuster is a foreigner like all foreigners, a *farangi*. Once I have made my first visits, the invitations will come pouring in; diplomats are courteous, welcoming, and cultivated people, they speak the languages I know and they play the same games. I could live happily here, Mr. Lesage, between games of bridge, tea, tennis, horse-riding, and masked balls, and when I go home in three years' time I would be rich, happy, tanned, and in the best of health. However, that is not why I came, Mr. Lesage."

He was almost shouting. An unseen hand, perhaps his wife's, discreetly shut the door to the sitting-room. He seemed not to have noticed and carried on:

"I came with a very precise mission: to modernize Persia's finances. These men have called upon us because they have faith in our institutions and the way we handle affairs. I have no intention of disappointing them. Nor of misleading them. I come from a Christian nation, Mr. Lesage, and that means something for me. What image do the Persians have of the Christian nations today? Ultra-Christian England which appropriates their gas and ultra-Christian Russia which imposes its will on them according to the cynical law of the survival of the fittest? Who are these Christians who have frequented here? Swindlers, arrogant, godless men and Cossacks. What idea do you want them to have of us? In what world are we going to live together? Do we have no choice to offer other than to be our slaves or our enemies? Could they not be our partners and equals? Some of them fortunately continue to believe in us and our values, but how much longer will they be able to muzzle the thousands who liken Europeans to demons?

"What will the Persia of tomorrow be like? That depends on how we behave and on the example we offer. Baskerville's sacrifice has made people forget the greed of many other Europeans. I have the greatest esteem for him, but I assure you I have no intention of dying; quite simply, I wish to be honest. I shall serve Persia as I would serve an American company. I shall not despoil Persia but I will make every effort to clean it up and make it prosper, and shall respect its government but without bowing and scraping."

Stupidly, tears had started to pour down my face. Shuster fell silent and watched me warily and a little confused.

"Would you please excuse me if I have hurt you, without meaning to, by my tone of voice or my words."

I stood up and held out my hand.

"You have not hurt me, Mr. Shuster, I am simply shattered. I am going to report your words to my Persian friends and their reaction will not be any different from mine."

When I left I ran to the Baharistan; I knew that I would find Fazel there. The moment I saw him in the distance I shouted out:

"Fazel. There has been another miracle!"

On June 13, the Persian Parliament decided, by an unprecedented vote, to confer full powers on Morgan Shuster to reorganize the country's finances. Henceforth he would be invited regularly to be present at Cabinet meetings.

In the meantime, another incident had become the topic of conversation in bazaar and chancellery alike. A rumor, whose origin was unknown but which could be easily guessed, accused Morgan Shuster of belonging to a Persian sect. The whole thing may seem absurd but the people spreading the rumor had distilled their venom well enough to be able to give the gossip an air of plausibility. Overnight the Americans became suspect in the eyes of the crowd. Once again I was charged to speak about it to the Treasurer General. Our relations had become closer since our first meeting. I called him Morgan and he called me Ben. I explained to him the subject of the offense.

"They are saying that amongst your servants there are *Babis* or acknowledged *Bahais*, which fact Fazel has confirmed to me. They are also saying that the *Bahais* have just founded a very active branch in the United States. They have deduced that all Americans in the legation are in fact *Bahais* who, under the pretext of cleaning up the country's finances, have come to win converts."

Morgan deliberated for a moment:

"I shall respond to the only important question: no, I have not come to preach or convert, but in order to reform Persian finances which are in dire need of it. I shall add, for your information, that I am of course not a *Bahai* and that I only learnt of the existence of these sects from Professor Browne's book just before I arrived, and that I am still unable to differentiate between a *Babi* and a *Bahai*. On the matter of my servants, of whom there are a good fifteen in this huge house, everyone knows that they were here before I arrived. Their work gives me satisfaction and that is the only thing that matters. I am not accustomed to judge fellow-workmen by their faith or the color of their tie!"

"I can understand your attitude perfectly well. It corresponds to my own convictions. However, we are in Persia and sensibilities are sometimes different. I have just seen the new Minister of Finance. He thinks that in order to silence the slanderers, the servants concerned, or at least some of them, will have to be fired."

"Is the Minister of Finance worrying about this business?"

"More than you think. He fears that it might jeopardize everything he has undertaken in his sector. He has asked me to brief him this evening on how I have got on."

"Don't let me delay you. You can tell him on my behalf that no servant will be dismissed and that as far as I am concerned the matter ends there!"

He stood up. I felt compelled to keep trying.

"I am not certain that that response will be sufficient, Morgan!"

"No? In that case, you can add to it: 'Minister of Finance, if you have nothing better to do than examine my gardener's religion, I can supply you with more important files to pad out your time.'"

I gave the minister only the gist of his words, but I am quite certain that Morgan himself repeated them to him verbatim at the first opportunity, moreover without causing the slightest drama. In fact, everyone was happy that common sense had been spoken with no beating about the bush.

"Since Shuster has been here," Shireen confided in me one day, "the atmosphere is somewhat healthier and cleaner. When faced with a chaotic and convoluted situation, one always thinks that it will take centuries to sort it out. Suddenly a man appears and as if by magic, the tree we thought was doomed takes on new life and starts bearing leaves and fruit and giving shade. This foreigner has given me back my faith in my countrymen. He does not speak to them as natives, he does not have any respect for people's sensitivities or their pettiness, but speaks to them like men and the Persians are rediscovering that they are men. Do you know that in my family the old women pray for him?"

46

I am in no way departing from the truth by stating that in that year of 1911 all of Persia was living in the "age of the American" and that Shuster was indisputably the most popular official and one of the most powerful. The newspapers supported his actions all the more enthusiastically when he took the trouble to invite the editors over from time to time to brief them on his projects and solicit their advice on some prickly questions.

Above all, and most importantly, his difficult mission was on the road to success. Before even reforming the fiscal system, he managed to balance the budget simply by limiting theft and waste. Previously, innumerable notables, princes, ministers, or high dignitaries would send their demands to the Treasury in the form of a note scribbled on a greasy piece of paper, and the civil servants were constrained to satisfy them unless they wished to lose their job or their life. With Morgan everything had changed overnight.

I will give one example out of so many others. On June 17 at a

Cabinet meeting, Shuster was presented with a pathetic request for the sum of forty-two million *tumans* in order to pay the salaries of the troops in Tehran.

"Otherwise a rebellion will break out and it is the Treasurer General who will bear the entire responsibility!" exclaimed Amir-i-Azam, the "Supreme Emir," the Minister of War.

Shuster gave the following response:

"The Minister himself took a similar sum ten days ago. What has he done with it?"

"I have used it to pay part of the soldiers' back pay. Their families are hungry and the officers are all in debt. The situation is intolerable."

"Is the Minister certain that there is nothing left from that sum?"

"Not the smallest coin!"

Shuster took out of his pocket a small visiting card which was covered with tiny writing and which he conspicuously consulted before stating:

"The sum the Treasury paid out ten days ago has been deposited in its entirety in the personal account of the Minister. Not one *tuman* has been spent. I have here the name of the banker and the figures."

The Supreme Emir, a huge fleshy man, stood up, bristling with rage; he placed his hand on his chest and cast a furious glance at his colleagues:

"Is this an attempt to question my honor?"

As no one reassured him on that point, he added:

"I swear that if such a sum is indeed in my account, I am the last to know about it."

There were some looks of incredulity around him. It was decided to bring in the banker, and Shuster asked the ministers to wait where they were. The moment it was indicated that the man had arrived, the Minister of War rushed to meet him. After an exchange of whispers the Supreme Emir came back to his colleagues with an artless smile.

"This damned banker had not understood my orders. He has not yet paid the troops. It was a misunderstanding!"

The incident was closed, albeit with some difficulty, but thereafter the state's high officials did not dare to pillage the Treasury to their heart's content, a centuries-old custom. There were of course malcontents, but they had to keep silent since most of the people, even amongst the ranks of the government officials, had reason to be satisfied: for the first time in history, civil servants, soldiers, and Persian diplomats abroad received their salaries on time.

Even in international financial circles people were starting to believe in the Shuster miracle. As proof: the Seligman brothers, bankers in London, decided to grant Persia a loan of four million pounds sterling without imposing any humiliating clauses of the type generally attached to this type of transaction — neither a levy on customs receipts, nor a mortgage of any sort. It was a normal loan to a normal, respectable, and potentially solvent client. That was an important step. In the eyes of those who wanted to subjugate Persia it was a dangerous precedent. The British government intervened to block the loan.

Meanwhile, the Czar had recourse to more brutal methods. In July it was learned that the former Shah had returned, with two of his brothers and at the head of an army of mercenaries, to try and seize power. Had he not been under house arrest in Odessa, with the Russian government's explicit promise never to allow him to return to Persia? When questioned, the St. Petersburg authorities replied that he had slipped out with a false passport and that his armaments had been transported in boxes labeled "mineral water," and that they themselves bore no responsibility for his rebellion. Thus he had left his residence in Odessa and with his men crossed the few hundred miles separating the Ukraine and Persia, boarded a Russian ship with all his armaments, crossed the Caspian Sea, and disembarked on the Persian side — all of that without arousing the notice of the Czar's government, his army, nor the Okhrana, his secret police?

But what use was it to discuss the matter? Above all, the fragile Persian democracy had to be prevented from crumbling. Parliament asked Shuster for credit and this time the American did not argue. On the contrary, he saw to it that an army was raised within a few days, with the best available equipment and abundant ammunition. He himself suggested that it should be commanded by Ephraim Khan, a brilliant Armenian officer who within three months would succeed in crushing the ex-Shah and pushing him back across the border.

In chancelleries throughout the world it could hardly be believed: had Persia become a modern state? Such rebellions generally dragged on for years: For most observers, both in Tehran and abroad, the response was summed up in a single magic word: Shuster. His role now went far beyond that of simply being Treasurer General. It was he who suggested to Parliament that they outlaw the former Shah and plaster "Wanted" posters, as in the Wild West, on the walls of all the cities in the country, offering significant sums to anyone who helped to capture the imperial rebel and his brothers, all of which succeeded in discrediting the deposed monarch in the eyes of the population.

The Czar was still in a rage. It was now clear to him that his ambitions in Persia would not be satisfied while Shuster was there. He had to be made to leave! An incident had to be created, a large incident. A man was charged with this mission: Pokhitanoff, former Consul in Tabriz and now Consul General in Tehran.

Mission is an unassuming word, for what was, in that context, a plot that was carefully carried out, although without much finesse. Parliament had decided to confiscate the property of the ex-Shah's two brothers who were leading the rebellion at his side. Commissioned to carry out the sentence, as Treasurer General, Shuster wanted to do everything with the utmost legality. The principal property concerned, situated not far from the Atabak Palace, belonged to the Imperial Prince who went by the name "Radiance of the Sultanate"; the American sent a detachment of the police and civil servants there, armed with warrants. They found themselves face to face with Cossacks accompanied by Russian consular officers who forbade the police to enter the property, threatening to use force if they did not speedily retrace their steps.

When told of the outcome, Shuster sent one of his aides over to the Russian legation. He was received by Pokhitanoff, who, in an aggressive tone of voice, gave him the following explanation: the mother of Prince "Radiance of the Sultanate" had written to the Czar and Czarina to claim their protection, which was generously accorded.

The American could not believe his ears. It was unjust that foreigners, he said, should enjoy the privilege of immunity in Persia and that the assassins of a Persian minister could not be judged because they were the Czar's subjects — but it was a time-honored rule and difficult to change; however, Persians overnight could place their property under the protection of a foreign monarch to deflect the laws of their own country — that was a novel and extraordinary process. Shuster did not want to resign himself to that. He gave an order to the police to go and take possession of the properties in question, without the use of violence but with determination. This time Pokhitanoff allowed it. He had created the incident. His mission was accomplished.

The reaction was not slow in coming. A communiqué was published in St. Petersburg stating that what had happened amounted to an act of aggression against Russia and an insult to the Czar and Czarina. They were demanding an official apology from the Tehran government. In a panic, the Persian Prime Minister asked the British for advice; the Foreign Office replied that the Czar was not playing games, that he had amassed troops in Baku, that he was preparing to invade Persia, and that it would be wise to accept the ultimatum.

Thus, on November 24, 1911, the Persian Minister for Foreign Affairs, with a heavy heart, presented himself at the Russian legation and shook hands fawningly with the Minister Plenipotentiary as he pronounced these words:

"Your Excellency, my government has charged me with presenting to you, on its behalf, apologies for the insult that consular officials of your government have suffered."

Still shaking the minister's hand, the Czar's representative retorted:

"Your apologies are accepted as a response to our first ultimatum; however, I must inform you that a second ultimatum is in preparation at St. Petersburg. I will advise you of its contents as soon as it reaches me."

He kept his promise. Five days later, on November 29 at midday, the diplomat presented the Minister of Foreign Affairs with the text of the new ultimatum, adding orally that it had already received London's approval and that it had to be satisfied within forty-eight hours.

Point one: dismiss Morgan Shuster.

Point two: never again employ a foreign expert without obtaining beforehand the consent of the Russian and British legations.

47

In the Parliament building the seventy-six deputies were waiting, some of them wearing turbans, others fezzes or hats; some of the most militant sons of Adam were even dressed in European style. At eleven o'clock the Prime Minister mounted the dais, as if it were a scaffold, and with a stifled voice he read out the text of the ultimatum and then mentioned London's support for the Czar before announcing his government's decision not to resist but to accept the ultimatum and to dismiss the American — in a word, to return to the tutelage of the Powers rather than to be crushed underfoot by them. In order to try and avoid the worst he needed a clear mandate; he therefore asked for a show of confidence, reminding the deputies that the ultimatum would expire at midday, that they had a finite amount of time, and that discussions could not drag on. During the whole of his speech he had kept glancing worriedly towards the visitors' gallery where sat enthroned Mr. Pokhitanoff, whom none had dared to forbid entering.

When the Prime Minister went back to his seat, there were neither boos nor applause but only a deafening, overwhelming, and oppressive silence. Then a venerable *sayyid* arose, a descendant of the Prophet and a modernist from the outset who had always given enthusiastic support to Shuster's mission. His speech was short:

"Perhaps it is the will of God that our freedom and sovereignty should be snatched away by force. But we will not abandon those principles of our own accord."

There was silence again. Then another speech in the same vein and just as short. Mr. Pokhitanoff made a great show of looking at his watch. The Prime Minister saw him and in his turn he pulled out his fob watch and held it up to read the time. It was twenty to twelve. He became panicky and tapped the ground with his cane, demanding that they move on to a vote. Four deputies hurriedly withdrew on various pretexts: the seventy-two remaining all said "no." No to the Czar's ultimatum. No to Shuster's departure and no to the government's stance. By this fact, the Prime Minister was considered to have resigned and he withdrew with his whole cabinet. Pokhitanoff also arose; the text he had to cable to St. Petersburg had already been drafted.

The great door was slammed and the echo reverberated a long time in the silence of the hall. The deputies were alone. They had won but they did not feel like celebrating their victory. Power was in their hands: the fate of the country and its young constitution depended on them. What could they do with the power? What did they want to do with it? They had no idea. It was an unreal, pathetic, and chaotic session, and in some respects it was childish too. From time to time someone came up with an idea, only to have it dismissed:

"And if we asked the United States to send us troops?"

"Why would they come, they are Russia's friends. Was it not President Roosevelt who brought about a reconciliation between the Czar and the Mikado?"

"But there is Shuster. Would they want to help him?"

"Shuster is very popular in Persia; but at home he is hardly known. The American leaders will not be able to appreciate why he has got on the wrong side of London and St. Petersburg."

"We could suggest to them building a railway. Perhaps they would be enticed to come to our help."

289

"Perhaps, but not for six months, and the Czar will be here within two weeks."

"And the Turks? The Germans? And why not the Japanese? Did they not crush the Russians in Manchuria?" Suddenly a young deputy from Kirman suggested, with a hint of a smile, that the throne of Persia should be offered to the Mikado, at which Fazel exploded: "We must be aware, once and for all, that we cannot even make an appeal to the people of Isfahan! If we join battle, it will be in Tehran, with the people of Tehran and with arms that are currently in the capital. Just as in Tabriz three years ago. And it is not a thousand Cossacks that will be sent to fight us but fifty thousand. We must know that we will fight without the slightest chance of winning."

Coming from anyone else, this disheartening speech would have aroused a torrent of accusations. Coming from the hero of Tabriz, the most eminent son of Adam, the words were taken for what they were — an expression of cruel reality. After that it was difficult to preach resistance, but that, however, was just what Fazel did.

"If we are ready to fight, it is solely in order to safeguard the future. Does Persia not still live in the memory of the Imam Hussein? Yet this martyr did no more than lead a lost battle. He was defeated, crushed, and massacred and it is he whom we honor. Persia needs blood in order to believe. There are seventy-two of us, the same number as Hussein's companions. If we die, this Parliament will become a place of pilgrimage and democracy will be anchored for centuries in the ground of the Orient.

They all declared themselves ready to die, but they did not die. Not that they weakened or betrayed their cause. Exactly the opposite — they tried to organize the city's defenses and volunteers, particularly sons of Adam, presented themselves in great numbers, just as in Tabriz. However, it was to no avail. After invading the north of the country, the Czar's troops were now advancing in the direction of the capital. Only the snow slowed down their progress a little.

On December 24 the fallen Prime Minister decided to take power again by force. Aided by Cossacks, Bakhtiari tribes, and an important section of the army and the police, he made himself master of the capital and had the dissolution of Parliament proclaimed. Several deputies were arrested. Those who had been most active, with Fazel at the head of the list, were condemned to exile.

The first act of the new regime was officially to accept the terms of the Czar's ultimatum. A polite letter informed Morgan Shuster that an end had been put to his functions as Treasurer General. He had only been in Persia for eight months, albeit eight hectic and dizzying months, which all but changed the face of the Orient.

On January 11, 1912, Shuster was seen off with honors. The young Shah placed his own car at his disposal, along with his French chauffeur Monsieur Varlet, to drive him to the port of Enzeli. There were a lot of us, foreigners and Persians, who came to bid him farewell, some in front of his residence and others along the road. There were of course no cheers, just the discreet gestures of thousands of hands, the tears of men and women and a crowd of strangers who were crying like abandoned lovers. Along the whole route there was only one insignificant incident: as the convoy went past, a Cossack picked up a stone and made as if to throw it in the direction of the American; I do not believe that he even carried through his action.

When the car had disappeared beyond the Kazvin Gate, I walked a little in the company of Charles Russell. Then I made my way alone, by foot, to Shireen's palace.

"You seem rather crestfallen," she said as she received me.

"I have just come from bidding farewell to Shuster."

"Ah! He has finally gone!"

I was not certain whether I had understood the tone of her exclamation. She explained herself.

"Today I have been wondering whether it would not have been better if he had never set foot in this country."

I looked at her with horror.

"It is you who are saying that to me!"

"Yes, it is I, Shireen, who am saying that. I, who applauded the American's arrival, I who approved every one of his actions, I who saw him as a redeemer. Now I regret the fact that he did not stay in far-off America."

"But what did he do wrong?"

"Nothing. And that is precisely the proof that he did not understand Persia."

I really was not following her.

"If a minister is right and the king mistaken, a wife is right when her husband is wrong, or a soldier correct and his officer off course, are they not punished doubly? In the eyes of the weak, it is wrong to be right. Compared to the Russians and the English, Persia is weak and should have known how to behave like a weak person."

"Until the end of time? Should Persia not recover one day and construct a modern state, educate its people and enter into the concert of prosperous and respected nations? That is what Shuster was trying to do."

"For that I grant him the greatest admiration. However, I cannot help thinking that if he had succeeded a little less we would not be in this lamentable situation today with our democracy destroyed and our territory invaded."

"The Czar's ambitions being what they are, that would have happened sooner or later."

"It is always better for a misfortune to happen later. Do you know the story of Mullah Nasruddin's talking ass?"

Mullah Nasruddin was the semi-legendary hero of all the anecdotes and parables of Persia, Transoxania, and Asia Minor. Shireen told the story:

"It was said that a half-mad king had condemned Nasruddin to death for having stolen an ass. Just as he was about to be led off for execution he exclaimed, 'That beast is in reality my brother. A magician made him look like that, but if he were entrusted to me for a year I would teach him to speak like us again!' Intrigued, the monarch made the accused repeat his promise before decreeing, 'Very well! But if within one year from today the ass does not speak, you will be executed.' As he went out, Nasruddin was accosted by his wife: 'How can you make a promise like that? You know very well that this ass will not speak.' 'Of course I know,' replied Nasruddin, 'but during the year the king might die, the ass might, or even I might.'"

The Princess went on:

"If we had been able to gain some time, Russia might have got bogged down in the Balkans or in China. What's more, the Czar is not eternal, he could die or be shaken by riots or revolts, as happened six years ago. We should have been patient and waited, used tricks, procrastinated, yielded, told lies, and given promises. That has always been the wisdom of the Orient; Shuster wanted to make us move to the rhythm of the Occident, he steered us straight to shipwreck."

She seemed to be suffering from having said that, so I avoided contradicting her. She added:

"Persia makes me think of an unlucky sailboat. The sailors constantly complain that there is not enough wind to move, and suddenly, as if to punish them, Heaven sends them a tornado."

We stayed silent for a long time, weighed down in thought. Then I put my arm around her affectionately.

"Shireen!"

Was it the way I uttered her name? She gave a start and then pushed me away as she gave me a suspicious look.

"You are leaving."

"Yes, but differently."

"How can one leave 'differently'?"

"I am leaving with you."

48

Cherbourg. April 10, 1912. The English Channel stretched as far as the eye could see, its surface flecked with silver. By my side was Shireen. We had the *Manuscript* in our luggage. We were surrounded by an unlikely crowd, completely Oriental.

So much has been said of the shining celebrities who set sail on the *Titanic* that we have almost forgotten those for whom these sea giants were built: the migrants, those millions of men, women, and children no country would agree to feed any more and who dreamt of America. The steamboat had to make a lot of pick-ups: the English and Scandinavians from Southampton, the Irish from Queenstown, and at Cherbourg those who came from further away, Greeks, Syrians, Armenians from Anatolia, Jews from Salonika or Bessarabia, Croats, Serbs, and Persians. It was these Orientals that I was able to watch at the harbor station, clustered around their pathetic luggage, in a hurry to be somewhere else and in a state of anguish from time to time, suddenly looking for a lost form, a child who was too agile, or an unmanageable bundle that had rolled under a bench. On everyone's face there was written adventure, bitterness, or defiance. They all felt that it was a privilege, the moment they arrived in the West, to be taking part in the maiden voyage of the most powerful, the most modern, and the most dependable steamboat ever dreamed up by man.

My own feelings were hardly different. Having been married three weeks earlier in Paris, I put back my departure with the sole aim of offering my companion a wedding trip worthy of the Oriental splendor in which she had lived. It was not a vain whim. For a long time, Shireen had seemed reticent about the idea of living in the United States and, had it not been for the fact that she was so disheartened by Persia's failed reawakening, she would never have agreed to follow me. My ambition was to build up around her a world yet more magical than the one she had had to leave.

The *Titanic* served my purposes marvelously. It seemed to have been conceived by men who were eager to enjoy, in this floating palace, the most sumptuous pleasures of *terra firma* as well as some of the joys of the Orient: a Turkish bath just as indolent as those of Constantinople or Cairo; verandahs dotted with palm-trees; and in the gymnasium, between the bar and the pommel horse, there was an electric camel, which, when you pressed the magic button, instilled in the rider the feeling of a jumpy ride in the desert.

However, as we explored the *Titanic*, we were not just trying to search out the exotic. We also managed to give ourselves over to wholly European pleasures, such as eating oysters, followed by a *sauté de poulet à la Lyonnaise*, the speciality of Mr. Proctor the chef, washed down by a Cos-d'Estournel 1887, as we listened to the orchestra dressed in blue tuxedos playing the Tales of Hoffman, the Geisha, or the Grand Moghul by Luder.

Those moments were even more precious to Shireen and me since we had had to keep up pretences throughout our long romance in Persia. Ample and promising as my princess's apartments had been at Tabriz, Zarganda, or Tehran, I suffered constantly from the feeling that our love was restricted within their walls, with its only witness engraved mirrors and servants with fleeting glances. Now we could take simple pleasure in being seen together, a man and a woman arm in arm, taken in by the same strange looks. We avoided going back to our cabin until late at night, even though I had chosen one of the most spacious on board.

Our final delight was the evening promenade. When we finished dinner, we would go and find an officer, always the same one, who would lead us to a safe from which we would take out the *Manuscript* and carry it carefully on a tour across bridges and down corridors. Seated in rattan armchairs in the Parisian Café we would read some quatrains at random, then, taking the elevator, we would go up to the walkway where, without having to worry too much as to whether we could be seen, we would exchange a passionate kiss in the open air. Late in the night we would take the *Manuscript* to our room where it spent the night before being placed back in the safe, in the morning, with the help of the same officer. It was a ritual that enchanted Shireen. So much so that I made it a duty for myself to retain every detail in order to reproduce it exactly the next day.

That is how, on the fourth evening, I had opened the *Manuscript* at the page where Khayyam in his day had written:

> *You ask what is this life so frail, so vain.*
> *'Tis long to tell, yet will I make it plain;*
> *'Tis but a breath blown from the vasty deeps,*
> *And then blown back to those same deeps again!*

The reference to the ocean amused me: I wanted to read it again, more slowly, but Shireen interrupted me:
"Please don't!"
She seemed to be suffocating; I looked at her worriedly.
"I know that *rubai* by heart," she said in a faint voice, "and I suddenly had the impression that I was hearing it for the first time. It is as if..."
She would not explain, however, and got her breath back before stating in a light and serene tone of voice:
"I wish that we had already arrived."
I shrugged my shoulders.
"If there is a ship in the world on which one can travel without

fear, it is this one. As Captain Smith said, God Himself could not sink this ship!"

If I had thought to reassure her with those words and my happy tone, it was in fact the opposite that I effected. She clutched my arm, murmuring:

"Never say that again! Never!"

"Why are you getting so worked up? You know very well that it was only a joke."

"Where I come from even an atheist would not dare use such a phrase."

She was trembling. I could not understand why she was reacting so violently. I suggested that we go back to the cabin and had to support her so that she would not stumble on the way.

The next day she seemed to be herself again. In order to occupy her mind, I took her off to discover the wonders of the ship. I even mounted the jerky electric camel, at the risk of putting up with the laughs of Henry Sleeper Harper, the editor of the eponymous weekly, who stayed for a moment in our company, offered us tea, and told us about his trips in the Orient, before introducing to us, most ceremoniously, his Pekinese dog which he thought acceptable to call Sun Yat-Sen, in ambiguous homage to the emancipator of China. However, nothing managed to cheer Shireen up.

That evening, at dinner, she was taciturn; she seemed to have become weak. I thought it best not to go on our ritual promenade and left the *Manuscript* in the safe. We went back to our cabin to go to bed. She immediately fell into a disturbed sleep. I, on the other hand, was worried about her, and unused as I was to sleeping so early I spent a good part of the night watching her.

Why should I lie? When the ship hit the iceberg I was not aware of anything. It was after the collision, when I was told at exactly what moment it had taken place, that I thought I could remember having heard a noise like a sheet being torn in a nearby cabin shortly before midnight. Nothing else. I do not remember feeling any impact and managed to doze off, only to wake up with a start when someone rapped on the door, shouting a phrase I could not make out. I looked at my watch. It was ten to one. I put on my dressing gown and opened the door. The corridor was empty, but from afar I could hear loud conversation, something unusual for so late at night. Without actually being worried, I decided to go and see what was happening, of course making no move to wake Shireen.

On the stairway I came across a steward who spoke lightly of "a few little problems" that had just cropped up. He said that the captain wanted all the first-class passengers to assemble on the Sun Bridge, at the top of the ship.

"Must I wake my wife? She has been a little unwell during the day."

"The captain said everyone," the steward retorted with the look of a skeptic.

Back in the cabin, I woke Shireen with the necessary tenderness, stroking her forehead and then her eyebrows, pronouncing her name with my lips fast to her ear. When she gave out a little groan I whispered:

"You must get up. We have to go up on the bridge."

"Not tonight, I am too cold."

"It is not for a promenade, they are the captain's orders."

The last two words had a magical effect; she jumped out of bed shouting:

"*Khodaya!* My God!"

She got dressed quickly and in a state of disorder. I had to keep her calm, tell her to slow down, that we were not in such a hurry. However, when we arrived on the bridge there was an atmosphere of turmoil and passengers were being directed towards the lifeboats.

The steward I had met earlier was there. I went over to him. He had lost none of his cheeriness.

"Women and children first," he said, in a tone that poked fun at the phrase.

I took Shireen by the hand, to try and lead her over to the boats, but she refused to move.

"The *Manuscript*," she pleaded.

"We would run the risk of losing it in all the crush! It is better off in the safe!"

"I will not leave without it!"

"There is no question of leaving," the steward interjected. "We are getting the passengers off the ship for an hour or two. If you want my advice, even that is not necessary. But the captain is the master of the ship . . ."

I would not say that she was convinced by that, but she simply let herself be pulled along by the hand without putting up any resistance — as far as the forecastle where an officer called me.

"Sir, over here, we need you."

I went up to him.

"This lifeboat needs a man. Can you row?"

"I have rowed for years in Chesapeake Bay."

Satisfied by that, he invited me to get into the boat and helped Shireen to clamber in. There were about thirty people in it, with as many places still empty, but the orders were only to load the women — and some experienced rowers.

We were winched down to the ocean somewhat abruptly to my taste, but I managed to keep the boat steady and began to row. But where to, or towards what point in this black void? I did not have the least idea and neither did the men handling the evacuation. I decided just to get away from the ship and to wait at a distance of half a mile for some signal to call me back.

During the first minutes everyone's concern was how we could all protect ourselves against the cold. There was an icy breeze blowing that prevented us hearing the tune the ship's orchestra was still playing. However, when we stopped, at what seemed to me an adequate distance, the truth suddenly dawned on us: the *Titanic* was leaning distinctly forwards and her lights were gradually fading. We were all dumbfounded. Suddenly there was a call from a man who was swimming; I maneuvered the lifeboat towards him; Shireen and another passenger helped me to drag him on board. Soon other survivors were making signs to us and we went to haul them out. While we were occupied with this task, Shireen gave out a cry. The *Titanic* was now in a vertical position and its lights had dimmed. She stayed like that for five endless minutes and then solemnly plunged towards her destiny.

We were flat out, exhausted and surrounded by forlorn faces when the sun surprised us on April 15. We were on board the *Carpathia*, which on receiving a distress call had rushed over to pick up the survivors from the wreck. Shireen was at my side, silent. Since we had seen the *Titanic* go down she had not spoken a word, and her eyes were avoiding me. I wanted to shake her, to remind her that we had been saved miraculously, that most of the passengers had perished, and that there were around us on this bridge women who had just lost their husbands and children who were now orphans.

However, I stopped myself preaching to her. I knew that the *Manuscript* was for her, as it was for me, more than a jewel, more than a precious antique — that it was, to some extent, our reason for being together. Its disappearance, come after so many misfortunes, had to have a serious effect on Shireen. I felt it would be wiser to let time heal.

As we drew close to the port of New York, late on the evening of April 18, a noisy reception was awaiting us: reporters had come to meet us on rented boats, and, with the aid of megaphones, they shouted questions over to us and some of the passengers cupped their hands to their mouths and tried to shout back answers.

When the *Carpathia* had berthed, other journalists hurried over to the survivors, all trying to guess which might be the truest, or most sensational, account. It was a very young writer from the *Evening Sun* who chose me. He was particularly interested in Captain Smith's behavior as well as that of crew members at the time of the catastrophe. Had they succumbed to panic? In their exchanges with the passengers, had they covered up the truth? Was it true that the first-class passengers had been saved first? Each of his questions made me think back and rack my memory; we spoke for a long time, first as we were disembarking, then standing up on the quay. Shireen had stayed for a moment at my side, still not saying a word, then she slipped away. I had no reason to worry, she could not really have gone far, surely she was somewhere nearby, hidden behind this photographer who was focusing a blinding flash at me.

As he left me, the journalist complimented me on the quality of my account and took my address in order to get in touch with me later. Then I looked all around, and called out louder and louder.

Shireen was no longer there. I decided not to move from the spot where she had left me so that she would be able to find me again. I waited for an hour, for two hours. The quay gradually emptied. Where should I look? First of all I went to the office of White Star, the company to which the *Titanic* belonged. Then I checked all the hotels where the survivors had been lodged for the night. However, yet again I found no sign of my wife. I returned to the quays. They were deserted.

Then I decided to set off for the only place whose address she knew, and where, once she had calmed down, she would know to find me: my house in Annapolis.

I waited for some sign of Shireen for a long time, but she never came. She did not write to me. No one mentioned her name any more in front of me.

Today I wonder: did she exist? Was she anything other than the fruit of my Oriental obsessions? At night, in the solitude of my overlarge bedroom, when doubt rises up in me, when my memory clouds over and I feel my reason waver, I get up and turn on all the lights. I rush and take out the letters of yesteryear which I pretend to open as if I had just received them. I breathe in their perfume and re-read some pages; the very coldness of the letters' tone comforts me, and gives me the illusion that I am experiencing anew the birth of love. Then alone, and soothed, I put them in order and dive back into the dark, ready to give myself over without fright to the dazzling sights of the past: a phrase uttered in a Constantinople sitting-room, two sleepless nights in Tabriz, a brazier in the winter in Zarganda. And this scene from our last trip: we had gone up on to the walkway, into a dark and deserted corner where we had exchanged a long kiss. In order to take her face in my hands, I had placed the *Manuscript* flat on a bollard. When she noticed it, Shireen burst out laughing. She stepped away from me and with a theatrical gesture she shouted to the sky:

"The *Rubaiyaat* on the *Titanic*! The flower of the Orient borne by the jewel of the Occident! Khayyam, if you could only see what a beautiful moment has been granted to us!"

Other titles in the series

From Chile:
The Secret Holy War of Santiago de Chile
by Marco Antonio de la Parra
trans. by Charles P. Thomas
ISBN 1–56656–123–X paperback $12.95

From Grenada:
Under the Silk Cotton Tree
by Jean Buffong
ISBN 1–56656–122–1 paperback $9.95

From India:
The End Play
by Indira Mahindra
ISBN 1–56656–166–3 paperback $11.95

From Israel:
The Silencer
by Simon Louvish
ISBN 1–56656–108–6 paperback $10.95

From Jordan:
Prairies of Fever
by Ibrahim Nasrallah
trans. by May Jayyusi and Jeremy Reed
ISBN 1–56656–106–X paperback $9.95

From Lebanon:
The Stone of Laughter
by Hoda Barakat
trans. by Sophie Bennett
ISBN 1–56656–190–6 paperback $12.95

From Palestine:
A Balcony Over the Fakihani
by Liyana Badr
trans. by Peter Clark with Christopher Tingley
ISBN 1-56656-107-8 paperback $9.95

Wild Thorns
by Sahar Khalifeh
trans. by Trevor LeGassick and Elizabeth Fernea
ISBN 0-940793-25-3 paperback $9.95

From Serbia:
The Dawning
by Milka Bajić-Poderegin
trans. by Nadja Poderegin
ISBN 1-56656-188-4 paperback $14.95

From South Africa:
Living, Loving and Lying Awake at Night
by Sindiwe Magona
ISBN 1-56656-141-8 paperback $11.95

From Turkey:
Cages on Opposite Shores
by Janset Berkok Shami
ISBN 1-56656-157-4 paperback $11.95

From Yemen:
The Hostage
by Zayd Mutee' Dammaj
trans. by May Jayyusi and Christopher Tingley
ISBN 1-56656-140-X paperback $10.95

From Zimbabwe:
The Children Who Sleep by the River
by Debbie Taylor
ISBN 0-940793-96-2 paperback $9.95

Titles in the "Emerging Voices: New International Fiction" series are available at bookstores everywhere.

To order by phone call toll-free 1–800–238–LINK. Please have your Mastercard, Visa or American Express ready when you call.

To order by mail, please send your check or money order to the address listed below. For shipping and handling, add $3.00 for the first book and $1.00 for each additional book. Massachusetts residents add 5% sales tax.

Interlink Publishing Group, Inc.
46 Crosby Street
Northampton, MA 01060

Tel (413) 582–7054
Fax (413) 582–7057